The Man Who Stole Himself

a novel of the Civil War

Thomas Thibeault

Ridgetop Press

www.ridgetoppress.org

Ridgetop Press
P.O. Box 1522
Swainsboro
Georgia
USA
30401

Cover illustration © Marielle Williams Singletary

Ridgetop Press ® is the registered trademark of the Ridgetop Press.

The Library of Congress has catalogued The Man Who Stole Himself as follows:

LCCN 2014908392

Thibeault, Thomas.
    The Man Who Stole Himself/Thomas Thibeault

ISBN   978-0-9836618-3-2

1 Civil War - fiction.   2. History - fiction.
3. US Navy - fiction   4. Afro-American History - fiction.

Cast of Characters

The People of the *Planter*

Robert Smalls, Harbor Pilot of Charleston and badge slave.

Hannah, his wife.

Their Children:

       Li'l Robert.

       Elizabeth Lydia.

       Clara.

Lydia Polite.

The Crew:

       Alfred Gradine.

       William Morrison.

       Sammy Chisolm.

       Abe Allston.

The Runaways:

       Lavinia.

       Annie.

The Sailors

Rear-Admiral Samuel Francis Du Pont, Commander of the South Atlantic Blockading Squadron.

Lieutenant Frederick Nichols, Commander of the USS *Onward*.

Lieutenant Alexander Rhind, Commander of the USS *Planter* and later of USS *Keokuk*.

Able Seaman Johnny Webb.

Carpenter's Mate David Collins.

Seaman Peter Postlethwaite.

Chief Petty Officer Murphy.

Captain John Rogers.

The Politicians

Gideon Welles, Secretary of the Navy.

Gustavus V. Fox, Assistant Secretary of the Navy.

Allen Russlynn, Assistant to Fox.

Charles B. Sedgwick Congressman from New York.

James Grimes, Senator from Iowa.

Mrs. Simmons, a socialite.

Part I

Robert Smalls

Dover Beach

The sea is calm tonight.
The tide is full, the moon lies fair
Upon the straits; on the French coast the light
Gleams and is gone; the cliffs of England stand,
Glimmering and vast, out in the tranquil bay.
Come to the window, sweet is the night air!

Ah, love, let us be true
To one another! for the world, which seems
To lie before us like a land of dreams,
So various, so beautiful, so new,
Hath really neither joy, nor love, nor light,
Nor certitude, nor peace, nor help for pain;
And we are here as on a darkling plain
Swept with confused alarms of struggle and
flight,
Where ignorant armies clash by night.

Matthew Arnold

Chapter 1

Dolphin Sunset

Sunset wrapped Charleston in magenta clouds. The bay was a parade of lazy ripples staggering to shore, and evening was the time for quiet strolls along the Battery and after-dinner gossip on white verandas. The troubles of a town under siege were set aside for tall glasses under the sultry circles of hungry gulls, and Charlestonians could forget they were in the second year of a Civil War and the tenth month of the blockade.

The evening paused for the ceremony of *Planter* leaving her berth at North Pier. Everybody loved the little boat tooting its whistle on its journey to the forts surrounding Charleston. The hour it would take for the sun to set would light *Planter* through her last harbor patrol of the day.

Her captain shuffled across the bridge and ignored the man standing at the wheel. He stooped over the chart table, leaning on his cane, and opened a book. He held the cane snugly under his left arm, picked up a pen with his right hand, and dripped black blotches onto a page. The little volume had been a lady's diary, but it had been pressed into service as the logbook of the *Planter*. Its calfskin covers opened to the same entry on every line, like a child's copybook. The lines almost confused the captain, and his hand trembled when he splashed the last annoying entry of the day, "CSS *Planter* - Harbor Patrol - May 12, 1862." He signed his name, "C. J. Relyea," and his title, "Captain," with the florid elaboration of people who wish to remind the world of their importance, and threw the pen onto the table. He stood staring at the table and mumbled, "Take her out, Bobby." The little black man at the wheel responded with an "Aye, Aye, Captain," and Relyea acknowledged the respect with a nod.

Bobby hated being called Bobby, for his name was Robert Smalls, and he was proud of it. Robert was a badge slave, officially "on release" from his master, Henry McKee, and had the papers to prove it. Master Henry allowed Robert to work on his own, for a price. Robert paid his master fifteen dollars a month for the privilege of earning his own bread by the sweat of his own brow. He called the money "the master's allowance," and joked about their owners being children grabbing at coins for candy. He knew carpenters and bricklayers who could earn as much as a hundred dollars a month over the allowance. When the coins jingled in Robert's pocket, it was unclear just who was the master. There was no confusion about the little badge on Robert's coat. The little circle of brass was his "permit to walk abroad," so the slave patrol wouldn't arrest him after curfew. The badge made him almost free. Robert liked it that way. He looked at Relyea's cane and smiled.

Robert and his wife, Hannah, seldom spoke of the masters. Other slaves were fascinated by every detail of their owners' lives, but in the Smalls family, visitors were careful to avoid the usual gossip of "Mah Masta Dis" or "Mah Missy Dat." Relyea's cane was different. Three scenes had been carved into its three feet of snakewood. "There's a bull and a bullfighter at the bottom, and the bull is worrying a cape." Hannah was enthralled by Robert's description of the "walking story" of the bull and toreador dancing through their deadly ritual. The scenes climbed up the cane until the sword gored the bull. The filagreed silver top was circled by Relyea's name etched in gold and metal claws clutched a compass set in rock crystal.

Hannah and Robert had speculated how such a wonder had ended up in the hands of such a cantankerous old drunk until one of the crew said, "His wife give it to him." Hannah's head nodded at the mention of a wife. "That gift is either a souvenir of Mrs. Relyea's travels in Mexico or a peace offering for their separation," she said. They grinned at Mrs. Relyea's youth, laughed at the husband's shortness of temper, and delivered their judgment that "Mexico was the farthest she could get away from him, and that stick was her ticket home."

Robert leaned over the ship's wheel, and with a voice as gentle and firm as his grasp on the wheel, whispered into the speaking tube, "Starboard Ahead Two." The tube connected him to Alfred in the engine room behind the bridge and below the deck. Robert gazed through the window to see Sammy in the bows, holding the rope that tethered *Planter* to the dockside. Sammy played out some slack as the giant paddlewheel revolved twice on the right side. Robert didn't have to look back to see Abe Allston holding the stern rope tight around a bollard, for *Planter's* bow swung gently away from the quay. Robert's voice snaked down the tube, "Ahead One Port." The wheel on the left pushed *Planter* clear of the dock. Abe relaxed his grip and cast the stern rope onto the dock, and *Planter* glided free upon the water. When Robert felt the ship shuffle itself into balance, he told Alfred "Ahead Five," and the wheels on each side set *Planter* into a gentle swim at five revolutions every minute.

Planter was a feature of Charleston, full of children's joys and grown-up worries. She was 147 feet of stout red cedar deck planking on a frame of rigid live-oak. The strength of the oak married to the cedar's suppleness allowed her to cut through the waves of winter gales far out to sea. For all her size and power, *Planter's* hull dipped only four feet beneath the water. Her two high-pressure steam engines allowed her sidewheels to push *Planter* out to the Sea Islands or skim through the plantation swamps. She was strong enough to battle a storm, but so light she could float the river shallows.

Before the war, she had been a cotton boat delivering the bales to the town's wharfs. With the feathery bales piled so high on her deck, people wondered how the captain could see to steer. Six months of the year *Planter* would ply the inland waters collecting and delivering the harvests, but during the planting and growing seasons, *Planter* was transformed into an excursion vessel. For a week, all hands would pick stray cotton strands from vents and sweep seeds from stairs and split planks. The crew would polish her wood and shine the brass, and what couldn't be cleaned was painted a gleaming white. As soon as she resembled a puffing swan, *Planter* was ready to convey squealing children and giggling belles to the picnics on Sullivan's Island amid the relief of sea breezes. The human cargo was more profitable than the cotton bales.

And the war came. The cotton and the crinolines of the quiet past were insufficient for the present troubles, so *Planter* was made a warship. Black hands scattered grey paint over her gleaming wood, and three short weeks of sea duty made her brass weep rust. The wood smoke from her stack dyed her stern a deeper shade of oily brown and sparks pitted her sides like smallpox. Balls of burning resin from the boilers showered her with amber hail, making her decks as slippery as ice. Now she wore a green necklace of river slime around her waterline, the final insult to a proud lady who had hit hard times.

The military decided to arm her, so *Planter* became *CSS Planter*, as if three letters and two cannon could magically transform a supply boat into a threat. The South was desperate for anything that could float and make a navy. Where cotton bales once stood on the foredeck, a 32-pounder cannon pointed over the bows. A 24-pounder howitzer squatted on the stern deck, like a sleeping toad. One lady giggled that "thirty-two pounds of cannon was a child's pop gun," but her husband enjoyed explaining that the thirty-two pounds was the weight of the cannon ball rammed into the monster's mouth. The cannon was a giant, pried from its embrasure at Fort Sumter and bolted to *Planter*'s foredeck.

The Union Navy had strung a line of ten warships across the entrance to the harbor "denying egress and access to the city in rebellion." When this was translated as "nobody can get in or out," the people of the town appreciated their plight. Their army was just strong enough to keep the Union soldiers bogged down in the swamps, but too weak to repulse a full-scale assault.

Charleston could not fight on the water. Neither side could win or lose, and the Charlestonians could not choose between fight or flight. There was just nowhere to go, so they took to building forts.

Gangs of slaves were driven from low-lying rice plantations and set to shoveling sand into mounds they called fortresses. The sandcastles big enough to house a few soldiers and a cannon were designated garrisons, knighted with names such as "Fort Defiance," "Thunder Alley," or "Rebellion Row." One pile of tidewater dirt was adorned with the title "Fort Never Surrender," but the soldiers consigned to that malarial cesspool christened it "Shit Britches Swamp." Thus plain old *Planter* became CSS *Planter*, "an armed supply vessel," delivering weapons, ammunition, food, drink, and not much else to the forty-seven forts, garrisons, batteries, and castles scattered around Charleston. She toted her heavy and useless loads in endless circles twice a day.

Captain Relyea knew a good thing when he saw it, and commanding Charleston's harbor boat was a very good thing indeed. Relyea would be eternally grateful to Brigadier General Ripley, Commanding Officer of the Charleston Garrison, for his commission as a captain of the South Carolina Navy and his appointment to command of CSS *Planter*. Captain Charles John Relyea was tolerated by his few friends as C.J. and reviled by his sailors as just plain Seajay. He could live with the joke that "Relyea's old lodge brother had found him an easy berth." With Ripley to protect him and South Carolina to pay him, Relyea was safely trapped. This was an excellent alternative to getting blown to bits in Virginia, for there was nothing to do in Charleston and everything to avoid in Virginia. "Let the young men be heroes. I'm too old for such shenanigans," he quipped. A besieged city was the perfect place to hide from a war. Seajay knew that "Bobby" was also a very good thing.

The day-slave knew every inch of the harbor and could guide *Planter* anywhere at any time. For five years, Robert had made

15

his way in the world by "grit and wit." He worked with his eyes and his memory because his hands were too small for a hammer and the monotony of laying a brick wall bored him. In his short twenty-three years of life, Robert had married and sired three children. He had also struck a bargain with Hannah's master and was adding to his stock of gold coins so he could buy his wife and their children. The water was Robert's fascination and his freedom.

When other children were taken to the sea to splash and jump, they demanded to know, "Who put all that salt in the water?" but little Robert had asked his mother what was under the water. She did not know, so he set out to wrestle the answer from the sea. He took every chance to study the bay and soon realized that he could remember just where the currents kissed the shore. From day-to-day, he could recall how the water changed color at different times. Momma Lydia sensed there was something extraordinary about her boy when he told her that the bay was "just like the quilt." He explained to her that the different squares in the coverlet she had sewn from scraps were just like the sea, "cept that the water has twenty-seven blankets... so far." The bay became a motley and familiar pattern to the child.

Lydia encouraged her son to look to the sky as well, and soon he could paint the clouds in his mind. When he could predict what would happen when the sky met the water, his mother had to acknowledge that something special was going on in his head. Her patience was as long as the summer evenings. She knew the water would be a kindly teacher. The sea rewarded Robert's persistence and revealed its sunken secrets. Robert grew with her knowledge, and it made him the most sought after pilot in Charleston harbor.

As they did every evening, Robert led *Planter* on her waltz around the harbor from fort to fort in the bay. The side paddles churned a lazy rumble, and Robert edged the boat just far enough away from the dockside to feel the water. Robert knew that the magic was in his feet. He grabbed the wheel with both hands, but that was just for show, for Seajay to think he was working. He shrugged his right shoulder to the setting sun and pointed the bow southeast to Fort Johnson sticking out into the bay like an angry pimple.

He held the harbor in his mind like a shimmering clock face, with its arms revolving from Fort Sumter in the center of the bay. *Planter* was swaying at nine o'clock, just past White Point, with the big church steeple rising over Robert's shoulder. A mile away at seven o'clock was Fort Johnson on James Island, and between them the Ashley River emptied into the bay. Robert's right foot felt the tiny bump when the Ashley current met the *Planter,* and he swung the wheel to the left to let the flow drift them to the fort. The Ashley had scoured the Main Channel leading to the open sea, but it had also thrust up the Middle Ground sandbar lurking only three feet beneath a low tide. *Planter* slid into the depths of the Main Channel, and Robert's left foot felt the ripple from the sunken bank slither under the keel. When the boat sashayed with the waves and the tides, Robert could feel the rhythms in his legs and his shoulders.

Seajay had once asked Robert why he didn't sit on a chair when he was at the wheel, and Robert had answered, "That's 'cause I steer with my ass," but he was careful to add "Captain." Seajay's laughter lasted all the way round their patrol, but its mirth evaporated when he bored his friends ashore with too many repetitions. Robert just thought that "Cap'n is simple in the head 'cause he has to say everything a hundred times." When Robert related the incident to Hannah, she laughed, "It's a wonder he can remember where he lives."

The wheel trembled to Robert's touch, so he settled into the boat's gentle yawing and dipping for the next mile. He glanced at Seajay fussing with the log book on the chart table. Robert smiled at the sparkles showering from the crystal compass stuck on the head of Seajay's stick. The compass was forgotten because Seajay only used the stick to walk or to poke people. It was easier to crack a skull with his cane than run away from a fight. Robert

17

had observed how people stayed four feet away from Seajay and well up wind from his temper.

Log book appeased, Seajay could now lean his chair against the bridge bulkhead and enjoy the trip. The last patrol of the day was always a leisurely affair. When they returned to North Dock, he could leave the boat for the dockside gang to load the guns and ammunition for the morning deliveries. This evening was for tall tales and taller glasses with Ripley and the boys at the Excelsior Hotel.

Robert trimmed *Planter* into the center of the Main Channel as the engines thrummed in harmony. His thighs felt the spring of ten fathoms pushing the boat higher in the water, and his legs swayed in time with the engines. Below decks, two giant steam machines powered the paddlewheels astride *Planter*. Robert once joked that if she rolled on her back, Alfred would keep those engines running.

Alfred Gradine had been set in charge of the engine room a mere three weeks ago. He had hair like a buffalo and eyes to match, and when he told Robert that engine grease was how he kept his mustache and goatee so neat, they had laughed their way into a friendship. Robert had surprised himself that he trusted the man so quickly.

Alfred's master had released him to the Charleston Steamship Company some years ago, thinking that Alfred would never be able to pay his badge fee. Alfred had worked his way from a log monkey, flinging wood into the boiler pans, to expert stoker, to something the company would have called an Engine Room Artificer, but the company gave titles only to whites - slaves were just casual labor. Alfred never gave a thought to what people called him because he was more concerned with the money in his pocket. He loved his new job and spent his shifts dodging the flywheels and taming the two prancing and puffing steam dragons.

The link between Robert on the bridge and Alfred in the engine room was as curious as it was simple. Robert at the wheel would talk into one end of the tube, and Alfred would listen at the other end in the engine room. The little whistle on the speaking tube was almost unnecessary. One blow into the tube and Alfred would know to set the engines to quarter turns. Three whistles was "Full Steam Ahead," and five shrieks meant "all hell is about to break loose, so get your ass topside before ya'll drown." Alfred kept his "black gang" running as smoothly as his engines, confident that Robert would not steer them to a watery grave. With the engines under such tight control, Robert could steer *Planter* through any trouble or around any obstruction, and keep all that water where it belonged, in the sea.

As they passed the batteries at Fort Johnson, Robert braced his legs and held the wheel tight. He stared straight ahead to keep the looming pile of Fort Sumter just in the corner of his left eye. This was how he knew to maintain a straight course over the gaping bay between the Fort and Morris Island to his right. The tide would whirl between the two islands, sometimes strong enough to pull the ship into its gaping mouth. Robert had heard of boats being eaten by unseen currents just off Cummins Point, when the sea was as flat as etched saloon mirrors. Sure enough, *Planter* lurched to the right, so Robert swung the wheel to the left and blew twice into the tube. Alfred jumped the power to "Half Ahead" and waited for the single whistle telling him to resume "Quarter Speed." Robert held *Planter* steady to the Point and when he could no longer see Sumpter or the cannons of Morris Island, he whistled once. *Planter* settled onto her bow, and Robert spun the wheel to the left to let the incoming tide swing them around Sumter and float them home.

Just off Sullivan's Island, Robert felt the surge forward as the tide swirled under his feet. He looked back to see the water spiraling white along the treacherous shallows called Drunken Dick's Breakers. The name had been submerged in time, but Robert was a curious child and had asked, "Who was Drunken Dick?" He pestered Momma Lydia with questions until she surrendered and brought him to Uncle Billy. Billy was so ancient no one knew just how old he was, not even Uncle Billy. The leather of the old man's skin fascinated Robert and Momma told him that Uncle Billy had been born "there," where there were no white people. Robert demanded to know, "Where's 'there'?" Uncle Billy chuckled and explained that "there" was "a place called Africa." Billy read the confusion in Robert's brows and confided, "That's the place where all we black people hail from." Robert pressed Uncle Billy to tell him all about "there." Billy did and closed his geography lesson with, "That's a good thing 'cause 'there' the black people are bad enough without learning from the white folks." Momma howled loudest at Uncle Billy's jokes, for he hid his wisdom beneath the laughter.

Uncle Billy smiled and leaned close in to little Robert's face to tell "the terrible tale of that no-account white man who had no sense at all. He found some rotted out boat and painted over the rot. After a skinful of skull-rot whiskey, he dragged that sack o' painted splinters into the water. His friends had a feast of fatback and more whiskey and cast their miserable hides upon the waters. Them waters didn't take too kindly to a passel of trash lunatics and promptly drowned them all. That boat just settled onto a sandbar, so it goes to show you that a man can drown in just a few inches of water."

Robert had heard other tales of that part of the bay, and Uncle Billy hid nothing from the inquisitive child. "People say those breakers is haunted. The haints of those fools rise every night looking for a drink. I suppose it gets mighty thirsty in the ocean." Billy leaned back and took his time to study the boy's face. His thumb pressed a crumpled leaf into the pipe bowl, "I seen a white fisherman pour a flagon of whiskey over the waters. When I asked him why he was wasting good liquor, he said it was for the souls of Drunken Dick. Those little white waves over the shoal is the sea laughing at Drunken Dick and his friends." That was how Robert knew all about Drunken Dick's Breakers.

When the water broke white, Robert recalled Uncle Billy, and the memory kept him from dancing with Drunken Dick. Such tales had taught him the bay beyond what his eyes and feet could discern. There was so much more in the shallows below the surface. When the wind was tracing crazy patterns upon the water, Robert could almost see Drunken Dick's skeletal arm waving to him in the moonlight.

Robert squinted toward the setting sun and saw the rumpled outline of Digby standing to attention at the bow, shouldering his shotgun. Robert shook his head and mumbled to himself, "That white boy sure loves to soldier."

Digby was the ship's guard. Seajay would grunt, and Digby would jump to eager attention. He was no more than seventeen, but he was already a veteran of three battles. One battle was enough to cure a dose of patriotism, but Digby's love of state and country only grew with every shot fired at him. When Robert saw Digby shining his gun's barrel, he had no doubt that "the boy is gun crazy."

It didn't matter if the weapon was a rusty pistol or a seven ton Columbiad, Digby was fascinated by anything that would make a loud noise and kill. Seajay told Robert that Digby's parents were in a hurry to get their son to the recruiting officer and that there were no tearful partings when they left Digby at the muster camp. Robert could only speculate why the parents were so eager to offer their child to the Moloch of war, but the more time he spent with Digby, the less he posed the question. Even Seajay grew tired of Digby's fawning.

To the crew, Digby was a young master. He would not look at anything black, and Alfred kept his head well down below the engine room gangway when Digby's feet marched past. Alfred had noticed that Digby's shoes made him walk with splayed feet and told Robert, "the first time those feet were shod with anything other than farm dirt and horse shit was when the army gave him his first pair of boots."

Digby's antics troubled Robert. Whenever they passed a flag drooping over a fort's parapet, Digby stood rigid on the foredeck and smartly presented arms. Nobody would return Digby's salute, even if they noticed him bobbing in the harbor over a mile away. His comrades and officers ignored him as just another village idiot.

Robert swung the wheel to point Digby and the cannon at the steeple of St. Michael's Church. From the bridge windows, Charleston's dark spires became splayed fingers across the sunset. All he had to do was let the incoming tide push the boat against the current of the Cooper River and aim the bow at one steeple after the other until *Planter* rested at her berth. He cared not a fig that the sticks piercing the clouds were Methodist, Presbyterian, Episcopalian or Baptist, for all led home to North Dock.

Robert would not speculate on which building was the preferred path to the Pearly Gates, for he had enough to concern him on this earth. The thought of what he was going to do frightened him. It would be useless to ask for forgiveness, for there was no power in this world or the next which would stay the hands that would punish his audacity. He would not be condemned for the deed alone; it was the very idea that would have to be exterminated. The only way they could kill the concept would be to utterly destroy his body and his memory. Robert knew full well that the unforgivable sin was having a thought. He steadied the wheel and jerked the fear from his heart.

The time for speculation was long past. Right now he had to concentrate on the outflow from the Cooper. The bow twitched up over the swirls of red river mud and knocked Digby into "at ease." Digby leaned against the guard rail and struck a picturesque pose with his arm around his rifle, as if it were a sweetheart. Robert blew "Half Ahead" down the speaking tube, and Alfred pulled the Johnson bar on a cylinder vent to increase the pressure. *Planter* dipped her stern and sliced through pink bow wash into the green eddies trailing the Cooper current like shoals of minnows. Robert whistled once to Alfred, and *Planter* swayed leisurely into the inner harbor pool.

Alfred left George and Eddy in charge of the engines and pulled himself up the engine room ladder to the deck. He shrugged himself along the guard rail to the bow. Alfred leaned forward and breathed deeply to cast the engine smoke from his lungs. He coughed oily soot and gazed into the bay before him. As if hearing its master's voice, a dolphin lunged through the air not three feet from the side of the boat directly under Alfred. Robert slowed *Planter* into a lazy paddle to prolong Alfred's pleasure. He knew that Alfred loved the creatures and did not wish to intrude upon the man's fascination. Knowing Alfred's joy was enough for Robert to linger on the way home.

Young Alfred had discovered a dolphin trapped on a sandbar by an indifferent and receding tide. He could not leave the creature struggling to find the water and had watched the strength fade with its life until the head drooped by its side and it surrendered to a welcome stillness. The creature died not fifty yards from where Alfred stood, but it may as well have been miles. He so wanted to drag the dolphin from the tormenting sun, but the water was wide and he had no wings to fly. He could not help the dolphin to live, and it was equally unable to die. The faint cries walking over the water screamed in Alfred's ears. He waited the whole day, keeping vigil until the next tide swept the body over the few inches of jagged rocks to sink in slow spirals down the unknown depths. The boy had mourned the passing of that dolphin for the weeks it took him to become a man and to accept what will happen to us all. And so, the man stood savoring the life playing in the harbor pool and smiled at his joyous blue oracles.

Some Irishman had told him that a dolphin was the soul of a drowned sailor, so eating them was cannibalism. Alfred nodded to the man and said he could never eat such a creature. Seajay snorted at "them sea-pigs." Alfred knew they were special creatures and was equally content to enjoy them just breaching a bow wave or offering their spectacular tail dance on the water. He never grew tired of their antics. Familiarity bred a gentle fascination which he neither could explain nor wished to spoil. He wanted them to keep their mystery and their charm.

Just as *Planter* turned home against the Cooper River flow, the dolphins cavorted back over the bow wash and headed down the deep channel. Alfred watched them punctuate the water until their fins receded into the distance like the faint dots and dashes on a telegraph. He did not raise an arm in farewell or even blink as his friends went home to the open sea. It was enough for him to know they were playing somewhere out there. With his hand trailing along the bridge wall, his unsteady feet dragged him back to the familiar thumping of the engine room.

Robert's eyes scanned to the west, and he relaxed into his knowledge that "blushing clouds calm restless waves." When he could see only a shrinking pool of cast-off jetsam between the hull and the wharf, he whispered into the tube, "All Stop." The paddlewheel blades snapped still and braked the boat into a gentle glide. Robert's hands were light upon the wheel, and he lurched to the window to see William Morrison standing on a jumble of ammunition boxes piled on the quayside.

William's gang of stevedores, as practiced as a chorus of dancers, lined the wharf edge between two iron bollards, waiting for his hand signals. Robert looked fore and aft to see Sammy and Abe at their positions at bow and stern, holding coils of rope, like cowboys fingering their lassos. William stood tall before the dockside crane, perched amidst a nest of powder barrels, and raised two coppery arms. Sammy and Abe whirled the ropes over their heads and sent the lines spiraling in graceful arches to shore. The two men at the bollards caught the ends of the lines, wrapped them once around the iron posts, and pulled in the slack. They knew *Planter* could be skittish. William dropped his arms and four men dangled intricate bundles of rope fenders over the water, to take the impact of the wheel covers amidships. At just the right moment, Robert pulled the wheel a quarter turn to the left, so *Planter* could nestle close and keep her sides from scraping to splinters on the dock's stone. The two men at the

24

bollards teased *Planter* closer. The hull sidled up to the fenders, the four men lowered their fenders, and the sea swell nudged *Planter* to her rest. The bollard boys played out enough slack, so *Planter* would not hang on taut lines when the tide dropped, and secured the rope ends under two half-hitches, as neat as a birthday bows. Robert whistled for Alfred to blow boilers and *Planter* sighed the last puffs of the day.

William's shore-crew rattled the gang-plank from the dock to the deck. William mounted the crane and swung the derrick over their heads to stand poised above the barrel of a 32-pounder waiting to be loaded. One of those cannons sliding out of the webbed cradle could crush a man, so they trusted to William's skill with the winch. They called him the Snake Charmer.

Seajay took off his straw hat and threw it onto the chart table. He donned a felt cap with a glittering peak, grumbled down the ladder to the deck, and waited for the gangway to thump before him. Seajay turned to see Digby standing guard behind him. "Boy, get rid of that thing," he commanded, and Digby stared blankly back. "You can't just walk into the Excelsior with a loaded gun over your shoulder." The boy blinked at this incomprehensible order. "Put the gun away and follow me."

There was so much Digby did not understand about this night, so he just said, "Yes, Capt'n," and did as he was told. He scuttled back along the gang plank to the arms locker behind the bridge. Robert listened to Seajay muttering, "bring a shotgun to meet a General." Alfred raised his head above the engine room ladder and watched Digby click the hammer to half-cock, remove the percussion cap, and put it in his pocket. The gun was now as harmless as a toy. Digby placed his gun in the locker, closed the doors, and tested the lock to make sure that all was safe.

Alfred ignored him clattering over the gang-plank to join Seajay. Digby's boots creaked with the spring in his step because he was being bodily assumed into the heaven of the higher ranks. An invitation to eat with his Captain and his Captain's General was a validation of Digby's soul which neither a woman nor a preacher could offer.

Planter snuggled at her moorings as Seajay stood on the dockside fidgeting with his cane. Digby ran up to him, waggled a nervous thumb over his shoulder at the dock crew, and asked, "What about them?" Seajay stared past Digby to see Robert standing in the pilot house doorway and rumbled, "Damn it, Boy, Bobby knows what to do."

Robert watched them march across the street and disappear through the door into the headquarters and residence of General Roswell Ripley. The door swung shut behind them and the last of the sun flashed over the polished brass plaque proclaiming that this was The Office of the Commander-in-Chief, Charleston.

Alfred and Robert had heard and studiously ignored every word. Robert nodded to William at the crane and the loading crew went about their business as if nothing had happened. All knew that *Planter* would be unguarded and the closest white man would be a block away in the snugs of his favorite boozer.

They stood gazing out to sea, savoring the beckoning twilight. It might be their last sunset because they had decided to steal the boat.

Chapter 2

Onward

Johnny Webb was enjoying his pipe. He paused between puffs to smile gratitude for his new commander. Lieutenant Nichols was a rare officer who appreciated that tobacco was one of the few joys of life at sea. When Johnny had been assigned to the *USS Onward*, he worried that it would be a hard ass berth. Every sailor dreaded the boredom of endless months of blockade duty. Nichols had told the new boys, "pipes at the for'ard gun." Johnny saw a 32-pounder near the ship's bow surrounded by a ring of water buckets. That cannon was always unloaded because it stood in the most useless position on a fighting ship. The Chief had quipped, "You couldn't hit a gale with a foc'sle gun." So, Nichols had turned the area into the one place aboard where sailors could congregate and light their pipes.

Fire at sea was more terrifying than drowning, so the Navy had simply forbidden any form of smoking. Nichols was different. He permitted a pipe but had warned Johnny and the replacements, "If I see or smell a cigar, you'll be sitting on it - while it's still burning." The man's tone, his stature, and his thoughtfulness had impressed the men, for he was as tall as a carrot and his voice was stick enough to command obedience.

Johnny heard footsteps scraping softly along the deck toward him. He grinned to hear Davey Collins asking him for "some of that Virginia Twist." Davey squatted on a rope coil and pulled a bent briar tube from under his squall jacket. This was Davey's usual greeting on Night Watch, for he knew Johnny would share his best tobacco with him. Johnny offered his pouch, and Davey packed his bowl. Johnny blew down the stem until the tobacco flashed sparks, so Davey could suck the flame and light his pipe. When the ember flared into a steady glow, Davey leaned his back against the gun wheel and sighed comfort. Hunkered down below the gunnels, a flashing pipe would not betray their concealment.

They had joined *Onward*'s crew four months ago at Beaufort and had taken station seven miles off the coast of South Carolina. Their duty was to catch any ship running the blockade in or out of Charleston harbor. They soon realized that their new commanding officer had his own ideas of seamanship.

The six replacements had been rowed out to the ship, where the crew held her steady, waiting for the shore boat to pull alongside. Before the last legs were thrown over the rail, *Onward* was under way. The six stood to attention beside their seabags in front of Chief Petty Officer Murphy's glare. They sweated for a half an hour, until an officer slowly walked down the quarterdeck steps and sauntered towards them.

Acting Volunteer Lieutenant J. Frederick Nichols paced the deck, casually looking them over. No head had to turn to know he was in charge of this ship. At a nod from Nichols, Chief Murphy scrambled them to the Number One gun position and started shouting commands. Nichols leaned against the foremast with his arms crossed over his chest, yawning. He watched Murphy drill order into this jumble of nervous young men. An officer may give orders, but they are useless, if the men can not perform their tasks. It was the Chief who commanded the ratings of the lower decks and kept everything in ship shape. Nichols valued Murphy because he was the best Chief he had ever sailed with.

Nichols smiled as Murphy blustered commands to Johnny and a tough looking fellow, "Man the ball cradle." He could see the arm muscles bulge through the new man's jacket sleeves. Nichols judged the boy capable of picking up a two-hundred pound iron ball and pitching it down the gun's muzzle.

Another new sailor held the muzzle puller, and the Chief commanded, "Receive." The man strained on the ropes, and screeching pulleys depressed the barrel to the deck. Johnny and his muscle-bound messmate stood on either side of the gun, grasping the handles of the ball cradle. The Chief growled, "Load," so they hoisted the cradle and slid the ball into the cannon's mouth. The sailor at the pulley played out the ropes, and the barrel raised itself and swallowed the iron sphere with a hungry rumbling. Johnny and the tough man moved to the rear of the gun and held two ropes steady. They hadn't expected gun drill in the first hour of joining the ship. Still less did they expect the gun to be primed with powder and ready to fire.

They all stood to their proper positions and seemed to know what they were doing. Nichols ignored their rigid postures, relieved that the new men had been mostly trained, at least in gun drill.

Onward lay at anchor a thousand yards from shore, and Nichols scanned an island through his telescope. He growled out of the side of his mouth to the new men. "What do you see?" The replacements stared at him, for this was the first time any officer had asked them a question. Nichols smirked at their awkward shuffling. "What do you see?" Murphy grinned and nodded permission. They wandered sheepishly to the rail and peered into the distance.

Johnny narrowed his eyes and heard Nichols' voice beside him. "What do you see?" The island was a bulge of scrubby timber, but his confidence bubbled up at Nichols' words, so Johnny said. "A woodpile, Sir."

Nichols casually paced behind the men, "Anybody else see it?" The rough looking sailor said, "It's to the left." Nichols stopped his pacing, pointed to Johnny and the other sailor, and commanded, "You two. Man the sights." Murphy scooted all six sailors back to the gun, placing Johnny and his partner at the rear of the cannon.

The Chief barked the commands, and Johnny turned the elevating wheel, raising and lowering the gun barrel. He squinted to line up the fore and rear sights with the distant rectangle of shredded bark. He jumped deftly to the side to let the other sailor check his aim, and they both stood to attention on either side of

29

the cannon. Murphy fitted the igniter into the gun's touch-hole and stood rigid to the right, holding the little rope in his fist. When Nichols saw that all six men were standing safely at their posts, he breathed, "Fire." Murphy pulled the rope, and the igniter spluttered sparks down the touch-hole to the powder. The gun spewed smoking embers, belched forth the ball, and recoiled four feet.

The replacements broke and ran to the rail. Nichols and Murphy indulged the men's joy and would not intrude upon the excitement of actually firing the gun. The men chanted, "One Mississippi, Two Mississippi..." for the six seconds it took the ball to sail from sea to shore. As their eyes followed its low, graceful arc, the woodpile came into sharper focus. What they had not seen before became more distinct as its destruction approached. The woodpile jumped and hailed tattered splinters through the forest of scrubwood, and the men cheered their success. Murphy poured a bucket of water down the throat of the gun, and the men turned to see its mouth splutter a boiling, grit-pebbled slurry. He forced a six-foot sponge rod into the gun barrel to cool its bowels, but heat shimmered up from the gun like a snake shedding its skin.

Nichols nodded to Murphy, who shouted, "To your stations." The line broke from the rail, and feet scrambled to stand beside the smoking cannon. Nichols nodded again, and the Chief commanded, "You three to port gun; the rest starboard gun." They sorted themselves into two confused lines on each side of the cannon and threw raised eyebrows to each other over the barrel. Murphy ordered, "put your hands on the barrel."

They had never heard such a command and shuffled from foot-to-foot. The Chief's eyes strangled any giggles, as his mouth bellowed, "Hands on barrel. Palms down."

Johnny stretched forth his arm and found that the metal had cooled but was still very hot. Nichols smiled along the barrel and looked each man in the eye.

"That was pretty good shooting," Nichols assured them. Savoring their pride, he quietly asked, "What did you hit?" He pulled his lips into a smirk at their silence. Murphy stood threading a length of rope between callused fingers, watching each man. Nichols waited a moment, gazed directly into Johnny's eyes, and repeated the question. Johnny felt he could neither take his hand off the barrel nor remain silent; both would be disobedience. "It was a log pile, Sir," he said through clenched teeth.

"How did you know it was not someone's house?"

"There were no windows and no chimney sticking up," Johnny said.

Nichols nodded to Murphy, who commanded Webb, "Number One Gun." Nichols looked to the gruff man beside Webb. "Did you see it was a house?" he demanded.

"No, Sir."

"So what was it?" Nichols demanded, sizing up the sailor.

"I thought it was a barn," the sailor answered.

"Why a barn?" Nichols quietly inquired.

"I heard a cow."

"What is your name?" The sailor caught the note of sincerity in the question.

"Carpenter's Mate Collins, Sir."

"You can saw wood when you're not on watch," Nichols told Davey.

He turned to Johnny. "And what is your name?"

"Gunner's Mate Webb, Sir," Johnny said, and Nichols caught the confidence in the voice.

Nichols turned to the Chief and commended, "These two assigned to Number One Gun Station."

The Chief nodded a polite, "Aye Aye, Sir," and turned to watch the hands splayed along the gun barrel.

Nichols eyed a young boy wincing through clenched jaws. The barrel heat rose into their wrists and forearms. "You never shoot what you can't see." He waited to see which replacement

31

would be the first to pull away his hand. He walked behind the line of three to the left of the gun and whispered into each ear, "You never shoot what you can't see." The young boy yanked his hand clear and shook it over his head, dancing with the pain.

Nichols asked him his name. "Seaman Postlethwaite, Sir."

"Number Four Gun," Nichols softly said.

The boy walked down the deck blowing air over his scorched fingers, and the men stopped giggling when Murphy threatened them with the rope end. Nichols continued his leisurely saunter and whispered to each sailor, "You never shoot what you can't see," until he had repeated the command five times.

Nichols finally nodded, and the Chief barked, "Stand To!" They all stood to attention pressing their burnished palms to their sides, holding back their tears. Nichols commanded Davey, "Show me your hands," and examined the callused palms. The hands spoke of rough work that could grasp hot metal. "You and Webb load and aim." Murphy assigned the remaining three to different guns. He knew why Nichols had chosen Collins and Webb for the lead cannon.

They never forgot the lesson and had the singed palms to remind them, "You never shoot what you can't see." Johnny suffered through Nichols' questions, and for the first time, realized he had excellent eyesight. Davey had also learned that the crazy officer with the quiet manner was more threatening than the Chief Petty Officer with the rope switch.

Davey warmed his palms on his pipe bowl and rose to peer into the distance. Johnny puffed out, "They forgot the light by the church." Davey squinted over the miles to Charleston. Johnny smiled to see Davey search the night until he picked out a dim glow amid the gloom that was the city. "Just like them to paint the town black and forget to blow out a candle," Davey said.

Indeed, Charleston's first citizens had decided that it was a good idea to "paint the town black." Somebody important had commented that "this city is too tempting a target for those people who do not possess the moral fiber not to bombard women and children." There had been such a hubbub about "barbarians hurling cannon balls through churches" that the City Council met in special session. They had squabbled over the expense of buckets of paint, until the mayor had made an executive decision and proclaimed that "all church steeples shall, henceforth, be painted black in order to confuse the enemy." This was easier said than done, for Charleston boasted so many churches, it had been dubbed "The Holy City." The civic minded and the desperate contributed their surplus servants, the few they had brought with them into town. After weeks of haggling over the cost of feeding "the artists," the councillors finally decided that "the work is a temporary war measure and will be paid for with the inevitable victory." House slaves were issued ropes and paint brushes and forced to climb the steeples. Gangs of slaves scuttled up and down the spires in a vain attempt to alter the city's profile, just in case the enemy fired on it. They joked about "rising in the world" and sang "Climbing Jacob's Ladder," but the laughter and the songs stopped abruptly when the first artist plunged two hundred feet to the fence railings.

Davey was as impressed by Johnny's eyesight as he was grateful for his tobacco. If Johnny could see anything on the horizon, he could always tell exactly where they were. Johnny took his talent in his stride and just blinked at the compliments. He turned to hear the regular shuffle of Nichols' feet, and they both stood to casual attention and greeted him, "Good evening, Sir."

"It's getting closer to morning, boys," Nichols answered. "Anything to report?"

"Completely silent, Sir," said Collins.

"Not a mouse a stirring," added Johnny, "except that one candle."

"Where do you think it is?" Nichols asked.

"It's in a window on the top floor."

"Why so?" Nichols prodded.

"It's too low for a church and too high for the street."

"Good."

They warmed to his approval. "Here's a present," Nichols said. He stretched forth his arm to offer them a book "courtesy of the Confederacy." Johnny clasped the volume and read aloud for Collins, "*Lady Audley's Secret.* Where did you get this?"

"Picked it off the captain's table when we got that last runner."

"The one from England?" Johnny asked.

"The very same," Nichols beamed.

The last three months of blockade duty had been bountiful, for *Onward* had captured three ships. Smugglers pinned their hopes on moonless nights with just enough wind to muffle their engines, but they hadn't reckoned on Johnny's eyes and Davey's ears. The commanding officers and the crew would eventually get their bonuses - after the government took the lion's share through the Prize Courts. In March, they had pounced upon the *Emily St. Pierre* and confiscated a cargo of Indian gunny cloth essential to baling the cotton that would be smuggled out of Charleston.

Onward was the only sail-rigged ship in a flotilla of Union steamships, but she had nabbed the best prizes. That Nichols could maneuver completely under sail was testament to his ability to think ten steps ahead and to the crew's mastery of rope, sail, and wind. Nichols knew that steam outruns sail in deep seas, so he had trained his crew to run the quarry into the shallows. Sail trumps steam when you're stuck on sandbars or rocks have ripped open a hull. In April, they had forced a schooner, the *Chase,* to run aground on Raccoon Key, and destroyed her. A couple of weeks later, she trapped the *Sarah* in Bull's Bay. *Sarah's* crew tried to scuttle her, but they weren't quick enough for the men of *Onward.* Johnny and Davey had been in the boarding party, and the months of monotony were punctuated by fifteen minutes of sheer terror. Nichols made sure that the cargo was transferred to *Onward* and took the book for his troubles.

34

The little red rectangle of pages was Nichols' greatest prize, for boredom was deadlier than either water or flames. When he first took command of *Onward*, he had to censor letters, and was intrigued by a midshipman's complaint. Nichols was at first amused to read the lines sent to a mother back home, "Go to the roof on a hot summer day, talk to a half-dozen degenerates, descend to the basement, drink tepid water full of iron rust, climb to the roof again, and repeat the process at intervals, until you are fagged out, then go to bed with everything shut tight." It was an accurate description of their life at sea, but Nichols scowled at "crew of degenerates." A young man with such an attitude could sink a ship. Nichols authorized the letter and then wrote out the "Transfer to Shore Duties." He hoped that the climate under a tin roof in the Beaufort depot would be more to the young brat's liking. Nichols later learned he had made the right decision, for the midshipman ran home at the first cannon shot.

The crew had accomplished three captures in as many months, when the usual quota was one per year, per ship. *Onward* was getting rich. The prizes would soon dry up if the crew took to entertaining themselves with punches and knives. The mail boat punctuated the doldrums, but it wasn't enough. He had overheard Davey ask Johnny at Mail Call, "Who do you know who can write, who knows you can read?" After that, Nichols kept a close eye on who received and who sent letters. Less than half the crew were literate. He immediately placed subscriptions with *Frank Leslie's Weekly*, *The Illustrated News*, and other publications.

The real weapon against deadly boredom was the serial story. Installments kept the crew wondering and were an endless source of conversation. He noticed that the weekly dose of melodrama made the work hum with gossip. Decks would be swabbed amidst speculations of what would happen next to the heroine of a dime thriller. The men could recite the newsprint doggerel and make up their own outrageous, but rhyming responses to "Verses In Humble Tribute to Our Gallant Troops." They had their fill of Dickens and Wilkie Collins, but didn't think much of "that Limey

Lord, Lytton." The best of the lot was Mary Elizabeth Braddon, for she kept the pot boiling and the crew yearning for more.

Nichols took command of the sheets and instituted a reading time after the evening meal. For an hour one sailor who could read would declaim three pages of murder, mayhem, and sentiment to those who could only listen. Johnny was a good reader, and the crew unanimously elected him *Onward's* "mouth-man." Nichols relied on the readings to maintain morale, and the crew saw mutual respect in the stories and the pipe buckets.

The men had been waiting patiently for the next installments to come down the blockade line from the literary pirates in New York, but getting the whole book was manna from heaven. Johnny thumbed through the pages as Nichols commanded, "Keep that in your hammock and don't read it too fast."

"Aye Aye, Sir."

Nichols listened with growing amusement as Johnny recounted the previous adventures of Lady Audley. Davey remembered only the broad outline of her story, but Johnny had a genius for details and for the family relationships which Lady Audley was systematically destroying. He would correct anybody who challenged his judgment that she became a lady by pretending to be a common slut "cause that's what them lords really like."

Lady Audley's adventures followed the rise of a simple maid in domestic service, who lied her way into a governess' job, married her master, killed him, caught herself a lord, and progressed up the social ladder through deceit, adultery, child abduction, and murder to become a lady. Davey had been fascinated by her criminal career and saw the dastardly deeds as her recipe for improvement. "She can kill the fathers just like she can breed their bastards," he pronounced. Nichols shared his opinion. "She'd be right at home in Georgia." The newspapers were full of women such as Constance Kent, who could rise above their stations by disposing of inconvenient husbands and discarding annoying children down wells. Johnny admitted, "I just can't believe that a woman would drown her own child."

"You 'ain't met my ma," Davey blurted.

They laughed, but Nichols wondered how this muscular carpenter could be so sensitive.

"Why do you think she did that?" he asked.

Davey was quicker off the draw. "Cause she'll do anything that gets her what she wants."

They chewed on their pipe stems and ruminated on the lady's character. Davey added, "Maybe she's just really selfish?"

"Takes a whole lot of that to make a woman kill. Men's easier," said Johnny.

"How so?" asked Nichols.

"We do that for a living and get medals when we kill the right ones." Johnny added, "Women ain't allowed to get at the business end of a gun."

"Good thing, too," added Davey, "If'n they did, there'd be none of us left."

They plunged into arguing over the relative merits of "mother," "wife," "woman," and "just a low-down plain old stinky."

Nichols smiled and left them to their discussion of the sins, wickednesses, and glories of the weaker sex. He slowly paced his rounds from stem to stern.

Onward was also caught between two women, fore and aft, for both her figurehead and stern crests were female. Under the bowsprit, Lady Liberty stretched forth her right arm miming "Onward" while clutching a bundle of wheat sheaves to her ample, flag-draped breasts. From the center of *Onward's* gracefully curving stern, the face of an Indian in a feather bonnet glowered over the ship's name. The crew thought the Indian was a woman and so jibed that they were "caught between the squaws and the deep blue sea." Under the Indian's hooked nose, *Onward's* motto was emblazoned in foot-high white letters: "According to Law."

Nichols had spent two years on slave patrol off the west coast of Africa thinking about that motto. He kept asking himself, "according to whose law?" while lying in wait for slavers running out of the coast. He had learned patience. He would let them move into the open sea, for he had studied their maneuvers. They thought the deeper the water, the safer they would be. Nichols anticipated their little games and relied on the wind and his own judgment to trap them.

Sometimes he would fire out of range and fall back, limping under wet sails. His quarry would believe they had made a clean break. He would simply turn south to catch the Trade Winds. *Onward* would be blown across the Atlantic and up to the Bahama Channel faster than the slaver's human-bloated holds could travel. He enjoyed their shock when they realized that *Onward* was the same ship they had evaded a month ago on the other side of the ocean. He could catch them within sight of a Cuban fort. That was the moment Nichols loved, to see their faces and to hail them with a raised arm and a clean shot across their bows, right at the moment when they thought they were safe.

Capturing the crew did not mean that the cargo was free. Both the ships and the slaves were to be taken to the nearest and "most convenient" port where a prize court would adjudicate and decide the fates of those who were things in the eyes of the law. As with *Onward*, everything was supposed to be "according to law," but he had been long enough on the high seas to appreciate low meanness.

Nichols was wise to their ways. Slavers would throw hundreds of people overboard, not just to get rid of the evidence of their trafficking, but mainly because the cargo was insured. They could make a claim that the cargo had to be sacrificed to save the ship. This satisfied the lawyers. Nichols had been a young midshipman of only seventeen summers when he had seen his first "cargo discharge."

They had sailed through a soup of sharks and human flesh. He looked over the side to see limbs and the leavings of headless bodies bumping against the hull. The sea had boiled pink. It had taken hours to sail clear of the rotting carcasses. An Old Sailor explained that the sharks were frenzy feeding, for "they ain't had such a good meal in a month o' Sundays."

Nichols remembered one persistent fin which had followed them for ten days. The Old Sailor nodded his head and laughed, "He be the greedy one. He thinks there's more where that came from." For the first time, Nichols knew that death was always just one rope length away. One slip and he would not last longer than the seconds it took for that fin to reach him. He shuddered to think of such a death, but the Old Sailor clasped a kindly hand upon his shoulder and said, "Just remember, one hand for the ship and one hand for yourself." The grizzled face smiling at him was evidence of survival and proof of the point. He had never forgotten those words and had developed into a fine officer by practicing what the old man had preached. The Old Sailor's advice had remained through all the changes of crews, and ships, and shores, and duties, and he had shared "one hand for the ship and one hand for yourself" with all the sailors, and officers, and chiefs he had ever known. That was Nichols' law.

Now he patrolled a new shore, but it was the coast of his own country. The Carolinas, Georgia, and the necklace of islands between them were Nichols' new mission. Africa was a dim memory of past duty, but *Onward* still sailed "according to law."

His orders were clear and simple; he was to "enforce the blockade of shipping." All the commanders in the squadron had been instructed by some lawyer from the Navy Department that "to comply with the Law of the Sea, a blockade must be effective." They resented being told what to do as if they were children, or worse, midshipmen. They had spent their lives according to the Law of the Sea, and now this civilian who never got his feet wet was telling them the obvious. With every ship they captured, the Prize Courts doled out the proceeds "according to law." The politicians harvested votes from the expertise of the sailors. Congressman or deck hand was each rewarded "according to law," and Nichols was a small wheel in a vast money machine.

He glanced up to watch the moon beams dance along the spars. All his questions of "whose laws?" seemed as futile as the sparkles floating upon the waves. Lately, he had been suffering returning headaches, which had nothing to do with the salt crusting over his eyes. He had been thinking too much. The tired masts and moist rigging glistened with webs of diamond spray. The sea was calm, and it rippled around the ship, blinking in the moonlight like a carpet of fireflies. Nichols walked back from the rail smirking that "we are to take comfort from the command and the promise of the figurehead." He laughed aloud at the motto emblazoned upon *Onward's* stern. Somehow, the words just didn't rhyme. "If we are going onward, where is the law? If we were to live by these bad laws, how were we ever to prosper?"

Lady Audley wasn't the only one to keep secrets.

Chapter 3

By The Rising of the Moon

Alfred and Robert stood on the deck of *Planter*, watching the dock gang load the cannons, ammunition, and supplies onto the afterdeck. Robert turned his back to lean against the guardrail, so he could see the dockside reflected in the panes of the wheelhouse window. His eyes followed Seajay and Digby crossing the street. Digby looked naked without his belt and bayonet as he followed Seajay into Ripley's headquarters. Alfred chattered loudly and Robert feigned laughter through a broad grin. They could hardly believe their luck; *Planter*'s officers and masters would be ashore for the night.

It had all started a month ago as the best joke in Charleston. Some slaves got themselves onto a garbage barge and slipped the ropes. Their screams and desperate shouts gathered a crowd to enjoy the spectacle. The further the barge drifted from the land, the louder its passengers hollered, "Save me," "I'se goin ta drownded," "Dat water be big." The audience held their sides, slapped their backs, and howled at the ridiculous scene of a Minstrel Show on the water. The barge drifted with the tide until it hit the Ashley current and picked up speed. The slaves howled in feigned panic and ostentatiously prayed for deliverance from their watery fate. As the barge drifted out of sight, the crowd turned their backs and went home to relate the tale of a "garbage scow full of jumping jacks," but the run-aways laughed loudest when they made landfall the next day and were picked up by a Union patrol. They had set themselves adrift and trusted to the future.

When Alfred had joined *Planter's* crew, the wandering barge was all the talk. Robert and Alfred had laughed as heartily as the rest, until Alfred said, "It would be a better joke if we took this tub bucket ourselves." Robert's determined lips strangled his glee, and the laughter abruptly ceased. He whispered, "If you are serious, come to my house, but keep your mouth shut." Alfred nodded, and he just happened to drop by Robert's room that evening.

Hannah had prepared biscuits and lemon water, and they spent that first evening considering all the angles for stealing the ship. The conversation grew more questions than answers until it blossomed into disappointed frustration. They were about to give up when Hannah casually asked, "I thought you had a wife and child in Alabama you wanted to visit?" Her eyes dredged up some of Alfred's courage. He could not hide from the hope in Hannah's question. "That's one smart wife you got."

Robert heard General Ripley's door squeak open behind him and looked into the window to see Ripley, Digby, and Seajay step into the street. The trio walked down the line of buildings and marched up the steps of the Excelsior. Robert restrained Alfred's eagerness with an open palm. "Wait." They turned to casually watch William work the crane.

They walked down the gangplank and gathered the crew. Robert looked over the long metal tubes waiting their turn to be hauled aboard and spoke straight at the men. "We're going to send the women on their way." The crew nodded and went about their business, carrying boxes of gunpowder and rolling cannon shells along the stout wooden planks to *Planter*'s afterdeck. They had already loaded three cannons and the ammunition was growing into a deadly pyramid.

Alfred and Robert began to walk home to the slave quarters where Hannah was waiting for them. They had plotted their every move, but they could not keep the lid on the gossip. Over three weeks, their chances slimmed as more people joined their little party. There was family to consider. They would not desert their loved ones to the vengeance of their success or the retribution of their failure. Hannah was terrified of wagging tongues, and her fear fueled Robert's caution. One word slipped into the wrong ear would be a death sentence. Two days ago, one of those tongues appeared like a flustered ghost.

*   *   *   *   *

Alfred and Robert were walking to the dock when two girls came running up to Alfred. The short one squealed and jumped to hug him, and he laughed. "Why if it isn't my Little Dee Dee?" The girl was so overjoyed to see Alfred that Robert looked closely at Little Dee Dee's taller companion. Alfred grinned and asked about everybody back at the plantation and sincerely hoped that he would see her again soon because he had to "get myself back to work." The two tripped off, turning to wave at Alfred, who waved back and whispered through his smiles, "Trouble." Robert walked beside him and breathed, "Hannah."

Hannah knew all about the likes of Little Dee Dee, but the tall one was new to her. Alfred explained, "the long streak is Sandy the Saint. Ol' Miss bred her too young, and when her baby come, she got religion. More like religion got her. As soon as she dropped that child, she hollered for the Lord, and nobody could shut her up. Then she commenced preaching to the chickens in the yard. When they would not confess their sins and wickednesses, she tore off their heads, and then started in on the children."

Hannah could see straight through the problem, but she sensed Alfred's need to talk, so she asked about "that short skit of a girl." Alfred signed, "Dee Dee is a massa pet." Hannah and Robert waited for Alfred's next words to crawl up to his mouth. He tried to make it a joke, but Hannah knew there was nothing funny about this sort of pet. "She hears everything and trades for pieces of candy," Alfred said, and the memories fought with his fear. "She has a sweet tooth and a poison tongue. To get the candy, she'll tell any tale, true or not." Worry pulled his lips straight, but Alfred shook off his anxiety, "The pair of them wouldn't make a decent half-wit." Hannah nodded but said, "Just enough brains to hurt and not enough heart to heal." The worry hopped from Alfred to Robert when she said, "Even idiots have tongues."

They held their panic in tight reins, but Hannah knew there was something Alfred was hiding, and Robert knew Hannah saw something, so he asked for more. Alfred sucked in his anger and related the goings on at Home Plantation. "She scouts for Tiny Tim," Alfred explained. Hanna and Robert raised perplexed brows. "He's the house master at Home Plantation."

"Why Tiny Tim?" Hannah prodded.

"Ol' Miss, she cried buckets about some family called Cratchit and then she fixed on the smallest of the slave children. The boy was well fed, but never seemed to grow, so she named him Tiny Tim. He followed her everywhere in his little gentleman's suit. He was always close by with a handkerchief, or a pillow, or riding post on her carriage team. She liked to brag to her friends that 'my boy's smile can light up the room on a cloudy day.'"

All four feet ten inches of Tim had never grown into his purchase price, so Ol' Miss had kept him as a house pet. He learned to attend her at table, and she beamed pride when her guests commented on how decorative were her servants. The slaves joked that Ol' Miss would "make Tim into a jockey," but added, "at the dog races." They toyed with the idea of having him stand at the gates with a lantern in his hand when guests arrived for a soiree, but gave up the idea because the driver "couldn't bend low enough to see that light."

What nature had withheld in stature, Ol' Miss had supplied in rank. She trained him as her major domo and placed him in charge of all the other house servants. Ol' Miss had told Tim that "I could not replace you for less than a thousand dollars," and Tim's chest swelled with pride in every penny of his worth. Henceforth, he was "The Irreplaceable" who kept the house slaves in line. This was just the way Master liked it because he did not wish to waste time training servants to both know and keep their places. Master simply called him "The Insufferable."

Tim's devotion to his mistress made him eager to satisfy her every whim. The child's smile decayed into a permanent scowl, and the sparkling eyes dimmed in hollow sockets. Having given up the struggle with height, Tim grew in viciousness and became the tyrant of the house, garden, and yard. To ensure that the other servants were as obedient to Tim as he was loyal to her, Ol' Miss gave him the two giants, Gog and Magog. And Dee Dee's thirst for approval made her Tim's perfect tool.

Little Dee Dee was just an annoyance carrying tales to the master, but Tiny Tim saw her use. When she would run up to the master to report, "That Casco messing wit' ladies." Master would smile, give her a sweet, and send her to Tim. Casco's services were such that the Master bragged to his lodge brothers, "If I let that boy loose, my property would increase ten fold in a year."

When the Master and Ol' Miss were away in Charleston, they left Tim in charge and out of control. One morning, Casco had been resting from his labors and could hardly stand, so when Dee Dee roused him from the kitchen floor shouting, "Missa Tim want you," all he could barely reply was, "Tell him I am not well." Dee Dee skipped back to Tim and reported, "He say you go to Hell." Tim cocked his head and raised an eyebrow until he resembled a startled parrot. But he nodded once to Gog, who shuffled towards the horse stalls. Magog loped up the stairs into the house.

Dee Dee grinned cold to see Gog return with four feet of droopy leather. Tim had commandeered a withered carriage whip and had threaded fish hooks under the lattices of the crossbands. It could no longer goad horses without gouging the flesh, so Tim presented it to Gog as his badge of office to scourge the house slaves. Gog windmilled his arm to limber the muscles, and the steady swish cutting the air called all the slaves to the yard.

Magog dragged Casco along the back porch by a rope halter twisted around the neck. Casco's arms flailed to catch the bannisters, but Magog twisted the rope tighter and dragged Casco scuttling down the steps, like a terrified puppy at the leash. Tim smiled at Casco gasping in the dust, as Gog stood ready behind him.

The slaves crowded an excited semi-circle just out of Gog's reach and held their breaths. Magog twisted the rope and leaned back to stretch Casco's neck. Tim nodded and whispered "One," and Gog's arm slashed a diagonal from Casco's right shoulder to his left thigh. Magog wrenched the rope to strangle Casco's scream, but he played out just enough slack for Casco to gulp a breath. When his lungs were half-full, Tim said "Two," and Magog hauled back the rope so Gog could cut another diagonal. Casco's fingers clawed at his neck, but Magog's grip ensured a gasping silence.

The crowd thrilled with Tiny Tim's every nod, for they were betting on how many slashes Casco could endure before his collapse or his death. This was the most profitable "fixin" they had seen in years, and the pennies cascaded hand-to-hand with every stroke of the lash. Gog raised his arm and held it poised for permission. One voice screamed, "I got two dollar. Who gimme two dollar five?" Greasy fingers fumbled coins to "two dollar twenty," and when the frenzy hit the two and a half-dollar mark, Tim grunted "Six" and the greed gaped through their splattered faces.

Tim conducted the duo of rope and whip and skillfully delayed his commands to raise the betting with the strokes. Magog's garrote held Casco quavering on his knees with his elbow bent back to ward off Gog's next hit. Tim turned his head to the crowd and waited. When he heard "three dollar," he ordered "Seven." Gog cast the next cut over the back and along Casco's ribs until the hooks caught. He waited for "three dollar fifty" to pull out the hooks. Magog loosened his hold into a merciful gasp which only increased the agony.

When the wager reached "ten, ten, ten, I got me ten dollar," Alfred could stand no more and ran to the farthest corner of the house compound. Casco gave up the ghost at eleven dollars and seventy five cents."

Alfred finished his story and his head sank beneath his silence. The night seeped through their skulls and Hannah pressed a palm to Alfred's quivering neck. She knew the men shared her revulsion and she their fear, so she shattered the silence, "Eleven dollars and seventy-five cents?" Alfred nodded "Uh-huh" and held his face as stone. She raised his head and whispered, "Never trust to color."

* * * * *

Alfred shook his head at a heap of rags on the floor. Hannah pulled back a corner of a burlap sack to reveal Little Dee Dee's childish face. Alfred sniffed the air and asked, "Asleep?" Hannah poked the bundle of snores to show Alfred that the girl was unconscious. Her breath was puffing through happy dreams and little bubbles of pleasure popped at the corners of her slack mouth. Hannah assured them, "Cock crow tomorrow won't wake her."

Alfred nodded to the half-eaten pie on the table and chuckled to Robert, "I always said Hannah is one good cook." Robert whispered, "She has a pie for every occasion." Hannah beamed and proudly recited the recipe of "flour, lard, honey, apples, a little water, and two cakes of laudanum." The pie had filled Dee Dee's stomach, but the drug set sweet visions prancing through her skull. Their muffled giggles hid their fear, and the laughter swelled their courage.

"And the long one?" Robert asked. "That girl is finding relief in the arms of the Lord," Hannah said, and they had to cover their mouthes to stifle their glee.

Hannah had understood that Sandy the Saint was as malicious as she was crazy. Hannah's pie would ensure Dee Dee's silence long enough, but she confessed to Robert, "We'll have to get that length of skittering religion out of the way." She had approached the Reverend Kenneth to "please take that poor girl, for she cries out for comfort." The Reverend had spent months planning his camp meeting. This would be his largest congregation, and he expected a bountiful harvest. Hannah shook with such genuine pity for that "poor soul" when she described the "strange shouts in the night" that Reverend Kenneth grew worried. He wrapped a comforting arm around Hannah's trembling shoulders when she spoke of "the voices that were not that girl's." Reverend Kenneth was no fool and would not judge whether this was a simple case of mania or a possession by the infernal powers. He had the cure of souls but little experience of ministering to lunatics. It was enough for him to know "that girl just ain't right in the head" and include her in the two days of prayer and scripture, good food, and better fellowship which was a revival. At the last minute, he had found a family who would would take the "afflicted one" with them and minister to her physical and spiritual needs. Alfred blurted, "Preaching is better than pie," and Hannah added, "by now she should be dancing before the altar, making many joyful noises unto the Lord."

They chuckled to see Little Dee Dee snoring on the floor and laughed at the thought of Sandy the Saint howling at the moon. There was quiet pride in solving such a complicated problem with such simple solutions, and that was half the fun.

Every slave started every journey with "the good sit," when they thought of all that was past and what would yet be. They settled down to wait. This would be the greatest journey of their lives, but they all knew that it could be their last. Robert dwelt on the ten short miles separating the dock and the Union ships. It was no distance for the ship; for them it would be an eternity. Robert had figured out the best time to go, so now they just had to wait for the tide to fill the bay and carry them away.

Alfred looked up at the far wall and watched the stream of moonlight dive through the haint hole to the floor. Slave quarters had slits for windows on walls facing the street. The masters said these ventilation slots were to "keep you safe from any wandering spirit seeking your soul in the night." The slow witted were grateful for this safety from the haints, but Alfred knew the windows were not to keep out the ghosts, but to keep in the slaves. He waggled a thumb at the window and joked, "That haint hole says 'you h'aint going nowhere.'" Robert grinned and softly whispered, "There's more than one hole." They watched the moonbeam crawl over the floor. On a clear night, the little rectangle of light was as accurate as a clock.

Hannah's mind mapped out her busy day. She had gathered her little flock at five points along a circular route from their room to the riverbank. Her daughters and their babies were waiting for her. She had left Little Robert, her last born child, at the last station on the way, so the child and his grown sister would have the shortest trip to the water.

The big question pinned Alfred to the floor. All he knew was that there was a woman with her child somewhere in Alabama. He had heard it was a big place, so he could not just go door-to-door asking, "Has anybody seen a beautiful woman about twenty years old, answers to the name of Lizzie? She has a lovely baby about a year old." He smirked to think of such foolishness, but he had no better plan. The baby would be about four years old now and would not remember him. He hoped Lizzie had a better memory. However big this Alabama was, Charleston was shrinking. Soon the town would be too small for him to even ask the question, let alone find the answer. He had to leave this place before it strangled him.

Robert watched the moonbeam bump against the table leg and said, "Time." They all stood and shook the knots out of their legs, and their feet knew exactly what to do. There would be no more hurts wrapped in memories, no more tales tied up in bundles of gossip. The time for thinking was done. They walked out the door and through the gate into the street, casting aside their yesterdays like infected rags. The moon rose into the quadrant that said 3:00 AM and glowed upon their silent steps. At the corner, Alfred and Robert turned toward the docks, while Hanna marched straight ahead across the street.

Robert and Alfred ambled into North Dock Street and saw *Planter* sitting high upon the tide. They could see she was fully loaded, and the relief stoked their eagerness. They willed their legs to keep a slow steady stroll, for their feet strained to march in time to their heart beats. The crew had lashed the cannons lengthwise along the afterdeck. They had placed the ammunition boxes tight around each cannon, so they would not roll when *Planter* got under way. The neat rows of boxes reminded Robert of babies' cradles, until he saw the two barrels of gun powder lashed tight to the farthest stern rail. They were the deadliest cargo, so William had placed them the farthest from the passengers. The extra weight made *Planter* heavy ended, and her bows rose two feet higher than her stern. Alfred whispered through the side of his mouth, "Will she carry?" and Robert forced an assured "Uh-huh" through clenched teeth.

Alfred's heart rose with the white wisps floating from the smoke stack. The engine gang had banked low glow in the fireboxes under the boilers, so that the embers could be pulled to a roaring blaze in seconds. The gentle hissing told them that *Planter* was ready for full steam as soon as they needed it. They refused the temptation to look at Ripley's headquarters, just in case Seajay's bladder had roused him from his stupor.

Sammy stood at the bows, holding the rope linking *Planter* to the dockside, and Abe was at his station in the stern. Bill Morrison and his cousin John were standing on deck grasping the ropes holding the gangplank in position. When Alfred and Robert stepped onto the deck, Bill and John silently swung the gangplank aboard and gently lowered it onto the deck. A week of practice and a fistful of grease had paid off in silence, for not a squeak or a thump was heard. The slightest scraping of metal would sound their doom. Sammy gripped the belaying pole under his right arm with its head just touching the side of the dock. Robert walked up the gangplank and nodded to Sammy. With the rope in his left hand and the ten feet of pole tucked under his arm, Sammy reminded Robert of a picture in one of Hannah's books about a knight of olden times. Sammy made a comical sort of knight without a horse.

Alfred jumped down the engine room steps and nodded to George and Eddy standing before the two boilers holding their rakes and shovels as if on sentry duty. Alfred turned his back on them and wiped the sweat from his face. He controlled the tremors in his leg and stood between the two giant pistons that would push *Planter*'s paddles into the unknown. He knew George and Eddy would feed the green logs into the fireboxes and keep the pressure high. With a final suck of air, he grasped the two levers that controlled the giant flywheels and waited for Robert's voice to jump out of the trumpet in front of his face.

Robert let his eyes grow accustomed to the moonlight splattering the harbor. As he always did at night, he would drag his gaze from the far to the middle distance, until his eyes could make out details on the water. When he could see the starless outline of Fort Sumter a mile away, he could focus on anything floating in the water between him and the looming island. He watched a branch turning on a rippling wave, and it reminded him of a hand waving or something drowning. Only then did he turn to see Sammy waiting at the bow rope for his signal. He nodded once.

Sammy set the tip of the pole on the side of the dock and leaned forward to push *Planter* clear. He heaved his shoulder into his joust with the land and played out the rope through his hand. *Planter* swayed two feet from the dockside and dipped her bow as Abe tethered her stern. Robert cocked his head out of the bridge window and saw Abe's white-knuckle fists pulling on the stern rope. He whispered into the tube, "One Right," and the sidewheel paddles stroked the water bubbling between *Planter* and the land. Tidewater swirled into the wet triangle widening between the deck and the dock. Abe braced his feet against the rail, tugged *Planter*'s stern toward the dock, and the bow inched toward the open sea. Sammy let the bow rope slither through his fist into the water. He usually threw the rope onto the dockside, but tomorrow, it would not be needed.

Robert let *Planter* slide into the current, and they waited for the sea to part them from the land. Digby had guided Seajay and Ripley home on staggering feet, and by now they should all be passed out. They had forgotten to close the curtains, yet again, and a shaft of candle light beamed from the top window of Ripley's headquarters. Robert needed to save his night vision, so he averted his eyes from the small flame that dappled the cobblestones from the window to the dockside.

The tide pushed *Planter* back, so Robert breathed into the tube, "Ahead One." Alfred's nostrils flared in the engine room. He grasped both piston levers and pulled them up one notch. George and Eddy steadied themselves with their boiler rakes as *Planter* waddled forward. Robert squinted into the darkness and held the wheel in a hopeful caress as his heart thumped in time with the paddlewheels. *Planter* inched forward, chuffing a lullaby. Her smoke stack passed across the glimmer of candle light as *Planter* slid into the bay, as if on velvet slippers.

Chapter 4

Night Patrol

Onward was riding a gentle swell with just enough wind to keep her few sails snoring, like an old lady napping. Johnny snapped his head to the left, and Davey stood quietly rigid. "What is it?" he asked, but Johnny was silent in concentration. Davey sucked deeply on his pipe and mustered patience, as Johnny's eyes searched the night. "It blinked," he said.

"Blinked?" asked Davey.

"Blinked."

As *Onward*'s bow swung toward the land, Johnny and Davey scampered across the foredeck and resumed their dark vigil. Nichols saw them dodge below the foremast ropes and stopped amidships to watch. He always stood beside the mizzen mast, for that was the very center of *Onward*'s deck, where nothing could escape his notice. Standing on the afterdeck beside the wheel was a good pose for painters of thrilling scenes of "The South Atlantic Squadron," but a real commander had to be everywhere at all times. Leaning his back on the spray-smoothed wood of the central mast allowed him to rest at "Alert" the whole night.

Nichols had to know why they had jumped to the other side of the ship, so he padded along the deck until he came up behind them. They knew he was there, but did not stop craning their necks to the distant harbor. "See anything?" Nichols sighed.

"It blinked." said Johnny.

"How many times?"

"Just once."

They stood for ten minutes searching for any twinkling, but there was nothing. This was unusual, and Nichols sensed trouble in anything out of place. They knew that some fool in town kept a candle burning with the curtains opened. It had happened three times in the past month, but the candle guttered, and the light was gone. Either light or darkness was normal. A blink was not. Nichols would have to ponder the meaning of this blink. Candles and lanterns did not blink. Nichols quietly ordered them to "keep a sharp eye and ear," and turned to continue his pacing. They did not acknowledge him with a formal "Aye Aye, Sir," because he wanted results not protocol. Polite behavior was for port and senior officers.

*   *   *   *   *

Robert's shoulders swayed in time with *Planter*, but his hands clasped the wheel to steady his nerves. George and Eddy raked the boiler fires as if nursing a friend with a bad cold, and the engines rocked in a stately waltz time. They kept the flames dancing in a light orange glow over green logs, so the sparks would not flare in the smokestack. The snorting crackles of a waking boiler could raise the dead. The sidewheels turned in lazy circles and silently cut the water, as Sammy and Abe stood in the bows guiding Robert the hundred yards to the *Etowah*.

Sammy waved his arm backwards and down, and Robert spoke into the tube, "All stop." Alfred halted the pistons and water gurgled gently beneath the taut paddles as *Planter* glided up to the side of the *Etowah*. Abe held a fender over the side for *Planter* to snuggle close to the other boat. Robert could barely feel the two boats touching. He stared through the wheelhouse window at Hannah's arm waving to him.

Because it was such a useless hulk, they had arranged for all the women and children to be collected on the *Etowah*. Her owner had convinced the authorities that his worm-rotted derelict would "come in handy some day," and he had pestered his friends on the city council to purchase the "hundred feet of spongy planking" and commission her the CSS *Etowah*. Forgotten at its lonely wharf and ridiculed as "graft upon the low seas," *Etowah* was the perfect hiding place for escaping slaves.

54

When Robert and Alfred had turned the corner to the docks, Hannah had marched straight on to her appointed rounds. She had gathered fifteen men, women, and children from the five points where she had stashed them. She had worked out a roundabout route along a wide semi-circle to the docks. The route had been dictated by the sleeping habits of the masters. Two women and their three children hovered in the shadows of Mrs. Johnson's house, because she was old and went to bed the earliest. Noisy revelers ignored an entire family squatting in the moon-shade of a tree in a brothel's garden. She had hidden two in a cemetery behind the ornate tomb, "Sacred to the Memory of Jedediah Quentin Sloane," with strict admonitions to "be quiet as the grave." Others huddled in the stalls of an empty stable, with no horses to scare. The last feigned a drunken slumber on the rotting dock planks beside the *Etowah*. Hannah skipped shadow-to-shadow, steering clear of the puddles of light left by clouds blowing across a full moon.

*   *   *   *   *

The clouds were passing in parade over *Onward*. Nichols squinted at the moonlight hopping along the swaying spars of all three masts. A visible full moon meant a quiet watch through a wave-cradled night because even the greediest fool would not risk cargo, ship, and crew under such an open sky. Moonless nights in a storm were the busiest. He looked over the miles of shimmering water surrounding him and felt assured that no danger would be coming out of Charleston. He had positioned *Onward* to maneuver on a wide sea to catch anything approaching from landward. It was rare, but he had kept alive all these years by preparing for the most unexpected event. There was safety in such wariness.

He had seen what the Gentlemen Rebels could do with a few bits of railroad iron. They had nailed the metal to a fast, screw driven harbor boat. Nichols saw it dart out of a river inlet, coming

55

dead straight for them. He immediately ordered a broadside, and the first cannonball split the metal apart, like wind through tall corn. The thing lay dead a hundred yards to port, hissing its death rattle, but *Onward* kept its distance. The boarding party's boat nosed around the iron clad ship, like a duck pecking at a dead egg. When the boilers blew, all that iron just kept the steam from escaping. Nichols forced open the main hatch and the scene reminded him of a lobster kettle. It stood only three feet above the water, but the sting was under the surface. Three fifty foot lengths of iron rail had been attached to the bows and merged into a point five feet below the waterline. It was a ram. It could punch a hole five feet wide through oak planking and kill a ship.

Nichols kept Webb and Davey on full night-watch with orders to look landward, just in case.

*   *   *   *   .*

Robert could not leave the wheelhouse, and Alfred was confined to the engine room, so Hannah was in charge of the passengers. William and the loading crew were as gentle with their human cargo as they were cautious with gunpowder. William stood on *Planter*'s deck as Hannah passed the four sleeping infants to him from the *Etowah*. Sammy guided a frightened momma as she climbed gingerly over the slippery rail, then waited beside her for Hannah to pass over her child. Abe led the pair to the stern and seated them behind an ammunition box. They carried on this bucket brigade of babies, until the stern was crammed with fifteen bundles of terrified hope. Hannah waited until the last. Abe stretched forth his hand, and she stepped from one ship to the other. Abe was startled by her step, for he hadn't expected such a large lady to be so light on her feet. This was going to be a night of many surprises.

Sammy pushed the dock pole until *Planter* drifted free. He felt the boat move under him and stood for a moment watching the boats drift apart. He let the point of the pole dip into the water. It was one of the funniest sights he had ever seen. Only his fist crammed into his mouth stopped him from laughing out loud. The pole was now the most useless thing, so he let it slide into the water with a dull splash. The pole floated, turning like a lazy compass needle, and he stopped laughing.

Hannah made Abe count the passengers and when they tallied, Sammy stepped along the deck and crept up the ladder to the bridge. He nodded to Robert and told him, "Mrs. Smalls say 'Go.'" Robert looked to the right and saw the dock pole glide past them. He waited until it looked no bigger than a fireplace poker, and knew that there was enough space between them and the dock to set their course and fire the engines. He calmly told the speaking tube, "All Ahead, Four," and pointed *Planter* towards Fort Sumter.

*   *   *   *   *

Nichols felt uneasy in his skin. Hanging from its fifty feet of chain cable, the anchor would not hit the sea floor. When the sea was calm, *Onward* would turn in long graceful circles at the end of her chain. At sunset, they had thrown out a drag anchor and bedded down the crew. The Night Watch above decks held her steady on station, and by midnight *Onward* was a rolling box of snores and swaying hammocks below decks. He had ordered that there be at least two officers on deck throughout the night, but he always took more watches than any other officer. On such a night, Nichols rested at the stern rail behind the helmsman. He felt the ship gently ride upon the tide and lazily swing to the light breezes of night.

In such peace, a man might nod to gentle dreams, but this was not Nichols' lot. The activity of the day, with its hustle and its ordered frenzy of sails and ropes, was Nichols' peace. Night brought either terrors or hate and frustration. He leaned his elbows on the rail and rubbed his hands against the cold. Night fired his detestation of the stupidity that had brought him to this place just ten miles from where the foolishness had all started.

He gazed back at the darkness of Charleston and sneered, "The idiots thought they could hide the place." He had shared a hearty laugh with the other officers when they realized that the rebels' church spires had been painted black. The exercise had been worse than useless, for the whole town stood out in silhouette against a starry sky. All they had to do was look where there was no silver peppered sky and they could see Charleston carved in darkness. The crew had guffawed when he announced to them that "the lair of the enemy is now as clear as if your little sister had cut its outline on black paper with a pair of blunt scissors." He had announced, "Three Cheers for Fools in High Places" and men and officers responded with three waves of enjoyable contempt.

But other stupidities crawled through his mind in the night. He had read of a fire-breathing senator who rose in Congress to announce, "I will soak up all the blood spilled in this war with my handkerchief," and waved ten inches of snot-rag above his head to a standing ovation. Nichols had frequently looked at the thousands of square yards hanging over *Onward* and saw them all dripping blood. He had once frightened a sailor with his scowl when he burst out, "Every sail in the whole navy should be crimson." The sailor didn't know that his commander was cursing the politicians.

Nichols leaned out over the stern to catch a wandering breeze and cool his brow, but the thoughts just heated his head. The sweat spread through the leather headband of his hat, so he grasped its peak and wiped his forehead with the back of his hand. A sweat bead splashed from his nose over the Indian's head below him, and he followed its trail to the ship's motto, "According to Law." He snorted and recalled a few mess-deck fights he had to punish.

All the brawls had been over politics, but the men never threw punches for the Republicans or the Democrats. Both the spats warranting a Commander's Trial had been over the ridiculous competition of "My congressman is twice as corrupt as your damned senator." When the evidence had been presented to Nichols as supreme judge at sea, he could hardly control his laughter. He sentenced both pugilists to "two weeks double watches and galley duties." He had purged *Onward*'s crew of the drunks, the lunatics, the wounded in mind and body, and the cowards. He heartily wished he could do the same to Washington. He laughed ruefully at "According to Law," turned, and paced back to Johnny and Davey at their posts in the bow, hoping they would improve his mood.

*   *   *   *   *

Alfred heard "All Ahead Ten" and pulled the piston levers two notches along their ratchets. Robert felt the bow lurch forward as the sidewheels turned ten to the minute. They would need the extra power, for the Ashley current wasn't strong enough to push them through the incoming tide. Robert listened to the mounting rhythm of engine and wheels, and when he felt the thrust, he faced *Planter* to the south channel between Sumter Island and Morris Point.

Hannah shuffled along the rows of cannons and boxes, her voice soothing each passenger in turn. Abe and Sammy were placing the men to squat on the deck between cannon barrels and boxes. The two barrels of gunpowder stood silently threatening them all. William tried not to think of what a stray spark would do, so he spoke in whispered orders to each man of his gang and to the male passengers. "You will sit quiet until I tell you to stand. Look at the floor. Nothing else." They obeyed with the belief that this man knew what to do and took refuge in their docility.

Hannah had put her trust in her pie, for each child slept as soundly as Little Dee Dee back at the quarters. A baby's night cry would be as deadly as a rifle shot. The mothers' panicked whimpering could be smothered until they were further away, so she made sure that they sat together gossiping under their breaths. The women were astonished to hear this older woman asking them about their men and were happy to brag in whispers about the boys they left behind and the men they hoped to meet. Hannah listened as if this was the most important talk she ever had and kept them softly prattling, waiting for the signal from William that they should all "hush now."

The moon stood fair upon the straits between the fort and the peninsula. Robert nudged the wheel to the left, pointing *Planter* at Sumter. He wanted to pass the sentry post close enough to be seen, but not so close as to be recognized. On the rare occasions that *Planter* had made a night run, he had noticed that the guard was usually asleep. Seajay liked to sneak up, hang on the whistle cord, and laugh at the stream of curses blasting from the guard post. Robert had decided to follow the captain's example. Waking the sentry was a low-down trick, but that was all the guards expected from Seajay.

Planter veered to within hailing distance of the sentry box hanging high on the walls of the fort. Robert reached above his head for the cord of the steam whistle, when he saw Seajay's straw hat lying on the chart table. He grabbed the hat and jammed it over his head almost covering his ears. With one hand on the wheel and the other on the whistle cord, he swung *Planter* into the currents rushing around the fortress island. The sentry box was dark, so Robert pulled three times. Two men jumped out of the wooden shelter, shaking their fists and hurling oaths and insults. "That damned fool!" "Seajay, get your stinking ass outta here!" Robert scrunched up his nose and roared Seajay's annoying nasal laugh as loud as he could. The laughter and the hat convinced the guards that Seajay was up to his old tricks, so they tried to settle back to the hour of sleep left in a short night.

Robert turned *Planter* sharply to trace a circle around the island, but hung on the whistle to leave one long screech behind him. Every guard on dock, fort, island or battery knew the signal was three short whistles and one long blast. Robert made *Planter* sing the right tune for the right time, to keep them guessing as long as possible. All he needed was a half hour of hesitation.

* * * * *

Davey felt Nichols creep up behind them and ask, "Anything?"

"A harbor signal," Davey answered.

"What was it?"

"Three short... one long."

Nichols had to know, "When?"

Davey took a breath and whispered, "About five minutes ago." Nichols pondered the strangeness of a signal in the middle of the night. Davey added curiously, "the long blast was longer than I would expect."

"Longer," said Nichols. "How longer?"

"I don't know. It was longer... It sounded like it was a joke."

Davey was not the sort to make up sea tales. Others would offer elaborate explanations for a branch rolling in the surf, but Davey always stuck to the facts. If he said the whistle was like a joke, there had to be an explanation. First, a blink. Now, three toots and a laughing whiffle. Something was going on, but Nichols would wait for more.

* * * * *

Planter chugged around the tip of Sumter Island, so that any sleepy eyes watching from Fort Moultrie on Sullivan's Island would think she was headed back to port. When he could feel the current from the Cooper River slow the boat, Robert told Alfred, "All Stop." The sidewheels ground to a halt, and they could hear only the engines humming to rest.

He had long known that the Hog Island Channel met the Cooper River current just off Sullivan's Island, but on this night

61

he trusted to the merging of the two flows to turn *Planter* around. The force of both rivers would be just enough to face them in the right direction without the thumping engines tattling to suspicious guards.

The fort was not more than fifty yards from their side, and the moon picked out every detail of the walls and the boat. He heard voices through the thrumming of the engines, but could not move to silence the gossips. *Planter* started to drift slowly back. Robert swung the wheel to the right and waited.

Robert felt the bow swing gently, and *Planter* heaved to the right with the current. She wallowed as if drugged, but the river water nudged her around. Robert eased the wheel back to center, and his throat ached. His fingers were slippery on the wheel as they picked up speed. He let *Planter* drift, and his heart slowed when he could see the parapets of Moultrie pass by his left shoulder. He kept his eyes straight ahead, searching for the little white serrations that betrayed the shoals beneath.

He nudged *Planter* to the right of the breakers blinking over Drunken Dick and his chums. He wanted to laugh aloud and whistle to the ghosts of those sodden revelers and tell them, "You'll have to wait for us to join the party." But he stifled his joy to feel the currents drag them back towards the Main Ship Channel.

Even if there were no moon, he'd know exactly where they were. This close to shore was as far out of range of Sumter as he could get without running aground. Once past the breakers, Moultrie was too distant to be wakened by their engines. The currents would throw them into the tide, and *Planter* would fight the flow all the way to the open sea.

He used the wheelhouse window to frame his course through the Main Channel. Just within the pane of glass, he could see the surf breaking on both Morris and Sullivan islands. Morris on the right was called Lighthouse Point, even though there had been no such structure for many years. On dark nights, one solitary lantern guided the English ships running into harbor, but tonight the shore was a necklace of moonbeams on sand and rock. He knew one trick that had saved his neck on many such nights. A tide would crest and spiral along its length, but there were also strange lights along its path. He cocked his head and saw the wave beams rippling green along the tidal foam, like limelight in a theater. When he squinted into the center of the window, Rattlesnake Shoals glimmered to the left and the smoke stack of a wreck popped above the water to his right.

He aimed at the blackness between the white shallows and the tide-washed cylinder, but his own reflection disturbed him. For a moment, he was caught by his own eyes looking back at him. The sight of his face was like a candle destroying his night vision. *Planter* thumped into the oncoming tide and cleared Robert's head. He welcomed the darkness and chuckled to think he was the best pilot in Charleston, even when he was almost blind.

The tide slowed them, and when Robert's head jerked back, he could just see his eyes beaming under Seajay's hat. He felt ridiculous and said, "I wouldn't be caught dead in this plate of moldy straw." He threw the stinking hat over his shoulder and commanded into the speaking tube, "All Ahead Half."

Planter churned over the rim of the tide. Her bows washed a filigree of dirty lace along her sides, as if she were plowing through molten lead. Robert held her steady and straight for the gap between the shoals and the wreck. With the channel below and the moon sinking behind them, *Planter* chuffed steadily into the night, trailing timber sparks behind her.

Chapter 5

Glory in the Mist

First light shot over the horizon into Johnny's eyes. Somebody had once told him that morning was "the rosey-fingered dawn," but they had never seen day break over a calm sea in Carolina. Nothing but the curvature of the earth stood between them and the sun streaming up the hull and over the whole crew standing for First Watch.

Nichols kept Davey close by on the quarterdeck and positioned Webb in the bows. Half an hour before dawn, Davey had hailed Nichols and said the one word, "Engine." Nichols scanned the ship and saw every man obeying his command for "Silence." Nichols found it comical to see one hundred men pussy footing over the decks and up the rigging, but they knew that silence was not only golden, it was safe. All stood poised and hung on their commander's words and Davey's ears. Neither Johnny's eye nor Nichols' telescope could see what Davey heard, so they must stand and wait.

Davey cupped his fingers around his left ear to snatch any distant vibration. He pressed his palm against the other ear to deaden the booming of the wind in the sails, but heard only the thrumming of his own heart. The blood coursing through his right hand drummed a steady rhythm, and his left ear picked out the faint throb of a distant ship. He closed his eyes, hoping the sounds would merge in his hearing. The ship's engine was getting louder. He waited until both ears tapped in time together and the harmony confirmed his hunch. Davey skewed his neck to Nichols and assured him, "No doubt about it," and thrust his arm into the remains of the night.

There was no use jumping to stations. Nichols would keep the crew at their morning routine, for sudden jerks under sail could sink them quicker than cannon fire. The sun shrugged off the night and yawned clouds. Nichols did not relish these morning mists, and if Davey was right, the middle of a morning fog bank was the last place he wanted to be. He thrust back his head and arched his voice up the mast, "Top Gallant."

The sailor swaying one hundred feet above the deck waved his arm to the east and bellowed, "Clear." Nichols now knew that the fog was a belt five miles wide and rolling into shore with the tide. They could easily retreat from this dawn murk into the open sea, so he commanded, "Face About" and *Onward's* crew turned her to the sun. Nichols kept Davey on the quarterdeck. "Stay here."

*   *   *   *   *

Robert saw the stars grow drowsy with every mile. They were clear of the shallows on either side of the Main Channel, but William was panicking. He jumped up the wheelhouse ladder and shouted, "They're chasing us." William was blubbering about "a boat" and "they'll catch us." Robert could not leave the wheel. There was no time to calm him before William ran back to the stern, so Robert had to turn a deaf ear to William's terror. The wailing of the babies and the screaming women ran through the boat and up to the wheelhouse.

He had to ignore the panicked cries and keep to the channel. He could not look back for everything pointed forward, but William had set them all screaming. Loaded down with cargo and passengers, *Planter* could not outrun any pursuer.

Then Robert saw it loom before him. The cloud of fog was a curtain straight ahead. Once wrapped in its smoky folds, he could not see ten feet in front of him. Whatever was behind them could not catch them, but they were far enough out to sea that Robert did not know where the sandbars lurked and sunken wrecks waited. If they hit just one, they would be trapped until they were captured.

He took one last look at the carpet of indigo water rushing through the channel and shouted into the tube, "Full Speed

Ahead." *Planter* disappeared into the fog. He did not know William could not tell the difference between another ship chasing them and the echo of their own engines.

*   *   *   *   *

When he heard the faint rumbling, Nichols' eyes followed Davey's arm pointing to the wall of cloud behind them. Davey kept repeating, "There." A steamboat was beyond their vision, but not their knowledge. Davey heard Nichols' order, "Face About," and saw the helmsman wait for the sign. The crew stood ready at their stations. Nichols nodded once, and the helmsman spun *Onward* sharply to the right.

Nichols had trained this crew to turn the ship with slow and graceful efficiency. Now that he knew there was something coming out of the harbor, he would not wait to be rammed. Whatever was coming, would have a surprise because he could hear them, even though they could not see each other. He would turn the ship around in a full circle, so there would be maximum wind in his sails heading toward the approaching vessel. With that much speed behind, *Onward* could pounce and the hunter would become his prey. No attacker expected to be attacked. When the maneuver was completed, Nichols would have the steamboat right where he wanted it, dead ahead.

Onward heaved over, and it was every hand for himself, with every sailor clinging to the rigging or mast. Nichols commanded, "Fly Ensign," and the sailor standing by the flag mast pulled a rope and released the American flag tied up in a bundle. Eight feet of Old Glory spread itself before the wind and danced in ribbons of red around the star-studded pole. Nichols had bought this very expensive flag with his own money, not out of patriotism, but because silk flew freer than soggy linen. A Navy-issue flag drooped in every wind. Silk caught each wandering zephyr and a glance at the flag staff told Nichols the exact force and direction of the wind. He thought of it as "the National

Weathervane," and it had allowed him to go anywhere the wind would carry him. The flag flew straight and perpendicular to *Onward's* hull, showing an onshore breeze of six knots. When he turned through the circle, Nichols could count on a steady ten knots of speed and be able to swing past any approaching ship.

He waited for the flag to fall and when it fluttered in a little spiral cone, he ordered "Sheets Forward." The deck crews sprinted to the stern, pulling the ropes attached to the spars fifty feet above their heads. The sailors standing on those tarred branches pulled on other ropes attached to the masts. Together, they turned all of *Onward's* sails into a line running above the deck from stem to stern. This was how the ship could sail against the wind. The prevailing stream would catch the sail and circle in its little cyclone, trapped by the cloth tethered to the spars. With nowhere to go, the energy would travel down the mast and push the ship forward into the wind. This would slow the ship down to half speed, but by rocking from side to side, the wind would circle on both sides of the sail and they could make headway. Nichols could stand confidently between the flag and the wheel, believing in both ship and crew.

*   *   *   *   *

Alfred was about to faint from the heat. The piston arms rose and fell like an insane guillotine and the boilers bulged in protest. George saw Eddy's jaw chattering, and he knew it wasn't from the cold. They had thrown more wood into the firehole and raked the embers to a fierce crimson glow. Alfred had kept turning the hose wheel to let more water into the boiler, but the pistons were very thirsty, and he had to keep fire and water balanced to ensure the steam kept pushing the paddles.

Eddy started to cry because he felt the worry oozing from Alfred, but George shook some of the fear out him with a firm hand and a soft voice saying, "Rake that wood." Eddy thrust the rake straight into the fire, and the heat crawled up the wooden handle to his hands. Just when he thought he could not hold it any longer, George shouted, "Pull," and they dragged their rakes in unison through the burning piles below each boiler. Immediately the pressure surged and Alfred pulled the levers to drive the wheels faster. The sweat collected at their shoulders and ran over their backs and chests. Alfred could barely hear Robert at the other end of the speaking tube. There was no telling how long they would have to endure, but continue they would.

Planter shuddered protests at this unfamiliar haste, and Robert saw swirls of brown mist spinning on each side of the boat. Wood smoke, flaming embers, and sea spray twisted and braided themselves into coils of sparkling ropes circling around the wheelhouse in the fog. He could not see any threatening patches of white rippling over knuckles of rock or wreck. They were running almost completely blind.

The right paddle hit the top of a sandbar, churning stones and crumbling marl inside the wheel-housing. Robert knew they were hitting shallows. The next turn of the wheels could be their last, and they would be stranded. If he slowed, whatever was behind would surely catch them. If he sped up, they could hit rocks, splinter and drown. Either choice would be the end, but he could not blink this decision. It would be better to die together in the water than bring them all back to a worse death on land. He stared straight ahead, with no other hope than the faith he would not hit something lurking beneath the waves.

His eye caught the glint of white to the left. He thought it was a branch, but it disappeared. Moments later, it was cutting the water, and the little semi-circle rose and twisted and was gone. It returned and looked straight at him. It was a dolphin. The fin was keeping pace with *Planter,* and the little show-off was darting in and out of the bow wash. Robert looked to the right and saw three more fins. Robert knew they were having their breakfasts, so they would not be diving in shallows. The best feeding would be in the deepest trench that held the fattest fish. They were feeding in the channel. He could keep in deep water simply by staying close to them. Salvation surfaced with this little troop of hungry clowns. He shouted into the speaking tube, "Pull White."

Alfred could not believe his ears and demanded to hear it again. "Pull White" snaked down the tube with an assurance of joy, but Alfred knew what that meant. He turned to George and Eddy and screamed above the thundering pistons, "Pull White." They stood in terror until he repeated "Pull White" and turned his back on them to grasp the piston levers in each fist.

They pushed their rakes through the flaming wood and heaped the embers at the back of the boiler pan. George looked to Eddy and nodded for them to pull together. They raked the inferno from back to front as fast as they could. The angry pyres burst into white flames writhing in a blue aura and the boilers groaned to hold the pressure. They stood back from the open fireboxes, and white light filled the engine room.

Alfred felt the heat sear his back. He pushed both levers forward until the piston valves were fully opened. He wiped his hands and turned to grasp George and Eddy. There was nothing left to do. The engines were running beyond full power, and the boilers would either take the strain or explode. They could pray or they could cry, but they had to wait. Whatever happened would be quick, and that was the only blessing left.

*   *   *   *   *

Onward turned through the last segment of the circle, and the wind at her back blew her toward the distant fog bank. Nichols looked up at the faces staring down at him from the spars and along the lines upon the deck and ordered, "Full Sail." The spars and sails turned to rest squarely across the center deck line, and the ship surged forward. Nichols ran to the bows and stood beside Johnny. "You're certain?" he asked, and took the returning nod as gospel truth.

Johnny was scanning the edge of the fog bank when he saw the smoke trail. He stretched out his arm and shouted, "There."

Nichols confirmed the report with his telescope and his eye framed *Planter* in the circle of the lens. He snapped the scope shut.

The target was two miles dead ahead, and *Onward* was ready for a quick and clean kill. Nichols yelled to the Chief, "Run Guns," and four cannons on each side of the ship screeched forward on metal wheels to poke their mouths through the wooden walls. The gun crews stood ready to fire. The cabin boys marched down the deck casting sand and sawdust from buckets, like sowers at Spring planting. The sand would help them keep a firm footing; the sawdust was to soak up the blood.

Each second gun was loaded with shot or shell. *Onward* would sail down the side of the approaching ship and fire each gun in sequence. The first gun sent a solid iron ball punching through the hull timbers, and the next gun fired an exploding shell. When all four guns fired in order, the target would be a bloody mass of burning splinters in less than a minute. Nichols had even made the gun crews chant, "Shot and Shell and Shot and Shell. As we pass by, you go to Hell." The sand and sawdust said this was no idle threat. Nichols stood at the base of the bowsprit and looked back to make sure the helmsman could see his hand signals. Johnny fixed his gaze on the approaching ship and told Nichols, "One mile." Nichols raised his left arm above his head, and the wheel juddered in the helmsman's palms.

*   *   *   *   *

Planter punched through the fog bank and the sun blinded Robert. He strained his vision back to daylight, shook his head, raised his chin, and opened his eyelids full to see a three-masted ship directly ahead. Relief rattled through his knees, and he smiled to see the dolphins were his escort. They had joined him out of the fog. Tempted by the water washing over *Planter*'s bow, they darted in and out of the stream, and Robert could feel their magical joy. He saw such hope in their sport, and he was happy

70

to follow them to the ship before him. Salvation beckoned with its three trees of white cloth, and he felt peace ripple up his spine.

*   *   *   *   *

Nichols dropped his left arm, and *Onward* swung gracefully to bear down on the strange vessel. They were in perfect position for the gun run, and Nichols could scan the ship with his telescope. His eye ran along the boat's hull to the stern and he saw that she was low in the water at the back. Cargo was stowed on the afterdeck, boxes and barrels piled in orderly fashion. No ram would be so loaded down at the stern. This was not expected of a warship stripped for attack. He demanded of Johnny, "Is the bow high?" Nichols stood perplexed with the answer, "Yes." With the bow high, the ram should be seen rising above the water. There was no ram. What was this thing doing?

It could be a suicide run full of explosives. They were crazy and desperate enough for that. Nichols ordered, "Prime" and the gunners inserted the igniters into the touch-hole of each gun and held the striker cords at firm attention. Nichols looked along the line of primed guns and saw the flag spread to the side of the ship. The wind had shifted, so it was flying perpendicular to the hull. Nichols leaned over the rail to examine the bow cutting the water and gauged the speed reduced by two knots.

*   *   *   *   *

Robert looked at the ship veering to the right. The American flag flew straight out and there was no greater joy than seeing its welcoming folds. He heard the roar of the passengers on the afterdeck. He turned *Planter* toward the flag's welcoming folds and was impatient to close the gap between them. The dolphins stopped their play, and he was sad to see them go.

*   *   *   *   *

71

Johnny screamed, "She's coming straight at us." Johnny shouted, "She's flying the rebel rag." There was now no indecision. Nichols held his right hand high. When it dropped, all guns would fire to the right.

* * * * *

Robert watched the dolphins follow the fish and swim away from the boat. The pilot house filled with lonesome uncertainty. He seldom had such feelings, and he thought it must be the terrors of their escape making him think about the creatures Alfred so loved. He could not shake the thought that he should follow them, but did not know why. He turned to the left to join the blue tribe cutting through the sea.

* * * * *

"They're turning," Johnny shouted.
"I see it," responded Nichols. Both stood silent. Nichols barked, "Hold Your Fire" to the gunners and slowly lowered his arm to rest his hand upon the rail.

* * * * *

William shouted into the wheelhouse, "I can't get the flag down." They were out on the ocean flying the Carolina flag. Robert had thought it was already down. He looked out the window and saw Hannah running along the deck to the bows. She stood in front of the cannon and bent over something at her feet. Hannah stood up and spread her arms wide, and Robert saw the white sheet. She was playing tug-of-war with the wind over the sheet, and it was about to fly away. William jumped down the ladder and ran to her. He grabbed the other corner of the sheet and together they held it fast in the wind. Robert looked to the dolphins circling the boat and shouted into the tube, "All Stop."

*   *   *   *   *

Nichols squinted at the figure standing in front of the cannon and the white streak and demanded, "What is that?" Johnny answered incredulously, "It's a woman." Nichols hunched his shoulders and declared, "Suicides don't take their women along for the ride." Johnny breathed, "They've stopped."

Nichols aimed his telescope at the stern of the boat and saw black faces staring back at him. He scanned the deck, and his vision swept over a crowd of people jumping, dancing, and hugging one another. Whatever this was, it was not an attack. Even Charlestonians couldn't get their slaves to blow themselves up. He turned to command, "Belay All Guns." The sailors snapped the igniters out of the cannons, but all eyes turned to the odd-looking boat. He glanced up at the mastheads and commanded, "Haul Main Sails." The ropes were dragged and pulled and the sails bunched up to the spars. *Onward* slowed, and the men's curiosity rose as they closed the distance between the two ships.

*   *   *   *   *

Alfred gave silent thanks when he heard, "All Stop." Immediately, he pulled back the piston levers and could feel the boat settle into a slow glide and stop. He opened all the valves and blew the steam from the boilers, and George and Eddy breathed freely. He didn't have to say, "Let's get outta here," before they all clambered up to the deck.

*   *   *   *   *

73

When they were within hailing distance, Nichols demanded, "Who are you?"

Robert shouted from the wheelhouse window, "*Planter*."

Nichols' eyes glanced over the boat's nameplate. "I can read," he retorted. "I asked, 'Who are you?'"

Robert gazed directly into Nichols' eyes not twenty-five feet from him and said, "I am Robert Smalls. Pilot of Charleston Harbor."

Nichols introduced himself with a shout into the wind. "I am Lieutenant Frederick Nichols. Commander of *USS Onward*." Every eye on *Onward* was turned to *Planter,* and when they realized that every face staring back at them was black, every voice was raised in shocked disbelief. Robert waved across the gulf between the two ships and spread his arms to the man. He heard Nichols order him. "Stay where you are. I will send a boat."

Nichols told Chief Murphy to "take Webb and Collins on the boarding party," and he ordered the cutter launched. Johnny and Davey rowed together, and all of the sailors were as curious as they were armed. Murphy was taking no chances, so every man sported a pistol in his belt or a cutlass in his hand. They pulled alongside *Planter* and clambered onto her forward deck.

The ship was a jumble of men, women, children, and babies. The people rushed their rescuers with alarming jubilation. Murphy ordered his ten men to take station, and they all jumped through a gaggle of whooping women to secure the ship.

A young woman tackled Davey by the neck and wouldn't let go. She was screaming something he couldn't understand when he heard an ominous pop behind him. He turned to see a flame jumping over the stern rail. He pried his head loose from the woman's frantic arms and pushed through the tangle of dancing joy. Flaming embers from the smoke stack were falling on a barrel of gunpowder tied to the stern. He ran through the dancers and jumped over the guns and boxes. He raised his cutlass and slashed at the ropes until the barrel rolled free. His hands grasped

74

the burning wood. Davey hefted two hundred pounds of instant death above his head and heaved it into the sea. It floated long enough to shake terror through his limbs, until the merciful water quenched the flames.

He turned to see ecstatic brown arms circle Murphy's broad shoulders and grateful kisses smother his shy face. A woman was clutching a baby who hailed the Chief with outstretched arm and splayed fingers and laughed, "Hwowah." Murphy felt ridiculous standing fully armed before such a dangerous foe and sheepishly sheathed his drawn cutlass.

Murphy pulled himself up the pilothouse ladder, and a black face smiled at him and said, "Good morning." The man touched the visor of his cap, but his salute only added to Murphy's confusion. Robert walked to the door and pointed back to the neat rows of gun barrels. "I believe I am returning some government property stolen from Fort Sumter last year." Murphy could only mumble, "I'll be damned," and Robert roared the laugh of the rescued. He was safe. They were all safe. Now they had to trust their new friends.

Alfred pushed himself through the jubilant throng. He was desperate to be alone and dragged himself to the bows. He pressed his hands onto the side rails away from the new ship and watched the dolphins skim through the water. His shoulders shivered, and he let the tears run through the soot and down his face.

Murphy composed himself and told Robert, "We will guide you to Port Royal. Follow the ship and stay slightly behind and to port."

"Do you want to take the wheel?" Robert asked.

"No, Sir," Murphy simply replied. "This is your ship."

He left Robert in charge of the voyage, disappeared down the ladder, and jumped to the rail facing *Onward*. He shouted across, "They're all contrabands."

"Contrabands" jumped from throat-to-throat along the rigging and spilled across the deck. *Onward*'s crew lined the rails waving their arms, or hung on the rope ladders screaming laughter and yelling "Contrabands" back to *Planter*. Nichols walked behind the lines of sailors slapping backs and raising a storm of praise and laughter.

Nichols looked over the watery gulf to the man at the wheel of the ship following them and nodded once. The man Smalls grinned back and raised his arm to the whistle cord. Nichols heard the one long blast playing bass to the cheers of his own crew. He watched *Planter*'s steam whistle spray a joyous cloud and said, "He was right. It does sound like a joke." Nichols looked up to the helmsman and ordered him, "Set course south by southwest." *Onward* veered slowly to the right.

His feet crunched past the cheering and along the sandy deck to the bow. He stood behind the figurehead feeling a long-forgotten pride shudder through his limbs. He looked over the bows to the feet of Liberty resting on a globe and said, "Whoever they are, these people have heard the murmur of a higher law and followed its faint whispers." Nichols' eyes rose up the figurehead to the wheat sheaves she clutched to her breast and he wondered if they would prosper in their refuge. Nichols shuddered to think this had been such a close run thing. One motion of his arm and the ship and the people would have been another cargo discharge. He looked along Liberty's outstretched arm, and her finger pointed to a chilly sun.

Part II

Rear Admiral Samuel Francis Du Pont

The Charge of the Light Brigade

Half a league, half a league,
Half a league onward,
All in the valley of Death
Rode the six hundred.

Someone had blundered.

Theirs not to make reply,
Theirs not to reason why,
Theirs but to do and die.
Into the valley of Death
Rode the six hundred.

Cannon to right of them,
Cannon to left of them,
Cannon behind them
Volley'd and thunder'd;
Storm'd at with shot and shell,
They that had fought so well
Came thro' the jaws of Death,
Back from the mouth of hell,
All that was left of them,
Left of six hundred.

Alfred Tennyson

Chapter 6

The Measure of a Man

USS Wabash, Port Royal, May 13, 1862

My Precious Sophie,

Twenty minutes past ten. I was interrupted by Rogers with such startling news that I must share it with you. Something like one of our steam tugs was coming down the river. We thought it was the Mercury or the Pettit; still she approached. An officer hails and reports it is the Confederate steamer Planter, mounting two guns and brought out this morning from Charleston by a party of contrabands who delivered her up to the blockading fleet. She is a lovely boat, has a fine engine and draws but little water and will be of the greatest use to us -- so that in herself she is a valuable acquisition, quite valuable to the squadron.

I sent for the hero, Robert, and he soon came, a pleasant-looking darky, not black, neither light, extreme amount of wooly hair, neatly trimmed, fine teeth; a clean and nice linen check coat with a very fine linen shirt having a handsome ruffle on the breast, part of the wardrobe of the Navy officer who commanded the boat but fitting him very well indeed.

As he did every night, Commodore Samuel Francis Du Pont lit a cigar and walked the deck of his flagship. He puffed to the clouds and looked up the river to see the ships at anchor on each side of the entrance to Port Royal. He always drew comfort from the sight of vessels safely moored in harbor, for such order was a relief from the chaos of war.

A small vessel was steaming at speed into the harbor, so he asked Rogers, his second-in-command, if she was the late mail boat. He was always anxious to receive letters from his wife. The strange ship approached, and they recognized Parrot, the Harbor Master, jumping on the deck and waving his hat over his head. The sight promised something curious, for Parrot was the most reserved of men. Parrot's boisterous shouts filled the harbor and reassured them he was not bringing more trouble.

Parrot guided the odd little craft alongside, and a stream of black people flowed into the decks of the *Wabash*. Du Pont swung his head to see Hannah fussing with a small child and sailors offering helping hands to more women and children struggling over the ship's rail. He stared into the face of a short black man and heard Parrot blubber, "Commodore, allow me the pleasure to present to you Robert Smalls, pilot of Charleston harbor." All the people froze to hear Du Pont's voice boom over them, "Captain Rogers, please make our guests comfortable." The sailors herded the people to the mess decks for a meal as Du Pont listened to Parrot's staggering account of Robert's escape. Parrot offered Du Pont the *Charleston Courier* dated the previous day, and this was proof that their tale was true. Du Pont immediately appreciated the importance of a pilot escaping with a boat and sent a message for General Hunter to join them.

Du Pont heard the bosun pipe new visitors aboard and rushed from his wardroom to see General Hunter swaying up the gangplank. Colonel Stowe and Major Adams, that twig of a genius, wobbled behind Hunter. Even though they were safely tied up to the dock, Du Pont waited for the Army officers to get their sea legs. They looked comically queasy on the steady deck. Du Pont knew the sailors gambled on which soldier would be the first to "muster his breakfast," and the largest bets were always placed on Hunter. Adams was rail thin, but as flexible as a tarred rope. Stowe looked like a tree that had staggered out of a forest.

When he was sure they were steady, Du Pont invited them to his wardroom, "for you must hear for yourselves this extraordinary account by a no less extraordinary individual."

*   *   *   *   *

Robert Smalls was more tired than he had ever been in his life, but they kept filling him with coffee and firing questions. One of them was really curious about Hannah and kept on about the children.

"So it was Hannah who flew the surrender flag?" Stowe asked.

"Well, she didn't exactly fly it," Robert answered. "More like she shook it out, like when she's doing laundry." He noticed that the big sailor laughed louder than the rest.

"But this woman is accompanied by three children. Are they all your children?" Stowe pressed.

"I am the proud father of two children," Robert beamed.

"So who is the father of the other one?" Stowe asked.

"You'd have to ask Hannah about that."

Hunter sat leaning forward, and Robert mused that the man's face looked like a well-scrubbed washboard. Hunter's palms smoothed the ridges from his brow to his ears, as if to put aside his confusion. "But are all these people your dependents?" Hunter asked.

"They are now," Robert casually added. "I also am father of another daughter, Charlotte, but she's a few months older than me."

Hunter's shocked face amused Du Pont. Stowe was too flabbergasted to continue the interrogation of The Family Smalls. Robert felt sorry for Hunter and tried to explain, "We have a different type of family."

"Is everybody on that boat related?" Du Pont suggested.

"Yes, we all know each other."

"But are you all blood relations?" Hunter pressed.

"You mean are we all from the same father?" Robert asked.

Du Pont waited through the awkward silence until Robert said, "We are all children of Our Father in Heaven."

"Well, yes, I suppose so," said Hunter.

"Oh, no. That's not the way it is," Robert was quick to add.

Stowe demanded impatiently, "If you don't have the same blood, you're not related."

They all shot embarrassed glances around the room. Du Pont was getting irked by the obsession with family ties which didn't match up. He was not willing to waste any more time determining which second cousin, twice removed, was from which plantation, with whose third child by their grandfather's master. This was worse than being trapped at a New Year's Ball by three maiden aunts chattering about the Du Ponts long residing in the family mausoleum. He cut through the awkward silence. "I think what the General is attempting to understand is that all of you have some sort of connection which is not dependent upon genealogical charts."

Robert did not know what a genealogy was, but he locked his ignorance behind a broad smile. Du Pont leaned over, and Robert heard him whisper into Hunter's ear, "it is evident by the variation of color that these people share a motley of parentage which defies our experiences of familial ties." Whatever that meant, Robert read Du Pont's signal to stop harping about the family and get down to business. He nodded his thanks to Du Pont and waited to find out what this business was.

Du Pont turned to Robert and asked calmly, "Now, Robert, tell us again about the barrels." Robert steadied himself to be quizzed again about "those infernal barrels."

"Yes, how big are the barrels?" asked Stowe.

"About up to my waist," Robert said, placing his hand on his hip.

"How wide?" Major Adams asked.

"They were well-fed."

"What?" blurted Stowe.

"They were stout, like a person had been used to good eating, but they weren't fat, like someone who is a glutton."

Robert saw the irritation seep through Stowe's clenched fists and raised eyes. Stowe had been promised a simple tale of thievery at high tide, but Du Pont had started talking about barrels of gunpowder floating in Charleston harbor.

Deserters had told him that the Confederates were mining the harbor "with explosive obstructions." Stowe realized this contraband had first-hand knowledge of the "infernal devices." He was desperate for any information about the torpedoes and wished he could pry it out of the wooly head with a lash or two. Stowe glared at Robert and demanded, "Were they kegs or firkins, or as big as a hogshead?"

"They were cracker barrels." Robert said, with presumptuous confidence.

"That doesn't tell us much," Stowe complained in disgust.

Adams tried to smooth the ruffled feathers and explained to Robert, "Each store sells its crackers in different barrels."

Robert tried to lighten their load and said, "Oh, that's just our joke because the barrels are so important to the Crackers."

Only Du Pont laughed. The others didn't know what a Cracker was. Stowe threw up his hands in exasperation and demanded of Adams, "You deal with this."

Adams pulled his chair closer to Robert. "Look, if we can figure out the size of the barrels, we will be able to calculate the size of the explosive charge."

"They can't tell a keg from a hogshead," Stowe rumbled.

"Do you know the difference?" Du Pont interjected. "I certainly don't."

Adams had picked up the scent of a solution and shot an observation over his nose. "Wine, and beer, and whale oil all come in different barrels."

"I am most happy to enjoy what is decanted on my table," Du Pont teased, "but how it gets there, I leave to the servants."

Du Pont could smell the frustration and feared it. Such vexation could have perfectly reasonable gentlemen grabbing at knives or pistols. He looked directly at the general and demanded, "Hunter, do you like beans?"

Hunter roused himself from his cross-armed pout to ask incredulously, "Beans?"

"Yes, beans," and Du Pont waited for all their heads to turn. "An army may march on its stomach," he said, "but a navy sails on its beans. Why, without beans no ship could travel a hundred miles without seeking further sustenance in some unfriendly port."

Courtesy demanded they pay attention to their host, even if they thought he was crazy. "I often think that Aeolus gave those sailors a bag of beans," Du Pont reminisced.

"I am not acquainted with this Ayloose," Stowe said through his scowl.

"Of course not. Your expertise is in the contemporary sciences, not in the classical past. Aeolus was the God of Winds. He gave Odysseus a bag full of wind to help him on his journey home to Ithaca - the one in Greece, not the one in New York. You see, Aeolus was rather taken with those sailors and gave them the bag of wind for when they were becalmed. Rather gentlemanly of him, don't you think?"

"And just what does all this have to do with beans?" Stowe demanded.

"Well, a bag of beans," Du Pont explained, "would be of infinite relief to a ship trapped in a windless sea. Forget steam power. A diet of beans would keep the crew healthy and the wind would always be in the sails."

Hunter and Stowe exchanged disgusted glances, but Adams beamed understanding. Robert laughed. Du Pont turned to him, like a slightly forgetful uncle. "Do you like beans, Robert?"

"Why, yes, I do. Hannah makes chicken with red beans and rice. Very spicy."

"Well, she must invite me to dinner," Du Pont said, "I so enjoy excellent cooking. I remember one cook on the *Porpoise*. The man was a genius with beans. His name was Pakah."

"Pakah?" Robert said.

"Yes. Pakah was some sort of Creole, but he could turn a handful of beans into haute cuisine. After one spoonful of his concoction, I had him brought to my wardroom and offered him a position back home at Louviers. Sophie wrote to me that he is a treasure, and she is encouraging him to experiment with potatoes."

Hunter and Stowe looked aghast at the Commodore of the South Atlantic Blockading Fleet waxing lyrical about beans and potatoes. Du Pont could almost hear them thinking, "The man's gone senile," but he savored the calm his ramblings had generated. Robert saw there was more to this old sailor than a hankering for vegetables.

Adams smiled at Du Pont's ruses and steered the conversation back to the harbor defenses. "What about a whiskey barrel?"

"Excellent idea," said Du Pont, and bellowed, "Steward!"

The door rattled and the Commodore's Steward entered, as eager to serve as he was to listen from the hall. "We would like some whiskey, please," Du Pont instructed, "And do bring us the whole barrel."

"The whole barrel, Sir?"

"Yes. We're rather thirsty."

The Steward returned to the wardroom carrying a tray of glasses and leading a procession of sailors manhandling a whiskey barrel. The sailors accepted the strange sight of so many high ranking officers ready to tie one on with some runaway slave. The Steward suspected they were up to no good.

"Excellent," Du Pont beamed. "Now stand it up on its end." The sailors raised the barrel onto its butt end, and the Steward pried off the lid. "Robert, please stand beside our refreshments," Du Pont requested.

Robert took his place beside the barrel, sporting a smile as mischievous as Du Pont's. The Steward hustled the sailors and himself out of the wardroom and shut the door. The peculiarities of officers were none of their business, he told the sailors, so they hurried back to the galley to avoid the shenanigans of officers in their cups.

"This is ridiculous," Stowe blurted.

"Why?" asked Du Pont.

"Barrels are all different."

Du Pont saw Adams itching to join the game and asked, "What do you suggest?"

"I disagree. Whiskey barrels are standard"

"Tell us more," Du Pont prodded.

"A firkin holds nine gallons of whiskey," Adams lectured, "and a hogshead holds fifty-four gallons, but a barrel contains thirty-six gallons. They are all proportional."

"How do you know so much about these obscure matters?" Du Pont asked.

"My family is in liquor," Adams admitted rather sheepishly.

"How jolly for them. And you have a mathematician's appreciation of the distillers' arts."

"I have made an extensive study of the subject in my leisure hours."

"So, all we have to do is figure out how much whiskey is waiting in the harbor," Du Pont smirked at Stow, "to blow our ships to smithereens."

"In essence. Yes," Adams concluded.

Du Pont walked over to the barrel and cast a sharp eye over Robert. He picked up the ladle and invited them to fill their glasses. Du Pont asked Robert, "What is your youngest child's name?"

"That would be Robert Junior."

"How old is he?"

"He came to us a year and a half ago."

"How tall is he?"

Robert bent over and his fingers drew a line across his trouser leg, "Not yet knee high." Du Pont grabbed a pencil and slashed a gray line across the barrel at Robert's knee. Adams caught the drift. "What about the next child?" Adams asked.

"That would be our Elizabeth Lydia. She's four years old."

Adams snatched a notebook and pencil from Du Pont's desk and casually said, "I suppose she's a bit bigger than knee high?"

"She's very forward for her age," Robert said.

"Show us," Du Pont demanded, and Robert's finger pointed to his hip.

"How tall are you?" Adams asked

"Five feet and five inches."

Du Pont ran the pencil across the barrel's staves at Robert's waist. "Now we're getting somewhere."

Adams was as happy as Punch and looked a little like the imp on the magazine covers. Du Pont exclaimed, "Gentlemen, please retire to chairs with your glasses." They all sat in a comfortable ring.

Adams' pencil scratched furiously at the notebook. "Is the smallest barrel in the harbor about the size of Robert Junior?"

"Yes."

"If you picked up the barrel, would it weigh about the same as Little Robert?"

"Now that you mention it, yes it would."

"This is very good," Adams assured him. "Now, Elizabeth Lydia. Is there a barrel about her size and weight?"

"Yes."

"Excellent. What about the biggest barrel?"

"That would a mite bigger than you," Robert said.

"In what sense?"

"Well, Robert observed, "you could squeeze into the biggest, but there would be room to spare over your head, if they put the lid on."

Adams squealed delight, lunged to the desk, and spread out sheets of quickly penciled drawings. They all crowded together around the desk.

Du Pont caught the excitement oozing from Adams, so he suggested, "Gentlemen, shall we retire topside for cigars?" The question was a welcome order. They started for the gangway ladders, when Du Pont, ever the considerate host, restrained them. "Please, first refresh your glasses. It would be a sin to waste this fine example of the distiller's art." They milled around the whiskey barrel.

The wind stood fair upon the straits of Port Royal. They could see a campfire winking to them from Hilton Head Island, not four miles over the water, and Robert especially savored the calm of the night. He thanked one of the officers for the cigar offered, but politely refused, saying, "I am too Small to smoke." Du Pont chuckled at the pun and again praised Robert's pluck. Robert was as gracious in receiving the Commodore's compliments, as Du Pont was in offering them.

The Commodore tapped his glass with his wedding ring, and they all gathered around him expectantly. "Gentlemen, I see that this barrel is marked as the produce of Oban, Scotland. It has made a very hazardous crossing of the sea to be delivered to us as contraband of war. Please join me in a salute to our contrabands, who have accomplished an even more astounding crossing of the waters to be our most patriotic guests this evening. To the crew of the *Planter*. Glory to all who sail in her."

*   *   *   *   *

Yes, it had been quite a night, one of the longest Du Pont could remember, but the day dawned pregnant with possibilities brought from the most surprising quarter. This Robert, this obscure slave with the audacity to steal a gunboat, had steamed into harbor bearing renewed hope and most welcome intelligence.

Du Pont looked at the litter of papers on his desk and started to organize them into neat piles. Adams' scrawled notes were gathered into a ragged collection to the left. To the right lay the numbered pages of his official report. He gazed down at the report's last page and reviewed his conclusion: "Smalls is intelligent, and what is in his head is much more valuable than the ship and the weapons he brought to us. He has knowledge of the infernal devices which the rebels have placed in the approaches to Charleston."

Du Pont smiled down at his letter to Sophie spread between Adams's notes and the report. The first word of the report was "Sir," and Du Pont snorted to think that he would never address a report to the Secretary of the Navy with the salutation, "My Precious Welles." Sophie's letters held more wisdom than all the politicians rolled together. His fingers pushed apart the report's pages until he could review his conclusion: "Robert, the very intelligent slave and pilot of the boat, who performed this bold feat so skillfully, informed me of the rebels' plans to place explosives in the channels leading into Charleston."

He thought over the impression which Robert had made on the officers and added, "The man Robert Smalls is superior to any who has yet come into our lines, intelligent as many of them have been. His information has been most interesting, and portions of it are of the utmost importance." Now that he had admitted Robert's usefulness to the Secretary, he had to decide just what to do with him. "I shall continue to employ Robert as a pilot on board *Planter* for the inland waters, with which he appears to be very familiar.

Your obedient Servant,

Samuel Francis Du Pont

Commodore.

Du Pont's eyes scanned his letter to Sophie and his report to the Navy Department lying on his desk. He carefully wiped his pen, so the nib would not soil the papers. He studied his letter home because Sophie was a stickler for grammar and spelling, and he did not like being corrected. Du Pont picked up the letter and the report and slumped into his chair. He swiveled his head between the two documents and smiled to see his own name at the end of both sheets. There was a certain comic formality in "Samuel Francis Du Pont" which sat beside the pomposity of "Commodore." He remembered that Robert bridled when Adams called him "Bobby," but even a commodore was secretly pleased when the sailors referred to him as "Uncle Sammy." Three decades of letters to "My Precious Sophie" had always ended with "Your loving Husband, Frank." To the Commodore, there was no higher title than husband, and if anybody had been stupid enough to press the matter, he would admit with pride that he would rather be Frank.

Chapter 7

The Office of Cargo Requisitions

Allen Russlynn was packing boxes of old office files. This was his last day as the Claims Clerk at the New York Office of Cargo Requisitions, and he had spent the morning sorting papers for the Prize Court. The beribboned bundles of claims for compensation made the air hang dusty with hope and disappointment. He would be glad to pass them over to his replacement, "that idiot Peter." He fished a letter out of the slim satchel lying on his desk and read it for the tenth time, "I have the honor to offer you a position as my personal assistant commencing immediately at Headquarters, the Department of the Navy." Russlynn's eyes lingered over the signature, "Gustavus V. Fox, Assistant Secretary of State for the Navy."

Gustavus Fox was too busy running the Navy to worry about details. His boss, Gideon Welles, was the Secretary of the Navy, but Welles spent his time fussing in the Cabinet. Welles unloaded his ideas on his assistant, but Fox needed someone who could translate Welles' notions into action. Welles had decided that the ships blockading Charleston needed some help. He had ordered twenty old hulks to be sunk in the channels approaching the harbor. When the derelicts would not cooperate and refused to sink, Welles' solution was to "fill them with rocks and they'll soon sink." Fox was tasked with finding enough rocks to sink the ships, but he couldn't waste time searching for ballast.

Two weeks ago, Welles had invited Fox to one of his interminable supper parties and seated Fox beside "that dreadful Mrs. Simmons." Welles enjoyed the spectacle of Mrs. Simmons pestering Fox about one of her protégés. She badgered Fox with her enthusiasm for "that brilliant young lawyer, Mr. Russlynn," who had quite caught her fancy. Simmons saw the twinkle in Welles' rheumy eye, caught the scent, and mercilessly nagged

Fox into a promise to "find something for this brilliant young man." Welles laughed so hard his wig fell off when Mrs. Simmons added, "For God knows, there are so few talented people where you work." Fox perceived something frightening about such an insistent woman, so he agreed to have Russlynn find enough rocks to sink the ships.

A week later, Allen Russlynn had appeared before Fox's desk, clutching a fistful of official looking papers. Fox shot an irritated scowl at the intruder and demanded, "What is this?" The man introduced himself. "I am Allen Russlynn, and these are the requisitions for blockade ballast."

Fox thumbed through the sheaf of "Accounts Outstanding" and listened to Russlynn explain how he had hired a contractor to collect rocks from farmers' fields. The rocks had been transported to Hartford and were waiting to be shipped to Du Pont's fleet at Charleston. Fox raised one eyebrow and took the papers and the young man to Welles, who asked, "Where did you get all these rocks?" Welles was pleasantly astounded by the answer, "From your constituents."

Russlynn had paid a contractor to clear the field stones from Connecticut farms, which all happened to be in Welles' electoral district. He had expressly instructed the contractor to tell the farmers, "the Navy needs your rocks," and to pay for both the removal of the nuisances strangling their harvests and the transportation of "the useless rubble" to the dockside in Hartford. Russlynn had also arranged for a front page article in the *Hartford Evening Press* celebrating the patriotism of local farmers under the headline, "He Also Fights Who Sows and Reaps." Welles had founded that newspaper six years ago and would reap many votes at the next election. Welles looked at the young man and saw such promise that he immediately created the position of Assistant to the Assistant Secretary of the Navy. He turned to Fox and said, "Your new assistant will be invaluable to your work." Russlynn accepted the position with admiring gratitude and a hint of embarrassment.

Welles dismissed them, and Fox shared their latest problem with Russlynn. Spies had reported "much hammering by the enemy in the Newport News docks." Out of the mists of smoky rumor sailed a stretched pyramid of metal loaded with cannon. The rebels had created a floating fortress they called the *Virginia*, The monster was frightening, even if her weak engines could not outrun a confused turtle. Welles had risen to the challenge and had hurriedly formed a committee called The Ironclad Board. Fox explained to Russlynn, "We countered this threat with our own design." He paused long enough to convince himself that his new assistant was completely trustworthy.

Russlynn kept nodding in the affirmative to everything Fox said about "our newest ironclads." Fox explained how "it is not enough that our *Monitor* can fight their *Virginia* to a stand-still." More was needed, "so we have commissioned new and greatly improved ironclads." Russlynn heartily rejoiced when told, "these weapons will win the war." Fox confided, "But there is a problem of coordination." Russlynn was perplexed, "I don't see what I can do to help, Sir?"

"Do you have any children?" Fox asked.

Russlynn was taken aback by the question. "I am a bachelor, but what would my marital status have to do with Navy business?"

"This is no assignment for a family man," Fox declared. "It will involve you traveling constantly between Washington, New York, and Philadelphia."

Fox finally admitted, "The problem is that Secretary Welles and I cannot spare the time to deal with both the Board and the construction facilities. That's where you come in." Russlynn pressed for details, and Fox's enthusiasm bubbled through his explanation. "I want you to be the link between the Board in Washington, the designers in New York, and the builders in Philadelphia."

"Where will I be based?"

"You will have an office here, but you won't be using it much."

Russlynn smiled and confessed, "I have been told that if one joins the Navy, one may see the world."

Fox laughed and added, "I don't envy you your new associates. They're a rather boring lot."

Thus, Russlynn had plunged into learning all he could about these new-fangled ironclads and had secreted the best material in his satchel. He had condensed all the reports, accounts, letters, and memoranda into three large piles under the headings "Design," "Costs," and "Construction Schedules." These he had reduced to three summaries of a single page each. Fox shuttled Russlynn to Welles, who liked a good lecture provided that it "wasn't as long as a sermon." Russlynn compressed hundreds of pages of details into a simple list of points, and Welles appreciated Russlynn sparing him the bother of so much boring reading.

Russlynn had spent two weeks on his first mission, and now it was time to pack up the old job and finish the move to Washington. The Office of Cargo Requisitions was almost bare, except for the desk and two chairs. He decided to leave an old statue as a moving-in present for the new clerk. Russlynn carefully placed his leather satchel on the desk. The worn leather clutched the most useful pages culled from the files. Years of reading the law had taught him, "Justice may be blind, but she's not deaf and dumb." He had learned to turn the gossip in a theatre's crush bar into gold, and even the babblings of The Widow Simmons were bankable. He had made friends in places high and low, gathering any tidbit which would further his clients' interest. His devotion to those interests would now be as patriotic as it was profitable, because his new client was the government.

The satchel bulged with the technical manuals of the *Monitor*, the new iron ship which would defeat the rebellion and win the war for the Union. Russlynn had carried all of this information between the three points of his new mission and used the train journeys as his reading room.

The design was genius; this vessel would make all wooden ships obsolete. One sentence screamed to him. "The iron requires specialist forging techniques available at two foundries." Fox's notes supplied the names and addresses of these two essential businesses. Mrs. Simmons' bankers told Russlynn he was "throwing his money into a hole in the sea," but as a special favor, they accepted his check for shares in The Continental Iron Works of Greenpoint and the DeLamater Works of Greenwich Village. Continental completed the *Monitor* in only 118 days, and DeLamater then installed the engines and propeller in one week. Ten days later, Russlynn's recently purchased stock increased by 500%. When the Ironclad Committee commissioned nine more ships, Russlynn's future was launched. This may be a poor man's fight, he mused, but it was definitely a rich man's war.

Russlynn pulled a file from the satchel and tossed it on his desk. This would be his last official duty, so he set about preparing the legal brief for the *Planter*. There were the usual reports and testimonies, and the newspapers had been touting the adventure for the last two weeks, whenever it was a slow war day. Russlynn had had his fill of "the plucky negroes" and was bored by their little bit of mischief. But it was the note attached to the file which irked him most. A small piece of writing tablet stated, "Expedite with all dispatch. Du Pont." Not so much as a "please" or a "thank you," just a peremptory command.

Russlynn resented these "sons of privilege" who were "all the same." It didn't matter if they were in business or in government; they expected his immediate attention to their desires. Du Pont was heir to the largest fortune in the country and was wealthy beyond calculation. Russlynn would be very slow in "expediting" this last file and proclaimed to the empty room, "I won't be pushed around by some millionaire and his passel of pet coons."

The office door crashed open, and Russlynn quickly closed the file. A sailor swiveled on a crutch into the center of the room, stood to attention on one leg, saluted, and mumbled, "Able Seaman Postlethwaite reporting for duty, Sir." Russlynn sighed and said, "Sit over there, Peter."

It was much easier to call this annoyance "Peter" than to get his tongue around "Postlethwaite." The man had arrived with orders to be "Transferred to Convalescent Duties, New York." The orders were signed by somebody named Nichols or Neckles or Nickels. Peter stood staring around the room. Russlynn really didn't want to bother with this problem, so he thrust the file for the *Planter* into the man's free hand. "Why they have given this position to a cripple is beyond me," Russlynn mumbled.

Peter had shown up for the past two mornings like a hangover. The Navy had assigned him as the new clerk and ordered Russlynn to train him, but the man was useless. Russlynn thought him mentally defective because he hardly said anything. The boy didn't seem to know where he was and just sat at the window all day. Russlynn had attempted to instruct the man in the work of the office, but decided "you may as well expect a dog to speak Latin." Russlynn commanded Peter to "sit," and Peter slouched into a chair near the desk. The crutch fell to the floor. Peter stared at it until he giggled, for the crutch was useless without him.

He looked vacantly at Russlynn sitting on the other side of the desk, and tried to remember who the man was. The man's face looked like it was carved out of butter with a hot knife. Peter could see milk flowing from his hair, so he stared at the pink bulges of the man's cheeks glowing through the creamy paste.

There was nothing left to do until the evening train to Washington, so Russlynn decided to wile away some time explaining the work, yet again. "Now, Peter," he began, "You know that this office prepares the documents for the Prize Courts." Russlynn spoke slowly to get Peter's attention, but the boy could not concentrate. Postlethwaite seemed incapable of remembering anything. He just sat there with that puppy-dog look, expecting Russlynn didn't know what. Approval? The time of day? "Let's try this again," he said.

Peter didn't like the man. Russlynn was always talking about things he didn't understand, and Peter wondered if the man himself even understood these strange words. Russlynn squatted his elbows on the desk and cupped his face between his hands. "There is a difference between civil and maritime law. At sea the law is *in rem*. Can you say that, Peter?" Peter tried to please this madman and spluttered "rem." "That's very good," the man said, "*In rem* means *against the thing,* and that means that when a ship is brought into the court, it is the thing which is on trial." Russlynn tilted his head to one side and waited for some sign of recognition. When Peter nodded, he continued, "But on land, the law is *in personam*. Can you repeat that?"

Peter's hand rummaged in the pocket of his pea jacket. His throat was tightening, and the man kept wanting him to say something. Peter's fingers clung to a small bottle, for he was about to cry. The man looked like he was praying, but his eyes were laughing. That wasn't right. If he were praying, they were in church, but this place was no church. People shouldn't laugh in church, but the face was laughing and telling him to repeat something he couldn't understand. Peter's hand trembled in shame that he didn't know the word, and he took a deep breath to shout out "person."

"Now were getting somewhere," Russlynn sighed. "On land, under *in personam*, the person is innocent until proven guilty, but at sea, under *in rem*, the thing, meaning the ship, is guilty until proven innocent. It is a very nice distinction, and that is what we do in this office."

Peter's hands were shaking so hard he couldn't pull the cork from the bottle. He bit into the cork and tightened his teeth enough to twist the bottle. Russlynn scowled at the screeching cork. Peter's jaws ripped open a seam in the cork, and a bitter liquid dribbled over his tongue and welled out of the corners of his mouth. After a few moments' silence, Peter decided the place was a church and the man was a preacher, because he would not stop talking.

Russlynn bellowed, "For the judge to make a decision he has to see the preponderance of evidence in the case." Words were spilling out of his mouth like men jumping off a sinking ship. Peter watched the words swim and struggle on the desk and started to cry because the words were so desperate to get away from the ship and they were screaming and sinking through the desk. He grieved for the drowned words and could not hold back his tears. "What?" Peter breathed.

Russlynn inhaled his irritation and slowly repeated, "It's the evidence which decides a case." Peter stared past Russlynn's shoulder, through the wall, and down the river to continents yet to be discovered. Russlynn stood up abruptly. The juddering chair legs jerked up Peter's head, and he winced to attention. Russlynn walked across the office, picked up a little statue of Justice and placed it on the desk. He sat behind the desk, leaned forward on his elbows with his palms joined over his mouth, and glowered over the statue.

Peter looked at the lady. She had been wounded and had a bandage around her head. She had been in some sort of fight because she held a sword in one hand and scales in the other. Maybe she was a cook and was measuring flour in the scales and was going to cut it with the sword. Peter watched Russlynn's head nod from side-to-side and thought, "This still feels like a church." The man was shouting at him again, "Look at the scales. You see the two dishes?"

The dishes were like the plates when they took the collection. Mummy always gave him a nickel for the plate, and he hoped that the money would be a blessing to someone. This man was taking the collection as he continued with the sermon. Peter nodded. "Good," Russlynn encouraged. "We put all of the evidence on the dishes." Russlynn tipped the scales with his finger. "That side says 'Yes.'" Russlynn moved his finger along

102

the balance bar of Justice, and the dish swung down. "And on the other dish, we put all the evidence that says 'No.' Preponderance of evidence is what tips the scales one way or the other."

Peter's head drooped with the collection plate. "Now, remember, here we start with the 'Yes' dish a little lower. That's 'guilty until proven innocent.'" He watched the man's finger go back to the 'Yes' dish, and the dish started flying around. The man was fighting with the lady because the dishes were going up and down. The man was robbing the collection plates. He wanted to make the man stop hurting the lady, but he was just too sleepy.

Russlynn looked at Peter and his lips smirked to greet an unexpected opportunity. This idiot was supposed to assist the Office of Cargo Requisitions, so let him deal with this last case. That would take him a few days at least. If Du Pont wanted this particular case expedited with dispatch, he could pester Russlynn's replacement. Russlynn grabbed the file and shoved a page towards Peter. "Now, Peter, I want you to copy out this page. It is very easy."

Peter heard a voice shouting in his ear and looked up to see the man's eyes glaring at him, "All you have to do is make a list. It's simple. The list is just one boat and its cargo. So just write down 'one boat' and then make a list of everything on the page." Peter looked at the paper and slowly read aloud, "In the Case of *Planter*..." Peter sucked at the bottle of medicine, but the man stood up and spluttered, "Oh, what's the use." Peter wrapped his arms around his head because the man was going to hurt him just like he hurt the lady.

Peter peeked over his elbow, but he nuzzled his chin into the soft wool of his sleeve. The man was offering Peter a pen. It looked very dangerous. The man put the pen on the desk and pointed the nib at Peter's head. Peter winced in case the pen fired at him, and the man kept shouting, "Just copy the damned list. Copy. Just make a copy." The man opened a cardboard file with sheets of paper held together with strings and he saw each piece of paper as someone tied at the neck and swinging from a tree branch. The man kept shouting, "Write the names. That's all you have to do. Just write down the names!"

Russlynn scrawled the name "Smalls" over the paper. Peter cowered, weeping into his arms. He peeped over his elbow to see "Robert" and "Hannah" tumble out of Russlynn's pen. They were soon joined by "Alfred," "Samuel," and "William," but he just heard the man shout, "Oh, what's the use!"

Russlynn looked at the incomplete claim paper and knew it would take many weeks for the Prize Court to adjudicate a submission prepared by Peter. He could see the bright side of this matter and was happy to leave the case in Peter's shaking hands. There would be many delays correcting the pages. Russlynn smirked and said aloud, "We'll see how much 'dispatch' this simpleton will give Du Pont." He picked up his leather bag from the desk and placed his hat upon his head. Russlynn smiled down at Peter, tipped his hat and wished him "Every success in your new post as Clerk to the Office."

The man laughed as he walked to the door and opened it to the loitering darkness. The man was gone, but Peter trembled in the stillness. The darkness took a step and a floorboard creaked. Peter raised the medicine bottle to his lips, and his mouth sucked gossamer webs over his tongue. He saw the shadows coming towards him. They had very bad manners. Shadows were not supposed to walk into people's rooms. The warmth filled his head and spilled down his neck to purr in his stomach, like warm bread or maybe even cake. A glow like icing tumbled through him all the way down his legs and made his left foot itch. He bent over to scratch his toes, but they weren't there. Maybe his foot had gone for a walk, because that's what feet do.

The shadows were very naughty and swept darkness over the floor. Peter told them to stop, but they just laughed and jumped from floor-board to floor-board. The black tide swept over the desk, and Peter wept to see it drown the lady. He stood and cringed from the cresting tide. He leaned on his crutch and could see the face of Nichols looking down at him.

Peter had been scrambling up the mizzen ratline when his boots slipped and he fell to the deck. He plunged only the height of a man, but his left foot smashed through a wooden cracker box. The lid splintered around his foot and held it like a bear trap. The Chief yelled at Peter "Stop. Stand still," but Peter panicked and tried to shake the box off his foot. His struggles only pulled the jagged lathes and nails deeper into his flesh. Nichols saw the blood flooding the box and immediately ordered Surgeon Prentiss on deck. Prentiss pulled a belt tight around Peter's leg and told Webb and Collins to "get him to the galley." The box had shredded Peter's ankle to the bone, and mercy demanded that the foot come off.

They laid Peter on the messdeck table, ignoring his protests. Prentiss shoved a square of opium between Peter's teeth and poured in a whiskey chaser. He flushed half the bottle over the plate holding his saws and knives and gulped a long swig. They waited for the hush. Prentice raised his knife and commanded Johnny and Davey to "hold him down."

He didn't care if it was the whiskey or the opium, but the snoring was the overture to Prentiss' duty. He worked fast, for the patient could wake at any moment. He pulled the belt tighter around Peter's leg just above the ankle and told Davey to "grab hold." Johnny stood behind Peter's head, pinning the arms to the table and watched Prentiss' knife scribe a red trail around the calf. Davey tightened the belt as Johnny pressed his full weight onto Peter's limp body.

Prentiss plunged his fingers into the mass of pulped flesh, feeling for good bone. He pulled the knife through the mangled muscle and pushed it off the table with a soggy thump onto the floor. The remaining skin was lying to one side, like a discarded, dirty stocking. He was careful to keep the Achilles' tendon and split it apart to form two tails. Prentiss gripped the leg above the opening in his left hand and wielded the saw with his right.

A butcher had taught him to separate pork ribs in five saw passes, so it took only four heaves of his shoulder to cut through both of the lower leg bones. His forefinger and thumb circled the bones, and he pushed back the flesh until he could see the ends of the large tibia and the little fibula. He used his little finger to push some marrow back into the bones. With his right hand, he tied the two bones together with the split ends of the tendon. His fingers slipped in the bloody fat, but he patiently pulled the bones together in a double slung knot of sinews. With a nod to Davey, he released the tourniquet and let the bones be sucked back into the quivering flesh.

Prentiss grabbed the whiskey bottle and poured libations over the quivering flesh. He passed a candle over the stump, and flaming spirals danced across the wound. He told Davey and Johnny to tighten their grips. With the nerves cauterized, he turned to the skin flap. He scissored the pelt as would a tailor cutting out a trouser leg. Prentiss filed the ends of the clasped bones into a smooth, beveled semi-circle, so the stump could swivel in the harness of the wooden replacement. There would be less pain, if the sailor survived. No use having him shuffle through life wincing at every other step.

He had left plenty of skin to cover the gaping maw. Davey sweated over the belt, waiting for Prentiss' needle to finish laying half-inch cross stitches along the seam of skin. When the flap was secure, he told Davey to loosen the tourniquet. Blood scrambled frantically along the veins to the dead-end. Crimson paste squirmed through the stitch holes and gathered in confused little bundles, like grumbling passengers waiting for a late train. Prentiss waited to see clots form over the stitches.

When he was satisfied the flap would hold, Prentiss picked up a mason jar with holes punched into its lid. He waved the jar like a salt shaker, and an enraged troop of maggots tumbled over the stump. He did not know why this was so, but he had observed that those patients who didn't bother to squash the insects tended to survive the operation. He conjectured that the maggots ate the pus and that this had something to do with the healing process. So, he spread his collection of hungry little friends over the clots and wrapped the wound in a wriggling poultice of clean linen. He was content to leave to nature what mystified his science.

He had finished his work in seven minutes.

When the screaming started, Nichols transferred Peter to the Sanitary Commission in New York. It was in Postlethwaite's best interest and for the good of the crew to get him off the ship quickly. Nichols complimented Prentiss on his skill and was told, "It was all I could do for the boy." Together they cursed shoddy footwear and marveled at the dangers of a box of hard-tack.

Peter flinched from the crawling darkness, terrified that it would hurt him as it had drowned the lady. He flung the papers at the angry shadows and turned his head away. A round window stared back at him.

This was not right. Rooms had square windows, but this window was round. He threatened the black tide with his crutch, but it would not heed him. He tried to sweep it away, but he fell onto his back. The strange window's golden glow beckoned him to its smiling circle. He obeyed and crawled towards it, the tip of the crutch screeching across the floor. He shuffled through the pain and threw his palm up to the window frame to steady himself. Sweat dripped onto the floor as he ran his hand around the cool, metal rim. The gold turned silver in his hand, but he could feel it was a real window.

How strange it was. He knew he was on land because the deck had stopped swaying, but this window was just like the port-hole of a ship. His fingers pulled him up to the circle. His hands traced the delicate webs holding the panes together. The window reminded him of a perfectly cut pie. Each segment of glass held a magical scene that was singing. Music came from every little triangle, and Peter saw the distant flaring of many furnaces and heard steam hammers crashing into molten iron. They flashed like shooting stars, and where they would not shine, there was a black arrowhead silhouetted against the sky. Peter could see men hammering squares to form a ship's bow. The men looked like ants stealing crackers at a summer picnic. The pounding smashed against the window frame and spun around his head.

He hunched his neck to look through a different slice of the pie and could just make out a distant wheat field of rippled brown. It was a long rectangle, and streaks of moonlight ran over the plowed furrows as gently as a lady's fingers jumping from string-to-string on a harp. The field called his eyes away from the noisy foundries. He could lie down and rest in those humid folds and sleep in wavy caresses. He pulled the lever on the side of the frame, and the wind blew the window back into the room. Peter clutched the sparkling disk like a shield.

The wind rushed in to attack burned-out candles and evict the acrid stench of a forgotten spittoon. The stink of this place whirled around him, jumped through the open door, and ran down the corridor. "Let the night run to rob someone else," he said, for he was tired of it. There was no comfort in its strangling embrace.

The faint strains of a patriotic march plunged through the port-hole. He pressed his palms harder along the curve of the frame and gazed past the foundries to a large building near a dock. A band was playing on the roof. He knew that tune; it made people, run, and jump, and kill. It was a nice song.

A different music wafted toward him from the river, and he imagined young women dancing in the halls that lined the Bowery. He could smell beer and remembered his mother's warnings about "ardent spirits." She would not like his medicine bottle. People had told him that such women were dangerous, but he liked the music and balanced on his leg in time to its rhythm.

The spasms started in his thigh, and the pain clawed its way across his back to lodge in his neck. Peter felt a tormented animal clawing up his spine under his skin. He pulled the medicine bottle from his pocket and held it poised before grim lips. A boat plowed the river with its portside lights shining upon the water.

The harbor lights mirrored the stars in the sky. The stars danced around the moon and pointed Peter to the sea beyond the city.

The medicine spilled over his chin and down his chest. He looked at the bottle and raised his head to gaze once again upon the magic vista. It was beautiful. He could smell everything on this wonderful wind.

He slid the bottle back into his pocket and invited this night to rest a while and be his guest. His eyes followed a train, shuffling along a glimmering ribbon. A clock blinked in a tower above a railroad station. It sang no song and played no music, so Peter waited for the clock's hands to grasp an axe above its head and kill the day.

Chapter 8

The Great Skedaddle

Hannah gripped Clara close to her body. "He's back," Clara whimpered. She pointed through the door frame.

They watched Sammy jump past them into the dusty yard and run at two huge men approaching their cabin. Abe picked up a stout log and sprinted after Sammy. Sammy barreled into the first man. Abe leaned into a swing and caught the other man on the side of the head. The wood splintered and blood gushed from the point of the blow. Sammy thrust his fist under the first man's chin, and the man tried to scream through the steel spike Sammy had driven into the bottom of the jaw. The man fell to his knees, and Sammy kicked him as savagely as he could. Abe and Sammy stood shaking over them. The two men stumbled away, and Abe threw the bloody, splintered stump at them. Sammy shouted a final warning, "You come back, we kill you."

That had been two weeks ago. Now Hannah stood in the same opening, leaning against the doorless frame, thoroughly hating this place. She looked around the four partitions of slatted boards and up to the sodden leaves that pretended to be a roof and asked Sammy, "How long are they going to be?"

Sammy shrugged. "They didn't say."

Since their escape, the Smalls family had huddled together in the contraband colony, fighting off the drafts that brought the fevers and their neighbors who brought the terrors. They lived within the hollow square of skeletal walls, waiting for the boards that would keep out the dirty winds. A piece of scavenged canvas torn from a cast-off sail stretched over the window hole. One of the Gullah people had shown them how to weave palm fronds to make a roof. Hannah was not impressed but conceded, "At least this thing keeps the sun off our heads, if not the rain." Hannah had organized the women into rounds of cooking, cleaning, and child minding. There wasn't much to clean, and they were getting sick from a steady diet of rice and beans. The men took turns protecting their refuge. Now they had to wait. She crossed her arms over her chest and cast her eyes to the nest of swirling dust clouds that was Hilton Head Contraband Camp.

Hilton Head was Union territory because of Du Pont's victory. The previous November, he had led a flotilla into Port Royal Sound and hammered two forts into submission. After endless defeats on distant battlefields, Du Pont's triumph at sea brought hope and confidence. Du Pont won the laurels, but to the Navy went the spoils. The newspapers screamed "Ships Capture Rebel Forts" and hailed Du Pont "The Hero of the Union" and "Neptune's Favorite Son." The Navy ferried thousands of soldiers south of Charleston and turned geography on its head. The reporters had difficulty keeping track of the capitalization to explain that "The North was now in a favorable position south of the South" and "The South will now have to turn south to defeat the North."

The Union flag again flew over Port Royal, Edisto Island, the Outer Banks of the Carolinas, and the hundreds of inlets between Charleston and Georgia. The soldiers marched inland to "reclaim our land from treason" and disappeared into the swamps. The putrid pools of Carolina swallowed more soldiers than the hurricanes at sea drowned sailors.

With the "Yankee desecration of our sacred soil," the richest rebels packed up their valuables and headed for Charleston or any place offering sanctuary from the invading barbarians. The house slaves were portable, but the rice fields were abandoned, along with the field hands. The masters lightened the load of their retreat by casting aside the old, the sick, and the very young. The unwanted were sucked into the vacuum, and in their desperation, scavenged anything jettisoned by their absent owners. Every empty mansion between Beaufort and Hilton Head echoed with the rejoicing of "The Day of Jubilo" and was thoroughly looted. They called the flight of their masters "The Great Skedaddle."

It started as a trickle. Two soldiers saw a black man walking towards them over the water. They both cried "Jesus," and a man's voice gurgled back through the water cypresses, "Hello there." The man approached with a most respectful bow, and they asked, "Can you walk upon the water?" "Only when I know where the land is," he laughed. They brought the "wet negro" to their officer, who realized that "these people know all the paths through the swamps." The soaked refugee was immediately designated "contraband of war" and pressed into service as a scout. His many cousins soon joined him. They also knew the routes through the flooded rice fields and they all had a friend or a relative who could give good service.

The trickle became a human tidal wave. Within a month, the solitary water walker became ten thousand homeless wanderers. They bubbled forth from plantations and seeped out of the rice fields to merge into a great river of leaderless hope. Some left to be free, but had no idea what the word meant. "Free" was wandering and taking in the new sights. "Hunger" was understood, and it drove them to knife fights over pots of boiling sweet potatoes. A full belly marched them a few more miles, until they started eating bark and demanding rice with menaces. Others just followed the crowd beyond the few familiar acres where they were born.

Those with a thought to the future dragged anything that would hold whatever they could scavenge. Robert had seen a magnificent coach hitched to twelve strong men coming down the road to Port Royal. He asked the lead negro, "Where have you come from?" to be told, "Don' know," and received the same answer to his question, "Where are you going?" The carriage was piled high with all the clutter that took their magpie fancy. A chest of drawers sat next to a plough covered with linen bedding. Iron pots held books with pages thumbed by dirty fingers that had scratched lice from mystified heads. A lady's ball gown was ripped into ropes to tie rice bags to a piano with rain-sodden keys. Robert could have sat there all day and found no reason for this confusion of cargo. Talking to the men in the harness would be as useless as a chat with the horses they replaced, so he stood aside to let the carriage sway down the road to all their uncertain tomorrows.

Such chaos frightened him more than marauding thieves. You could kill a thief.

Port Royal became the coaling station for the South Atlantic Squadron and Beaufort the Headquarters of the Army of Reoccupation. The contrabands quickly outnumbered the Union soldiers and became "a plague upon the Quartermasters' Stores."

General Hunter was put in charge of the deluge. His haggard staff grew weary of his exasperated question, "Where do they all come from?" Soon the soldiers thought they were now godparents to all the slaves in the South. They told the newspaper people, "All we have to do is free them and send them all back to Africa, the war will be over, and we can all go back home." It was useless to explain to them that their ten thousand wards were "nothing compared with the four million of them out there somewhere."

Most soldiers had never seen a black man, let alone three of them offering to "Carry yo bag, Masa?" or "Let me help you with that firewood," or "I can hold that musket of yous. It sho look heavy and yo is sweating something fierce." Before too long, a patrol of twelve soldiers was followed by fifty of their "attendants." Five contrabands could transform a Kansas plowboy into a master, and it didn't feel all that bad. Hunter started to comprehend what was happening when a soldier was brought before him charged with "Sleeping on Guard Duty." The soldier's defense was, "Yes, Sir, I was asleep, but Sambo was looking out for me." Hunter pronounced sentence of "one month in the stockade," with the proviso that "the prisoner is not to take his slave with him to do the hard labor for him." Hunter designated Hilton Head as the collecting point for contrabands, until he could figure out what to do with them.

No prison could hold the ten thousand, and it would take more than five loaves and two fishes to feed them. Hanging a few as a threat to the many would only spark rebellion. They couldn't be whipped into shape because they feared no chastisement. Hunter could not cope with his colonists because they simply ignored his orders. Thousands of men released from restraint jumped hundreds of women, and rape became casual amusement. Theft was to be expected, but the soldiers kept their weapons on full-cock when the murders mounted. Typhus brought panic in its wake. Hunter detailed more of his men to guard his guests than he sent to fight the enemy.

Salvation sauntered into the camp on the high head and broad shoulders of Brother Brantley, wearing a stovepipe hat, a clawhammer coat, just enough trousers to satisfy decency, and little else. He strode into the hoard of the curious brandishing a shovel in one hand and waving a Bible over his head, and bellowed, "I bring the good words to the darkness." The multitude parted as if before Moses. "I will tumble you through the Book of James," and tumble them he did. For four hours a torrent of scripture "lashed their wickedness" and "scourged you of your sins." He screamed that "faith without works is dead," and they gathered round him as ducklings begging a ride on their mother's back. He assured them, "the righteous shall labor in the fields of the Lord" and "will reap rewards that ye can not count," but the lazy and the idle will be "cast into the lake of fire and snakes will crawl under your skin." They shuddered to hear that "Satan shall burn your toes with brands torn from your own flesh," but he also promised that "the cooling drafts of Lazarus shall pour over you a gourd of pure water." He shook the shovel in their faces and scorched their souls with "the glory of the Lord's work," and had them baying for the tools of salvation. One sinner shouted, "We Massa, Now!" and Brother Brantley's eyes shone bloodshot damnation through the crowd to the unbeliever. "Thou stiff-necked fool. There is only One Massa and He is the Righteous of the Lord." He threw the shovel at the blasphemer's head and commanded, "Repent ye and get you' black ass up that sand hill and dig holes for the white folk to hide in." He led them to the edge of the camp, and in two days, five thousand happy hands had erected Bastion Number One. Brantley had accomplished with his tongue what Hunter could only order with his threats.

Hannah had to contend with the dregs which would neither fear Brantley nor heed Hunter. Sammy would protect Lavinia, and Abe had taken a shine to Lavinia's friend, Annie. The two big men Sammy and Abe had chased away had been sniffing around the new women and were especially drawn to Clara's youth of only fourteen years. Hannah trusted her own men, but she had to find relief from the anxiety.

Hannah turned from the door frame to see Li'l Robert fussing in Clara's arms. She thought of their ages and wondered that she was almost forty years old and Clara was so young. Li'l Robert was new to Hannah and Robert, and time was all a jumble. She would not think of Clara's father but was happy that Clara accepted Robert. That was as it should be, but few men would step into the traces as Robert had. It was just one of the many things about him that made her heart swell with pride. He was not like other men; that was a good thing.

Hannah gathered her motley brood and led them to the sea shore. Sammy and Abe followed and ensured they would not be bothered. They walked into a grove of palm trees, and Hannah breathed deeply of their moist perfume. The smell and the shade were such a relief from the stinking noise of the camp, and they had worn a little path through the fronds to the sea. Taking the children to the beach was the best way to leave the men to whatever they had to do.

Clara's toes dug deeply into the sand to push herself and the baby up the incline of the first dune. Clara stood beside her to ask, "When are they coming back?" Hannah quietly reassured her, "When they've finished what they started," and left Clara to be satisfied or not with the answer. Hannah could feel the waves of worry surging from Clara, so she said, "They'll be back soon." Clara's eye threw questions at the horizon. "They won't be alone."

Hannah wanted to comfort the girl, but her desire tangled with the need for discretion. "They're bringing friends," she said, and sensed her daughter's relief. "You go play and I'll wait for them," she commanded. Clara was happy to obey and trundled down the dune with her little burden to join Susan, Lizbeth, Lavinia, and Annie dodging the surf. Hannah stood at the top of the rise to meet the sea breezes. Her body felt cool, and she let the wind dry her.

The palm trees wouldn't grow past the first dune, and Hannah had chosen this spot as much for the privacy as for the shade of its green umbrella. The high grove also provided an excellent view, so she could keep an eye on the young ones and see anybody approaching along the wide flatness between the dunes and the rippling water.

She heard Li'l Lizbeth's joyful squeals rise above the gentle roar and narrowed her eyes to see the child scamper just ahead of the water chasing her. Lizbeth turned and scolded the water, while she marched it back to the sea, only to turn again and run from the next pursuing surge. Lavinia joined in the little girl's game, and Hannah was content to watch their antics. Lavinia had chosen well, for Sammy would protect her with more than a nail and a fist. The boy was a puzzle to Hannah. He seemed to be the usual young man, and she laughed to remember Alfred's judgment, "more between his legs than between his ears." But Sammy had insisted that Lavinia come with them and told Hannah, "No Lavy, no Sammy." They needed him to cast off the ropes and get them out of the harbor, but he would not throw away that little chit of a girl. Hannah decided that there was more to that pair than met the eye, and when she saw how carefully Lavinia cared for Elspeth and how quickly she joined in the child's play, Hannah knew what it was. The girl wanted to be a woman and had chosen Sammy as the man. The choice was the proof of the person.

Vague figures in the distance strolled along the beach towards her. As they approached, they trailed tall and short shadows behind them, but she knew Robert by his stride. The long shadow revealed Alfred, even from so far away. The man walking between them would be their guest, but the two men further back were strangers. She stood to greet the little group.

Robert playfully made the formal introductions. "Commodore Du Pont, I take the pleasure in presenting you to my wife, Mrs. Hannah Smalls."

Du Pont removed his straw hat and offered his hand. "It is a pleasure to make your acquaintance, Mrs. Smalls." Hannah smiled, grasped his fingers, and thanked him for all his help. "It is the least I could do, Mrs. Smalls. I have much more reason to thank you."

"My husband tells me that his knowledge of the harbor was of great benefit," she said, and Du Pont picked up the suggestion in her tone. "The information your husband has shared will save many lives."

Hannah liked the man's open face and refined manner. She felt he wanted to be on friendly terms with them. Hannah was fed up with uncertainty and hoped there was something more than warmth in his hand. She looked at the two sailors who stood guard behind Du Pont and said, "You gentlemen look familiar." They waited for Du Pont to nod his permission to speak, and the taller one said, "We met when you first came to visit." Hannah's face flashed happy recognition, "That's right," and she looked at the shorter, stockier man to say, "You threw that barrel into the sea."

Davey's face beamed. "Yes, Ma'am. That was me."

Du Pont was quick to conclude the formalities, "These gentlemen are Able Seaman Webb and Carpenter's Mate Collins. They have volunteered to help you settle in." Hannah looked at the pistols dangling from their belts. This "settling in" was Du

Pont's way of giving them protection. Hannah looked at the man they called Webb. He carried a sheaf of newspapers draped over his forearm and he reminded Hannah of a well-trained waiter. Du Pont selected one of the newspapers and shuffled the pages to show them a photograph of Robert. Hannah gaped, and Du Pont explained, "You are all famous. As famous as *Harper's Weekly* can make you. People all over the country are reading this report."

Hannah looked at the portrait of her husband filling one side of the folded page alongside a sketch of the *Planter* and the thrill of reading their names in the print smothered her worries. Alfred was shaking his head, as if to throw off his broad smiles, and Johnny and Davey were itching to hear the news they brought. Du Pont asked Johnny to "please read for us." Johnny stood to intone, "One of the most daring and heroic adventures since the war commenced was undertaken and successfully accomplished by a party of negroes in Charleston."

Hannah sat on the sand dune reading the same edition spread over her knees. She swallowed the insult that Du Pont thought she couldn't read, and her eyes followed Johnny's every word. Davey stood with his thumbs in his gunbelt, enjoying every twist in the tale.

Johnny's voice sailed over the pages covering his face, "The following are the names of the black men who performed this gallant and perilous service: Robert Smalls, pilot; Alfred Gradine, engineer, Abraham Jackson, William Morrison, Samuel Chisholm. They brought with them the wife and three children of the pilot and the wife, child, and sister of other members of the crew. The balance of the party were without families."

Robert stood gazing over her shoulder at his own image staring up at him from the page in Hannah's hands. He remembered those men who asked so many questions just a week ago. The reporters had come to the island and quizzed everybody about "the adventure." They had papers with them that looked very important, but they wrote down everything Robert and the crew said. Sammy started strutting and spluttering a whole load of nonsense, until Alfred took him aside and warned him to "hush up. We don't know who these people are." They scribbled for a whole day and Robert had no way of knowing if they would tell the truth. They took him into a tent to take his photograph, and this frightened Robert more than their escape. The man took off his coat and tie and told Robert to "put these on." Robert obeyed, and the man seemed surprised that Robert knew how to tie his tie. Robert sat on the tails of the coat, so it would sit tight around his shoulders, and the man fidgeted with something behind Robert's back. Robert felt a cold claw grasp the back of his neck and the base of his skull. The man told him, "This clamp will keep you from squirming. You have to sit for seven minutes. Don't move."

The man hid under a black cloth at the back of a box, and Robert stared into the eye gazing back at him. He could see the distortion of his eyes splayed over the glass dome of the lens, but he listened to the voice in his head condemning him for "bringing your family to this terrible place." He felt such shame that he had risked so much for so little. They had abandoned their quiet life for this rag-tag uncertainty.

After the weeks of building trust, the crew had been scattered along this dune, unable to tell friend from foe. Before, they could believe that the white folks were "them" but now, "them" was every shade from marbled white to deep copper to coal black. There could be no more trusting to color, or to anything else. People said one thing and did another. Hannah had warned them to "smile at everyone, but trust nobody." She had learned to play the fool when she was a waitress, and so she was not fooled by the present game. She ordered her brood to "look to what they do." Her words pulled Robert through the grim stillness, until he heard the screws squeak behind him and the clamp spring open and release his head.

The face in the paper betrayed no hint of Robert's anxiety. The eyes were clear, and determination seeped from the corners where he thought only tears should well. His own face spoke to him, "Do not concern yourself with what is done." The words said what was done, and the pictures showed just how they had "undertaken and successfully accomplished... one of the most daring and heroic adventures since the war commenced." The face in the paper fluttering through Hannah's fingers was enough for Robert to ignore the face in the lens.

Hannah looked down the page to see an illustration and a caption in big capital letters: "FEEDING THE NEGRO CHILDREN UNDER CHARGE OF THE MILITARY AUTHORITIES AT HILTON HEAD." The picture showed a skinny granny ladling rice out of a pot to a crowd of children in the yard. They were being fed like chickens. She squinted at the picture and saw that the artist had placed a chicken pecking its way through the children squatting in the yard dirt. Hannah felt the insult and thought, "I suppose we can only feed our own children from the pot they give us." In the background was an old black man leaning on a stick. He was wearing some sort of Scotch hat. She had only seen such a hat at a Fancy Dress Ball while waiting on tables at the Excelsior Hotel. The hat looked ridiculous on the rich white folks, but now it made the old man in the picture look both stupid and foolish.

Johnny was reading a list of the cannons they had taken with them, but Hannah was more interested in the picture on the next page of the newspaper. She scowled at the cartoon of a large black woman standing behind a three-bar gate. The woman's face was as vacant as Little Dee Dee's drugged on their floor. There was a bubble coming out of the woman's mouth, and Hannah read, "Oh! I'se so glad you is come. Massa says he wish yen was in de bottom ob de sea - but you ain't in the bottom ob de sea, you is he'yar an I'se so glad to see yer." Of course, the woman had fat hips and looked as stupid as the two children playing beside her. Hannah's anger rose with the bile from her stomach, but she kept her indignation locked behind her smile. She silently cursed the dunes around her and thought, "one minute we are heroes and the next page we are imbeciles who can neither talk properly nor feed our children." She raised her chin to catch a sea breeze that might dry her eyes.

Sand flew into Johnny's mouth as he spluttered, "various plans were proposed," and he stopped to wipe his face. Alfred raised his eyebrows and wondered how the newspapers knew about their plans. Du Pont urged Johnny to continue. "But finally the whole arrangement of the escape was left to the discretion and sagacity of Robert." Du Pont looked over Robert's embarrassment and saw they were all perplexed when Johnny added, "his companions promising to obey him and be ready at a moment's notice to accompany him."

Robert snapped up his head and protested to Du Pont, Johnny, and Davey, "We did this together."

Du Pont assured him. "There is no need to be shy."

"They did not 'accompany' me," Robert insisted. "We did it together. I didn't escape. We skedaddled with the property stolen from the government."

Du Pont recognized Robert's annoyance. He knew all too well that the distance between the deed and the tale in the papers involved a very tortuous route. He blushed to think of all the things he had read about himself after the victory at Port Royal and how he had to explain to Sophie all the "heroic feats" that had wormed their way through the reams of newsprint. He decided to keep his mouth shut, for the moment.

Johnny was winding down to the stern of the article. "The crew had been sent forward to Commodore Du Pont." Alfred winked at Du Pont, who seemed to be just as pleased by the mention of his name. "The families of the crew have been sent to Beaufort, where General Hunter will make suitable provision for them." Alfred swiveled his head over the group and along the sand dunes and said, "This sure doesn't look like Beaufort."

Du Pont chortled and asked Johnny to continue. Johnny clearly spoke the last sentence, "The crew will be taken care of by Commodore Du Pont."

Johnny fell as silent as them all, and Du Pont exclaimed, "I do apologize for the delay in finding suitable quarters. Please gather all your possessions, for you will be moving immediately to more salubrious accommodation in Beaufort."

Hannah was stunned. The man was so polite, and this was the answer to her prayers. Anything would be better than this place. Du Pont waved his hand and casually said, "Able Seamen Webb and Collins have agreed to stay with you." Hannah could have kissed him. Her eyes dragged her gratitude from Du Pont's smiling face to the eyes of Johnny and Davey. She lowered her eyes to their pistols and knew they would be safe.

Du Pont stood tall and said, "There is one other matter." Alfred was suspicious because he was always waiting for the sting in the tail of good news. "I have arranged for your case to be sent to the Prize Court." Du Pont listened to the hubbub of questions and realized they were completely ignorant of prizes. "A Prize Court," he explained, "will decide the amount of money you will receive for delivering the ship to us."

Alfred blurted, "You mean you are going to pay us for stealing the boat?"

Du Pont held his sides and laughed. "Young man, that is the perfect definition of the function of a Prize Court. Yes, you all will receive money for your deed. I have instructed the commissioners that the compensation be awarded to all the people on the boat."

Robert and Alfred turned to march over the dunes and collect all the people and their few possessions, but Hannah stayed back with Du Pont. She did not know what to say to him and could not voice any one of the hundred questions she held tight in her mind about this man. Du Pont broke the silence. "I look forward to tasting your beans and rice. Robert tells me they are a treat."

"Yes, Sir," was all Hannah could think to say, but it took a few moments to fathom that Du Pont was inviting himself to dinner.

"I would be honored for you to be our guest."

He smiled and said, "Thank you," and turned away. Hannah wondered if she could stomach one more dish of beans and rice.

Chapter 9

All Hands to The Pumps

USS Keystone State, off Georgetown S.C. 19 May 1862

My Precious Sophie,

On Sunday morning the Connecticut arrived bringing large mails and the captain brought aboard such official letters, some of them important, as are not put in the mails that have to go to the post office. We sent a boat over to Hilton Head and your lovely letter was there.

We went ashore and it was a relief to have a good long walk. The visit with the soldiers was not so healthy as the air. They invited us to 'stop in' and meet Colonel Rich, who kept us waiting for some time, came in with a cigar in his mouth, kept his cap on, while the rest of us were without ours. Had hardly a word to say on the news of the day; took a seat at a distance from me and the whole scene was typical of our impressions of Army officers. Drayton tried to convey to them, now and then, some of the proprieties of life.

Drayton came on board about ten, and he and I discussed things on deck until twelve when he left. He is one of the best talkers I know and is very sensible in all professional matters, on the war and the politics of nations, etc., and I have not had a more intellectual pleasure for some time. His comments are admirable and he has a practical view on the subject of slavery, as you seem to infer, except that he cannot see the end of the war without its extinction. General Hunter's order freeing all the slaves in South Carolina, Georgia and Florida was read to the troops yesterday. Drayton thinks that most unnecessary, remarking every Negro who comes in is practically a free man, and so with everyone

124

within our lines, and never can return to slavery. This is perfectly true; so why make declarations that cause discussion, revive the issues, give the South renewed cause to excite their people. The death knell of slavery was sounded when that first gun was fired on Fort Sumter. He made another remark in speaking of the South attempting to hold out, and a guerrilla warfare, etc. that the element for guerrillas with them were our friends, the slaves; that they had the knowledge of the locality, of the forests, of the waters; for no white man in the South can handle a skiff, are stupid and awkward on water, while the Negroes are skillful and daring.

Du Pont had been true to his word and moved the Smalls into a derelict store in Beaufort that same afternoon. Davey shouldered open the front door, and it scribed a screaming semi-circle into the wooden floor. Johnny led the family into their new quarters, and Alfred sighed, "picked over cleaner than a Sabbath Gospel Bird." The floorboards creaked up a fine, white dust. Hannah sniffed and said, "They sold flour." The flour would have been the first to go, after the whiskey.

Johnny pointed to the exposed brick. "They even took the plaster," and Robert added, "but they left the stairs." Davey bounced up the stairs, and Hannah followed him until her head was level with the upper floor. She saw a bed too big to be easily moved, and Davey speculated, "This must be the hammock deck." She crept back down to the main room to find Robert examining empty crates and two barrels. Johnny swiped his finger over the rim and tasted dried sorghum syrup. Clara released L'il Robert, and his delighted screams echoed off the walls. Johnny stomped after the pitter-patter of the child's bare feet to the rear of the large room, where a double row of cargo doors ended the chase. Johnny pried up the iron latch and pushed open the doors on shrieking hinges to reveal a back yard. They all gazed at a litter of broken bottles, rusted hoops, and smashed boxes bounded by brick walls on two sides right down to a rickety dock at the river bank.

Lavinia herded all the children to the center of the room, as Sammy and William stepped carefully through the debris in the yard. They could all live in the echoing chamber between the street and the river. Robert saw that goods could be unloaded straight from the water's edge into the main hall. Hannah had to turn an empty wreck into a home, but as she looked from the ceiling to the sailors, she knew their new home was dry and safe.

When their owners skedaddled, the slaves flew in like crows. They ran through the mansions, and what they could not eat, carry, or sell they smashed, ripped, and threw to the side of the road. The sailors arrived to restore order, found one drunken white man passed out over a barrel in the middle of Bay Street, and promptly helped themselves to whatever the freedmen had ignored. When the soldiers arrived to declare martial law on the sailors and the contrabands, there was very little left of value for the Army. Bales of cotton were too heavy to move and the buyers were long gone, so the Department of the Treasury sent agents to "confiscate abandoned property for government use." The sailors, soldiers, and contrabands understood grabbing the cotton, but when the "Washington vultures" packed up the books in the town's library, they were mystified.

In two weeks, they had their new home in ship-shape. The children and girls slept upstairs. Hannah and Robert camped at the bottom of the stairs. Davey and Johnny shared night-watches at their "guard stations" at the front and back doors. Being "assigned to shore duties" was far better than hauling sail on blockade patrol. The bricked-in yard between the back doors and the bay made a perfect summer house, minus the roof, so Hannah transformed this three-sided haven into their kitchen and laundry.

Robert bought an iron skillet from a back-alley peddler for ten cents. The silver one-dollar coin sparkled in Robert's palm and lit avarice in the looter's eyes. He offered three tin pots as change. When Robert proudly presented his purchases to Hannah, she shook her head and laughed, "some people don't know when they're well off."

One morning, she opened the front door to a handsome sailor offering her an envelope. Robert and Davey craned their necks to see her read a note from Du Pont expressing his desire for "the honor of your company on Thursday evening at eight bells." She demanded of Robert, "He's coming here... tomorrow?" Hannah didn't like being hurried, and Robert explained how Du Pont had hinted about "a plate of rice and beans." Robert had extended a vague invitation, and Du Pont had turned their polite chat into a definite date. Hannah clutched the page and read, "If it will not inconvenience you, may I bring two friends who are most anxious to make your acquaintance?"

Johnny was quick to add, "I didn't know Commodores had any friends."

Through their laughter, Davey caught the edge in Hannah's voice. "You mean I got to make a fancy meal for them?"

"No," Robert protested, "He just wants simple fare."

"Simple fare for five," Hannah complained.

"If he brings two more, it's important. Hang the expense, throw in another potato."

Hannah had two days to turn their camp house into a dining room fit for company. She grabbed her bonnet and commanded Davey, "Get your hat. We gotta go fetch." Robert looked out the door to see Davey running after Hannah all the way down Bay Street and knew she was enjoying her problem.

Davey caught up with her and had to know, "Where are we going?" He was no wiser with her one word answer, "Lydia." He'd find out whoever or whatever was a 'Lydia' when Hannah ceased bounding down the street. Davey's boots crunched beside her, until she slowed her pace enough to demand, "And just what is an eight bells?"

Davey tried to explain, "They ring the ship's bell once every half-hour, so two bells is one hour."

"You mean he's coming over at four 'o the morning?" she said.

"No. The bells start at mid-day for four hours," he said, and added, "and then they do it all over again, except for the Dog Watch."

"Sound like you have mean dogs on that boat of yours."

"No dogs. Dog Watch happens from four to eight. But we have lots of cats on the ship."

Hannah calculated that by eight o'clock tomorrow evening she had to devise some way of turning a handful of moldy rice and a few slabs of fatback into a pretty dish to set before important guests. She grumbled, "You people sure have a complicated way of telling the time."

"What would you call it?" Davey asked.

Hannah raised a pair of fingers to the horizon and said, "two fingers of summer sun." Davey curled a lip to stifle a laugh and kept his mouth shut.

Hannah stopped at the end of the street and turned them away from the bay. She led him along the alleys between prosperous houses snuggled behind privet hedges, but she seemed to know where she was going, so Davey gawked at the silent buildings that were once family homes. He had no reason to be in this part of the town, but after all the clatter and clanging of a crowded port, the little islands of tidy domesticity were a relief. He guessed that some of the houses were mansions, but they also passed wood-frame dwellings needing a lick of paint. He saw holes in roofs hanging over porches and thought that two planks and twenty nails would keep the rain off their heads.

Hannah halted before a wall of green shrubbery surrounding a two-storied house. She grabbed a branch and pulled it to the side to make a gap in the hedge and held the hole open for Davey. They stood in a neatly trimmed back yard, and Davey looked up to see white walls gleam against the pine trees. An old lady rose from the grass. She beamed at Hannah and included Davey in her smile. "I thought you'd be over today."

Hannah simply said, "Davey, Lydia," and offered nothing further. Lydia was tiny, and her wrinkled arms looked like bronzed rifle barrels. The wrinkles started at her brow, flowed around her mouth, and didn't stop until they reached the ground. Davey thought it best to put some distance between the two women and stood under a tree. Lydia hopped spryly around the back yard, and Davey's eyes followed them up the back stairs until they disappeared through an open door.

Davey wandered to the corner of the building and saw officers lounging against the porch railings. They were chatting over cigars and snifters of something strong, so the house was definitely "Off Limits to Other Ranks." Officers could be unpredictable, especially when they were off duty, so Davey rounded the corner, where he could not be seen, but they could be heard. Their laughter drifted around the porch. Davey heard them salute, "those Bitches Boys had a nerve."

They must be talking about *Onward*'s crew, he thought, for her busty figurehead had inspired the nickname throughout the fleet. Temperance fanatics, anxious for the sailors' morals, had forced the Navy to abolish the "foul practice of dispensing ardent spirits aboard ship." *Onward*'s crew had written a letter of protest directly to Du Pont, who sent it back to Nichols. Nichols called the crew to General Quarters and told them, "The Commodore will compensate the men for the loss of their rum ration," and added, "according to law." Davey heard another voice float over their spluttering guffaws, "that Nichols is a bit of a pistol himself."

He shuffled to the bottom of the stairs. Lydia's voice floated through the open door, telling Hannah, "this'll be enough to keep a'fire most of the day." Lydia complained, "can't even hit the spittoon," and Hannah added, "those carpets are like wet ice." Their laughter tickled Davey when he heard, "They won't notice an' those who do will be too drunk to mind."

Hannah and Lydia walked down the steps carrying two iron pots in each hand. Davey stepped out of the shade to help, and

Lydia pulled her lips into a mischievous smile flavored with conspiracy. "Nice that you've brought along such a strong, young man. You going to help us?"

Davey relieved her of the pots, which were heavier than he expected. "Of course, Ma'am." He hefted one of the pots, and it jingled with the silverware they had borrowed. Lydia held open the gap in the hedge, and they rattled their way back to Bay Street.

They returned home to find Johnny worrying the windows with a rag and some vinegar. They looked through a window to see Robert and Alfred staring back at them. Hannah tapped a pane and asked, "How'd you get 'em to shine?" and Johnny showed her a fistful of soggy newspapers. "I kept the page about our adventures."

They walked into the house, and Hannah joked, "Do I live here?" Robert produced a packet of Navy issue coffee, "compliments of Captain Rhind," and Lydia took it into the yard to "scald up a pot" for them all.

Alfred was eager to burden them with ships' scuttlebutt, and Johnny was especially curious about *Planter*'s new commander. He quizzed Robert about his first day with the new man. "He was honest enough to say what he couldn't do," Robert said.

"How so?" asked Hannah. Johnny and Davey leaned in for Robert's answer.

"He told me he's a blue water sailor."

"That's a real good sign," Johnny said.

"Said that he's not Mud Turtle Navy."

"That means he doesn't like working inshore," Johnny was quick to add. Davey and Johnny cast approving but skeptical glances over their tin mugs.

"He said that in deep water, he was captain, but when we are in the shallows and rivers and creeks, 'then you are Captain and I am First Mate.'"

"This Rhind sounds like he knows his business," Johnny said with relief, and Robert knew that was the sailors' way of saying,

"This officer won't get us killed." The business of the Navy was staying afloat and alive.

Davey brought his cup to the yard and returned with two longs sticks. Lydia examined them and saw a deck brush attached to one and a bundle of old sacking around the other. "What'chya goin to do with this?" she asked.

"Swab the deck," Johnny said as he hoisted a bucket and walked to the river.

Lydia was mesmerized by the sight of men cleaning floors. Davey cast a pail of water over the floor and impaled a bar of lye soap in the broom-brush. She watched him scrub two strokes along the grain of the floorboards, swing his shoulders twice from side-to-side, and take two steps back. Johnny followed him with the same dance, soaking up the slurry with the stick-rags, and wringing them into the bucket. They marched backwards in time together, and Lydia winked approval at Hannah, "These men know how to work."

Halfway through the room, they paused, and Johnny proudly showed Lydia his bucket of oily filth. "It's a start," he exclaimed, walking to the river to change the water.

Hannah and Lydia sat on the old boxes finishing their coffee. Lydia didn't bother to whisper just because Davey could hear. He felt included in Lydia's complaints about the the officers at the white house. "They sleep and they drink and sometimes they do both at the same time... but they pay good."

"Cash money?" Hannah asked.

"A golden circle. Not that scrip. Least the sailors are quiet. Not like those preacher women."

"You mean those ladies from up North?" Hannah asked.

"The very same."

"They were in the house?"

"Yup. A whole month with nothing to do," Lydia sighed. "Came down from Boston and New York to teach us how to read and write."

"Well, isn't that's a good thing," Hannah said.

"And teach us to grow cotton," Lydia smirked, and they both laughed.

"I heard they were a handful at the island."

"Whumph. Every one of them could start a fight in an empty room. You know what they were arguing over?"

"Dresses?" Hannah suggested.

"Kneeling."

"How can you argue over kneeling?"

"Can't tell but they started fussin over who was kneeling during their prayers and that blew up into a knock-down, drag-out cat fight. They were rolling around on the floor, throwing the crockery and screaming like pussy on a skillet. They pulled out so much hair I saved some to stuff a pillow." Lydia looked up to Davey, leaning on his stick and drinking in every word. "No disrespect, Young Man, but there ain't nothin' uglier than a fighting white woman."

Hannah stood, smoothed out of her calico dress, picked up a satchel, and headed for the door. Davey scuttled after her, demanding, "Where are you going, Mrs. Smalls?" Hannah smiled at the boy's enthusiasm and said, "I need to find some groceries."

Robert picked up Davey's brush-stick to help Johnny, and Davey held the door open for Hannah. He marched escort beside her until she told him, "You don't have to come with me."

"I'd like to, if that's OK with you," Davey shrugged back. She realized he was just plain bored when he asked, "What are we doing?"

"We're after the fixins for a feast." She was glad when Davey threw his cap ribbons over his shoulder and squared his cap to march beside her, eager for a treasure hunt. The man seemed interested in everything they did.

Davey asked about the worn leather bag Hannah was carrying. "That's my 'maybe'," she replied.

"Maybe?"

"Yeah. I take this bag and maybe I will find something to put in it."

Davey admired the hope she found in an old sack. "Just what are we 'maybeing'?"

"Something for a Head Man Sailor to eat, only better." Davey smiled to think that "only better" summed up the Smalls family. He hoped some of that "better" would find its way to him.

Hannah's eyes scanned the river. When she spied a man in a skiff, she walked to the edge and yelled down to him, "What you got?"

"Melon and peaches," he echoed back. He shrugged at the pole to set the skiff gliding towards the bank. He picked up a watermelon and pried it open with his thumbs. Hannah knew if he could open it without a knife, it had already been holed. The sellers stabbed the melons and then cooled them in the river. It tasted fine, but two hundred yards upstream was a latrine. Holed melons made people sick.

"Throw me a peach."

"They not ready," he objected.

"I'll be the judge of that." Hannah tossed back. She caught the fuzzy ball and ordered, "Nine more. Just like this." She took a few steps along the shore and Davey saw the skiff saunter beside her. The man hardly touched the pole and Davey saw the man move his little craft merely by shifting his weight from foot-to-foot.

"You crazy woman," the seller protested. "Ain't ready. Give you the squitters."

Hannah tossed him a dime. "Suit yoo'self," he surrendered. Davey bent over and spread the maybe's mouth wide. The man tossed nine peaches at Davey, but the skiff stood perfectly still. The man leaned away from her, and the skiff settled beside his next customer. Hannah turned away and ignored the man yelling after them, "A fool and her dime soon parted."

She guided Davey through the salt-and-pepper throng of noisy peddlers and desperate white women. An alley-merchant thrust greens under her nose, and Hannah cast them aside with a dismissive hand and a snort at their suspicious stink. But the pecans she wrangled out of a girl's burlap poke were worth the twenty cents they finally agreed upon. She had a pleasant gossip with an old slave-man whose smile was brighter than the new quarter she gave him for his sackful of beans.

A white woman at the corner stood guard over a bucket of Irish potatoes. Hannah smelled the earth rising from the bucket at the woman's feet and saw the hurt in her eyes. The woman was clutching her last grain of respectability, and Hannah wished to relieve her pain at being reduced to hawking spuds. "My oh My oh My. Are those from Edisto?" Hannah asked with genuine enthusiasm.

"Yes," the woman coughed.

"I've hankered after them for an age."

The woman's eyes softened enough to say, "Home grown."

"Better than anything I've seen in weeks. How much?"

Hannah let the woman take her time to enjoy the haggling and revel in the simple joy of making a good sale. Davey poured the whole bucket of potatoes into the maybe and heard the woman say, "Thank you."

"I'll be back in a couple of days," Hannah assured her, "I hope you have some more."

The woman jingled the two quarters in her dirty palm and said, "You can count on it."

Davey waited until they were out of the woman's earshot and asked, "Do the best potatoes come from Edisto?"

"They do now," Hannah smiled.

"How did you know she was from Edisto?"

"White women there wear very big bonnets. They don't like too much sun."

They wandered down an alley, and a man approached them with three dead chickens hanging from a stick over his shoulder. "How much the three?" Hannah asked.

"Dollar each," he said with dismissive contempt. Davey did not like the man's sneering manner.

"They not worth fifteen apiece," Hannah shot back, but the man grinned to know she wanted them. "Maybe two dollar to you. Maybe nothin."

Davey pulled the chickens off the stick and stowed them in the bag. He pulled three quarters from his pocket and dropped them at the man's feet.

"Keep the change."

The man tensed to lunge, but Davey pushed his face back and whispered, "You learn to be nice to ladies." The man turned, and Davey's eyes bore into the back of the man's head to make sure he kept going. Hannah followed Davey back to the corner.

She stopped to chat with a gaggle of young women and Davey was lost in their shrieking confabulations. One woman said something about "linkumpig" and he thought they were cussing the President. Hannah explained that they were looking for links of sausages. There were other incomprehensible discussions about the "best joloff" and arm-waving arguments of "ngubas spoil the meat." Davey heard a woman ask, "e nayam yampig?" and Hannah shrugged back, "It won't keep." Another woman clasped her hands on her swaying hips and smiled over Davey from head to foot. Davey heard her croon, "Dis nice buckra yo bohboh. Enty tittuh?" Hannah scowled back when she saw the smile turn greedy and linger in places that made Davey blush. Between his rosy cheeks and his knuckles whitening around the straps of the maybe, Hannah knew it was time to head for home.

Hannah broke the silence as they returned. "What do sailor men call such women?"

"Dock wives," Davey admitted with a guilty smile.

"Anything else?" Hannah pressed.

"Some call them 'stinkies.'"

"But you don't," she was quick to add.

"No, I do not."

Davey's curiosity loosened his clenched jaw. "What's a bohboh?"

Hannah raised an eyebrow. "A boy."

Davey sensed she was holding back, so she told him, "She asked if this nice white man is your son." They laughed together. "We have a saying, 'Every grin don't mean a laugh,' but you grin when you laugh and that's a good thing."

She stopped and pointed Davey to an old woman squatting before a pile of woven mats. She asked for three, and the woman counted out a trio of circles woven out of seagrass. Hannah gave her fifteen cents for the bundle and explained to Davey, "This is a fannuh."

Davey waved the pliable disc in front of his face. "You mean like a fan?"

She grinned back at him. "You can use it like that, but fannuh come in handy in all sorts of ways." Davey wondered what she would do with all these different things, but kept quiet until they returned home.

The day had been as busy as a fleet review, and Johnny was glad Hannah was in charge. Davey's arms beat the dirt of decades out of the floor, and Lydia transformed the yard into an open air kitchen.

Hannah called from the yard for Davey's help, and he saw Lydia walking around the enclosure with one finger raised to heaven. "Put that bigun here," Lydia ordered, and Davey trundled the largest iron pot to the spot her finger selected. "Fat one, you live here." He followed Lydia to the door, carrying a smaller pot, when Lydia again pointed to a cloud and then shook her finger at the pot and ordered, "Little Boy, you stay here." There was some method in her wanderings, but Davey could not fathom why she chose those places for the pots to "live." She gathered stones into her apron and placed them around the pots. This could be black magic, but Davey was curious to delve into the old lady's secrets.

Johnny gathered every piece of rectangular, cubical or flat lumber he could find and placed five tea chests in a roughly even row to serve as a table. He had taken careful note of Du Pont when they were at Hilton Head, so Johnny trundled the stoutest of the crates to where he thought Hannah would seat the guest of honor. He jumped on the crate to test it, and when he was satisfied that it would support a large man said to himself, "Can't send a Commodore home with his ass full of splinters." He carried a slightly taller, more delicate box to the other end of the table, sure that Robert would sit opposite Du Pont. He placed one box next to Robert's seat for Hannah, but he would wait for Hannah to tell him where she would place the two other diners. He looked through the back doors to see Lydia fussing with some kindling, so he picked up the bucket and walked out to the yard.

Hannah raised two fingers to the sky and watched the sun dip below the distant trees on Lady Island. The forest scattered sunset over the water. She looked over the busy yard and let confidence flow through her cheeks. Tomorrow would bring more work, but now was the time to rest and to savor the company of trusted friends. She smiled at the delight shining in Lydia's eyes. Davey and Johnny laughed like children at their chores, and when she saw the boys hovering around Lydia, she shared their joy of a new adventure.

Chapter 10

The Wonder of the World

Allen Russlynn was enjoying his new position. The traveling was tedious, but the voucher assured him a First Class seat on the New York-Washington Express. He sat digging his elbows into the upholstered armrests and pressing his palms together over his nose. Every time the Conductor opened the carriage door, the wind curled sparking smoke over the passengers. The aisle carpet was slippery with tobacco juice. Russlynn breathed through his steepled fingers, for the furnishings were less offensive than the Conductor, standing so annoyingly above him and demanding his ticket.

The wretched man insisted on punching his ticket, when Russlynn had already told him, "I don't need a ticket." The Conductor had heard this excuse as many times as he had thrown stowaways off his train, but this one refused to budge. Russlynn offered him a letter bearing the seal of the Department of the Navy, clearly stating that he was "traveling on the business of the Government of the United States." Still, the man demanded a ticket, so Russlynn almost shouted, "I don't need a ticket." He thrust the paper up to the Conductor's nose, "This is a Travel Warrant. It is better than a ticket. I don't have to pay for a ticket. The Treasury pays for the ticket." The Conductor was fed up with this well-dressed scrounger demanding a free ride, but he was also wary lest the man was telling the truth. He slowly scratched his head and then used the same finger to sound out the words, "entitled to travel, unrestricted and at government expense, on any appropriate means of conveyance." Russlynn closed his eyes and sucked his exasperation through his fingers. The Conductor sincerely hoped this passenger's next "means of conveyance" would be a ferryboat sinking in the Hudson River. He punched a hole in the letter before Russlynn could snatch it from his grasp.

The Conductor resisted the temptation to break this passenger's nose and walked down the aisle with a cheery, "Tickets, please."

Russlynn opened the satchel he used as his portable desk. He drew forth a slender file marked "Monitors. Passaic Class." The file outlined the designs and the costs of the Navy's newest ships. The *Monitor* had been such a success in high places that they decided to create more of the iron wonders. That the things could float was astonishing; that they could move on their own steam and fire their guns was a miracle. Russlynn had organized a demonstration of the newest ironclad, the USS *Keokuk*, at the Washington Navy Yard. Even though he had memorized the day's events, he studied a list outlining the "Schedule." The exhibition would astonish Welles and delight Fox.

Russlynn had crammed his diary with two weeks of meetings in three cities to prepare for this display. When he wasn't riding the over-night cars, he crouched at the center of humming telegraph lines. The many consultations in New York and Philadelphia were exhausting, but highly profitable.

Three days ago, Fox had presented Russlynn's account of the new ship to Welles, and they had enthused over the phrase "miracle of bellicose buoyancy." Welles ran his finger across the page to quote, "This vessel will bring retribution upon the waters into the very lair of rebellion." Welles grinned, "this is exactly what we need," and Fox added, "just when we need it most." Welles tapped the report. "This is good news, indeed, and most providential." The captains were wary of ironclads and chortled that they were "swimming castles." Below decks, the sailors laughed at the "floating turd buckets." Politicians were desperate for victory, so they grasped at iron.

Russlynn had caught Welles' enthusiasm for "these instruments of Providence," but was unsure whether the Secretary was referring to a congressional district in Rhode Island or to some higher constituency. It didn't really matter. The more people dismissed "Welles' Follies," the higher Russlynn's

139

stock rose. Welles reminded Russlynn of a diminutive beau in a fly-away wig offering his hand to the ugliest girl at the ball.

Russlynn swelled with confidence, for Welles had confessed to Fox his appreciation of the young man's enthusiasm. Russlynn blushed demurely when Wells complimented his efficiency. He chortled with just the right flavor of embarrassment when Fox joked, "It seems that dreadful Mrs. Simmons has finally gotten something right."

The engine shuddered the cars to a hissing halt inside the cathedral of the Baltimore and Ohio depot. Russlynn held back until the platform was almost clear, clutched his satchel under his arm, and dodged the islands of giggling women. He strode through the hall and under the arches of the main door into a chilly Washington morning.

Russlynn fumbled in his pocket for his watch and checked it against the clock beaming down from the station tower. "Exactly fifteen minutes past six," he mumbled to himself, and saw he had forty five minutes to walk to the Department of the Navy. He could have taken the new streetcars, but that was much too long to sit beside yet more chattering strangers. Rather than risk his new shoes and his trouser crease to the mercies of other passengers, he sauntered along New Jersey Avenue to admire the incomplete dome of the Capitol.

Russlynn had dined out with many a monumental joke at the building's expense, but raised the heartiest laughs when he quipped, "One can not determine whether it is a volcano which has already erupted or one which is building up to its next explosion. Rather like the members who will sit below it." Two giant cranes, like a pair of stringy midwives, lifted cut stones into place, and each week the ribs grew closer together. In the midst of war, rebuilding the Capitol was an act of faith, for nobody knew who would use it when, if ever, it was finished. The President had taken such an interest in the work that he was once seen talking to the stone masons and the carpenters. They were eager to explain their work and delighted by his more ribald stories. Russlynn had collected such anecdotes under the heading of "The Wit and Wisdom of the Original Gorilla," and what he could not remember, he composed.

He turned down Pennsylvania Avenue, and the screeching of the cranes faded behind him. The few people on the street made his march down 17th Street to the Navy Building enjoyable. He slowed his pace, for one did not appear before one's superiors dripping in street sweat.

The guard lounged at the main door, and even though he knew Russlynn by sight, he demanded his "Pass." The guard took his time studying Russlynn's *carte de visite* and spat out a bored, "Good Morning," followed by a surly, "Sir." Russlynn was fed up with ticket takers and door keepers, so he thoroughly scraped the soles of his shoes on the doormat, just to remind the guard that he was nothing more than a mudsill, and casually walked down the hall to Fox's office.

Fox looked up to see his assistant hovering in the door frame. "Ah, Allen. I'm glad you're here. Welles is in a foul mood and the demonstration is just what the doctor ordered."

"In that case, I am happy to bring the medicine."

"Is everything set up at the yard?"

"I waited for a telegram from Boswell before boarding the cars last evening."

"Boswell didn't produce any of his customary problems?" Fox asked, nonchalantly.

"He promises to have Captain Rogers sail *Keokuk* past the reviewing point at precisely 8:00 a.m."

Fox looked relieved. "I am very grateful for all your hard work in this matter."

Russlynn confessed over shy eyes, "All in a good cause."

"In the cause of the Department," Fox added.

Russlynn appreciated how vital this project was to both the war effort and the honor of the Navy. Fox was eager to get to the Navy Yard, so he led Russlynn into the corridor. "Have them bring round the carriage," Fox ordered. He turned towards Welles' office. "I will fetch the Secretary."

"Yes, Sir." Russlynn listened to the diminuendo of Fox's footsteps and walked to the front entrance. "Bring the Secretary's carriage to the front door," he told the porter, and exited the building to wait for both the horses and his bosses.

Fox led Welles out of the building and down the steps to Russlynn standing beside the open door with his arm poised to help Welles into the carriage. The driver sat impassive on his seat as Fox admired the matched pair of geldings in the traces. "Good morning to you young Allen," Welles greeted. He slouched his sixty three years of assorted ailments into the seat, asking, "I hope your train journey was not unpleasant."

"I'm used to the traveling, Sir. It's all part of the job."

"Does it look like rain?"

"There may be a few showers this afternoon, but we will be back before the clouds burst."

"We could do with a good soaking," Welles mused. "The rain will scour the houses and clean the streets. I like it when Washington looks clean."

Russlynn agreed. "So many pretty houses; it's a shame to hide them under dust."

Russlynn gently closed the carriage door and climbed up to take his place beside the coachman. They drove the three blocks to the Navy Yard at a walking pace, for Russlynn had given strict orders that "nothing shall bother Mr. Secretary's lumbago." The coachman knew enough about Russlynn to keep the reins of the two horses tight in the four slits between his fingers. The lead reins wrapped around his thumbs kept the animals under the strictest control.

The horses weren't the only things under the thumb, for Russlynn had impressed upon Commander Boswell that there were to be "no last-minute hitches." Russlynn threatened, "Your prospects depend upon the success of this exhibition." Boswell knew how things worked in the Navy and how they didn't work in the Yard he commanded. He resented this young upstart giving him orders. He had been put in charge of the demonstration and supervised every preparation for this morning's inspection. Boswell was keenly aware that those who shoulder the responsibility for success are often forced to bear the blame for failure.

The carriage approached the Navy Yard, and its walls sweated the morning mists through a decade of coal soot. Russlynn ignored the white gloves of the two Marines guarding the gates but took their salutes to the Secretary's carriage in his stride. The coachman drew the horses to a halt beside a dock, and Russlynn jumped down to attend to his superiors.

Keokuk, the prototype of the new class of warships, had been launched only three weeks ago at Jersey City. Boswell had received telegrams from "the Assistant to the Assistant Secretary of the Navy" and had barged into the Navy Department enquiring about "the identity of the anonymous civilian" and demanding, "By whose authority am I receiving peremptory orders via Mr. Morse's Magic Show?" The clerk had explained that "Mr. Russlynn is the special assistant to Mr. Fox." Boswell's irritation flew flares over his cheeks as he assaulted the clerk's ears, "I don't give a Tinker's Dam if he is special assistant to the Vicar of Hell." The clerk had deflected Boswell's rage with a sympathetic smile and a long-suffering sigh, "We have the same problem, Sir." Boswell had laughed at the absurdity of a Commander grumbling with an Able Seaman. The young clerk had leaned into a conspiratorial confession, "Between the decks, Sir, I'd rather be on ship's station than dealing with the assistant." It was just enough to tell Boswell something was in the wind and he'd better be careful. A casual gust of office gossip had blown many a career onto the rocks.

Boswell guided the party from the carriage to the end of the dock. "Would you like a chair, Mr. Secretary?" Boswell asked.

"No, thank you, Captain. I do too much sitting as it is."

"In that case, I will have the signalman start the proceedings." He nodded to a sailor standing at attention with his flags at the ready. Welles watched the young man's arms windmill his message and squinted to see an answering gyration of flags across the Anacostia River. They heard a low, distant grumble grow into a roar, and a dark iron stain spread itself over the river. Boswell offered his commentary, and Fox stood in wonder at the thing. "*Keokuk* is two hundred feet long and has a beam of forty six feet."

The elliptical monster spluttered towards them, and Welles was quizzical.

"What's that sticking up behind the gun turret?" Fox asked.

"Another gun turret," said Boswell. "To be more precise, they are floating bastions."

"You mean this is not another *Monitor*?" Welles demanded.

"It is an improvement, incorporating all we have learned from previous ironclads."

Russlynn heard his cue and asked Boswell, "Could you explain to the Secretary these improvements."

"With pleasure. The *Monitor* has one turret, which revolves to place the guns on the target. *Keokuk*'s guns rotate inside those bastions. These iron towers give added protection because they do not move."

"What is the advantage?" Russlynn asked, knowing the answer.

"We can have thicker plates of iron on a bastion than we have on a revolving turret."

"How does the thing fire?" Welles queried.

"The guns roll on fixed tracks so they can fire to port, starboard, or ahead."

"Is that why there are two bastions?"

"Yes. *Keokuk* can fire to the sides, to the front, and to the rear."

"So, it doesn't have to turn around to shoot."

"Precisely."

Fox was unable to restrain his admiration. "And the sheer size is enough to instill fear."

"That's exactly what we want," Welles answered.

"Mr. Ericsson's mind is most fertile," Fox said.

"His designs are truly revolutionary," Russlynn added.

"Yes, but he's a finicky sort," Fox added.

"I've noticed that is the way with geniuses," Welles said. "Mr. Ericsson is sensitive because of a supposed slight and neglect by the Navy Department. I made it a point to Admiral Smith, the Chairman of the Board, and especially requested that Ericsson should be treated tenderly."

"No use ruffling feathers when so much is at stake," Fox said.

Keokuk glided over the water like a black swan and slid into a lazy halt near the dock. Boswell signaled to the squad of sailors standing behind him, and they wheeled a gangplank to the end of the dock for the party of dignitaries to board the ship. Russlynn offered his arm and guided Welles delicately over the rickety wooden bridge to the deck. Welles was surprised by the slipperiness of the metal and clung to Russlynn's arm. Fox worried he would fall and make a fool of himself. A sprawling pratfall in front of the blue jackets simply would not do.

Boswell stood nearby and made the introductions. "Captain Rogers will give us the grand tour." Rogers saluted and walked them around the deck. Welles looked up the sloping sides of the bastion, which resembled a sugar cone with the top lopped off. Rogers explained that the angle of the walls was calculated to deflect solid shot. Welles tapped the forward bastion with his cane, and Rogers was relieved when he did not hear a salty voice respond, "Who's there?"

Rogers led them to a hatch behind the smoke stack. He told Russlynn to descend first, "so as to assist the Secretary. Mind your head, Sir." Russlynn tore his pant leg on the metal ladder and crouched on the lower deck to help Welles down into the bowels of the boat. There was hardly room to stand upright, so they all hunched in a file like tunneling trolls. Rogers led them to the engine room in the stern, and the heat was as excruciating as the noise was deafening. Welles dripped sweat beside the double boilers that powered the propellers. He was unable to concentrate on Rogers' account of the propulsion system. Rogers saw their discomfort and led his little party forward to the captain's cabin in the bows.

Rogers pulled a lever on the ventilator and flooded the cabin with river air. Welles felt restored but was grateful that Russlynn was standing behind him in case he passed out. Rogers claimed their attention with a raised finger. "There is one innovation which you may find amusing," he said, and opened a louvered door. They all gazed at an iron cylinder with a wooden lid. "Mr. Ericsson has incorporated the latest in conveniences. Behold." Rogers lifted the wooden lid to reveal a little pool of bilge water.

"Is it a well? Fox asked. Rogers laughed to think of a well sunk into an ocean and exclaimed,

"Watch this." He pulled a chain beside the cylinder. The machine gurgled and spluttered water into a little cyclone and disappeared. Welles peered down the hole as if looking for the rabbit in a magician's hat. "What is it?" he asked.

"It's the Captain's Commode," Rogers said with mischievous pride.

"You don't say," Welles sputtered.

Rogers threw his handkerchief into the iron mouth, pulled the chain again, and they all watched it disappear.

"Amazing!" exclaimed Welles. "I have been told that Jefferson Davis has such a device in Richmond."

Russlynn was quick to add, "We can bring him another convenience."

"When he sees your ship," Fox said to Rogers, "he'll need two of these marvelous devices." Welles' lips suppressed a laugh and his smirk was an invitation, so Russlynn said, "Now every Captain is a Commodore." Fox and Welles joined in the laugher, but Rogers turned and led them back up the ladders to the deck.

146

He waited for them to ascend and escorted them to the gangplank.

It took them a few minutes of leaning on their canes to get back their land legs, and Welles commanded Boswell, "Please continue with the demonstration."

"Captain Rogers and the crew are at their stations," he assured Welles. "All is prepared."

Welles looked up to see Rogers standing high atop the forward bastion, his head and shoulders rising above the semi-circle of eleven-inch-thick iron that was his only shield from wind, waves, and cannon balls. It was possible to steer the ship from this position, but more probable to be blown to bits. Welles turned his head to Boswell, who waved to Rogers, who shouted something incomprehensible, and *Keokuk* nudged away from the dock. Her propeller churned like a giant egg beater, and *Keokuk*'s stern dusted the dock with river spray. Boswell's lifetime at sea had inured him to the droplets beading over his chin and chest, but Russlynn had come armed with an umbrella to open for Welles.

Duty ashore drained Boswell, but this invasion of politicians was a torture. He had been devising ways to get back to sea or to resign his commission. One did not retire in the middle of a war, so victory was the quickest way home to Massachusetts. He did not share the others' faith in the "expensive tin cans," for he knew too much about the new-fangled contraptions to believe in them. He trusted only to the men who would sail in these "Iron Coffins." There was something human about a wooden ship. You could bend with the forest of masts and strike a deal, saying, "I won't push you, and you won't throw me into the sea." Life was a bond with rope, timber, and tar. There was no talking with a boiler.

Welles' and Fox's eyes followed *Keokuk*'s waddle to the middle of the river. Boswell nodded to the flagman, and the message "Open Fire" fluttered from shore to ship. A clanking shriek screamed over the water, and they all held their breath as an explosion bounded over the water and smoke hid the ship. A black sphere arched gracefully into the sky and tumbled to the water. The cannonball spun up, splayed into the river to surface again, and careened along the glassy ribbon. It bounced four times before finally plunging through a crown of spreading circles.

Welles waved like an excited schoolboy, and Fox was clapping as if he were in a theatre. Russlynn padded his hands together with a gentlemanly approval of "Well done."

Boswell clenched his jaws at the smoke spewing from the gunports. The cannonball had skipped along the water because the guns could not be raised to full elevation without the shells exploding inside the bastion. The designers said, "It will be a simple matter to cut extra holes in the gun ports," but they had not fulfilled their promise. *Keokuk* ignored their applause and glided gently away, trailing greasy clouds of coal dust and burnt powder.

Welles was so delighted he shared a little cabinet gossip. "Mr. Lincoln refers to these vessels as 'a cheesebox on a raft.'" Russlynn guffawed with just enough of a smirk to laugh at either the joke or the joker. Welles grinned at Russlynn's amusement, and Fox exclaimed, "this cheesebox will deliver victory."

Boswell knew what was happening inside the gun deck. The men were blinded, and some would be deafened forever. The cost of one shot would be three sailors nearly suffocated and two more with punctured eardrums. That was why it took seventy-five men to run this ship; they had to change the gun crews every five shots just to keep the thing firing.

"We should return to the office," Welles said, "There is much to discuss."

Fox thanked Boswell for "this most interesting exhibition," and Boswell saluted with the "thanks of the whole Yard for the honor of the Secretary's visit." As Russlynn led his superiors to the carriage, Boswell returned to his duties and to plotting his escape. Russlynn helped Welles mount the steps and seated him facing the driver. Fox sat in front of Welles. Russlynn gently closed the carriage door and turned to sit beside the driver. Welles stopped him with the invitation, "Please, join us, young man. It's too drafty up there." Russlynn offered his thanks and uneasily took his place beside Fox.

The carriage bumped along 17th Street, full of Welles' excited statements that "This marvel of engineering gives us limitless advantages."

"And undreamed-of possibilities," agreed Fox. "This will enable us to take Richmond."

Welles saw the dead pan expression flood Russlynn's face and sensed skepticism in the blankness. He knew Russlynn would not be so ungracious as to express an unsolicited opinion, so Welles prompted the reticent assistant. "What do you think, young man?"

"It is not for me to say, Sir." Russlynn responded with exquisite deference.

"It certainly is," Welles said.

"Yes, what is your opinion of this new development?" Fox encouraged.

"In that case, may I be so bold as to ask, why Richmond?"

"If not Richmond then where should we deploy these ships?" Fox almost demanded.

Welles and Fox were stunned by Russlynn's one-word answer, "Charleston."

Fox's face beamed triumph at Welles, who cast a stoney gaze at Russlynn. Russlynn suffered through their silence, unsure if he had overplayed his hand. This one word could sink his plans or launch him to a glittering career. He looked directly at Welles, unblinking in his confidence and his terror, his eyes as inscrutable as the flesh rippling across Welles' brow. Russlynn did not breathe until he heard Welles say, "You're absolutely right."

Russlynn quickly inserted the point he had been honing for weeks. "With these ironclads, we can sail right into Charleston harbor and demand the surrender of the city."

"The fall of Charleston is the fall of Satan's Kingdom," Fox agreed.

"But it can't be done with a single vessel," Russlynn qualified.

"Then we shall have more of them," Welles said.

"And give the rebellion a solid thrashing," said Fox.

"How many do you envision?" Russlynn asked. "Five?"

"Why not seven, twelve," Welles said. "We'll commission a whole fleet." Fox reveled in their decision. "As many as it takes!"

Russlynn beamed admiration at Welles and said, "Just imagine. The Navy sails right into Charleston Harbor, treason is vanquished, and this terrible business is ended."

"These new ships are the wonders of the world," Fox enthused.

"And so much cheaper than armies," Russlynn contributed.

"War is the most terrible of human endeavors," Welles reflected. "It is left to us to finish treason once and for all."

"I don't see the Army ending the war," Russlynn said, spurring Welles to his favorite theme.

"That's because of their confounded generals. They have an interest in prolonging the war. After all, what's a general without battles to fight and glory to be won?"

"A glory that is traded for votes," Russlynn reminded them.

"Generals are dangerous in a democracy," Welles concluded.

Fox's eyes bridged the gap to Welles, and his cocked brow suggested that Welles was being most indiscreet, but before Welles could take the hint, Russlynn asked, "But could not a sailor pose an equal threat?"

Welles confided to Russlynn, "I have had to remind Du Pont just who is the Secretary of the Navy." Fox knew that Welles had the bit between his teeth, and his tongue would run away with his discretion, so he leaned back in his seat, banished from their conversation.

"Du Pont may not see it that way," Russlynn said.

"Du Pont is a skilled and accomplished officer," Welles admitted, "but some people in New York think he should be running the Navy." Welles leaned closer to Russlynn and grumbled, "Du Pont is a courtier, with perhaps too much finesse."

"That's just his manner," Fox said. "He was like that when I sailed with him."

"Oh, he has a fine address," admitted Welles. He added to Russlynn, "You should see his wardroom."

"A commodore can decorate his flagship to his taste," Fox defended.

"He's turned our ship into his personal palace." Russlynn nodded agreement and carefully hoarded every nugget Welles dropped. "Like many naval officers, he is given to cliques. It is clanship. Secession took off some of the worst cases, but there are symptoms of this in the South Atlantic Squadron." Russlynn heard Welles complain that the Northern royalty of the rich is as dangerous as the slavocracy of the rebellion and claim, "This evil I have striven to break up."

Russlynn was all too aware that Du Pont was the scion of one of the country's wealthiest families; he was equally well informed of the family's political capital. He heartily agreed when Welles said that "officers should not only respect but have an attachment to their commanders, but not with injustice to others, not at the expense of true patriotism and the service." Russlynn shared Welles' loathing of wealth and the influence it exerted, but he was determined to have both. Russlynn thought Welles' opinions of the Du Pont family were as accurate as his criticisms of the Commodore's style.

"Du Pont resorts too much to subordinate influences to accomplish what he might attain directly," Welles added.

"But you are the Secretary of the Navy," Russlynn assured him.

"Some people think the Secretary of the Navy should be covered in tar."

Russlynn laughed aloud at the image of Welles as a black-faced powder monkey with calloused hands. Welles assured Russlynn, "Certainly, while he continues to do his duty so well, I shall pass upon minor errors and shall sustain Du Pont in his command." Russlynn supported Welles' opinion and confirmed his belief that "a ship is no place for monied aristocrats." He gave Welles a moment to reflect and said confidentially, "Du Pont and his kind are a threat to our republican form of government."

Fox squirmed at this private gossip masquerading as discussion of public policy, but he was used to it and assured himself he could deal with Du Pont. After all, they were old friends. The sun scorched Welles' wet wig, and it slithered over his right ear when he nodded enthusiastic agreement. "Just because he fights with us doesn't mean he's on our side."

The driver turned into Constitution Avenue, and the empty bowl of the Capitol dome loomed behind Welles' head. The screeching of the cranes made the horses whinny, so he held the reins tight. The steam rose from the horses' flanks, and the driver yearned for a good scrubbing when they were stabled. He looked back over his shoulder, and the huge cranes reminded him of gigantic storks building a nest. He was used to hearing his passengers' complaints about the construction, and their conversation made him wonder if the dome should ever be finished. If all work stopped right now, the people could see all the hot air rising from the blatherings of the politicians. This thought had led him to christen Congress "the Tower of Babble." But if the dome were completed, we would not know what they were planning inside. Maybe it would be better if the people didn't know all that happened behind those ornate doors. He wavered between the two opinions each time he drove the Secretary and his friends around town. He was still undecided when he loosened the reins and gave the horses the freedom to trot home in time for dinner.

Chapter 11

Dinner at Eight Bells

Hannah lugged the satchel past Johnny, and he followed her into the yard. Lydia grinned and pulled three bundles of feathers from the maybe. She passed them to Davey to "please pluck these good to the skin." Davey crouched on the weedy grass, fumbling with the chickens in a cloud of feathers, while Lydia and Hannah clucked about "peaches and hardtack." Davey laughed at his attempts to juggle the three carcasses. Lydia commanded, "Pile those birds on this fannuh," so he placed the chickens on the yellow circle beside him.

Johnny cocked his questioning head at the birds. Davey ostentatiously told him it was a fannuh and casually confessed, "If I stay here too long, I'll forget English." Davey rolled the fannuh into a funnel and took great pleasure in explaining to Johnny just what could be done with the tube of delicate strands. Johnny then demonstrated what he would do to Davey with his broom handle, and the two set about their horseplay.

Lydia started weak fires under the four pots and cast a woeful look over to Davey. "We're gonna need some more." Davey tapped his forehead, jumped up to the woodpile, and returned with a big log of pine. "My oh my, you sure have strong arms," Lydia effused. "Can you turn that pole into kindling?" Davey squatted cross-legged with the log held between his chest and his feet. He drew his rope knife and pushed it down the log, raising curling spirals of wood over his blade. "Like scraping through butter," Lydia complimented. When he had planed down to heartwood, he hammered cross-cuts along the white core, scattering small squares over the tangle of shavings. Lydia was amazed at how quickly he reduced the log to kindling and demanded, "How come you can do that?" Davey caught the sincerity and simply said, "I'm a carpenter."

Lydia's curiosity and confidence were satisfied enough. She left him to "scatter that chop-wood evenly under all them pots," and rose to supervise Johnny, who was carrying buckets of water from the river.

Lydia walked him through the yard, filling the pots to different levels. Davey rolled logs to the pots, and she charged Johnny to "make sure they stay filled and the strong one will keep the whittling coming." The pots were soon boiling clouds that reminded Johnny of the volcanoes he had once seen off the coast of Nicaragua. They watched Lydia raise her finger to the sky and kick some more rocks into a circle near the wall. She picked up handfuls of Davey's chop-wood, spread them evenly within her rock circle, and asked Davey to "catch some fire from your bacca." Davey blew flares from his pipe into the kindling, and when it caught alight, Lydia scraped a stick through the crackling flames to make a round carpet of glowing embers. "Keep doing that 'til we got one hand's high."

Hannah sat breaking hardtack into a wash basin snuggled in her lap. She thrust the base of a tin cup into the chunky mound and ground it a fine power. She looked up to enjoy seeing the boys happy in their work and heard Lydia tell Johnny to "get a pail of clay and a long river reed." Hannah sliced thin slithers of a peach into her mixing basin and watched Johnny search along the river bank until he returned with a reed pole over his shoulder and his bucket brimming red and wet. Hannah rolled the hardtack and fruit into a wobbly ball and poured a bottle of Navy-issue rum into the basin. With the bowl tucked into the crook of her arm, she stood up and squished her fingers through the mush, as she walked over to Lydia fussing with the fire.

Lydia stuffed fistfuls of Hannah's rum mix into a chicken and dumped it into the pail of wet clay. Her fingers caressed the carcass with the sticky paste. She spread more of the grainy slurry over the bird until no skin was visible through the clay, and then added "some more for good measure." She nodded to the reed and ordered Davey. "Cut off three pieces, one hand high each." Davey's knife fluttered through the reed, and he offered her six inches of hollow pipe. She scowled at the slice and threw it away, telling him, "Cut the next one to a point." Davey's knife flashed an angle through the reed, and Lydia smiled as she fingered the sharp point. She drove the tube through the clay and into the heart of the chicken. She slathered more clay around the protruding reed and then gently placed the gooey ball of flesh on the glowing embers.

She soon formed the three chickens into a line and then spread the smoldering chips over them with a stick. Lydia sucked on her forefinger, touched the air, and piled five rocks on one side of the circle. She had left a space between the two biggest rocks and placed her foot over the opening. Davey watched the crimson wood chips grow tired and weaken to a dull orange. She arched her foot to let the wind blow through the hole. The bed of embers blushed red, and the pyre burst into flame. Johnny saw that she had found a prevailing wind and was guiding it through the tunnel of stones to make a flue. She asked Davey, "Can you make sure the wood keeps firing steady?"

"Sure," he said. "How long?"

"Most of the day," she smiled back.

Davey sucked on his pipe and settled down to guard duty over a slow fire. They worked through the rest of the humid day.

Hannah stood on the street looking into the house. They had ransacked their bedding to cover the boxes and barrels Johnny had turned into a dining table and seats. The boys had burnished the floor until it reflected the flickering storm lamps they had placed around the table. The silverware Lydia had temporarily liberated from the officers' quarters blinked with the sparkles Davey had coaxed out of them with fistfuls of wet sand. She could see all the way through the room and into the yard, where Lydia wandered from pot-to-pot, threatening the fires with a stick. Hannah marveled once again at the diamond glitter of the front windows and craned her neck along the street. She held up two fingers to the setting sun and peeked through them to see Du Pont walking along Bay Street with a middle-aged man and a small woman. "Right on time," she said over her shoulder to Robert.

Du Pont approached them with a grin, removed his hat to shake their hands, and presented the newcomers. "Mr. and Mrs. Smalls, I have the privilege to introduce the Reverend Mansfield French and Miss Laura Towne." Robert took their offered hands and invited them in.

The guests squinted at the dimness but could not disguise their surprise when they saw a formal table with a complete service and cutlery set for five on a gleaming white cloth. Hannah sensed their awkwardness and offered lemon water in tin tumblers. She noticed that the tight bun on Laura's neck couldn't pull the waves out of her hair and she caught a whiff of something that reminded her of islands. Robert and Hannah were very attentive to Laura's explanation of the Macassar oil in her hair. Du Pont looked enthralled by Laura's account of "the very therapeutic aspects of coconut and palm oil." He was also intrigued by his knife, fork, and spoon, which he recognized as Navy issue. He raised his tumbler and toasted "this evening of good company," and Hannah seated the party.

Du Pont explained that "Miss Towne has come to us as a teacher from Philadelphia."

Laura turned a slightly embarrassed smile to Hannah, who assured her, "There is much to learn here."

Du Pont saw Robert cast a quizzical glance at French and added, "Reverend French has been a most active advocate of abolition for the last thirty years." Hannah smiled straight into French's serious face and decided he didn't have enough flesh to keep his bones from making him look angry. Robert compared the height of the skinny minister with the short plumpness of the teacher and thought they made a comical pair, but he was careful to keep his mirth hidden behind the friendly smile suitable for important white folks. Du Pont was anxious to assure Robert and

156

Hannah that "these people are friends." Reverend French toyed with his fork and said, "We at the North are ready to take action to improve the conditions of the Freedmen."

"The Reverend and Miss Towne firmly believe that faith without works is dead," Du Pont commented.

"We've heard much of the same recently," Robert added.

Hannah already knew they were just two of the many volunteers who had journeyed south to set up the Colonies of Freedmen on the plantations emptied by the Great Skedaddle. The Reverend wanted to talk about "the contrabands raising their own cotton for their own benefit," and Du Pont listened intently to French's account of the "many specialists in agriculture who have so magnanimously offered their services, their time, and their expertise to ensure the success of the Port Royal Plan." Robert wondered how they were going to perform such miracles on Hilton Head.

"Miss Towne is an accomplished physician," French said.

"I practice therapeutic medicine. It is called homeopathy," Laura explained.

"That will be very good," Robert assured her, "People here will think you are a witch."

Laura's shock escaped her gaping mouth, and Du Pont could not control his laughter, as he had a momentary vision of the little lady straddling a broomstick and flying high over the islands. Hannah was quick to add, "That's what people 'round here call a 'healer,'" and shot a scowl at Robert. Hannah paid a little more attention when Laura spoke enthusiastically about home-grown medicine and how "you can find cures in your back garden."

The Reverend seemed anxious and wanted to draw the conversation into the practicalities of cotton production. Hannah decided that they were so keen to talk about what interested them because they were uneasy being in a contraband's home.

Du Pont heard footsteps behind him and turned to see Johnny and Davey march to the table carrying a large metal platter that looked suspiciously like the top of a burnished ammunition box.

French and Towne bored their confused brows at the three half-moons of wicker the boys placed on the table. Robert and Hannah smiled at their perplexity. Hannah caught the sparkle in Du Pont's eyes and sensed he was enjoying the promise of some mischief. He ran an inquisitive forefinger around the semi-circle and discovered a knot holding the two sides together.

"What is it?" he asked, with evident delight, and Robert told him to "Pull the string and you'll get a surprise." Du Pont squinted to see a small bow of ribbon at the zenith of the arc. He pulled it and the half moon of the fannuh fell open before him, offering a warm circle. The guests rose and leaned over the table to see a ball of baked clay with a tube sticking out the top. Laura and French pulled the other two strings, and a heady mist rose from the three little islands on the table. French was so flabbergasted he forgot to say the grace.

Du Pont's finger tickled the tuft of sea grass rising from the top of the tube. Hannah told him, "Now you pull out the stopper." His fingers trembled over the tube holding the little tuft of grass. Steam billowed to his nose, and a sweet cloud of cooked rum and chicken engulfed his head. "My Word, it's a little steamer," Du Pont exclaimed.

"Doesn't smell like one," Hannah assured him.

"What do we do?" French asked.

"Will you do the honors, Commodore?" Robert said as he offered Du Pont a hammer. The merriment in Du Pont's eyes reminded Robert of a little boy at a birthday party. Du Pont shrugged and confessed, "I must defer to the head of the household, mainly because I haven't the foggiest idea what to do."

Robert laughed and raised the hammer above Du Pont's dinner. He let it fall with a gentle tap and the clay ball cracked neatly into two halves. "I have never seen such a thing," Du Pont exclaimed, and Hannah smiled over their confused faces.

"It's called 'Poacher's Delight.' When you catch a bird and don't want to get caught with the feathers, you bake it in clay and nobody knows what you've been doing. We took off the feathers for you."

"But how do you eat it?" Laura asked. Hannah scraped some meat out of the half shell with her fork and dipped it in a bowl of creamed potatoes. Laura was kneeling on her seat with her elbows on the table and her face shoved into the plate. Robert passed the hammer to her, and she eagerly entered the game of "smash your supper." She was too delicate and only cracked the shell, so Robert pried it open with his knife and fork.

The Reverend was a bit too energetic and shattered his ball into meat-encrusted shards. Hannah divided the remains among the five diners and suggested, "Everybody share a forkful of the Reverend's bits." They were soon scraping and circulating their dishes and enjoying the simple fun of playing with their food.

The Reverend commented, "I met a woman yesterday whose child has the most peculiar name of 'Road.' Is that a family name here?"

Hannah assured him, "I know that girl," and turned to Du Pont. "You are her godfather."

Du Pont laughed, "There may be many bridges in my family, but I am certain there are no roads leading from us." The quip was lost on the diners, so Du Pont asked, "How does a sailor make a road?"

Hannah grinned to him and explained, "You are talking about Mary, the child's mother. Mary was running to Bay Point to see the big gun fight."

"The what?" French asked.

"That's what we call the day the Navy first came here."

"You mean the attack on Port Royal last November?" Du Pont asked.

"Yes. The big gun, the cannon, and the shooting is the fight. That's what we call the battle, 'The Day of the Big Gun Fight.'"

"I do not see the connection," French admitted.

Hannah enjoyed their eager interest in her tale. "Mary was running to the point when the cannons fired, and she birthed that child right in the middle of the road, so the child is called Road."

They all smiled to think that the baby would be named after such an event, and Du Pont said, "So in that sense I am the godfather of this child."

"Exactly," Robert assured him.

"Well then. That is a great relief. I would have some difficulty explaining my new status to Mrs. Du Pont."

Du Pont aimed his eyebrows at French, but Robert caught Du Pont's pleasure in embarrassing the Reverend. Robert became serious when he told them, "That is a very special child, and she's sometimes called Freedom for the same reason."

"Because she was born free," Laura said.

"No," Robert clarified, "because she was birthed by the big guns that started the Great Skedaddle."

"We are free only because the masters ran away from the big gun fight," Hannah added.

Du Pont knew what Laura and French really wanted to hear, so he asked Robert and Hannah to "please regale us with the account of your extraordinary adventures." Robert retold the story as Laura and French savored the tale and their chicken. Hannah explained how she had organized the escapees, and the Reverend took special interest in how Hannah had used brothels and graveyards as hiding places. Laura's face flushed with admiration when she realized they had all been willing to either escape or drown together.

Du Pont beamed, "Robert gave me both the rebel and the South Carolina flags as souvenirs."

Laura asked, "Didn't you fly a white flag of surrender?" Hannah's smile bubbled into a laugh when she said, "We surely did," and then noted, "It's our table cloth this evening."

They sat in silent wonder. When Robert and Hannah finished their tale of freedom, the Reverend tried to steer the conversation back to bondage. He spoke of his church and how his

160

congregation "eagerly endorsed the writings of Mrs. Stowe which have brought your plight to a wide public audience."

Robert looked impassively at Du Pont, and Hannah hid her annoyance behind the rattling of her fork. "Not all masters are like the people in that story," she whispered.

"Of course, there are exceptions," French conceded.

An insistent edge bubbled through Robert's voice when he said, "We know all about such exceptions."

Du Pont looked to Hannah to vanquish the embarrassed silence.

"We wouldn't be married without them," she said.

Laura turned to Hannah, her curiosity jumping ahead of her confusion. "I thought it was illegal for slaves to marry."

Robert laughed, "Well, there's legal and then there's legal."

The guests sat up, and Du Pont asked what they all were thinking, "But how could you marry?"

"Over the broom," Hannah simply said. Laura pressed for details.

"We meet at a place and vow to love and cherish and then we step over a broom to say that we will clean house together. That means we will work together for the rest of our lives."

"No preacher?" French asked aghast.

"Preachers talk a bit too much. I suppose that's why they are called to a vocation of the mouth," Robert said.

"All that 'honor and obey' you folks say we change to 'love and cherish,'" Hannah told them, "The only way to do that is to work together, so we jump over the broom."

"So you just stepped over a broom and considered yourselves man and wife?" French said.

"Husband and wife," Hannah corrected, looking at Robert.

"That was a fine Christmas," Robert recalled.

"So you got married at Christmas?" Laura asked.

"Mr. McKee, he was my master, opened his house on Christmas Eve and we broomed in the parlor. There were fireworks that night, but all the neighbors thought it was for Christmas."

"That's why Mr. McKee had it done that night," Hannah said.

Listening to this woman was the revelation Laura so desperately sought; she was grateful for the gift. She detested this rebellion because it was such a betrayal, but the war had given her an opportunity that was both a challenge to her beliefs and a call to action. She sensed something lurking below Hannah's quiet manner. Laura was trying to put her finger on it, but the idea kept slipping from her.

Hannah had been watching the astonishment rise in Du Pont's face, and she looked over to Robert. He nodded back. Hannah informed them, "It's also illegal for slaves to own property, but my husband is a man of property."

"What do you own?" Du Pont asked.

"My wife," Robert said.

"And our daughter," Hannah added.

"You own Hannah and Lydia Elizabeth?" Du Pont blurted.

Robert was glad the man remembered the name of his daughter. Robert judged that Du Pont needed something to ease his shock. He said to Hannah, "Show them the papers." Three necks twisted to follow Hannah's quick steps up the stairs. She bounced back down offering a little leather wallet to their incredulous stares. French and Du Pont leaned across the table to see her pull out and smooth a single sheet of paper.

Laura stated, "This is a property deed," and Robert passed it to Du Pont.

"Sure enough," he exclaimed. He read aloud, "title to one Hannah Jones, spinster of this parish and property of Mr. Samuel Kingsman, is hereby transferred to Robert Smalls." Du Pont's eyes darted between the page and his hosts, and he saw they were enjoying his astonishment.

"The price was eight hundred dollars?" he asked.

"That's what I am worth," Hannah smiled back.

"At a dollar a month," Robert added.

"It's all true," and Du Pont shook his head in amazement. "It says you will pay one hundred dollars to Kingsman and the remainder at your mutual convenience."

"So it is really a mortgage," said Laura.

"Mr. Kingsman agreed with my master, Mr. McKee, and we struck a deal."

The Reverend asked what happened with the remainder of the money and Robert explained, "Mr. Kingsman skedaddled and we stole the boat."

"So you could say we went our separate ways," Hannah said with a laugh.

Hannah sensed Du Pont straining to understand the incomprehensible, and she struggled with her own suspicions of the man. He was a powerful person, but she had seen many of the "Great and the Good" who were neither. Robert had told her how Du Pont had helped organize the Hilton Head camp, but that wasn't much of a recommendation, when they had to fight off the worst of their own kind and be grateful to Du Pont, who was supposed to be the best of his own kind. No matter what they wanted to do in the name of some high-minded idea, Hannah grasped her duty to judge what was in front of her face. There was no use believing what Du Pont's kind said, when so many of them had never lived up to their own words. But what was this man doing right now? He was sitting at her table and listening to them both. She could see that his questions were sincere and that he both wanted and needed her answers. His need was greater than her suspicions. Hannah was pleased he had brought a healthy appetite to her table and felt pride in his enjoyment of the meal. But she wondered why he had washed down his food with six glasses of lemon water.

She saw the weariness in his arm when Du Pont fumbled for his cigar case, and she offered relief with the suggestion, "Let's all step into the yard."

Du Pont quickly rose. "Thank you, Hannah. My legs could use a stretch." He strode through the open doors biting off the tip of his cigar. Hannah noticed Du Pont's tired feet squirming beneath him and pondered, "There's something amiss with that man." She asked Laura to tell her more about the herb medicines, so "the big man could have a little time to himself."

The shadow of Du Pont's huge figure filling the door frame covered Davey, so he jumped up to attention and snatched the pipe from his mouth. Du Pont assured him, "Be Easy, young man," and Davey slouched into the regulation stance. "I mean to take it easy. Collins, isn't it?"

"Yes, Sir. Carpenter's Mate."

"May I draw fire from your pipe?"

Davey offered the pipe he was hiding behind his back. Du Pont puffed the flame from the glowing bowl, and his cigar lit up a smile on his face.

"How are you enjoying this new duty?" he asked returning the pipe, stem forward.

"Excellent berth, Sir, excellent berth."

Du Pont nodded and sucked on his cigar, as Davey respectfully stepped back the regulation three paces from his most senior officer.

Du Pont reflected on these astounding people. They had vanquished his ignorance of their ways, and he steadied his resolve to help them. He rolled his cigar between his fingers and thought of French and Laura attempting to make a paradise out of chaos. He admired them for the effort and for their belief, even if he doubted their abilities. He would do his utmost to make their dreams come true, but he also knew that Robert and Hannah held the secret to any success. Together, they had prospered. They had been owned by others and yet they had negotiated the most infernal laws to make themselves one. "Married over the broom," he said aloud, and marveled at the intelligence that could find so simple an answer to such a complex problem. The answer had been in the vows they had exchanged. He thought of his wife, and "love and cherish" was perfectly clear to him. But the Smalls' vows were cunning in their subtlety. They had cast aside "honor and obey" because they already knew that without "honor," both "love" and "cherish" were impossible. He puffed a cloud to the sky and told himself, "Forty-five years of service has made me the master of 'obey,' but I only love and cherish Sophie." He raised his cigar to his lips and kissed the memory of home.

He heard a harbor whistle and looked up to see a boat steaming down the bay. He pulled out his watch, read the dial by the light of the cigar, and said to Davey hovering behind him, "Ten o' clock. That will be MacAlister ferrying troops to Stono. Right on time." He looked over his shoulder to see Johnny and Davey standing just out of earshot. He knew they were from *Onward* and wondered if they had signed the letter he had received demanding their rum tot. "Welles takes away their spirit ration, but doesn't break their spirits," he joked to himself. "Those boys have the right sort of cheek." He laughed to think that they had fed him their confiscated ration by stuffing it into a chicken. "Yes," he thought, "it was a pretty dish to set before a Commodore."

He looked up to a clear night sky and cocked his head to the constellations. They were his oldest friends. "You took me to Europe, and China, and Japan, and you brought me home," he sighed. He puffed halfway down his cigar and said to himself, "I could sail the entire globe by your lights, but I might never understand what is happening in this yard." He heard Hannah's soft footsteps approach. "These people have shown me the currents of their hidden lives, but it started by sharing their chicken." He thought how blessed he was to have been invited into their story and he was curious to see how their adventure would play itself out. He turned and saw Hannah. The eyes of this extraordinary woman flashed assurances that they were willing to trust him.

Chapter 12

Blood and Treasure

Fox was grumpy and wanted his lunch. His office stank of stale paper, forgotten cigars, and frustration. The morning had been a tedious parade of documents, bills, reports, and accounts. He was glad that young Allen was so efficient. The man drew everything from his little satchel in order from least to greatest importance, so there was always a pleasant surprise at the end of their interviews. His little files relieved Fox of so many burdens.

They had spent the morning creating a new fleet. Welles smelled victory in the ironclads, and Fox was certain that the Navy would deliver the prize of peace.

Fox welcomed the diversion of another of Russlynn's tales, and the boy's impish grin promised a laugh or two. He leaned towards Russlynn and had to ask, "You actually saw this with your own eyes?"

"As you well know, Mrs. Simmons is somewhat a patron of the arts," Russlynn pronounced.

"I hear that brownstone of hers is a veritable museum."

"She has filled the place with expensive bric-a-brac, some of it rather amusing."

"And she showed you this statue?"

"Yes. She had her men place it out of sight, for decency's sake."

Russlynn paused and smiled to wait for Fox's prod. "Tell me more."

"She led me through her cast-offs and introduced me to a very large crate in her garden. One side had been hammered open, and she told me to 'just look at that. Disgraceful.' And there was the statue in its pineboard arbor."

"She actually told you she had purchased it?"

166

"Yes, she did," Russlynn assured him with playful incredulity. "She was furious that it had been shipped all the way from Paris, 'at frightful expense,' and now she was outraged."

Fox's head reached back to cast laughter to the ceiling. He wiped his eyes of the moisture of Russlynn's tale. "I can just see her righteous indignation. Whatever shall she do with the 'disgraceful' thing?"

"She has let loose her lawyers on the dealer. They're demanding compensation in full, for purchase, shipping, and shock."

"Shock?" demanded Fox.

"She complained bitterly that 'when the thing arrived, you can imagine my shock when I discovered that it has no arms.'"

"Are you serious?"

"'Pon my word. She also was relieved to return the statue because 'the damaged goods were indecent,'" Russlynn related with the hint of a wink.

"Indecent?"

"The statue was of a woman, naked from the waist up. Mrs. Simmons was spared even greater embarrassment by the 'old towel wrapped around her from the waist down.'"

Fox spluttered, and Russlynn eyes beamed merriment through the cigar smoke. He waggled his head back-and-forth over his fingers steepled under his chin and gauged Fox's reaction to the anecdote. When the laughter cleared, Fox sighed them back to work. "I wish the solution to our problems was as simple as Mrs. Simmons."

"Well, you can't get much simpler," Russlynn quipped.

Fox smiled the smile of the truly perplexed. "Anyway, we have a war winning-weapon, if we figure out how to use it."

"However the ironclads are deployed, it must and will bring victory."

"The sooner the better."

Fox passed his palm over his mouth and lingered just long enough to decide if he should trust his assistant with confidences.

167

Russlynn's sympathetic ear glowed with Fox's political and military problems. He believed Russlynn's eagerness to help and was gratified to have such an intelligent listener. His thumb and forefinger scraped the tobacco juice from his lips and dropped to pull his goatee to a point. "The President is fed up with the generals' delays and excuses."

"As well he might be," agreed Russlynn.

"He even asked McClellan if he could 'borrow the army, since you're doing nothing with it at the moment,'" Fox confided.

"I hear Mr. Lincoln is a master of drollery."

"McClellan sent in the usual requisitions to replace exhausted horses, and Lincoln asked him, 'What have the horses been doing lately to so fatigue them?'"

Fox and Welles valued the attentiveness of their young aide, and Russlynn hoarded every morsel of their gossip. His polite hanging on their every word produced a surprisingly accurate view of the relations in the cabinet. Russlynn could relieve the boredom of their meetings, and his superiors enjoyed the young man's humor, since it reflected their own words.

"The country can see no end to the fighting," Fox exclaimed. "They're weary of the Army doing nothing."

"Then it is left to the Navy to do everything."

"You're absolutely right and Welles agrees with you. He has informed the President that this stagnation on land has drained the people's belief in the Army."

"That was exceedingly brave of Mr. Welles." Russlynn observed admiringly.

"Yes. It was a risky business. The cabinet is hiding behind the newspaper headlines - "On to Richmond" - but nobody knows how to get there."

Fox's annoyed glare glimmered through his cigar smoke, but his eyes beckoned a response.

"If I may be so bold," Russlynn queried, "why can't the Navy change the destination?"

"What do you mean?" Fox asked.

"Let us leave the Army to repeat the battle-cry, but instead of Richmond let's have the Navy go 'On to Charleston.'"

Fox enjoyed Russlynn's aggressiveness and reminded him, "Secretary Welles is intrigued by the suggestion you offered at the Navy Yard."

"It seems fitting that *Keokuk* should be sent where she can do the most good, or to be more precise, the most harm."

"Allen, audacity such as yours is what is missing in our officer class."

"That is one characteristic we share with the Army, I am sad to say."

"The real question is, 'How?'" Fox demanded, eager to be convinced.

"Capturing Charleston with one ship is a pipe dream."

"How do we make this dream come true?"

"With seven."

"Can't be done."

"Must be done," Russlynn pronounced with conviction.

Fox warmed to Russlynn's confidence. This was just what he wanted to hear. He was sick of the defeatism seeping throughout the country. People no longer believed the battle was worth the fight, and their indifference left the recruiting offices empty. The government had resorted to offering bounties to any body willing to stop a bullet. He glared directly at Russlynn and had to know, "How would you convince Secretary Welles to order such an attack?"

"You mean a gamble?"

"If you will."

"I would demonstrate to the Secretary the cost of not making the attack."

Russlynn dangled the stakes before Fox's eager ears. He offered the construction costs as a saving to the government, "especially when we consider the massive expenditure in bounties." Fox couldn't fathom what shipbuilding had to do with bounties, but Russlynn was quick to explain. "A recruit for the

Army can count on $300 from the state, to be matched by another $300 from the Federal Treasury."

Fox understood the basic arithmetic of the fight. Volunteers had been cheap, but now that they were deserting the recruiting offices, the Army was filling the deficit by offering money. The government was making mercenaries of its own people.

"I have taken the liberty of drawing up an account sheet." Russlynn offered Fox one sheet of paper divided into two columns under the headings "Army" and "Navy."

Russlynn watched carefully as Fox studied the sheet. As Fox's eyes lowered down the page, Russlynn had the answers ready.

"How did you devise these figures for the Army?" Fox asked.

"I simply multiplied by twelve the monthly cost of maintaining the Army. I then took the recruitment objectives for the coming year and multiplied by 300 to find the aggregate of the annual payments for bounties. Add the two together and we have the total cost of continuing the war for another year."

"We are spending two and a half million dollars a day?" Fox gasped.

"Multiply that by 365 days and in one year the bill will total $912,500,000," Russlynn added.

Fox brooded over the numbers in astonished silence. There was no denying that Russlynn was correct. If he could come up with this sum, any newspaperman who could count would arrive at the same conclusion. He could see the headlines, "Treasury Bankrupt." "No Money for Troops." "Hang the Politicians." "Ruin!" Russlynn waited for the shock to seep in, so he would have Fox's full attention. He cast a sidelong glance at the office door and almost whispered, "That's why I have a suggestion."

"There is hope in the midst of this debacle?"

"Most definitely. Compare the cost of the Army with that of the Navy." Fox studied the two columns until the confusion pulled his eyes into narrow, searching slits. "You'll find that the sea service is only one fourth the cost of the land service, a saving of seventy-five percent."

"The Navy is much smaller than the Army," Fox stated.

"But, you see," Russlynn expounded, "we have plenty of money for ironclads, if we don't waste it on soldiers. A fleet of ironclads could sail into Charleston harbor and demand the surrender of the city."

"What if they refuse?" asked Fox.

"We burn the whole place."

The audacity of the concept was matched only by the ruthlessness of its execution. Fox lightened the atmosphere and smiled. "Young man, there's a bit of the pirate in you."

Russlynn laughed in recognition of the compliment and the permission to continue. "We are looking at this the wrong way. Everybody expects a decisive campaign on land to finish the war. I say, take the battle to the sea and have the Navy finish the war in the very place it began."

"Hence, Charleston," Fox mused.

"Yes. Charleston. Richmond is just a dot on the map." Fox perused the paper, and Russlynn let him savor the prospect of the naval victory he was offering. "How did you think of this?" asked Fox.

"Bounty jumpers." Russlynn waggled his head from side-to-side like a playful conspirator. "A very lucrative business has blossomed around the bounty. The "recruits" are now matching their frequent enlistments with repeated desertions. For the negligible risk of a quick court martial and a quicker firing squad, a multiple recruit can make thousands."

"I thought such things were rare."

"So did I, until I looked into the matter."

"The President has discussed this in cabinet, but he told us one of his interminable 'interesting tales' and rounded it off by showing us his son's pet goat. They've named the thing 'Jumper.'"

"How apt for the livestock of the White House," Russlynn said.

The naming of the pet was Lincoln's way of dealing with the dead. He spent hours in the telegraph office watching the operators' fingers dance upon their keys. He was mesmerized by the frantic rise and fall of the tiny brass lever hammering out the lists of the dead and he called the infernal machine "our democratic guillotine." His mind was haunted by a clock that measured time and money. He saw the nation's debt rise with every sweep of the minute hand and was powerless to make it stop. The debt and the dead became a mountain he could never climb and patriot graves became money pits.

Fox was captivated by this turn of expectations. The Navy had been fighting with the Army for every scrap cast from the tables of the Treasury. Russlynn might be offering him the very solution they had overlooked. "What else have you unearthed?"

"Bounty Jumpers with a mind for long-term dividends have invested their capital in tracts of federally owned land which Congress has so generously offered at $5.00 an acre through The Homestead Act."

"So, the government pays them to fight, they abscond with the money, and then they buy land from the government?"

"At very attractive and exceptionally low prices."

"Amazing."

"Not really. It's just good business. The deserter exploits what the government makes possible. We should be thinking of this war the same way the bounty jumpers do, as so much money invested at so much risk for so much of a return. In our case, calculating the cost of victory."

Welles and Fox were desperate for anything which would bring glory to the Navy and budget allocations from Congress. The ironclads were the answer to both their prayers.

"I found one item which may amuse you, if it doesn't disgust you," Russlynn offered.

"Go on."

"A very enterprising fellow took his federal, state, and city bounties from Detroit. He was an honorable chap, so he fought one battle before he deserted. With a thousand or so dollars in his pocket, he went to St. Louis, bought a train of cars full of cattle, and sold it to the commissary department for ten thousand dollars."

"He swindled the government out of ten thousand dollars?" Fox asked.

"That is the standard rate offered by the Treasury for a trainload of cattle," Russlynn explained. "If he swindled anybody, it was the owners of the cows."

"You mean a deserter is feeding the army?"

"I'd say that an extremely shrewd man is supplying us with beef."

"Tell me more," Fox commanded.

Russlynn took his time searching in his satchel, and Fox stared at the file Russlynn offered with trembling fingers. "What's this?" Fox asked.

"A solution to our spending problem, and a fairly cheap one at that."

Fox opened the cover, and his eyes danced over a heading "Accounts Pending - Keokuk." Russlynn guided his attention slowly down a column of figures. "I have an estimate from Whitney's shipyard." Fox looked over the bill, and Russlynn intoned "A mere $228,244.63 for *Keokuk*. Considerably cheaper than the *Monitor*, which cost $275,000."

"No sixty-three cents?"

"I couldn't find any small change."

Fox gazed at the sheet of paper, which offered him so much, for so little cost. "You are absolutely correct. This is why we have to present an argument in dollars and cents, not just a strategy and stories about Jumpers."

"In that case, I have prepared this."

Russlynn fished another file from his satchel. He read out his litany of wartime expenditures. "Mr. Welles will appreciate that the war is costing two and a half million dollars a day. Dividing by twenty four, we have 104,166 dollars and twenty four cents per hour. The cost of this vessel is really just a little more than the cost of two hours of war. Ten of these warships would cost less than one day's fighting."

"You've calculated that?"

"As a matter of fact, I have. Ten ships cost a mere $2,282,446.30."

"And that would be?" Fox smiled.

"A saving of 217, 553 dollars... and 70 cents."

Fox howled with the accuracy down to the 70 cents and his smile praised Russlynn's work. "I'll talk to Mr. Welles when he is in a better mood, and we will set up a meeting. I would like you to present this to him just as you have to me."

"I would be honored, Sir."

They relaxed into Fox's decision to bring Russlynn and his bold plan to Welles, and Fox asked, "Have you heard anything about the First Lady and some new-fangled scheme to keep her in clothes?"

" Yes. It's all Wanamaker's doing."

"Wanamaker? The man who owns that store in Philadelphia?"

"Yes. It seems that Mrs. Lincoln takes her *modiste*, a mulatto called Keckley, on shopping trips, where they raid the houses of high fashion."

"She's a notorious spendthrift."

"Yes, but Wanamaker is no fool. He had her sit for a portrait and then gave her one hundred cartes de visite with a price printed on the back."

"I don't see the point," Fox grumbled.

"The price is a guarantee of credit. The First Lady merely hands a card to the sales assistant and the purchase is complete."

"No money involved."

"Neither cash nor check," Russlynn explained. "Wanamaker has turned the *carte de visite* into the *carte de credite*."

"How did you learn this information?' Fox asked.

"If Mrs. Simmons was insulted by her armless statue, she was furious over Wanamaker's refusal to offer her the same terms as those he extended to Mrs. Lincoln. Nothing more talkative than a woman scorned."

"Do you think Whitney would accept such an arrangement for the new ships?"

"I'd be happy to ask him," Russlynn volunteered, "but do you really want your face staring out from a bond issue?"

They savored the humor, and Fox made a note of Russlynn's tale for the next dinner engagement. The table would roar at the foibles of Simmons and the Mad Woman of Pennsylvania Avenue.

"I have another request," Fox exclaimed.

"Yes."

"Du Pont has been pestering me about compensation for that *Planter* incident. Can you tell me anything about it? Cargo Requisition was your last position before joining us here, was that not so?"

"Yes, I was with the OCR for six months. The *Planter* claim was my last duty."

"It seems that they have been rather tardy."

"I think my replacement took his time in familiarizing himself with the procedures of the office."

"Well, it seems that Smalls and his people are not going to receive anything for the boat," Fox said.

"I expected that would be the case."

"How so?" Fox asked.

"The Prize Court cannot make an award to Smalls."

"Why is that?"

"Those people are slaves," Russlynn stated. "I calculated their cost as part of the value of the ship. I think I erred on the side of generosity and submitted a figure of $1,000 per slave. The actual adjudication of *Planter* would be the combined totals for the ship and the cargo."

The implications to the Smalls family sank in, and Fox knew there would some unpleasantness with Du Pont. The man had something of an obsession when it came to this *Planter* business. "You mean they will get nothing," he said.

"They can't get anything," Russlynn explained, "because they are cargo."

"Du Pont is not going to like this."

" I'm afraid that is the final decision of the court and it is the only decision it can make according to law.

"There will be Hell to Pay when Du Pont is informed."

"Would you like me to talk with him?"

"No."

Fox closed the files, threw them onto his desk and stood up. "That's enough for one morning. Excellent work, young man." Russlynn accepted the praise with a demure twist of his head and a joyful twinkle in his eye. "Thank you, Sir," he said. He turned to walk out of Fox's office with complete confidence in his shares in Whitney & Co.

Chapter 13

Debits and Credits

Captain Rogers heard the cursing blowing through the mist before they reached the flagship. The liberty boat chuffed against a lee tide, but the nearer they steamed to *Wabash*'s hull, the more distinct the oaths became. When they bumped into the side-ladder crawling up the ship's sides, the sailors grinned with admiration at the stream of profanities, appeals to the infernal powers, and amusing threats of physical violence escaping from the Commodore's wardroom. Creative vulgarity was a maritime art, and the sailors appreciated Du Pont's virtuosity.

The bosuns wielded long grappling poles to pull the boat to the loading dock below *Wabash*'s side stairs. The waves danced the ship and the boat to-and-fro like shy lovers, and Rogers stood with one foot poised on the boat's gunnels for his jump to the dock. He leaned one arm forward to catch the prickly bannister of the rope ladder and launched his legs over the side. When he was standing on the ladder's broad lower rung, a bosun swung Roger's seabag after him, and with one hand for the ship and the other for himself, he climbed the slippery steps to *Wabash*'s quarterdeck.

The Marine Gunnery Sergeant at the rail saluted smartly and said, "Welcome Aboard, Sir." Rogers' eyes smiled at the friendly face and the helping hand stretched forth to carry his seabag. The sailors found it funny that such a senior captain would prefer the luggage of a common rating, but it was just another of Captain Rogers' endearing eccentricities. They knew he was every inch the gentleman, and a sailor to the bone.

The Gunny escorted Rogers along *Wabash*'s companionways to the Commodore's wardroom, more out of curiosity than duty. They shared a grin as the gale of bad temper bulged behind Du Pont's door. Rogers could not stifle his merriment and winked at the Gunny.

"Shall I announce you, Sir?" and the Gunny's tongue dripped with schoolboy mischief.

"We'll let the squall pass," Rogers assured him.

They waited for a lull, and Rogers finally hammered the three regulation knocks at his superior officer's door. "Permission to attend upon the Commodore, Sir." The Gunny turned about face when he heard Du Pont's gruff, "Enter, John."

Rogers obeyed. He carefully opened the door, stepped into the room, and said, "I take it you have news from Washington." Du Pont's laughter exploded through his cigar smoke, and he greeted his favorite captain, "Damn them. Damn them all to Hell, and may all the devils of Satan play 'Hide and Seek' up their unworthy asses."

"The Rebels, Sir?" Rogers prodded.

"The lawyers."

"Well, Sir," Rogers mused, unsuccessfully containing a broad smirk, "such condemnation would be undeniable proof of the existence of a just God. What perfidy are they up to now?"

"This," and Du Pont offered him a sheet of paper, as if it were scrofulous.

Rogers immediately saw it was a legal brief from the Office of Cargo Requisitions, for he had received such documents every time he captured a prize. While Rogers read, Du Pont intoned, "Pursuant to some mumbo-jumbo their booze-addled brains have vomited, 'request denied.'"

"Denied?"

"Denied without so much as a 'respectfully denied.' Damn their eyes."

"Have they given any reason?"

"Reason?" Du Pont spat. "They are incapable of the act."

"In that case, how about an excuse?"

"Their excuse," Du Pont sneered, "is that 'Smalls is not a person under the law' so they 'cannot make payment to a non-person.'"

Rogers took his time reading the legal foolscap, so Du Pont could vent more righteous indignation and puff his cigar. When the air was as blue with tobacco fumes as with expletives, he coyly baited. "That's ridiculous."

"That's the opinion of a bunch of Stay-at-Home, cowardly, conniving, ignorant Brown Hatters."

"So, Smalls is not considered a human being," Rogers said.

"He is considered property. Therefore, he stole himself."

"How did they come up with this nonsense?"

"Since he is a slave, he is a thing which can be bought and sold. Therefore, he is property 'in the claim of *Planter* before the Prize Court, the slave called Robert is commercial cargo.'"

Du Pont waited for the idea to light Rogers' fuse.

Rogers glinted at the OCR report. "By the same reasoning, we must be on our guard against mutinous coal. We must put extra locks on the hold hatches. There's no telling when the quarterdeck will be invaded by murdering packing cases!"

"It gets worse," Du Pont growled. "Since he took the boat more than three miles from shore, he can be charged with piracy on the high seas."

Rogers' laughter surprised Du Pont. "From thing to property to pirate to 'enemy of all mankind.' My, my, how quickly has our Robert evolved," Rogers reflected.

"We must do what we can about this stupidity," Du Pont vowed.

"We'll need a lawyer."

"All you have to do to find a lawyer," Du Pont grumbled, "is shout 'fire' in a Molly house."

"In that case, we will need a maker of laws."

"You mean go directly to Congress?"

"I mean go indirectly to a member of Congress who has both a brain and a conscience."

"I think I know of such a rarity," Du Pont mused. "By the way, what are you doing here?"

"I have been ordered back to the Washington yard."

"Problems?" Du Pont asked with arched brows.

"The guns."

"What wrong with them?"

"Too big."

Du Pont threw his head back and laughed to the rafters of his wardroom. "I told them so."

"It seems that somebody forgot to widen the gunports when they fitted the larger 15-Inch guns."

Du Pont's amusement disappeared into a vision of exploding turrets. "We did put on a good show for Welles and Fox, but, in their opinion, 'she's not quite ready." Rogers brought him back to the problem in hand. "I'll be at loose ends in Washington while they fix these 'minor problems .'"

Rogers waited for Du Pont's mind to jump ahead. "What is a *Keokuk* anyway?"

"I think it's an Indian chief. Something about the Black Hawk War, but I'm as in the dark as you."

Du Pont became dangerously quiet, so Rogers waited. He was accustomed to Du Pont's ruminating and he relaxed through the long silence. Others found the Commodore's pauses peculiarly unnerving. Rogers knew there was something in the wind when Du Pont quietly muttered, "This is most providential."

"How so, Sir?"

"Wouldn't you like to pay a few visits while you are waiting for *Keokuk* to float?"

Rogers was alert to the suggestion because he knew this was the Commodore's way of issuing orders to friends. "I suppose I will have some time on my hands."

"I want you to call on one of our abolitionist friends at the Capitol," Du Pont grinned.

Du Pont rose from his chair, thrust his hand into the crook of Rogers' arm, and gently guided him to the door. He opened it to fresher sea breezes and pointed to the seabag slumped against the wall. Du Pont's toe nuzzled the bag as he stood in the door frame. "Visit the galley and come back in an hour."

Rogers left Du Pont thumbing through papers and wandered along *Wabash*'s decks. To pass the time, he went to the galley, but he lost his appetite when he saw a cook's thumb leave a black streak in a bowl of potatoes. He found the Gunnery Sergeant lounging at the taff-rail near Du Pont's wardroom and asked, "How fresh is the water?" The Gunny respected this age-old invitation to chat without deference to rank and led Rogers to the ship's scuttlebutt, lashed to the rails amidships. He removed the cask's lid and plunged a gleaming copper dipper into the barrel. Rogers knew you could tell the health of a ship by looking at the barrels of fresh water. If the scuttlebutts stank, the sickbays would be full.

"This came down with ice packed in sawdust." The Gunny proudly offered the ladle. Rogers felt the cold seep into his fingers and tasted winter on his tongue. "My, that is good. Have one yourself." The Gunny dipped for his draught and launched into the ship's gossip. Rogers' ears could hardly keep up with the Gunny's account of "those contrabands full of jam. You know they got away with the whole powder supply for Sumter?"

Rogers ignored the exaggerations but caught the pride in the Gunny's voice. He did not have to ask for his opinion, for amazement and admiration bubbled through his every word. The man could not hide his respect for Smalls. After two more ladles of ice-melt, Rogers had a clear view of how the tale of escape had threaded its way through all the lower decks in the fleet.

Rogers heard the creak of the Commodore's door and thanked the Gunny for the refreshment. The open door framed Du Pont's beckoning grin, and Rogers followed him into the wardroom.

Du Pont stood squaring the stacks of papers on his desk. He grimaced and laid the OCR report face down on the desk. "You are to take these to Congressman Charles Sedgwick at the Capitol." He waved a letter and envelope before Rogers' face. Du Pont placed the letter behind the report and piled both on the open cover of a portfolio. "You will ensure that Sedgwick receives these in the order I have arranged."

The last piece of paper was an advertisement for Mr. P.T. Barnum's *American Museum*. Rogers wondered what General Tom Thumb and a two-headed mermaid had to do with a Commodore's dispatches to a congressman, but he had learned to keep his curiosity to himself. There was always method to Du Pont's madness; one had to be patient to discover the reason lurking below the tomfoolery.

Du Pont gathered the papers into a neat pile, closed the covers of the portfolio, and carefully tied the ribbons together. "Make sure you seal the letter before you present it to the Congressman."

Rogers understood the Navy tradition that a letter was only private after it was sealed. Du Pont wanted him to read everything before he delivered the portfolio. Rogers assured Du Pont the bundle would "relieve the tedium of the voyage." Du Pont rummaged in his wardrobe and turned wielding a shotgun. "Put this in your seabag."

Rogers was puzzled by the command to travel armed. "Has Washington become such a dangerous place?"

"Wrong sort of weapon for what we're hunting," Du Pont chortled. "The Congressman will appreciate this gift."

Rogers smiled at the oil-gleaming barrels. "Is it loaded?"

*　*　*　*　*

Rogers was lost in the maze that was the Capitol. Crews of workmen swarmed through the building. Warped doors lay across saw-horses cluttering the corridors. He waded through curls of wood spiraling to the floor from carpenters' planes. The clanging of masons' hammers on chisels teasing ornate petals from reluctant blocks of marble assaulted his ears. Clouds of choking plaster dust wafted around him. After the quiet order of a ship on blockade station, Congress was a pandemonium of bellowing, chalky faces. Rogers joked to himself, "I could use a fog-horn in this mess."

A voice called from the mist, "May I be of assistance, Sir?" Rogers looked down to see a small boy dressed in the hand-me-down black suit of a much older man. The smeared jacket cuffs fell a full foot below the boy's fingers. The urchin sported a soiled white shirt, its collar held to his scrawny neck by an elaborate black silk tie. The child looked as if he could have crawled out the trouser leg and left the coat, pants, shirt, and tie standing to attention for its next duty.

"Where is the office of Representative Sedgwick?"

"Ten cents will get you there." The boy raised his arm above his head, so his hand could wriggle free of his sleeve. Rogers shuffled in his pocket for a coin to feed the hand and held his seabag over his other shoulder with a firmer grip. The dime disappeared into the folds of the boy's coat. His guide took Rogers in tow by his coattails and dragged him along the hall.

"Sedgwick, Charles B., New York, 24th Congressional District, Republican. He'll be in the pond."

"Does he have no office?"

"He's lucky to have a seat. He wasn't renominated, so he's now lame duck. We keep him in the pond. That's what we call the Annex."

The boy piloted Rogers up slanting stairs, over floors sticky with tobacco juice, under swaying scaffolding, and across springing plank walkways to a puddle of marble-dust slurry welling before a door. Rogers asked how he would find his way back to the main hall, and the boy assured him the return service would only cost him twenty cents.

Congressman Sedgwick was most pleasant to Rogers. His constituents had evaporated, along with their votes, and it was something of a relief to receive a visitor, especially one bearing gifts. Rogers was relieved to hear Sedgwick say, "I have read everything I could find about their adventure." Rogers believed the man's enthusiasm was genuine and offered him the portfolio.

Sedgwick examined the papers in the order Du Pont had placed them. Rogers saw the scowl appear when Sedgwick read the report of the Office of Cargo Requisitions. There was no mistaking the Congressman's disgust. Rogers remembered that Sedgwick was a lawyer and reasoned that the man had picked up subtleties and legal quibbles hidden from a sailor's understanding.

Rogers watched Sedgwick's knife disembowel the envelope containing Du Pont's personal letter. The wrinkles around Sedgwick's nose flattened as he read. When he finished, Sedgwick put down the letter and sighed, "Du Pont is quite correct."

Sedgwick returned to the open portfolio and held up the advertisement for the *American Museum.* "What's the meaning of this?"

Rogers admired Du Pont's strategy of leaving the most lethal charge for the last. "The Commodore wishes to remind the Gentlemen of Congress that Robert Smalls and his gallant crew are not to be exhibited in Mr. Barnum's freak show."

Sedgwick studied the illustration in his hands. A diminutive, stooped, black man wearing a grass skirt gazed quizzically from the paper. The "curious negro" leaned on a spear, and his elongated skull identified him as one of Barnum's "extraordinary pin-heads."

Rogers watched Sedgwick's eyes follow the title in bold letters, "What is it? Man or Monkey?" Rogers waited for the picture to fill his skull with a thousand words. Sedgwick scowled as he read aloud from the flyer, "this most singular animal combining characteristics of both the human and brute species."

Sedgwick added, "I have seen the same illustration issued as a political pamphlet against Mr. Lincoln."

"What? Is the President some peculiar amalgamation of the human and the animal?"

"That is what his opponents wished the electors to think."

"What is your opinion?"

"My opinion is clear from my voting record. That is why I was not renominated and will be gone this fall."

Rogers could not tell whether Sedgwick's fingers trembled from rage or indecision. Whatever the man was thinking, there had to be action. Rogers pointed to the advertisement. In as soothing a voice as he could muster after years of howling orders through gales, Rogers said, "The Commodore is of the opinion that, in the matter of fair compensation for Smalls, Barnum's question is also posed to Congress."

"We must do something practical for these people," Sedgwick exclaimed. "I shall take this to Senator Grimes and consult with some other members of the House and the Senate. Grimes and I are both on the Navy Board. Du Pont is quite right. A freak show is no place for heroes."

Rogers face did not betray his feeling that the man's decision was a credit to Congress. He opened his seabag and said, "You may wish to take this to Senator Grimes." Sedgwick stood rigid as Rogers pulled out the shotgun. Rogers assured him that it was not Open Season on Members of Congress. "The Commodore thought you would appreciate this souvenir."

"What is it?"

"It is the rebel guard's weapon from the *Planter*."

Congressman Sedgwick was thrilled to have Digby's pop-gun as a trophy. He walked around his office aiming the "magnificent fowling piece" at anything which caught his eye. Rogers sat relieved that the gun wasn't loaded.

*   *   *   *   *

Du Pont stood on the quarterdeck. He held Sedgwick's letter, and the lightest of morning breezes fluttered the pages. *Wabash* rode at a single drag-anchor with every door, hatch, port-hole, and gunport beckoning relief from the heat. The ice in the scuttlebutt had melted, and he feared the fevers that came with rancid water.

He was very proud of Rogers, and this letter was testimony to the success of his mission. Congressman Sedgwick and Senator

Grimes had pushed a bill through both houses of Congress. Grimes was the perfect ally because he had more of a future in Washington than Sedgwick. Grimes had shamed Congress into creating the Medal of Honor, so the politicians could recognize the valor of the citizens. It was so like him to honor the Smalls crew with an Act of Congress.

Planter was to be "appraised by a board of competent officers." The matter would not be left to some Office of Cargo Requisitions which had dismissed their bravery as monkey business. Du Pont himself was the competent officer in command, and he would "cause an equitable apportionment of one-half of such value to be made to Robert Smalls and his associates."

Du Pont drew out another page from his morning handful and ran his eyes over his list.

Robert Smalls, Captain	$1,500
Alfred Gradine, Engineer	$ 450
J Samuel Chisholm	$ 400
Abraham Allston	$ 400
William Morrison	$ 384
Annie, unattached woman in the party	$ 100
Lavinia, unattached woman in the party	$ 100
Total	$3,334

A bead of sweat dripped from his nose and splashed a black crown onto the page. Du Pont held the sheets away from him to let the sun dry the blot. So much of the Navy was held together by pieces of paper. Fire might be a sailor's greatest fear, but water destroys even the memory of their lives. When a ship goes down, the water washes away its life. The ship and all who sail in her become arabesques of ink swirling in the currents that drowned the authors. Time will destroy all the reports, letters, requisitions, diaries, every scrap, but this Act of Congress will last as long as the ship of state stays afloat.

Du Pont savored the pleasure of forcing the Abolitionists to put their money where their mouth was. It was one thing to weep over photographs of a whip-scarred back. It was quite another to pay the slave who had contrived his own freedom.

The Act stipulated that Smalls' share of the prize money was "to be invested in United States securities for the benefit of such individual, the interest to be paid annually." They were paying on credit. The usual practice was to award the prize money in cash. Du Pont did not like this arrangement. What good was a check to an illiterate? To the freedmen, a bank was just a holding cell for their mortgaged lives.

He held the papers as he walked back to his wardroom for a good think about the matter. Before he reached his own door, he said aloud, "No." He would have the Paymaster debit his account and make-up purses of ten-dollar coins in gold for each of the crew. This would be something they could hold in their hands and bright for all to see. What they did with the money was their business. Du Pont was adamant that freedom must be more than changing cages.

Chapter 14

Mille-Feuille

Sophie had insisted, so Du Pont had submitted to the torture of paying calls. He was the master at sea, but she commanded the ceremonials of society.

She sat beside him in the carriage, holding her little box of *cartes de visite* on her lap, as they drove through the compass points of Washington's best houses. He noticed that the carriage always turned to the left. Sophie plotted their stately trot through a wide elliptical of the town, and at each stop on her circuit, she extracted a card, which the driver delivered to the house servant opening the front door. The cards sat nestled in their carton like cannon balls in their racks, and Du Pont understood that Sophie was firing at every residence she deemed a suitable target. Each little fort capitulated to the request, "Are you 'at home' to Rear-Admiral and Mrs. Samuel Francis Du Pont?"

Their first call was to Mrs. Welles at C Street. Du Pont sat balancing the regulation cup and saucer, listened to Mrs. Welles recount the achievements and ailments of her children, and let the lady's effusive praise of his promotion wash over his quizzical brows. He had enjoyed the tea because it washed down the scones. When they turned onto Third Street, it was a joy to hear the latest news of old friends and new enemies from Mrs. Fox. The horses' heads predictably veered to the left when the driver guided the pair of matched geldings into Ninth Street on a bearing for H Street, but as they passed G Street, Du Pont asked, "My Dear, are you attempting to teach me the alphabet?" She slapped a glove to his thigh and smiled to see him navigating her route and figuring out her plan. Du Pont whispered, "In geometric beauty curved, And in an orbit sailed."

Sophie smiled and chided, "You need not quote Mr. Melville's lines. One will think you vain."

They had visited the wives of officers and cabinet members, and Sophie took no prisoners. Over the teas and gossip, she ensured that all knew of her husband's promotion and his services to such a "grateful nation." Du Pont smiled when he heard her repeat his own words that "the opportunity only brings out the character of the man." There were "so many who have risen to the occasion posed by this dreadful war, as your husband has," and "my husband is only one of such a noble band."

At the beginning of their week in Washington, she had steered him to Mr. Gutekunst's emporium of images and demanded that he sit for his portrait. He had reminded her that "only my great love for you will sustain me through the ordeal," and she had giggled like the girl he first loved three decades ago. She watched Gutekunst's assistant carefully seat her husband in a chair and place his right elbow on a table. Mr. Gutekunst moved his curious apparatus to the side to show the insignia on Dupont's shoulder straps and stepped back to ponder his composition. He thrust Du Pont's right hand into his open waistcoat to give a full view of the golden cuff bands of a Rear Admiral. Du Pont smirked to think he resembled Napoleon on his way to exile. The assistant clamped Du Pont's head into the neck brace that would ensure the seven minutes of absolute stillness necessary to capture his image. Gutekunst removed the lens cover with a flourish of his wrist and Du Pont was bathed in the frustrations of the last few days.

He had made the usual rounds of the Navy Department and the government bureaus, but the encounters had filled him with increasing dread. From every office came the cry, "On to Charleston," and his still, small bellow could not outshout their enthusiasm for the ironclads. Their mania for the things infected them with confidence and made them deaf to his warnings. He told them all that, even though the ships' decks and turrets were almost impregnable, they could not fire enough shells to subdue a fort. Capturing an entire city from the harbor alone was simply impossible. The boats were excellent for defense, but they were useless at aggression. The only way to take Charleston was through a combined attack by land and sea. The Army and Navy had to cooperate. But the bureaucrats had turned blank eyes to his reasoning. They looked ready to collect firewood to burn the heretic.

The assistant released Du Pont's neck, and Gutekunst was eager to show them the process of creating a photograph. He removed his magic box from its stand and led them into a small darkened chamber. He took out the wet glass plate and submerged it in a tray of chemicals that reminded Du Pont of befouled bilges. Gutekunst agitated the tray, and they waited for the alchemy that could grasp a single seven-minute moment. They bent to watch the image slowly appear under the ripples. The little waves becalmed, and Du Pont's face gazed up at them from the sulfurous pool.

Sophie noticed that the wallpaper in the background looked like the puffs of exploding shells. She did not share the superstitions of other sailors' wives but raised a silent prayer that this was not an omen. She searched her husband's face for the hope she needed. He looked older and much more care worn, but Gutekunst had captured the merriment in his eyes. She ordered a thousand of the little pasteboard rectangles.

Sophie told the driver to halt in front of Mrs. Simmons house, and she took her husband's arm for the last call. Du Pont could not fathom why they were making this visit and had to ask, "My Dear, I understand the tactics, but your strategy evades me. Why are we here?"

"Mrs. Simmons is the busiest of the bees."

"Bees sting and create a most annoying noise."

"They also lead to the honey."

"Ours is not to reason why," he surrendered and looked up to see Mrs. Simmons beaming welcome at her front door.

Mrs. Simmons was flustered by their unexpected visit, and she babbled up a storm. Du Pont winced at her high-pitched screech whenever she threw her hands to her shoulders and asked, "Just what is a Rear Admiral? Is that an Admiral who is not to the fore?"

"My Dear Mrs. Simmons," Sophie confided as to an old friend, "It is a new rank in the Navy."

"The Department has reinstated some of the higher ranks of the service which have not been used since the Revolutionary War," Du Pont added.

"Oh, my," Mrs. Simmons chirped, "that is something new."

"A Rear Admiral is the highest Naval position," Sophie explained.

"The illustrious John Paul Jones was a Rear Admiral," Du Pont recalled.

When Mrs. Simmons understood that a Rear Admiral was something very good with gold-tasseled epaulettes, she made a mental note to pay a call on Mrs. Jones. Du Pont let the women have their way with him.

"You are new to Washington?" Sophie asked.

"Since my husband passed away, I have decided to keep a residence in the capital to facilitate my charitable work."

"Mrs. Fox speaks very highly of your endeavors for the Sanitary Commission," Sophie complimented.

"Mrs. Fox is such a dear friend."

"Were you involved with the auction of the socks?" Sophie prodded, and Du Pont cocked a curious ear.

"Why, Yes, I was. I even knitted ten pairs myself."

"What a marvelous idea," Sophie enthused. "The ladies knit their own socks and auction them to the highest bidder."

"The proceeds allowed us to purchase twenty thousand pairs of socks from Lowell," Mrs. Simmons preened. "It would be impossible for the ladies of Washington to be so productive."

"It is exhausting work," Sophie praised.

Du Pont was confused, so Mrs. Simmons subjected him to a detailed account of their program and an itemized list of the charitable profits it had realized. He wondered just what was produced with such effort and asked, "So, you knit one pair of socks, sell them at this auction, and then buy one hundred pairs for each pair you personally knit?"

"That is exactly what we do."

"But who buys these socks?" he demanded.

"Patriotic gentlemen in the government, clerks, just about anybody who wants to keep their feet warm in this dreadful city."

"Why would anybody spend so much on your socks when they could just as easily make a contribution to the Sanitary Commission to make the purchases?" he asked, dumfounded.

"Oh, we embroider the name of the winner and the amount of his contribution on the socks."

"A completely new form of currency," Sophie said.

"One could call them shinplasters," Du Pont joked.

"Oh, no. They are much longer than the shins," Mrs. Simmons corrected.

"At least they keep one's feet warm, unlike these new bits of paper money," Sophie commented.

"And who chose the color green for this money?" Mrs. Simmons complained. "I would have chosen something milder, a nice light blue or a design like a Turkey carpet. So much more colorful than this thing they are calling 'greenbacks.'"

Du Pont imagined the trouser legs of Washington raised in gentlemen's clubs and at Taltavul's bar to display their owner's largesse and grumbled to himself, "May as well stuff ten dollar bills into your shoes and call it patriotism."

The floorboards creaked behind him, so Du Pont craned his neck to see servants passing in review over the drawing room threshold. Two servants carried in a low table and placed it before Du Pont, Sophie, and their mistress. More servants set the table with a full service for high tea. Du Pont heard a screech and turned to see the butler push in a table on wheels. It looked like a very superior wheelbarrow of varnished mahogany. But it was the tray on the cart which caught his amazement. A servant stood with tongs poised behind a silver rectangle, with three circular tiers of pastry rising from the center. It reminded him of a brig in full sail or a frozen pine tree and he judged that the tray held a Christmas treat for the whole crew of the *Wabash*.

Mrs. Simmons greeted the monstrosity with squeals of delight. "My friend, Mr. Russlynn, has introduced me to the most talented baker, a Mr. Guisling." The butler loaded three plates with rectangles of sugared cream, and Mrs. Simmons' eyes bulged in anticipation. The hearth blazed, and Du Pont felt the perspiration collecting under his hair above his ear. He examined the strange confection on his plate.

"I just love these milfies," warbled Mrs. Simmons. "They're French."

"We call them *mille-feuille*," Sophie said in the French accent she reserved for jokes.

"I've never been much for foreign things, but these are yummy."

"They are called mille-feuille because of the layers of pastry," Sophie said.

"How is that?"

"Well, 'mille' is a 'thousand,'" Du Pont explained, "and 'feuille' is a sheet, so they have a thousand sheets of pastry."

"I see only five," Mrs. Simmons said, with a suspicion that Mr. Guisling had cheated her.

Du Pont examined the brickwork of his dessert, and indeed there were five layers of pastry separating cream, custard, and marzipan built on a foundation of strawberry jam. Mille-feuille had been a special treat his mother reserved for birthdays and Christmas. He had always loved the delicacy of the cream between the buttery pastry topped with the chocolate brushwork in white icing. The thing Mrs. Simmons thrust toward him was really five slices of shortbread keel-hauled through sugared lard. Out of the corner of his eye he saw Sophie's nostrils rebel at the assault of almond extract, but her blink told him he had to eat it. He might fight his way through this horde of nutty treacle, but the indigestion would leave him dead in the water for days.

The spectacle of Mrs. Simmons wielding her fork as if it were a cutlass fascinated him until she said, "It is just marvelous that you will be going to Charleston." Du Pont clenched his jaw, but Sophie sat as calm as a cat at the saucer.

"Oh it will be just wonderful to read about our gallant ships sailing into Charleston," Mrs. Simmons thrilled. "Imagine, to the very heart of treason." Du Pont heard Fox's words slither through the mouthful of whipped cream, and the anger welled to his throat. It was not done to hit a woman, but he wanted to take the lash to her.

"And that new boat. What's it called?" Mrs. Simmons asked, "Oh yes. The *Kokook*. I hear that it is a veritable monster."

Du Pont blanched at her mangling of the the ship's name. That she should speak of such matters over her tea jug was appalling, but that she should even have such information disgusted him. His mind conjured burning sailors swallowed by a sinking ship. "It just shows you what Yankee ingenuity can do," Mrs. Simmons insisted. Du Pont wanted to inform her that the inventor of the monster was Swedish and wondered if Ericsson's genius could devise a mute for this chatterbox. Even her ghastly cream puffs couldn't keep her mouth shut.

"It certainly is big," was all he could say, and Sophie dared not look at him. The bead of sweat trickled along Du Pont's unbelieving ear, and he swallowed the custard to suppress his bile.

"I am so glad Mr. Fox took my advice," Mrs. Simmons casually mentioned.

"What did you advise?" Sophie asked, brimming with feigned excitement to hide her real interest.

"I merely brought to his attention the talents of Mr. Russlynn. I hear that the dear boy has been invaluable to Mr. Fox and Mr. Welles."

"I am not acquainted with the young man," Du Pont admitted.

"In that case, I will have to introduce you. He is brilliant, simply brilliant."

Du Pont smelled the sweaty maneuverings of office seekers. Sophie had told him how Mrs. Simmons was making a name for herself as a Washington hostess, and he had snorted, "Let her serve cakes," but he trembled to think such buffoons were placing their protégés in the department. Sophie had never put herself forward as these women did, and she frequently hid behind an ailment to avoid being tarred with the recommendation for a disastrous mediocrity. Sharks circled in such teapots, and Du Pont's contempt of meritless promotion made him gaze upon "the apes beneath the velvet." Mrs. Simmons and her busy tongue were more dangerous than the infernal devices waiting for them. That woman had an infinite supply of gossip, culled from those velveteen harridans.

Sophie rescued him with the casual comment, "we are at the Willard... I promised them we would not be tardy for supper."

"Oh, the Willard." Mrs. Simmons rose at the name. "Such a pleasure to share your company and, once again, Admiral, congratulations on your promotion."

"Thank you, Mrs. Simmons. The afternoon has been most enlightening."

Sophie tendered profuse thanks for Mrs. Simmons' hospitality, and their hostess basked in the celebrity of her guests. She could hardly wait to tell Mrs. Ellison of her triumph of actually having a Rear Admiral to tea. She could just picture Sour-Puss Ellison's toothy smile, beside herself with jealousy.

Sophie clutched her husband's trembling arm as they stepped over the threshold. She guided him to the carriage, and each step took the same effort as pacing a rolling deck. The driver helped him up the carriage step, and Du Pont collapsed into the seat. Sophie saw the pursing of the driver's lips and trusted to the man to get them home quickly. Du Pont grasped the carriage sill and held himself ramrod straight. Sophie saw the redness rise in Du Pont's face and commanded, "All haste, please."

She knew sugar and gossip were equally deadly, but she was relieved when he grumbled, "That stupid woman talks to everyone."

"But nobody listens to her."

Du Pont's fingers crept along the seat until they found Sophie's hand, and the warmth of her grasp calmed his nerves. His nostrils sucked enough air to stretch his chest and pull apart some of the knots in his stomach. "She thirsts for flattery. She will be so enthralled by the attentions of the newspapers that she will tell all she knows, and what she doesn't know, she will make up."

The driver tugged the reins to the right and goaded the geldings into a determined canter. Heads turned to the rhythmic clatter of their hooves and saw the Du Ponts' carriage glide along Pennsylvania Avenue. Washington's public buildings and stately homes circled around Du Pont's head and bent forward to look at him. He was so fatigued he did not care and dismissed the scowling houses with, "Damn your impertinence." Sophie likewise demanded her head to stop its complaining, and the pain crawled from her eyes to cower at the back of her skull. She felt the torment spreading through his body, and her clenched fist burst the seams of her glove. He could be dead, but he would always sport that lovely smile promising mischief. She was grateful to the driver for gliding the horses to a gentle halt close to the doors of the Willard Hotel.

The driver jumped down to open the door and hand Sophie to the sidewalk. She thanked him, and the look in his eyes said he didn't believe her when she said, "We can manage from here." He grasped the Admiral's upper arm and felt the muscle tighten to his grasp. Du Pont stood beside Sophie, and they were rigid as the figureheads on matched schooners.

The driver looked for an excuse to accompany his passengers into the hotel and spied the box of visiting cards, forgotten on the seat. "I'll just carry these in for you, Ma'am," and he followed them up the main stairs. The driver kept his distance, just in case the Admiral would fall backwards, and briefly wondered if he would be crushed by the weight of such a big man.

They marched along a corridor, and Sophie stood before a door. The driver held it open, and Sophie gently guided Du Pont into their suite. The driver carefully placed the box of cards on the table. Sophie sensed the man's concern. He did not expect a coin for his consideration and respectfully took his leave when he saw that she was mistress of the situation.

Du Pont's forehead glowed, and Sophie pulled at the buttons until she could peel the coat from his back. She felt the heaviness of the gold epaulettes pulling the shoulders to the floor. Sweat seeped through Du Pont's linen shirt, so she dumped water from a jug into a ewer to soak a towel. His eyes bulged, and his mouth gaped as he lunged for the window. Sophie flung up the sash, and Du Pont sank gasping to his knees. He pulled the night air into his lungs, but the stream was too shallow to relieve the pain. His chest heaved, but his throat could only rattle like an anchor chain.

Sophie pulled back his head to let his jaw drop and sat vigil beside him, praying for the pain to pass. His breathing lurched through spasms, but the ache in his stomach drained his strength. Sophie placed her hand over his chest, rising and falling in shallow swells. She suffered through his seizure until it crested and sank into a less violent flow. Sophie gave thanks to hear him curse, "That stupid politician."

She pulled him to his feet and led him to a large leather chair. He sank into its smooth glove, and she stroked his head with the wet cloth. He was like a tired child, angry to be put to bed. She heard him rail against the land sailors, "licking the cream at home," and blessed each epithet that pulled more air into his lungs. She made him rant that Washington was a game of uniformed clerks scrambling up the rope ladders of their invented ranks, building careers, layer upon slippery layer, "while we were eating dirt at sea." Sophie felt his anger tear at his resentment and was grateful for the purge.

197

Now the politicians had stopped issuing rum to the men at sea. This was supposed to be out of concern for the men's moral development; there would be no sin, if the temptation were removed. Du Pont knew the decision was the Navy's budget. Money was at the root of all altruism, and making places for relatives and hangers-on was the real object of this mean-spirited act. He railed, "Doing away with the spirit ration for the men just so they can pay their secretaries." Comfortable offices ashore are not earned by sea service. The Navy manned the desks with the undeserving, "Those places are all given over to be filled by sons and nephews. As far as the public service is concerned, they are not worth their salt, let alone their salaries."

She gazed at the man she had loved for so many decades and the pride swelled her breast as the tears welled in her eyes. He had served in all oceans and survived, shot and shell and storm and gale and had always come home to her with the same lovely sparkle in his eyes. He seemed to know what she was thinking and gently whispered to her, "Wouldn't it be funny, if I were to be done in by a milfy."

Chapter 15

Reflections in a Golden Circle

Robert shrugged his shoulders deeper into his squall jacket and dodged the Atlantic winds. His nose rubbed the musky comfort of new wool, for his head was a nest of knots.

Hannah had stayed in the cabin for the two days of the voyage, nursing Li'l Robert's cough, and Robert blamed himself for taking his wife and son on such a journey. For all the huffing and puffing of the engines, they were not making much headway. The paddlewheels were out of phase, so the boat had yawed from side-to-side, like an exhausted swimmer, all the way from Port Royal. *McClellan* was a fitting name for such a vessel, for she was as slow and cumbersome as her namesake. His tongue caught a snowflake and melted the exotic chills wafting through the rigging. Robert leaned against the stern rail, rubbing the knots out of his legs He looked down the deck to see the Reverend French dragging himself hand-over-hand along the side rail to avoid sliding into the masts or slipping into the sea. He smiled at the thought of French with a skinful of whiskey, for the man loathed liquor almost as much as he hated slavery. French's face was as green as the sea, but the hope they would soon be in New York brightened his habitual scowl.

French steadied himself beside Robert and said, "I suppose this is your first winter."

Robert assured him, "this is the farthest we've been at the North."

The Reverend was eager to get to dry land and a surer footing. "When will we arrive?"

"The Captain said we will dock in mid afternoon."

"I will be most happy to see Reverend Garnet and hope that this inclement weather will not keep him waiting too long."

Robert gauged the wind to make sure French was in the right position, in case he lost his breakfast, but the man had pluck.

French had spent three months organizing this trip to New York. He had written a stack of letters to his friends, and there was to be a big meeting. They invited "Robert and the family Smalls" to their church. Robert was to give a speech at the Shiloh Church. The New York people assured French they were "looking forward to meeting both Mrs. Smalls and young Robert."

The wind shifted and Robert could see land thrusting through the fog on either side of the ship. To the left must be Staten Island, so Robert reasoned the pilot was weaving them between it and Brooklyn. The glimpse of land let Robert assure French, "I don't think we'll keep your friend waiting too long." He added to himself, "If this rattletrap doesn't break down dead in the water."

French wanted to talk politics, so Robert listened. "Since Mr. Lincoln has put his Proclamation of Emancipation into the newspapers, great interest has been stirred." Robert would have added, "and all Hell broke loose," but restrained his tongue.

"Some say it will not free a single slave," Robert said provocatively.

"Don't believe all that whofafa from the South and their Northern sympathizers," French admonished.

Robert recalled his talks with the officers when word of the proclamation first surfaced. "I hear it's all a'chatter way over in England and France."

"Our friends recognize no borders when it comes to Abolition, and neither should we." Robert nodded in enthusiastic support, but kept his skepticism to himself. He knew the white people were going crazy with either joy or terror, and sometimes both. Mr. Lincoln had shoved the ferret down the rabbit hole, and there was no telling what would pop up out of the ground. "Old slavers were new-minted 'bolitionists," he thought, and the rich people were collecting enough money from the war to buy every slave in the country. The mouths opened and spewed forth so much gold you'd think Ali Baba was shouting at every street corner.

French had cried "Open Sesame," and the doors of churches in New York and Congress in Washington were flung wide for Robert. The Abolitionists even paid the price of the trip to strange places to meet stranger people. When he was first asked to go North, Robert had taken his worries to Du Pont. The excuse was seeking permission to be relieved of pilot duty for as long as French needed him, but the reason was to get some good advice. Du Pont knew these people and had navigated their shifting attitudes.

Du Pont had been kindly, but Robert was more concerned that the Admiral would think less of him for the asking. "The Reverend French is a friend to you and to your race," Du Pont told him, but added, "I see some dangers to you personally."

Robert was confused. "What dangers are there in New York City which we have not faced in Charleston?"

Du Pont splashed his most knowing smile over Robert's perplexity to tell him, "You escaped a besieged city. Now you are invading a hornet's nest." Robert was not understanding, so Du Pont took another tack through the murky thoughts. "Robert, you have seen how the Navy officers have treated you." Du Pont let the matter soak in. "They have all been gentlemen," Robert assured him. Du Pont beamed like a teacher at a bright pupil and added, "More importantly, they have not made a fuss of you."

Robert sniffed Du Pont's hint. "The newspapers make a fuss over people, but quickly abandon the heroes of the front pages to the consequences of such attention." Robert listened carefully to Du Pont's confession of his own fame for capturing Port Royal. "People even gave me a most expensive sword in appreciation of my efforts." Du Pont's fame was nothing more than what people wanted to hear. They needed heroes to endure the war. Now, it was Robert's turn in the newspapers because some people needed a hero for abolition.

Robert carefully listened to Du Pont explain that the sailors' reactions had been very different from the readers of newspapers.

The sailors respected Robert for what he had done, but his picture in the papers had not impressed them. "It is your seamanship and your devotion to your family which make you one of us." If Robert had run away without Hannah, he would just be another contraband. But because the whole family escaped together, the sailors recognized their own values and honored Robert and Hannah.

Du Pont finally pulled Robert to the main point and almost commanded, "If you remain as you are now and don't get spoiled by the abolitionists, the officers will always be your friends." Robert now understood that Du Pont was looking for more than the subservience he could get by his rank. Du Pont wanted a choice and a pact between equals. "If you are back in a month, Robert, I will take you on again as pilot."

"I won't go, unless the Reverend promises to have me back here in three weeks."

Du Pont smiled a satisfied grin, because the deal was just the tip of their friendship.

When Robert shared Du Pont's advice with Hannah, she brought him down to earth. "Let's not make promises other people can't keep," she said, as she started packing.

The river traffic grew with every twist of the *McClellan*, so Robert knew they would soon be docking and assured French, "We should get everybody together and collect the bags."

"Just call me when it's time to land," French replied. "The servants will take the luggage."

Robert led Hannah and Li'l Robert down the gangplank to meet French on the dockside. The man had rushed along the planking as if it were the Promised Land and pumped the hands of a crew of well-dressed black men. Robert had some difficulty remembering just who was "The Reverend Garnett," "The Reverend Wake," "The Reverend Gloucester," "The Very Reverend Johnson," "Professor Wilson," and "Mr. J.J. Zuille," who didn't seem to merit either a "reverend" or a "professor."

202

Hannah introduced "our son, Robert Junior," and the reverends drew candy from the pockets as quick as gunslingers. Li'l Robert beamed at the outstretched hands bearing sweets and smiles, and Hannah took charge of the gifts before the child could load up a bellyache. They bustled the family Smalls to waiting carriages in a gaggle of invitations and schedules, closely followed by "Big George" pushing the luggage cart behind them. Robert wondered if George was their new servant.

The next three days were a dazzle of more introductions, more photographs, more meetings, interviews, breakfasts, lunches, dinners, and suppers, with more talk than Robert could digest. Hannah used the meals to train Li'l Robert in table manners, and Robert followed her to "start with the furthest fork and spoon and work your way in." He studied Professor Wilson and copied the man's way with cutlery. Robert clasped the fork with his left hand to stab the meat, so his right hand could slice it with his right, like a good European. The professor's etiquette was as elegant as his suit. The eating soon got in the way of the listening, and Robert became so exhausted that he had to "nap between loadings."

When he was bombarded with compliments, he wondered why should he guard against "getting spoiled" by such accomplished and educated people? Du Pont could be frighteningly direct, but it was when he hinted and insinuated that he was the most dangerous. Even though it had confused him, Robert appreciated the man's subtlety. Now he was beginning to understand Du Pont's warning. Everywhere they went, they were "The heroes of Charleston" or "The Pirates of the *Planter*" or "The Plucky Negroes." The *Planter* had somehow changed from a supply boat to "the most valuable asset of the rebel navy," and even the old photographs of themselves started to look like strangers.

After the second reception, the warning became clearer as he looked carefully at Hannah and L'il Robert. Robert had first thought Du Pont had told him not to become proud and arrogant.

Anyone who knew Robert knew that this would not happen, but Du Pont had a more sensitive understanding than most white men. The fear was not that Robert would become "uppity," for Hannah would give him a smack for that. He sensed that Du Pont loved his wife, Sophie, and that she was even more important to him than the Navy, so it must be something about Hannah that concerned Du Pont. Clearly, the Admiral respected Hannah, for what wasn't there to admire? Robert had joked that he had married her to "keep me in line." For most of his life, Du Pont had been away from home, either at sea or on some assignment where he couldn't take his wife. Mrs. Du Pont was some sort of invalid, but whatever was wrong with her body had not affected her mind, for Robert gleaned from Du Pont's stories that "Mrs. Admiral" was as sharp as a knife. Maybe Du Pont had married her, so she could "keep him in line."

Robert had frequently smiled at how easily people accepted the joke about Hannah wearing the pants in the family. Whatever roost they had, they ruled together, because they could not make what they had alone. That was it! It was the "alone" Du Pont had been talking about. Robert could not have accomplished the escape alone, and neither could anybody else. No one could steal a boat single-handed. Robert reminded himself of his own words on Hilton Head, "We did this together." But the glory had been given to Robert. Maybe the white folks could not imagine black people who were both intelligent and courageous like Hannah. All the attention they paid to Robert took the shine off of everybody else, so the newspaper people could believe that Robert was the lone exception. If Robert were unique, it just proved that all the other contrabands were just dumb-ass idle.

By the final meeting of the trip, his thoughts became as clear as if he were piloting home waters. Big George drove them to the Shiloh Church, and French ushered them into the vestibule. Robert looked through the open doors to see the men they had met lining the stage and facing the packed hall. French instructed them to "wait for Reverend Garnett," so Robert listened to the

204

speakers while Hannah walked along a row of portraits with Li'l Robert.

The Reverend Gloucester was delivering his "review of the colored race in this country," and Robert heard of "Crispus Attucks murdered in the streets of Boston for his hatred of England and his insults to British soldiers." Gloucester raised his hands high to recall the "righteous rebellion of Joseph Cinqué who did not waver to plunge his knife into the breast of the tyrant who stole his freedom." He was relieved when Gloucester finished his "notable instances of courage and manly resolution," and let Professor Wilson rise to speak of "the condition of the colored people of the South."

It was news to Robert that the "slaves will remain permanently where they are at present, perhaps on the plantations they were now cultivating, and which they would finally possess." Robert wondered if the professor had ever been to a plantation when Wilson claimed that "the colored men will obtain their livelihood as hitherto by the cultivation of the soil and eventually by purchase from the government or individuals or by confiscation they will acquire the land in parcels." The speechifying crested until the people could no longer restrain their feelings. Robert saw people weeping and heard their prayers pierce Wilson's sentences. The professor was helping them release something manacled inside them and their joy was as if they had been visited by loved ones long dead. Hardly anybody heard his closing prediction, "The destiny of the southern states is inseparably connected with the black race, which is the bone and the marrow of prosperity."

Reverend French led Robert, Hannah, and Li'l Robert down the central aisle and through the throng of cheering people to the men clapping them forward to the stage. Robert, Hannah, and Li'l Robert stood facing the salt and pepper faces making deafening but joyful noises unto the Lord. The Reverend Raymond stood and prayed the jubilation to respectful silence.

Mr. Zuille walked onto the stage, and Hannah and Robert craned their necks to see what was on the cushion he carried. Zuille raised his voice to the rafters. "It is my privilege to present to our honored guests this medal in token of our appreciation." Zuille picked up the golden disk and handed the cushion to Garnett. He read aloud the medal's inscription, "Presented to Robert Smalls by the colored citizens of New York, October 2, 1862, as a token of their regard for his heroism, his love of liberty and his patriotism." He handed the heavy orb to Robert, who saw the *Planter* steaming towards him. Fort Sumter was in the background, and the little boat was chugging to the welcoming Union fleet. Their moment was forever held within the shining metal, and Robert pondered the admiration in all the faces staring up at him.

Now he understood the insistence that Hannah and Li'l Robert join him to New York. They were integral to Robert Smalls, "Hero of the High Seas"; they were the family Smalls. That was what Du Pont had been talking about. The danger to Robert personally was the danger to his family. If they put Robert to the front, the others were obscured by his shadow. The Navy officers had not made a big thing of him. They accepted Robert and the others as people who could do the job and, after their initial surprise at the escape, just took it for granted that the extraordinary was normal. That was what Du Pont had been getting at. "Don't get spoiled" meant "be like us." Keep your family together, and take the extraordinary in your stride.

Reverend Garnett stood before the assembly holding a sheet of paper covered in neatly sculpted cursive script and read, "Resolved. That the colored people of the City of New York cordially welcome Mr. ROBERT SMALLS, of Charleston, S.C., as a representative of the loyal people, comprising four millions of black Unionists, now living in the rebel or semi-rebel states."

Hannah drank in the words and found her answers in the arabesques of Garnett's voice. These people were honoring them. She saw some rough faces in the crowd, but they were softened

206

by the evening. Even the Rev. French was smiling to show his back teeth. Garnett's strained to throw his voice to the back of the hall and keep his emotions under a tight rein. He intoned:

"Resolved. That Mr. Robert Smalls has nobly represented this loyal population."

"First: By achieving his own liberty and freedom from the despotism which now broods over the South."

Li'l Robert was frightened by the noise of thousands of hands clapping and hid his face in the folds of Hannah's dress. She bent down to whisper, "Look at the people, My Sunshine, for they surely want to look at you." The child picked up the comfort and the command in his mother's voice and turned his head to the serried ranks of faces all smiling at him. Hannah waved his little hand to the audience and said, "It's just like the thunder on the sea; it won't hurt you." Hannah was talking as much to herself as to her son, for she had never experienced such adulation.

"Secondly: By securing the liberty of his wife and children and of those of the crew of his vessel, thereby carrying out most gloriously and promptly the doctrine of immediate emancipation."

These people were so happy to see them, and she did not fully understand why until she saw their eyes darting from Robert, to herself, to Li'l Robert. The people had met escaped slaves and listened to their tales of derring-do, but this was the first time they had seen a whole family. Usually it was the men who went, leaving their women and children behind. More likely they had no families to leave. They were solitary, but *Planter* was a whole family. She remembered how hard it was for Du Pont and Mr. French and Miss Laura to understand that their ties were longer than marriage papers. She laughed to think of how French had been so shocked that they were married "over the broom." He could not understand that a family consisted of all the connections to all sorts of people. There was no blood tie even though so many people wanted to bind them together only with their color. These people before her understood what she had always just accepted as naturally as the moon rising and the sun setting. They were not lonely runaways; they were a family, and they had liberated themselves. That was what the Reverend was talking about, liberating ourselves.

"Thirdly: In that the act of seizing the gunboat and passing successfully the six forts, which environ Charleston harbor, he developed a capacity for military and naval conduct excelled by nothing which has occurred in the present war and equaled by only a few events in any other war."

This was as terrifying as the trip out of Charleston, but she knew this would end with handshakes and not with bullets. These people had been working for years and there had never been an evening like this, with all the newspaper people and the reverends' speechifying and all those people in their seats. This was supposed to be a black church, but there were so many white faces looking up to her. She could see sapphire tears rolling over rosy cheeks.

"Fourthly: By presenting to the Federal Government the valuable prize won by his prowess, he has shown in his own behalf and of those whom he represents a faithful devotedness to the cause of the American Union which ever has and ever will illustrate the conduct of the black citizens of the United States."

Robert knew they were making him "one of us" and felt a sudden panic weave through his body. He imagined Nichols, Johnny, and Davey sitting in the crowd and reminding him that he was one of them too. With Hannah and Little Robert on that stage, they were one with many who could not see they were both part of all.

"Fifthly: Our brother SMALLS has by this one act proven beyond any man's gainsaying the safety, the justice and the easy possibility of the General Government's accomplishing immediate and universal emancipation."

Robert felt the current of their feelings flood through the church, and then he realized that many of these people could never say what they themselves had done. Recognition would put an end to their labors, for they had to keep their good works secret. Silence was both the secret of their success and their punishment. The Underground Railroad had to run silently. But this thunderous applause was their one chance to celebrate in the open, to bring to light the goodness they had to do in darkness. The celebration was not just of Robert Smalls, but of all the people who had done so much and received so little recognition.

Reverend Garnett spread his hands wide and confessed, "I have always hated South Carolina, but I have reason to change my mind if Mr. Smalls represents the kind of men that sorry state contains. We understand that Mr. Smalls will proceed to Port Royal on Monday and will become the regular pilot of the *Planter*, receiving the government pay and allowances. According to the decision of the government, he will receive a one-quarter interest in the vessel, equal to $7,000."

Robert was the first to rise when Garnett commanded, "Three Cheers for Admiral Du Pont." The congregation rose as one at the name of Du Pont, and Robert was filled with pride to be numbered in such company. He was happy that they could thank Du Pont, for they must acknowledge the man who had done so much, so quietly, and so graciously to make this evening a reality for his family. Now he could rise to thank and praise the comrades who were forgotten in this praise.

At the third cheer, Garnett kept them standing to inform them, "the authorities in Charleston have offered a reward of $4,000 for Smalls." The golden disk trembled in Robert's hand as he raised it shimmering above his head. The medal dazzled every eye, and every ear heard Robert's voice declare, "I will offer my services to conduct a Union fleet into the harbor of the cradle of rebellion." A chill went through Hannah's frame, and she held her son tighter.

Chapter 16

The Red Thread

Rhind crossed his legs, cuddled his pipe in his fist, and leaned back against *Planter's* rail. His face told Robert something was up. The man could gaze out to sea for hours, but Robert would not intrude upon his meditations. He appreciated Rhind's thoughtfulness and wondered what was rolling around in his head. Whatever he was thinking, their new captain would keep the water out of the boat and them out of trouble. Robert had noticed that whenever Rhind felt embarrassed or apprehensive or annoyed, his eyebrows skewed an angry diagonal across his forehead, so he asked, "Something pecking at you?"

Rhind blew out a stream of relief at the question, and his teeth scraped a stray tobacco strand from his tongue. His thumb pressed the burning ash deeper into the bowl, and Robert waited for trust to fill his eyes. Rhind spit into the water, "I have to ask you something."

Robert sensed the seriousness oozing from Rhind's casual tone. "Sure."

"Will you pilot the new boat?"

"Sure," Robert agreed.

"That's all? Just 'Sure.'"

"Sure."

"Sometimes you can be maddeningly helpful."

Their humor was their one reliable bridge. Rhind's rough manner kept the distance between them, but it left enough closeness to work the ship. Now, however, was not the time for friendly jibes. Rhind took a deep breath and said slowly, "I've been assigned to command of the *Keokuk*."

"Isn't that the new ironclad?"

"The newest," Rhind grumbled. He paused to let Robert's curiosity bubble up and added, "Somebody thinks a gun tower is such a good idea, they put two on *Keokuk*."

"What's that to do with me?"

"She coming here," he stated. "I need a crew."

"Can't you get enough sailors?"

"We can't get enough of anything. You know yourself, sometimes we steam on bunker dust."

"So what do you want me to do?"

"Can you talk to Alfred and the gang?

"Sure."

"There you go again with that 'sure.' Just tell them we need them."

Robert understood that the Navy needed more men than it had, in order to do everything that had to be done. It made sense that Rhind would ask for Alfred and the gang; the ships were always short of engine room crew. Rhind was never happier than when he could not see land, but why did he need Robert to pilot some seagoing steel monster?

"Where are we going?" Robert whispered.

"Charleston."

Robert slouched forward from the rail to stretch the knots out of his back and took a step towards the engine room, "Well, I'll see you in the morning."

Rhind blew a smokey "Sure" in reply, and Robert waved a glove in farewell. Rhind heard the clanging of a boiler rake scuttering along the engine room floor and saw Alfred lunge out of the door. Sammy and Abe appeared behind him, wafting auras of wood smoke, and William scampered from the bow to join them at the gangplank. Rhind watched them walk along the wharf. Alfred shouted something at Robert, but the dockside clatter drowned out his words. Their waving arms and shaking heads reminded Rhind of a Frenchman ordering dinner and told him that Robert had delivered the request. They wove their way through the maze of cluttered cargo and out of his sight, leaving him to puzzle over these curious people.

Most of the slaves had been happy to follow the soldiers flooding the land and find a shovel and a job, but otherwise they had done nothing to change their condition. Rhind reflected on how different were Robert and the crew. Their escape had been dramatic, a truly heroic action, and Rhind had tried to understand such heroism. His respect increased with his understanding, but there was always something just out of reach about them. They accepted orders eagerly. There was no grumbling as with white sailors, but he had not made the mistake of thinking they were passive vessels to be moved by white hands. And they showed neither resentment nor anger when the glory went to the white men. They never directly challenged his authority, but neither would they follow blindly. They always found some way of subverting his more stupid commands. Now they had to make their own decision, and he was pleased to offer them the opportunity. He wondered how they would go about making up their minds.

Possible answers slipped through Rhind's mind like a greased rope. He could not comprehend the world of a slave, so he tried to understand the world they had escaped. He turned to lean over the rail and peer down the bay and over the years to see himself, the boy midshipman of seventeen years, clambering aboard the *Ohio*.

Back then, Lieutenant Du Pont had literally shown him the ropes, the ones Little Alex Rhind could tie before he could even walk. He could have chosen an easy berth on any of his father's ships plying the trade from New York, but he had left his city and his family for the *Ohio* and his country. Robert had left his city with his family and the boat, but he did not have a country. What these people left behind determined what they would become. This idea intrigued Rhind. And then he recalled the last blockade runner he had captured.

Six months earlier, Rhind and his crew had boarded the *Amelia* from Liverpool via the Bahamas, expecting a prize cargo of weapons, ammunition, and medicines. He had watched two sailors hoist a crate, but it was so light they stumbled and dropped it to the deck. More out of curiosity than greed, they pried it open to reveal dresses straight from Paris. Rhind ordered them to inspect the contents of one hold and they found more high-fashion frocks, boxes of expensive perfumes, thousands of cigars, and military hats for fifty gentlemen. Charlestonians still had money for such things, and the smugglers had soon learned that the rarest articles fetched the highest prices. Basic staples might be scarce for the lower orders, but there were more important things than biscuits and gravy. The laws of taste demanded that a lady be properly and enviously dressed for the charity balls, where they raised the money to buy the British blades their menfolk needed to "Present Arms" at parades. No lady could tolerate her husband saluting her with a second-rate sword, and every officer took pride in his wife's gown. Swords and wives had to be dressed to the hilt. Rhind swung his lantern over the splintered crates in that dark hold. His eyes followed the fan of light running over such frivolous trade and saw that they had chosen luxury over necessity. Charleston was doomed. Wars were not fought with satin. There was no future for a people who could waste so much money for so little purpose.

Rhind laughed to the echoing clouds when he realized that Robert already knew this. They hadn't jumped from a sinking ship. They had escaped a shrinking city.

He lit his pipe and sucked the ember into flame. The warmth seeped through the bowl into his palm, and he felt the same glow of pride at figuring out their escape as he had when he was a schoolboy with a page of correct sums.

He knew why they had left Charleston, but why did they stay with the Navy? The newspapers were all quick to scream "freedom," but that didn't mean anything to Rhind. Two years of war had drowned the big ideas and when he heard "Union," "Freedom," "Rights of the People," or "Save the Government," they were just cargo bobbing in the sea, surfacing from a wreck. The only big word that made any sense to him now was "Duty." But these free men owed no duty, no allegiance to the flag that had flown over their bondage. He had volunteered for service, when they had been "persons held to service." Now they were contracted to the fight from day-to-day and could leave at any time. They were free to go, yet they stayed.

* * * * *

Hannah fisted the jug of lemon water and plodded around the circle, filling their cups. William gulped the whole cup and jiggled it for more, but Sammy stared over the rim, as if he were pleading into a wishing well. The room was stifling, so they had opened both doors to welcome any wandering river breeze. William squatted on the threshold, his shoulders hunched against the jamb to keep the door from swinging shut. Hannah dragged the evening's coolness into her nostrils and sucked in the scent of lilac to soothe her throat. She tipped her jug towards Robert's outstretched cup, and sitting on the edge of a crate with his palm on his knee, he looked like a besmirched statue. Abe lounged on the ground, looking bored. Alfred stood with arms crossed staring into the bay, defying them all to ignore his bold statement, "You know what will happen if we get caught." Robert wanted to hide, but Alfred sought him out and would not let go. "You got $4,000 on your head alone."

"It's my head."

"Mine too," whispered Sammy, and Hannah wanted to cuddle the boy.

They had all seen the reward notice in the Charleston newspapers "for the return of the runaways alive who have stolen government property." They all knew what "alive" meant. They had danced defiance, so their bodies must pay the piper. Now Rhind was asking them to return and risk a terrifying vengeance. It was too much. They had done enough already.

"You were there when they killed that child," Alfred accused. All the slaves and the soldiers of Charleston had been herded to the Arsenal to witness the execution. A skinny boy trembled on the Arsenal wall with a rope around his neck. He had been caught

214

"goin' home." His final service would be a warning to all tempted to disobedience. He had been so frail, his friends had to pull his legs to strangle him. "If they think so little of their own people," Alfred said, "what will they do to us?" Hannah squirmed at the memory, but nodded her agreement.

The wind quickened and blew last autumn's leaves in a happy spiral through the yard. William swung his legs into the room and let the wind blow the door to his back. Hannah walked over to open it and longed for the room to cool. But Alfred insisted, "You know what they're asking of us," and she heard the panic coiled behind his whisper.

"I know," Robert answered, and the shortness triggered Alfred's anger.

"Then why the hell are you asking us to do this?"

Robert locked his answer behind clenched jaws.

"It's what it is," Hannah blurted, "We have to deal with it."

"You want to lose a husband after all this?"

"Don't do that, Alfred," William warned.

Ashamed of his meanness, Alfred's fingers pulled at his neck, and his chin fell to his chest.

"I'm sorry," he whimpered.

"We're all a bit het up." Hannah comforted everyone as she poured more lemon water. The drink cascaded over gravelly throats into a bubbling silence.

"You know what's waiting for us," Alfred gasped.

"I know as well as you do," Robert admitted.

"But those Navy people, they don't know," Alfred stated, "They didn't pay much attention when we tried to tell them."

"How could they?" Robert defended, "We could hardly believe it and we put it there."

"Believe it or believe not," Alfred said, "there's still an old boiler waiting in the harbor to blow us all to Kingdom Come."

"You don't have to tell me it all again," Robert replied with the sharp edge of his tongue.

It was almost their last job before the escape. The masters had improvised the biggest of the infernal devices. They had filled the largest iron boiler they had with all the gunpowder they could find, and made *Planter* tow the rusty monster into the bay. "You said there was over two thousand pounds of powder in it," Alfred reminded him.

"Could be more," Robert answered.

"It was bigger than our boat," Sammy added.

"That was a lot of work," Abe chimed in.

Alfred paced before them and conjured the image of Du Pont's incredulous face. On that first, exhausting night, Robert and Alfred had tried to explain the bomb lurking a mere ten feet below the harbor's surface. Whether from disbelief or ignorance or simple fatigue, the officers greeted their tale with blank stares and suspicious frowns.

"We told them all about it," Alfred continued, "and they didn't believe us."

"They didn't believe us because it is unbelievable."

"Why? They too stupid to understand?"

"Nobody can understand this new thing because it is so new," Hannah assured him.

"We didn't even know what it was until they bragged it was the biggest one they'd ever made," Robert admitted.

"And now we're going back there," said Sammy.

Alfred slowly dragged his head from fear to anger. "That's as dumb as a hound sniffing a porcupine's ass."

They imagined the explosion that could disintegrate an entire ship, and their fragile bodies trembled in the afterglow of their visions. Fear throttled their words, and Sammy looked to Hannah, but her face was rigid. He begged for courage from William's eyes, but found only the reflection of their terrors.

Alfred demanded, "Why should we risk so much for them?"

"We're not doing it for them," Robert said. "We do it for us."

"We gotta prove that we're just as good as a white man?" Alfred smirked.

216

"They already know that," William shot back.

"And some of us need reminding." Sammy joined in.

"So what's the point of doing it all over again?"

"Because they asked," said Robert.

"What?" Alfred fumed.

"They didn't order us to go. They asked us."

"Turns out the same, just a bit more polite."

"What white man ever 'asked' you before?" Hannah asked.

"Didn't have to ask," Sammy said.

"Well now he has to," Robert added. "We can say 'yes' and we can say 'no,' but we are the ones doing the saying."

"Just like that. We do the saying?" Alfred shook his head in hurt disbelief.

"Just like that," Robert simply stated.

Alfred turned his anger toward Robert, "Face up to it, Robert, you want to go because you shot your mouth off to those people in New York."

"You don't have to remind me," Robert shot back.

"We don't have to go just because they gave you some gewgaw trinket," Alfred accused.

"We all know about that," Sammy said through an accusing grin, "and I don't remember you complaining."

Hannah so wished to convince Alfred that they could refuse, but they had to decide together, and Robert knew their decision was the real battle. Robert and Hannah stared down Alfred's anger. There was as much fear lurking in their hearts as there was powder waiting for them in the harbor. She was impatient for Alfred to understand that Rhind's request could only be asked of free people. Rhind had not ordered them to volunteer. Neither had he assumed they would obey. He had asked because they were needed, but they could refuse. There was the honor of free choice on each side, but Alfred could not appreciate the invitation.

Robert's quiet voice tethered their panic. "We towed it out just beyond Drunken Dick."

"And it took most of the day just to get it there," Alfred recalled.

"It was another two days to fill it," said Robert. "You remember how many barrels?"

"I lost count."

"I didn't." Robert said, "There were two hundred and forty seven... a hundred pounds of powder each."

"That's two hundred and forty-seven more reasons not to go."

"Then it was another day to sink it 'cause they couldn't keep it down."

"So?" Sammy asked through his confusion.

"Then they will have even more trouble getting it back up," Robert observed.

"What the hell are you talking about?" Alfred blurted

"They can't move it. We know where it is. All we got to do is steer clear of it."

This simple fact was the challenge they could not ignore. Alfred searched Hannah's eyes for an escape. "You would risk this?"

"We already have," she answered. "Second time around won't be so bad."

"Hannah, you are not going on that new tin can," William said.

"They won't let you," Alfred added.

"They can't stop me," Hannah simply said.

Their breathing wove a web of silent accusation. If Hannah had not been there, fists would have flown. Sammy raised himself to squat closer to Hannah, but he remained silent, drinking in their every word.

They watched Hannah's hand fumble behind her apron. She looked like she was rubbing her belly, and Alfred felt ashamed he had caused her agitation. Robert watched her slowly withdraw her hand, and Alfred squirmed at the knotted bundle of red ribbon spilling over her hand. She clasped the ribbon loosely to her chest. Sammy watched her thumb force the end of the ribbon between her fingers, and the red point held him like a snake. William looked from her hand to Sammy's face. He knew that Alfred had to win and was desperately spluttering excuses they would accept.

"This is different," Sammy replied. "This is a big gun fight."

"It's my fight too," Hannah said.

"You can't do this," Alfred insisted.

Hannah pulled the ribbon between her thumb and forefinger to straighten out the curls and kinks. Sammy's eyes were welded to the red thread hanging from her fist. "I already made the trip when we come here."

"We were together then."

"You think I'm not with you whenever you go away?"

They watched her slowly wind the ribbon around each of her fingers and raise her hand in reply.

"What about him?" Alfred demanded, pointing to Robert.

Hannah slowly pulled out a few more inches of ribbon and offered the end to Robert. "Where he goes, I go."

Robert welded his eyes to Alfred's face, stretched forth his hand, and gently pulled the ribbon towards him. Hannah and Robert stood up together and gazed at Sammy and William. Sammy shook the tension from his legs, and pinched the ribbon. His cheeks swelled into a laughing grin of resignation as he whispered, "Me too." Abe stood beside Sammy, and his finger gently touched the ribbon

Alfred sat stubborn in defiance and demanded, "What is the matter with you, Woman?"

Hannah's voice was soft with kindness. "You know we're together, even if we're not in the same place."

"Oh don't gimme that mumbo jumbo," Alfred protested.

"Maybe you been too long with the white people," Sammy said.

"It's time you remembered," said William.

William stood up, turned his shoulders to Hannah, and stretched forth a frightened fist to the ribbon. Robert tightened his grip to stop William's fear running along the tape. Each grasped the ribbon between taut thumbs and trembling fingers. They turned their eyes, brimming with fear, pride, and invitation towards Alfred.

*　*　*　*　*

Rhind jerked half-awake, swung his legs out of the bed, and lit a candle stub to wait for sunrise. He sat admiring his new boots.

The old servant who ran the Officers' Quarters had giggled like a school girl when he called her "Miss Lydia," so he never missed a chance to use the title, just to hear the music of her laughter. Miss Lydia had brought him a cobbler who made him two pairs of boots for twelve dollars, "one pair for show and one for blow." Rhind picked up one sea boot and examined the sole and the upper with his thumb. The cobbler had expertly married the soft leather to the hard bottom, and Rhind ran his finger over the three rows of double stitches marching along the welt. The strength of the threads told him these boots would survive any sea. He flipped the boot in his left hand and reached for a wire brush with his right. He worked the brush's sharp teeth in rough spirals over the smooth cowhide to roughen the sole and give him a solid footing. Slippery soles had cost many a sailor's life. His nose smelled the cloth lining, and he remembered the cobbler's boast, "I put in some red silk 'cause it gets mighty cold where you work."

Miss Lydia had commanded him to "put on your new brogues" and squatted before him. She thrust her hands into a tin pail, and her fingers slathered whale oil over the new boots. Her fingers smeared the lazy fluid into the tongue, and her thumbs shoved the greasy paste deep into the instep. Her hands massaged the heels and toes until Rhind could feel her palms spread the heat through his feet. She sat back to admire her handiwork and then rose to bring him his pipe and a glass. He smiled in mock submission when she told him to "bide a time for the drying." He sat back to bask in the old lady's care while his boots formed around his feet like an extra skin.

He picked up the other pair of boots to admire the contrast. The sea boots were as rugged as these "land slippers" were delicate. The cobbler's masterpiece was as pliable as ballroom pumps. "Now you can dance from here to Jubilo." These were shore shoes, so he laced them with a cross weave to hold them firm to his feet. Sea boots needed a different pattern of lacings. Rhind threaded the lace through the holes down one side of the boot and up the other, so the laces crossed evenly over the tongue. His careful arrangement was more than vanity. A ladder of laces could be cut with one swipe of a knife point, if he had to get the boots off quickly before they drowned him. He pierced the last hole and pulled the lace through the little circle of red ribbon Miss Lydia had sewn into the tongue, "so's you'll always know these are yours."

So it was with confident steps that he marched from his quarters to the dock, half-expecting it to be empty. He rounded the corner and saw *Planter* puffing to the morning watch. He walked up the gangplank and told Johnny and Davey to "Be at Your Ease," and they slumped their backs to the forward gun snuggling their coffee cans. He looked up to see Robert glance down from the wheelhouse window and climbed the ladder to join him. Robert extended the steaming cup for Rhind to suck the brown fumes and blow away the night dreams.

They hardly spoke during First Watch and went about their business according to their morning routine. Rhind stuck his head out the window and looked back to see Sammy and Abe sitting at the bow gun, ignoring him. Rhind asked, "Engine Crew?"

Robert's eyes didn't move. "All present."

Rhind looked down to see Alfred slouching against the engine room door jamb and blinked away his astonishment.

He had half-hoped they would have all skedaddled. He needed them, for ships did not move of themselves. But this next job was no simple supply trip. It would be the sharpest end, and they had no reason to follow him. But here they were. Their presence was their agreement that they would stick with the ship and with him. He had what he needed for *Keokuk*'s mission, but he didn't know what they needed. They could have disappeared, and he had asked, precisely so they could refuse. If he had ordered them to their posts, their disobedience would have been a mutiny. But he had requested, so they would have the option of refusing. They had accepted. He wanted to tell them how much he admired their decision, but that was impossible. They had shown courage in the choice, and he hoped the same valor would carry them through the ordeal ahead.

Chapter 17

Night Signals

USS New Ironsides. off Charleston. 5 April 1863

My Precious Sophie,

We have just anchored here and Sumter is in sight. I trust we shall have the Sunday undisturbed, though I am apprehensive when the Keokuk goes in to lay the buoys at the bar, the batteries on Morris Island may open fire upon her, at very long distance, but she will not return it. Rhind and Robert will make Keokuk behave. The ironclads are all up, but since they anchored the wind is rising and the monitors are already awash. The Ironsides, like a floating castle, will be the target for all. I have considered maturely about where I ought to go.

Du Pont leaned back into his chair, and his tired fingers clutched the Excelsior pen. He squinted at the golden nib, a gift from Sophie, which had traced the many lines and contours of their lives. The little stick seemed to suck the ink into the handle, so he did not have the annoyance of continually dipping into the inkwell and risking a blot. He carefully wiped the nib and his fingers with his handkerchief and placed his pen on the desk. This letter must not be soiled, for it might be his last.

The desk held his letter book, the Order of Battle, piles of requisitions, a sheaf of telegrams, and a small prayer book. His elbow rested beside *The Daily Food*, their little collection of devotions. Sophie would have her copy opened to 6 April 1863, and its crammed pages were more intimate than a kiss. For a decade, they had shared the daily scripture readings, so there were never any awkward moments wondering about the other's thoughts.

His elbow slid along the desk, and the book fluttered to the floor like a tired butterfly. He leaned over to retrieve it and saw the random heading from Hebrews. The quotation assured him that "the word of God is quick, and powerful, and sharper than any two-edged sword, piercing even to the dividing asunder of soul and spirit, and of the joints and marrow, and is a discerner of the thoughts and intents of the heart."

He ignored the Order of Battle waiting impatiently for his signature. It was a formality, for all the captains and the crews knew what they would do on the morrow. Still, it was his duty to affix his name to the commanding document. Tomorrow there would be too much of dividing asunder. Tonight was for reflection. He picked up the book and ordered his desk to set his letter before him. The other papers would wait their turn, as would the ships entering the harbor.

He rose, walked to his bed, and knelt. He pulled a handle and opened the sea drawers beneath his mattress, revealing a long burlap sack. Like a boy discovering hidden presents, Du Pont sat with the parcel beside him on the bed. He skinned back the rough cloth, and a wooden case gleamed on the quilt. Du Pont blinked at the polished brass plaque proclaiming, "By these presents, The People of Wilmington, Delaware, Honor Commodore Samuel Du Pont on his Great Victory at Port Royal on the 7th of November 1861." His thumbs touched the clasps. They clicked in time to his heart, and the lid sprung open. He slowly raised the lid and gazed upon a ceremonial sword.

He stood and wielded the sword. This was no store-bought trophy. The people of Brandywine had commissioned this splendid memorial, and he had frequently extolled its beauty to his officers, men, and favored guests. The Brandywine people had collaborated on its design, and he was thrilled that they had chosen a naval sword and rejected the more usual rapier. Rapiers were for pirates and actors, but this gently curving blade was regulation U.S. Navy. Somebody had made the effort to discover the proper sword for an American sailor. They had displayed it in the window of Ziba Ferris' jewelry shop, so the whole town could see how their money was being spent. Sophie had told him that members of the Du Pont family were forbidden to contribute because this was the gift of his neighbors. The Du Ponts may be the richest family in the state, but the people insisted this was their own endeavor. They wanted to honor him without currying favor with the family. Such consideration was sharper than the blade's single edge. Their thoughtfulness commanded his respect, but he would not be spoiled by their adulation.

The warmth of boyhood play with a broomstick seeped into Du Pont's palm, but the years of service had engraved the commands of the "Manual of Arms" upon the mind of the man. "Officers on all duties under arms are to have their swords drawn." The book did not have to remind him that "swords were to be drawn without waiting for any words of command." He dropped his right hand to the seam of his pants. The handgrip nestled between his thumb and first two fingers, and the blade rested comfortably on his shoulder. He stood at "Carry" and slid his hand inside the guard to firmly grasp the handle. With an effortless sweep of his arm, he raised the hilt to his lips in mocking "Salute" to the papers on his desk. His letter to Sophie called him back from his play, and his arm drooped to "Order Arms."

He rested the sword across his desk, a paperweight for his labors. The light from his reading lantern shimmered along the blade, picking out the filigree of gold on silvered steel. Du Pont gazed long at the metal basket forming the handguard, admiring the talent of the swordsmith. He had molded an eagle's head where the hilt met the blade, and curved the gilded guard to the dolphin's snout biting the heel of the handle. The grip was loose around his large hand, and the graven creatures were a reminder that his service was between the sky and the sea. He chuckled to remember Sophie's objection to a tiresome guest's oily compliment, "Your husband is very 'down to earth.'" She had been quick to correct, "My husband is a sailor, so he must be 'down to water.'" He wondered if the sword's artist had heard the anecdote, for the eagle and the dolphin perfectly represented his high ideals and his practical seamanship.

For a moment, he was caught by the reflection of his own eyes looking back at him. The gray bags reminded him that he was no longer the sprightly lad. The sight of his face disturbed his memories, like a candle destroying his night vision. His mind thumped against the ebbing tide of his years, so Du Pont shook away his fears to clear his head. He welcomed this night, for with the first shot tomorrow, all their plans would be useless. The deck tilted beneath him, and his eyes followed the light edging up the blade to shine upon the white shallows and black grooves of "Du Pont" engraved into the handle.

The candle guttering in his lantern told him to go on deck for some air. The bustle of the gundeck was a relief from his wardroom. He calmly strolled the deck so as not to disturb the men at their work. Such purposeful activity always filled the night before a battle, for this was when the fight was won or lost. Hannah and Robert had called Port Royal a "Big Gun Fight." Du Pont gazed along the tunnel of the gundeck, watching the sailors at their tasks, and was glad such men would operate those big guns. He mounted the companionways to the upper deck and walked to the stern looking for a breeze.

The wind had shifted to a cooling draught at the stern flag mast, and he drank the calming zephyrs of the sea. Sweet is the night air! The tide was full, and the water swelled beneath them like a kindly mother's arm. He tilted his head to the clouds to gauge the moon lying fair upon the straits.

Ships alone could not lay siege to a city. There had to be boots on the ground. He had warned them of failure, if the Army would not cooperate. Fox would not listen. Du Pont knew the attack was doomed. They were to be sacrificed to a silly idea. Weather and wind augured well for them, but nature did not win battles. Men must use the winds and waves, no matter how foul or contrary, to achieve their ends. He had been commanded to achieve the impossible, and he must obey. A cloud blushed a drunken crimson gleam, trailing a distant rumbling from behind him.

He turned to the bows to see the muzzle flashes of Sumter glimmering in the tranquil bay, and relief swelled across his face. Firing into the night was not only stupid, it was a waste of ammunition. He mumbled through his mirth, "Let them use up their shot plucking up their courage. They'll have less to fire at us." He laughed to recall that night firing was more for the hunter than the hunted. At this distance and in this darkness, they could never hit even a ship of the line, so all their booming bluster was useless. He would not be tempted to return their fire and give away his position. Let them tire themselves, for the tables would be turned with the morning tide. His "Order of Battle" would form the ironclads into line-astern, offering the sharpest point to those impatient cannons.

A distant popping burst to seaward, and he swung his head to watch a Coston flare shower white sparks upon the far horizon. That would be *Onward* taking station on the outer ring of their position. Du Pont was confident that Nichols was a steady man, as ready to pounce upon the enemy as he was prepared to rescue flailing survivors. The little flares were a wonder.

He had worked with Benjamin Coston in the Philadelphia Navy Yard, and their efforts blossomed into a friendship cut short by his early death. Du Pont's admiration for the Widow Coston exceeded his respect for her late husband. Martha had been left with three young children and no pension. When she was sorting through Coston's papers, Martha found a drawing of a strange tube on a single sheet of torn wallpaper. The penciled notes surrounding the picture told her it was her late-husband's idea for a signal flare. She recalled the excited evening when she could barely understand his cascade of frenzied words. She had waited for him to catch his breath, and he spurted forth, "If we can use fireworks for the Fourth of July, why not use them on ships?" Martha had wondered if sailors shared Mr. Coston's enthusiasm for pyrotechnical patriotism; she had seen their distinctive ways of celebrating with rum and tobacco. Coston explained that "the fireworks would be launched as signals," and Martha had asked, "You mean like flags?" Delighted by his wife's question, he had exploded, "Yes. The very thing. Fiery flags at night." Martha had borrowed enough money to hire a chemist, and together they had created a flare which could be launched from a steady hand. Nobody paid any attention to "that silly woman," so she took herself to France, where they appreciated feminine intelligence, and filed a patent. Her flares had saved thousands of lives, and the sailors had devised a code of many colors to pass messages. Many a blockade runner had been captured under the red, white, and blue of "Mother Coston's Fireworks." Du Pont mused aloud, "Tomorrow's flashes will be horizontal."

Du Pont retraced his steps to his wardroom. He slouched into his chair and grasped the Excelsior to finish his letter. He felt pride that he would not leave Sophie to the mercies of the land-sharks of the Navy Department. Their wills were safe in the family accounts, where chance, fraud, and legal quibbles could not rob her. Sophie was the complete sailor's wife, and she would deal with whatever happened tomorrow. The many funerals of old friends mourned and enemies forgiven had prepared them for the eventuality.

Rogers was his best commander. He would lead the attack in *Weehawken*. That was their best chance to clear the obstacles for the rest of the flotilla. Du Pont would take position to the right of the line in *Ironsides*. They would obey their orders and run up against the impossibility of capturing Charleston. But then what? Then they would have to break off. *Keokuk* would be the last in the line, so that when they all turned, Robert could lead them all to safety. But Du Pont had to tell her the truth.

I must assume the responsibility which no one else can. Therefore, I will stay with the Ironsides just to the side of the line of ironclads.

She would already know that he would be in danger, and he knew the waiting was the worst. He tried to comfort her with the pen.

Rogers has been so concerned about where I should be during the attack. I told him that there seemed to be an idea that the Ironsides was not safe, but I feel it my duty to share with any and all the dangers involved. At the same time I have never had any mock heroism, never showed off, that I am willing to be where I can best discharge the duties of my position.

Over the years, they had worked out a simple code. Every New Year, they gave each other identical copies of *The Daily Food.* If he lived, he would telegraph a short line in French. If he should die, a friend would simply telegraph the verse for the next day. She would know, and the torture of the vigil would end. Today's verse was Isaiah 59:19. "So shall they fear the name of the Lord from the west, and his glory from the rising of the sun. When the enemy shall come in like a flood, the Spirit of the Lord shall lift up a standard against him." He reflected how they would attack with the sun behind them on a flooding tide. The scripture was as clear as the maps they had studied. He doubted the much promised glory.

I mention these things so you may not be worried if any disaster should arise. In October, Welles told me the country was yearning for Charleston but I told him the day is gone for taking it. He sent orders to take the town and that was before he sent me more ironclads.

The attack was as stupid as the defense was strong. Charleston was now the most heavily defended port in the world. He had been commanded to steam into Charleston harbor and demand the surrender of the city. No one believed Goliath could stand up to their new-fangled David.

With wooden ships I would not have hesitated to affirm that the place could not be taken. But the country believes these vessels invulnerable. I felt a certain degree of hope but never confidence.

He had tried to convince Fox that the mission was impossible, but his reasoned objections were brushed aside by the belief of the convert. It was as if the iron turtles had cast their spell upon the people. Welles and Fox and all the rest were in a land of dreams, glamoured by the iron machines simply because they were so various, so beautiful, so new. Du Pont knew the lies that lurked beneath the decks, where there was neither joy in a sailor's craft, nor love of ship, and precious little light. The newspapers had vaunted ironclad invulnerability, and now the people expected victory with untested certitude. There would be no peace, nor help for the pain these things would give. But their belief had ignored his warning, "Charleston is a good deal like a bag made from a porcupine's hide, with the quills turned outside-in and sewed up at one end." He had to confess to her.

Tomorrow, if God in his mercy does not take us under the shadow of his wings, I do not see how it is possible to succeed.

She would know what the night firing from Sumter meant, and it would be a comfort for her to hear there was more bravado in the rebels than the sense to keep their powder dry. She could understand such things as well as any captain, for she had always wanted to know what he was doing. It was no wifely politeness, for she read books on seafaring and asked him detailed questions.

The enemy has already seen our ships and my flag. Their flags are flying defiantly on Sumter, with guns going off in all directions.

But she knew more than the range of a Parrot Rifled Gun. She understood the plays behind the curtains which had so beguiled Du Pont when he was a young man. Many times she had warned him of the duplicity of a friend, and he had ignored her signals to his peril.

It seems hard that after a life of long and successful service and at my age, this should be forced upon me. Indeed it is literally forced, for no man of honor can withdraw in time of war from hazardous service.

She knew the frenzy for "Charleston" and appreciated how powerless they were to refuse an order. They had pledged themselves to service, even when they were commanded to serve those unworthy to lead. It was the price they had to pay, when the people hired pipers who could not play in tune.

Our failure will be an enormous victory to the enemy; our success will gratify a sentiment of hate on the part of the nation, not unnatural, but containing no results.

He had to affirm the creed that bound them together. He looked at the next verse in *The Daily Food*, the verse that would end the worst of the waiting, and read aloud, "The Redeemer shall come to Zion, and unto them that turn from transgression in Jacob, saith the Lord." He had turned from transgression and hoped his little sins would not weigh too heavily upon him. Sophie had cured him of cursing around her friends, but their well-mannered outrage showed only their ignorance of the talk of sailors. But that was such a little sin in face of their fidelity. The sailors had clung to the flag and the country. Their honor kept them true to one another, but few would see that ship and country were the same.

He heard the distant clanging of anchor chains, but there was no alarm in the footsteps scurrying along the sandy decks. This night there would be no struggle, and none would flee the morning's trials. Now they stood upon this darkling water, ready to act upon their faith. What was it that Robert and Hannah had vowed? To love and to cherish. They were like the Navy, and so resembled Du Pont and Sophie, for they knew what to cherish and had chosen to honor the things they loved. Du Pont did not think he would be killed in the coming battle, but he must be prepared. They had never hidden their fears beneath their love. Now was the time to tell her.

10 P.M. Sunday night. Precious, these may be the last words I shall ever address to you. We shall move in the morning at eight o'clock in the Ironsides where my staff all prefer to go, and on the whole it is best. I shall be in the center of the line, four in advance and four behind her. The weather seems most propitious and it may please God to cover our heads and give us success, but I think all is in His hands.

I shall not be able to add to this in the morning and will close it now, by expressing the extreme love I bear you, the extreme gratitude I feel for your devotion to me through life, the comfort and happiness you have ever been to me. I pray that God will give you strength to meet any trial with resignation and to live to cherish and protect my memory. I am surrounded by the warmest friends and Christians, who sympathize in all that concerns me.

He slumped back to catch his breath. The sword beckoned before him like a friend. His legs pushed back the chair, as he rose and reached out to grab the hilt. He clutched the handle and thrust the point behind him to "Reverse Arms." He knew what would happen and forced his fingers into a fleshy vice around the handle with all his strength. He could feel the heat welling through his hand from his iron wrist to the tips of his burning fingers. He stretched forth his arm and returned the sword to the desk, so he could spread his hand before his eyes. He peered into his palm, not for the tracery of a charlatan's prophecy; that was for fools to pass silver over a gypsy's lies. The swordsmith had engraved the Du Pont family motto into the reverse side of the handle, so he searched the swelling redness to read "Rectitudine Sto." That was expected of every Du Pont and was emblazoned over the doors of their homes, a warning to foes and a greeting to friends. He would follow the family, and Sophie would stand at his side or march behind his coffin, but they would both proclaim, "Upright I Stand." No matter if the cynic would snigger or the false tears would flow, they would stand together. His fingers spread around the pen for the last benediction and a final, loving command.

Adieu, chérie de mon coeur - que Dieu te protegé, te bénisse. Ton dévoué mari.

Frank

P.S. Do all you can for Roger's children if he falls.

Chapter 18

And the Last Shall Be First

The cannon balls screamed along her sides, and *Keokuk* shuddered under the iron hail. The spheres shattered on the towers, and twisted shards clawed the deck. A ball ricocheted off the wheelhouse walls and skipped over the water.

Robert crouched to peer through the eye-slits and looked into the eyes of the man trying to kill him. The gunner on the fort poked his head around the sides of the embrasure, and they played a deadly game of peek-a-boo. Robert sprang to the side and pressed his back against the curve of the iron wall. Rhind calmly paced the deck behind Johnny at the wheel. Their concentration numbed the terror.

Rhind and Robert were holding *Keokuk* at her station between Sumter and Sullivan's Island. Robert stretched to gaze over the parapet at the stone castles on either side of them. The other ships in the flotilla had veered off and were calmly reversing against the tide to get out of range. *Keokuk* was the last in the line, and the dents and scars along her armor made her resemble a feverish child with a bad case of the chicken pox. Rhind and Johnny stood composed at their posts, but Robert knew they were all drinking courage from their show of studied indifference. Ninety balls had hit them so far.

Robert counted fifty guns firing at them from Fort Sumter, not more than five hundred yards to their left. Rhind saw thirty guns firing steadily from Fort Moultrie to the right. He calmly informed them, "Moultrie is firing low. Must be nervous." As if to prove his point, a shell flew into the water behind their stern, spraying a murky fountain over the rear tower.

"Fifty plus thirty equals eighty," Robert calculated, and Rhind and Johnny laughed at the absurdity of the arithmetic. Johnny giggled like a schoolboy reciting his sums, "Times two shots every five minutes," and Robert proudly answered, "Equals one hundred and sixty." Rhind glanced at his pocket watch to add, "We've been here for thirty minutes."

"Hang on," said Johnny.

"Which makes?" Rhind quizzed.

"Thirty divided by five equals six, so," Johnny said.

"One hundred and sixty times six makes..." and Rhind waited for Robert.

"Nine hundred and sixty."

Rhind dryly observed, "If we stay here much longer, the entire rebel army will run out of ammunition."

Rhind slid down the tower ladder into a cloud of gunsmoke. He heard no screams and did not trip over any bodies sprawled over the deck, so the gun crew was safe for now. He stopped long enough to admire their frightening choreography. Davey was lifting a fifty-pound power bag as if it were a sack of flour. He shoved it into the gun's muzzle and stepped back one pace, leaving just enough room for the Rammer to charge the barrel. The Rammer turned aside, and Davey bent forward with the Gunner's Mate to lift the ball cradle and feed the hungry mouth. The Chief waited with crooked elbow to pull the igniter chord.

They danced through the ballet of the "Manual of Drill," and the scene reminded Rhind of the little figures in a cuckoo clock striking the hour. He shuffled along the sloping circle of the wall, skirted the backs of the crew, and climbed down the hatchway ladder into the engine room.

A quick glance made his duty clear. Most of the lanterns had been blown out. Men were forcing blocking frames over the holes in the hull. He saw William and Sammy wedging beams between deck and wall to stem the deluge, but there were just too many punctures. They were too frantic to notice him. Rhind waded shin-deep through water to the engine block and, by some miracle, the boilers were still working. Alfred and his gang were raking a boiler pan, but the rest of the room was a frenzied fight with the invading sea. The men forced hand pumps below the waterline, waggled the wooden handles, and fought to hold the flood below the engine platforms. Those not pumping or bailing dodged the galloping rods and pistons, desperately splashing oil over the propeller gears. Their measured frenzy gave *Keokuk* almost enough power to escape.

Rhind pleaded to Alfred, "Can you keep them working?"

Alfred shouted back, "As long as water don't meet fire."

Rhind turned to climb to the wheelhouse and, as his head rose above the deck, he commanded Robert, "Get us out of here."

Robert cast calm assurance back to Rhind's imploring eyes and said, "We'll pull back and let the tide turn us around."

Rhind hollered down the hatchway, "All aft." His command scampered along the steel tunnels as the gun crew passed his order down to the engine room. Robert felt the lurch as the twin propellers fought to pull *Keokuk* away from the forts. They were carrying tons of water, but the engines strained and made some headway in reverse. The sluggish juddering frayed their nerves, and Rhind could not trap his impatience behind clenched jaws. "Come on, come on," he ordered and prayed, but they could not coax any more power from this giant snail.

They shivered at the dull thud of something hitting the hull. The thump was too slow to be a cannon shot below the waterline. Rhind and Johnny turned to Robert, and he quietly soothed them, "We're rubbing up against an old wreck." Rhind and Johnny cursed to think that they had come this far only to be grabbed by the rotting spars of some sunken garbage. Robert called down the hatch, "All stop."

The silence wrapped them in icy wonder, and they could feel the ship bumping against whatever was below them. Robert told them "The wreck will hold us steady. The tide will turn us round." He knew what was below and beside them, but refused to tell them they were pressing up to that monster boiler set to explode. It could all be over before they knew they were dead, so Robert kept his knowledge to himself to spare them the terrors.

Ever since they entered the harbor, Robert's eyes had been searching the water, seeking the sea-marks that would reveal where they had sunk the boiler almost a year ago. When he saw the sun twinkle over Drunken Dick's Shoals, he knew the boiler was directly below Du Pont's flagship, the *New Ironsides*. While they were waiting for *Keokuk*'s turn to enter the fray, *New Ironsides* had moved back into the Main Channel. Nothing had happened. There was no explosion. No fractured ship rose into the air dropping sailors into a burning sea. The enemy could not have resisted the temptation to kill the biggest ship in the Union Navy, when it was sitting directly above their largest infernal device. Robert figured that they had either moved the boiler or something had gone wrong with it.

Robert told Johnny to "Hold steady," and he rose to his full stature to look over the starboard side of the ship. He gazed down to ignore the firing from Moultrie and peered into the depths. If Robert could unwrap the truth, it might just save their skins. He could see nothing below the surface. He looked up to see the white ripples over the shoals and begged Dirty Dick to wave a ghostly arm. He felt *Keokuk* drift to the right, and a second thump shuddered up his legs. The tide water rippled around them, leaving a peaceful pool to the right. Robert squinted into the still water and spied one tiny ribbon of bubbling foam. His nostrils caught the scent of sulphur. The boiler was leaking powder, but it was holding them fast before the circling tide.

Keokuk began to turn around the submerged pivot. They stood in wonder and relief as the bows veered away from Sumter. Rhind could not bear to look at the island fortress, for he would not let the smoke and flame intrude on this stately arc upon an unknown axis. Johnny and Robert stood to either side of their captain, their eyes fixed on the point before them. The fort passed out of their line of sight, and the clouds glowering upon the horizon beckoned them home.

Rhind could feel the hull lift as she drifted free of the wreck. If they had thrashed the propellers, they would have been trapped. But the thing that would have drowned them now pushed them to the narrow safety of deeper water. Robert felt their caged panic when he saw Rhind's jaw tremble once and order, "Get to the main channel." Robert knew their patience was their only choice. They had to endure this sluggish weaving out of harm's way.

Rhind was astonished that it had only taken thirty-two minutes for this worse-laid plan to split apart at the seams. He laughed at the simpletons in high places who had convinced themselves that nine ironclads, "the pride of our victorious fleet," could sail into Charleston harbor, blasting the cannons to the right of them and smashing the forts to the left of them, to demand the surrender of "Satan's lair." His seven-year-old nephew had devised just such a plan with his present of toy boats. Little Colden had spent Christmas morning under his bicorn hat of folded newspapers, commanding his tin flotilla. Rhind blew out the candles, so the boy's navy could sneak up the carpet to attack the tree. Little Colden was proud of his uncle and reassured him, "soon you'll be an admiral too, even if you only have one boat."

Rhind had grumbled in disbelief when he read Du Pont's "Order of Battle." Someone had blundered. Robert was the only man who could guide them through the shallows into Charleston and Robert had been assigned to pilot the *Keokuk*. Some fool had forgotten this saving fact and had positioned *Keokuk* at the end of the line. When Rhind had pointed out the mistake, he received only an eyebrow cocked over an annoyed pout and the icy sigh, "your ship is an experimental craft." Robert would not be leading the flotilla to any victory, and they both knew they were steaming into a disaster. One glance along the channel cluttered with punch-drunk and foundering ironclads confirmed that the experiment had failed.

All three savored their calm within the panic, for each man had made his separate peace. They had decided to cast aside both their petty hates and their future hopes, and stand still within their time. They could think of no regrets and refused to mourn their stolen tomorrows. Here stood the simple courage of men freed

238

from all that had passed and merely curious as to what was yet to be.

Johnny heard the banshee wail and lunged at Robert and Rhind. He tackled them to the deck as molten needles sprang through the eye-slit and clawed along the iron wall. An iron flake gyrated around the wheelhouse walls. Johnny spread his arms around them, but none could tell who was shielding whom. The iron disc clattered to a stop beside them. They looked at the thing hoping it was dead. Rhind pulled himself free, and the blood dripped onto his two companions. The fragment had gouged his temple over his ear. Rhind calmly pulled his handkerchief from his pocket and pressed it over the wound.

Johnny could hear their own heartbeats echo off the walls.

The nearest bastion on Sumter was only fifty yards from them, and now they were level with the gunners' eyes.

Rhind staggered along the wall to the door. He leaned on the handle lever, and the door flung open to clang against the outside wall. Rhind steadied himself in the opening and looked at the amazed face of the enemy gunner. Rhind put his pipe in his mouth and rested his shoulder against the door jamb. He crossed his arms and legs and stared straight into the faces of the enemy. The gun fell silent. Robert saw Rhind posing as if for his photograph. Johnny looked at the startled faces filling the slit in the fort's wall. Some laughed, others cursed the man's coolness, but all looked at the crazy officer calmly standing in the doorway of his floating tin can, as if taking the morning air. The blood trickled around Rhind's ear and furrowed little creeks through his beard.

Rhind grunted over his shoulder, "Any leeway?"

He heard the relief in Robert's voice with the answer, "Maybe ten feet."

Rhind almost whispered down the hatchway, "All Ahead Full," and did not wait for his words to be echoed to the engine room.

When he had gone below, Rhind had seen a bulkhead bulging toward him. If it burst, the hull would split open.

Keokuk had been pierced from stem to stern, and Rhind cursed the jokes about a cheese box on a raft and spluttered, "Swiss cheese." They had to keep out enough water to float out of range. The gunners on Sumter thought Rhind's pose was spectacular bravado. The shock stayed their hands just long enough for *Keokuk* to pass them in stately progress. Robert sensed the buoyancy in his legs and told Johnny to steer right ten degrees. Johnny could see they were leaving the channel and shouted, "We're headed away from the buoys."

Robert touched his shoulder to steady the wheel. "That's because they put them in the wrong places." The bow cut an even wash. When he was a child, Robert had learned that uneven bow-wash meant a sandbar below. White caps streaming down both sides of the hull confirmed deeper water. Rhind left the open door to stand behind Johnny, and to keep an eye on the fort behind them.

They passed into the Main Channel, and Robert saw Du Pont standing on the quarterdeck of the *New Ironsides*. He felt sorrow for the man who had done so much for him, when so little had been expected. Du Pont stood rigid as one of the statues in his ancestral mausoleum, but when he saw Robert at his station, he smiled and waved his arm in salute. That Du Pont could stare at the ruin of his hopes and still offer a small kindness was a sign that honor remained afloat. Rhind saw the salute and whispered to Robert, "That's our Gentleman Frankie."

Robert kept *Keokuk* plodding through the green water, and two miles from Sumter, they passed the *Patapsco* stuck on a bar. Rhind hailed her captain to offer assistance, but was told "All hands safe. Go on."

Robert could have taken any of the finger channels out to sea and to deeper water, but he didn't know how long *Keokuk* could stay afloat. If he headed to sea, it would take an hour to be rescued, but they would sink before help arrived. If he veered closer to land, they would be beached and captured. Rhind and Johnny knew exactly what Robert was risking. They had read all the newspaper articles offering the "$4,000 reward to anyone returning Robert Smalls and his gang." There would be no simple hangings, for vengeance would be torn from their bodies in public butchery.

Rhind looked for the Main Channel curving around Fort Wagner on the nose of Morris Island. Rhind peered straight into Robert's eyes and commanded, "Set your course along the extreme seaward edge of the channel." Robert knew that Rhind was saying, "Keep out of range of Wagner's guns, even if it means we sink in deep water." The journey away from land would take more time, but Rhind would risk all of their lives to spare "our sable volunteers." Robert obeyed with a grateful heart, and Johnny swung the wheel further out to sea.

Robert was dredging his memory for a place to beach the boat, but it had been almost a year since he had last piloted these waters and the tides would have carved new figures in the seabed. There was no telling where they might strike land.

When they were safely past Wagner, Robert decided to run straight for shore. The less time they spent pumping and bailing, the more lives could be preserved, including his own.

Rhind ordered every man to the pumps, and the gun crews scuttled out of their iron bastions to do battle with the sea. Robert rose to peer over the wheelhouse shield and saw Davey take his position on the port side of the deck. He swung his shoulders, pushing the handle back and forth, hoping he could pump enough water to quench a thirsty sea. Robert scanned the horizon, desperate to recall a distant shore, but it was almost as useless as the pumping. The waves circled them like a war party eager for scalps, and the pumps trickled hopeless streams. Davey could push and pull on the slippery wood all day and it would do little good.

The sun slumped low behind the shore, and Robert's eyes followed the long shadows over the dunes until he saw a grove of

241

three trees. His mother had taken him there for a picnic. They had rolled up their pants and skirts and walked far out to sea and joked about "walking on the water." They had won a steeplechase with the incoming tide and fell panting under the cool branches. Robert had been fascinated by how the wind had brushed the branches to one side. He had pointed up to the well-groomed crown, and Momma had laughed when he told her, "Those trees have been to the barber shop."

Robert told Johnny, "Head for that clump of trees." Johnny's eyes scanned the approaching shore, and aimed for "the ones standing by themselves." Their hope welled within Robert's memories of a childhood adventure.

Robert yelled to the deck crew, "All Stop," and *Keokuk* shivered into a gentle glide. Robert saw brown wash rippling up the port side. There was the sandbar, three miles past Wagner and almost a mile from the shore. Robert could see the little river separating Folly Island and Morris Island and thanked its tidal wash for keeping the sandbar just where he and his mother had played. With certainty in his voice he turned to Rhind. "We'll hit in a hundred yards." Rhind ordered all stations to "Brace for Beaching."

Johnny didn't have to hold the wheel when the bow rose and *Keokuk* slid onto the sandbar. She lurched onto her side, her propellers churning the water in lazy circles. Rhind told Johnny to "Fire Signals Forward," and Johnny grabbed a satchel of Coston flares. He slithered down the ladder to the deck. Johnny pushed himself up to the bow and wedged his feet into the anchor chain to keep from sliding off the tilting deck.

Rhind jumped down the companionway ladders into the stoke hold to see Alfred, William, and Sammy shoveling water away from the boilers. The Chief Mate said they could keep the screws going, but not for long. They needed the propellers to keep them from sliding from their sandy perch. Alfred told Rhind that the boilers were hanging at too high an angle, so firing them would cause an explosion. There was just enough pressure left to power the propellers for ten minutes.

At the bow, Johnny fumbled a foot-long brass tube out of the satchel and held it firmly in the crook of his right arm. He gently twisted off the top to reveal a slack wire. The thing looked like a child's pop-gun, but the Coston Rocket was a lifesaver. Johnny raised thanks for Nichols' drilling them with the flares, aimed the tube at the sky, and pulled the wire. The explosion jerked him back, but he raised his head to follow the screaming smoke trail into the sky. He sucked his breath until he saw the red sparks shower the clouds.

Alfred and Rhind heard the screech and looked up through the hatch opening to see the splintering flare. Rhind sighed relief at the rocket's red glare, calling all ships to their distress. Johnny would continue firing the Costons through the sequence that wrote their troubles on the clouds. Rhind bellowed, "Everybody on deck, now," and the engine room crew waded a line through the water and up the ladders. Rhind held back to be the last man up, but a thought flashed and he asked Alfred, "Can you give us fifteen minutes?" Alfred nodded once and gently prodded a rake into the tilting boiler pan.

Robert looked down from the tower to see the hatches disgorge sailors like rabbits from a flooded burrow. Sammy and Abe were pressed in the middle of a huddle of men clinging to the guardrail. Rhind herded them to the bow and called down to Alfred for more propeller spin. They had to keep *Keokuk* from the hungry sea and let her sink slowly into the sand. The engines surged, and Rhind felt the shudders tremble along the deck and up his legs. The propellers found some purchase in the water, and the bow ploughed a furrow into the sand. *Keokuk* rocked and rolled, clumsily seesawing on its little island. Johnny was caught between a wave and a very hard place, and his hands shook as he launched the second flare.

The engines roared again, and clouds of burning coal dust coughed through every hole in her smokestack. *Keokuk* lurched further up the sandbar. The stern rose and two bronze jaws spun into the air. *Keokuk* fell back, and the whirling monsters gurgled like a suicide happy to drown.

Robert turned and saw Davey clinging to the pump handle on the heaving deck. He ran from the bastion door to bring Davey forward. Robert slid along the oily surface until he crashed into the base of the rear tower. He tried to crawl to Davey, but the propeller surge lifted *Keokuk* and sent Robert sprawling to the guardrail.

Davey felt the final roar when the deck fell beneath his feet and sent him sliding to the stern. His hand grabbed the metal rail, and he dangled above the water line, clinging to the ship writhing in her death throes. The engines whined, and *Keokuk* twisted her spine up the sandbar. The surging deck wrenched his screaming body. His free arm clawed the air for anything to keep him from sliding into the shining teeth. Davey forced his torn muscles to hold the rail. His legs dangled over the side like a damp flag, and his feet thrashed at the metal until he found rest upon a rivet.

Davey hung above the propellers by four fingers and an oily boot. He thrust his right arm at the rail, but his grasp exceeded his reach. His fingers touched safe metal, but he felt the rivet move. He heard a soft squeak like a loose tooth, and the rivet snapped. His body pulled the torn tendons of his arm, and he tumbled down the deck. The edges of the plates ripped his flesh and his mind collapsed into a frayed memory of boyish slides down snowy hills. He opened his mouth to take his last gasp and fell to the water.

He kept his eyes open because he was curious to see what death was. The propellers sucked him into a cloud of swirling sand. His left leg took the first bite. It was not as painful as he had imagined. It was so quick he did not have time to bid his life adieu.

He blinked and wondered how he could blink when his body had been mashed to fish food, but he could only see a cloud of gray bubbles. An eye was looking directly into his eye. This must be Saint Peter peeping through the Pearly Gates. Peter smiled a toothy grin, the gates swung open, and Davey was sucking bubbles into his lungs.

Davey screamed, and Saint Peter cast a sorrowful eye on him. Davey wanted to tell the eye that he was "so sorry for making such a fuss, but this really hurts." Why would there be hurt in heaven? This was not right. The pain circled his leg. The cloud under him was soft and firm. He felt Peter hit him over the head and Davey raised his arm to ward off the saintly blows. He peeked under his elbow and saw the eye looking back at him. Something was terribly wrong. Why did he have arms? He pulled his right arm to his leg. He could feel his leg and then the other leg. He pried open his eye. The lids separated and dragged needles over his eyeball. The pain spidered over his skull and gathered in a throbbing knot behind his neck, but he mustered enough courage to look.

The eye was still staring at him, but this time it was laughing. How could Saint Peter be so mean? Then Saint Peter spit at him and it was the last straw.

Davey screamed "Just who the hell do you think you are?" His throat burned and he coughed grainy blood. The torture was flooding in his chest, and he could feel his own weight falling through the cloud. This must be some trick, giving him a glimpse of Heaven just before he started the slow spiral down to Hell.

He pulled his fingers in despairing betrayal and felt his nails dig into sand. The shock of knowing he was alive almost killed him.

Water exploded over his head and back, and he could turn his neck just enough to see the eye. The eye was black within a golden circle in a round blue head cocked curiously to one side. The head funneled into a long, toothy smile, and Davey finally understood. It was a dolphin.

He wanted to laugh, but his lungs could not raise even a giggle. He rolled onto his right side and his breath rattled from his chest. The head rose to meet his gaze. Davey found just enough air to say, "Hello." The creature seemed to understand and it smiled to the blunt tip of its merry nose. The snout waggled at him and sprayed a fishy, comforting stream over Davey's head and shoulders. The dolphin was laughing through the bubbles and enjoying its new playmate. He tried to follow the dolphin with his eyes but could not turn his head any further. It swam to the left and disappeared. Davey pulled his head back to search for his savior. He could see two of everything, as if through broken binoculars, but one image was red and the other murky. He took deep breaths to cough up water, blood, and sediment, and every hacking torment was more proof that he yet lived.

He shielded his eyes and saw the ship in the distance. He could not tell how far away it was, and neither did he care. It was so small and meant so much less to him than the head that had plunged up to greet him. He fell onto his back and kept his eyes open. The sky tumbled over him, and a green fringe was hanging from a cloud. Even if they were upside-down, they were trees and they were much closer than the boat. The wind whistled through the branches, and he heard their tremulous sighing answer to the rhythm of the waves.

There was a long line of spray behind him. A beach. The insistent chattering pulled his ears back to the sea, and the dolphin sported in and out of the water. It was not circling him. It was riding in a circle before him because there was not enough water to swim round him.

Davey realized he was on a sandbar about fifty feet from the shore. The waves pulled sand around jagged rocks. Pebbles tumbled after the waves, and he could hear a grating roar. The waves were sucking up pebbles and flinging them back. Each wave passed the little rocks to the following crest and returned them to the sandbar. He listened to their antics stop, and start, and crash around him, until he felt an overwhelming sadness in the sound. It built to a roar, and he could see the dolphin twisting itself high upon the water. He wanted to cry from the sheer joy of listening to the water and looking at the dancer. The dolphin did not leave him.

This little concert of sea, sand, and rock was an incoming tide. If he dallied much longer, he would drown. These waves would grow and march across the sandbar, and Davey would be added to the pebbles they played with. But he no longer cared. The dolphin jerked its head to a distant explosion and together their heads lifted to see glistening sparks fill the sky. This last Coston rocket was blue and signaled, "We are coming." The dolphin tilted its head to enjoy the sapphire shimmer fading into the sunset.

Davey pushed himself to the edge of the sandbar and sat facing the ocean. The surf played around his feet. The water had reached its limit, and so had Davey. The slow, trembling cadence matched the shudders running over his body. He could see puncture marks along his upper thigh. It was painful, but it was not bleeding. He figured that if the wound was deep, he would have already bled to death. The line of holes was as neat as he could drill into new pine. He turned the leg and saw a corresponding line below his knee. He gazed back out to sea and a row of teeth smiled back at him. The propeller had not even touched him. He had no idea how it happened, but the bite marks and the smile were proof that the dolphin had grabbed him by the leg and thrown him onto the sandbar.

There was no understanding. There was only the wonder of this miracle. The animal had plucked him from the depths and carried him into a mystery he could not fathom. Neither would he try. He just watched his friend turn away. Davey raised one hand in thanks to the departing fin etching a little line of white arrows towards the welcoming sea.

Part III

USS Wabash

Beware the People Weeping

But they killed him in his kindness,
In their madness and their blindness,
And they killed him from behind.

...

But the People in their weeping
                Bare the iron hand:
Beware the People weeping
  When they bare the iron hand.

Herman Melville   1865

Chapter 19

Down to the Raisins

Welles glowered over the page as he read, "I send Commander Rhind home with this dispatch, whose vessel sank this morning from the effect of the bombardment yesterday and who will give the Department all the information it may desire."

Fox cringed as the redness flushed under Welles' wig and filled the folds of his brow. With every hour of waiting for news from Charleston, their worries fed their fears. But this report only added insult to anxiety. Du Pont had sent them less than a page and had the audacity to entrust the report to one of his subordinates. Welles grumbled to himself, "Lincoln is getting better information from the Richmond newspapers."

Welles scowled at Rhind, sitting too relaxed before his desk. "Didn't you say that *Keokuk* was an excellent vessel.?" Welles challenged. Rhind refused to be intimidated. "I used to believe in the ironclads, but now I see they are almost useless. They are a greater danger to us than to the enemy."

"The monitors have proved their power to resist enemy shot," Welles fired back.

"But not their power to destroy the enemy," Rhind corrected, "and *Keokuk* is at the bottom of the sea."

Welles had never been spoken to with such rudeness. The man sat there, sneering at him, and were it not for the bandage circling his head, Welles would have boxed his insolent ears. Du Pont had sent Rhind with express orders to recount the battle in his own words, and Rhind was not holding back. Welles held his temper and reminded Rhind, "The ships were to sail past the forts and threaten the city."

"It was impossible," Rhind said in vexation.

"Why?" Fox asked.

"The channel is rigged with obstructions."

"You were supposed to avoid such obstructions," Welles complained.

"And run aground?"

"There was plenty of room to maneuver."

"There was just enough water to stay afloat." Rhind leaned into Welles' face. "I know because I personally laid the buoys marking that channel."

"You must have marked the wrong channel," Fox retorted.

"Impossible," Rhind blurted with disgust. "The pilot was Robert Smalls. He knew every gouge of that channel, and we checked his memory with the lead lines to the exact depths he said. In every instance, he was correct. We had better knowledge than at Port Royal or Savannah or the Ogeechee. The channel wasn't wrong. The target was wrong."

Fox worried that Welles would have Rhind arrested and charged with insubordination. The newspapers would feast on Fox with photographs of a wounded warrior in legirons and manacles jumping from the front pages. He could not smother such a publicity disaster, so Fox shivered his head at Welles. They had no choice but to suffer through Rhind's lecture.

"There is no way that the ironclads could accomplish the task you set them," Rhind said adamantly.

"Are you criticizing the judgement of this department?" Welles demanded.

"Yes."

Welles' arm pumped the air to convince this fool of the obvious fact that "those ships are the most well constructed vessels and have cost the government considerable amounts of taxpayers' money." He had a duty to those taxpayers, and he expected his subordinates to do their duty. Rhind's eyes narrowed at Welles, and Fox had only seen such looks in sailors' eyes seconds before knives were drawn.

"The Secretary means no disrespect to the service," Fox cut in, and Rhind puffed a cigar to cool down.

Welles smirked to deliver his final point. "In this great fight the accounts speak of but a single man killed and some ten or twelve wounded."

Rhind bristled, for it sounded like Welles was saying it wasn't much of a battle with only one dead. "Only because Admiral Du Pont refused to order us back into that trap. If we had resumed the attack, your accounts would have to be revised considerably."

Fox was cornered. He knew all about Du Pont's criticisms of the attack, but Fox had not informed Welles. Finding fault with the ironclads would be like spanking one of Welles' favorite children.

Welles resented Rhind's overbearing tone. That Du Pont had the boldfaced effrontery to entrust his report to a lunatic Welles took as a calculated and personal insult. He would not rise to the bait. They would not shoot the messenger. Welles spread his wrinkles into a smirk and said, "We must go to the President. Commander Rhind will make his report in person."

"Fine with me," Rhind said, and stood to place his cap at a jaunty angle over his bandage.

Fox rose to leave and immediately saw Welles' ploy. Much better to let Rhind make a fool of himself and show Lincoln that Du Pont was making fools of them all.

It would take more than a lick of paint to resurrect the Executive Mansion as The White House. Anybody could enter the grimy building during the day and demand to see the President, so hoards of office seekers burst through the doors, cluttered the lobbies, and flooded the halls to lounge on the stairs. They wanted everything from a job as the local postmaster to an appointment as an ambassador, and it didn't matter where. Lincoln quickly comprehended their tenacity, but their desperation frightened him.

In the first week of his presidency, one disappointed hopeful told him, "If you can't give me a job, how about a new pair of pants. I've worn these out waiting for you." Lincoln hid his disgust behind his humor and quipped, "Too many pigs and not enough teats."

Russlynn ushered Rhind into the President's office, and Lincoln requested, "Please sit down, Commander. We are all anxious to hear your tale." Rhind sat in the chair at the end of Lincoln's finger, and Russlynn stood deferentially beside the door. Welles and Fox sat wriggling just out of Rhind's line of sight. Lincoln pointed to a stylish man sitting beside him and told Rhind, "I have invited Senator Sumner because he is an aficionado of sea tales." Sumner inclined his well dressed head, and Rhind wondered if Sumner's hair and Welles' wig shared the same barber. He had reported calmly to Admirals, but his nerves tightened before a President. Rhind noticed the archipelago of age spots on the President's stringy hand. Lincoln smiled, and it looked like all the flesh on his face was flowing around his questioning eyes into his waiting lips. "Tell us of your service, Commander," and he curled his feet around the legs of his chair. The face begged for knowledge, and Rhind's words flowed with the assurance that Lincoln was listening intently to every one of them.

Lincoln squirmed at hearing Rhind relate the danger of waiting for the attack, but he thrilled to hear how Rhind had faked such disarming aplomb standing in the pilot house doorway. "They were so shocked they didn't fire, just stared back at us and by the time they fired, they missed." Rhind had heard that Lincoln liked getting information "from the horse's mouth rather than the other end of the horse," and the anecdote spurred Rhind to hold nothing back. He was adamant that the ironclads could not take Charleston and convinced Lincoln that the whole sorry business was a fool's errand.

Welles was compelled to interrupt. "We expected Admiral Du Pont would pass Sumter and the forts and receive their fire, but not stop to encounter them."

Rhind snorted, "We had to stop, or get blown to bits." Lincoln sat forward, hungry for Rhind's knowledge. "The rebels have sunk piles into the channel bed and placed barrels of powder on them. The ironclads are only iron on top, and the hulls are wood, so any submarine explosion will send any of those ships to the bottom." Lincoln appreciated that the soft underbelly was the boat's weakest point and nodded in agreement.

Senator Sumner added, "It looks like the Army will have to capture Charleston."

Lincoln laughed when Rhind replied, "How are they going to get there? Take an ironclad?" The Senator was not used to his social inferiors speaking their minds, and Lincoln was amused that Rhind treated Sumner as an equal. The sailor's highest compliment was the senator's greatest insult. Russlynn forced himself to keep still by the door and watched Fox shuffle in his chair.

Welles sighed, "What's done is done. I have sent most of the ironclads south to the Gulf. They will be a great help at New Orleans."

Rhind was quick to remind Lincoln, "They'll have to be repaired before they can make such a journey." Lincoln wanted figures, and Rhind told him that one ship was already sunk, his own. "We only survived because the pilot knew where to beach us."

"Who was that?" asked Lincoln.

"Robert Smalls."

"The same Smalls who got away with the *Planter* and his whole family?"

"That's right." Rhind was surprised by Lincoln's knowledge. "Without him, I would not be here and neither would be our entire crew."

257

They could almost grasp the question floating through the room, "If Smalls can get out of Charleston with his whole family, why can't we get in with our whole Navy?" But it was left unspoken.

Rhind saw something fleet across Lincoln's eyes and heard him whisper to Welles, "Why have you sent the survivors south?"

Welles spluttered, "To attack the forts along the Gulf coast."

Lincoln's fingers combed his beard as he observed, "After they have failed to capture the forts on the Atlantic coast?"

Lincoln sat rigid, and Rhind watched his eyes bore through the fog at Welles and Fox. Lincoln remembered the confusion of two years ago when the Navy sent conflicting orders to the ships relieving Fort Sumter in 1861. The mix-up ensured the failure of the expedition and the start of the war. Now Lincoln sensed yet another muddle.

Lincoln smiled at Welles and said, "That reminds me of a little girl back in Springfield who celebrated her birthday - " Welles plastered a smile over his jaws and prepared to be assaulted by yet another of the President's tales. Rhind turned a puzzled face to his Commander-in-Chief, who continued, "by eating very freely of many good things, topping off with raisins for dessert." Lincoln paused to cast discerning eyes over his audience. He could feel Sumner groan and took pleasure in the Senator's embarrassment when he added, "During the night she was taken violently ill, and when the doctor arrived, she was busy casting up her accounts." Rhind's jaw dropped to hear Lincoln tell of a child mustering her groceries and sat fascinated as Lincoln continued, "The genial doctor, scrutinizing the contents of the vessel, noticed some small black objects that had just appeared." Fox gritted his molars, glad that there were so few people to hear this confirmation of the Presidential vulgarity. Rhind waited for the point of the tale when Lincoln got to the punch line. "The good doctor then remarked to the anxious parents that all danger was past, as the child was 'down to the raisins.'"

Welles and Fox burst into well-rehearsed laughter, but they had no idea what Lincoln was talking about, other than digestion. Russlynn memorized every word, for he would dine out on this anecdote for many weeks. Rhind caught Lincoln's drift when he explained, "I tell that story to the boys in the telegraph office. When I reach the message in the pile which I saw on my last visit, I know I need go no further for like that greedy little girl, I am 'down to the raisins.'"

And just like the little girl, Lincoln would get to the bottom of this confusion of conflicting orders sprinkled with hints of treachery that Welles and Fox were serving to him. He would write to Du Pont directly, so there could be no ambiguity, no matter how useful the muddle was to some people's little plans.

Lincoln thanked Rhind for the clarity of his report and hoped his wound would soon be healed. Rhind stood and saluted Lincoln with more than the regulation formality, and Lincoln nodded in reply. Somehow it was a compliment, but Rhind couldn't figure out just why he felt so good. Rhind turned and walked out the office, glad to be leaving the White House for a stiff drink and a mellow pipe. When he left, Lincoln told Welles, "There must be no confusion. The ironclads stay on station at Charleston, as soon as they are able to float."

Lincoln fiddled with his glasses and turned to Du Pont's report. Welles looked at Fox, who nodded to the door, and Russlynn followed them back along the corridor. Fox had learned that Lincoln was the most dangerous when he said nothing. Fox confessed that the meeting was very anxious, and Russlynn assured them, "These are anxious times." Fox nodded concerned agreement and left them to make their own way home.

Welles grasped Russlynn's offered arm and shoved himself into the carriage with a grunt. "Join me, young man." The coachman snapped the horses into motion, and Russlynn slid into the seat facing Welles. Welles complained, "What wooden or unarmored vessel could have come out of such a fight with so few disasters?"

"Only a monitor could have accomplished such a feat," Russlynn assured him, and added, "So why did they fail?"

"What do you mean, Allen?"

"I am merely observing the facts reported by Du Pont's messenger. The flagship suffered no serious injury. I doubt Du Pont's ship even joined the fight."

"You mean Du Pont skedaddled?"

"Rhind told us Du Pont moved the *Ironsides*."

"So he could get a better view of the battle."

"And the best view was out of harm's way."

Welles toyed with the idea of Du Pont's complicity in the defeat, but the carriage ride to his house was shorter than the progression of his thoughts. Young Russlynn may be onto something they had not considered. There had been every indication that Charleston would yield, but the attack had been a complete failure. There had to be some reason for such a catastrophe, and it was not in the ships themselves. Therefore, the causes must be in the men who operated those ships. The horses' hooves stamped in front of Welles' house and jerked him from his reverie.

Russlynn's hand stretched forth to guide him to the curb, and he stood for a moment and then invited, "Come take tea with me." Russlynn nodded over his beaming smile and followed Welles through the door held open by the beckoning servant and into the sitting room. Welles studied Russlynn's face as boiling flagons of Darjeeling and rattling Beleek china cups were set before the master and his guest. Welles scratched his head as he probed Russlynn's suggestion.

"Rhind is a brave man."

"I would not presume to doubt the man's courage," Russlynn confessed, "just his confidence."

"How so?"

Russlynn steepled his fingers under his chin and pasted his brows with thoughtful concern. "He is rash and impulsive. More importantly, he has lost all confidence in armored vessels."

"What makes you say that?"

"I have read his file and note that before Charleston he had unbounded faith in the monitors, when he took command of the *Keokuk*," Russlynn stated.

"That is certainly not his present position," Welles grumbled.

"Rhind had too much confidence in his vessel before entering the harbor."

"And has too little in any vessel now."

"Wasn't Mr. Fox of the same opinion?" Russlynn added.

"I agreed that speed was valuable, but the monitors were formidable."

"The problem is not with the ship, not with the man, but rather with the master."

"You mean the President?" Welles queried.

"I mean the Admiral."

Welles poured his tea from the cup into the saucer. Russlynn raised his cup in mock salute and said, "He thinks wooden vessels with great speed would do as well as ironclads." Welles blew cooling ripples over his saucer and ruminated on Russlynn's suggestion. Russlynn waited and delved deeper into the problem to tickle a solution. "Du Pont has been allowed to decide for himself in regard to proceedings. He has selected the best officers and vessels in the service, and his force is in every respect hand-picked and personally chosen."

"Perhaps I have erred in not giving him direct orders," Welles admitted. "We have to consider the possibility that I have given Du Pont more responsibility than he can handle."

"But his chief responsibility was to accomplish the mission with which he was entrusted," Russlynn said.

Welles watched Russlynn's lips kiss the rim of his cup and his brows arch into a knowing suggestion. He understood Russlynn's reluctance to criticize, even when it was his duty to find fault. He shared Russlynn's pity for Du Pont's condition, but reminded himself this was no time for misplaced compassion. Du Pont had failed when success was all that was expected. Welles was thankful that Russlynn could both understand his situation and appreciate his dilemma. Russlynn's willingness to share the burdens of office had earned his trust and allowed Welles to confide his opinions.

"I have for some time felt that he wanted the confidence that is essential to success. His constant calls for more ironclads has been a trial. He has been long, very long, getting ready, and finally seems to have come to a standstill, so far as I can learn from Rhind, who is, if not stampeded, disgusted, demoralized, and wholly upset."

"But why Rhind?" Russlynn interjected.

"It was, I apprehend, because of this change and his new appointment to armored vessels that Du Pont sent him to us with the dispatches. Du Pont should have sent him home to howl."

"Or with a howl," Russlynn suggested.

"I do not exactly understand."

"Rhind has been tutored." Russlynn paused to gauge Welles' confusion and suggested, "If Du Pont sent Rhind with this report, to strengthen faith in himself and destroy our faith in the monitors, the selection was well made."

"Then this messenger is just another of Du Pont's intrigues?" Welles asked.

"It could be the Admiral's way of snubbing his nose at the Department."

"You mean he purposely sent this man Rhind to puff himself up?"

"At the expense of the monitors and of the Department."

"He has no idea of taking Charleston by the Navy," Welles coughed in disgust.

There was so much invested in Charleston, that to blame Du Pont for this failure was to brand him a traitor. Russlynn smiled to think that Welles had caught his hint of disloyalty.

Welles gazed at a tray of cakes surrounded by teacups and offered, "Try one of these. They are excellent."

Russlynn shook his hand in deferential denial and said, "I don't think I should."

"Watching your weight?"

"No, Sir. It's just that I can't stomach raisins."

Welles formed his lips into a smirk and mumbled, "Raisins."

Chapter 20

Handy Andy

Russlynn peered through the cloud forming around Fox's head. The hurried sucking at the cigar was a sure sign that Fox was worried. Russlynn could gauge the level of vexation by the volume of smoke. He wanted to open a window, but this was not done in the office of a superior. Fox may have boasted about blowing smoke in Lincoln's face, but Russlynn did not wish to be known for impudence.

Russlynn glanced at two piles of papers, sitting on Fox's desk. He knew one was the report of Stimers, the engineer Welles had commissioned to assess the technical advances of the ironclads. The other was the account of John Fulton. Fox had sent Futon to Du Pont to observe the attack on Charleston. Fox waved an exasperated hand over both documents, as if hoping they would just go away.

People were asking the questions which dredged up embarrassing answers, but Fox had smothered his panic under bland smiles. He had clutched at his cigar case when a political opponent graciously offered, "You can count on me when you're called before the House Committee on the Conduct of the War."

Fox squirmed in his chair as if it were a keg of powder. "There'll be hell to pay when word gets out," he sighed. Russlynn let Fox's words sail through the vapors and waited to ask, "How can I help?"

"I'm not sure there is much help for it."

"People will understand."

"The hell they will. We'll be crucified," Fox confessed.

"It seems to me that in order to accomplish such a task, one needs at least two pieces of wood and three nails," Russlynn assured him.

"What does that mean?"

"You can't get crucified, if they can't make a cross."

"Oh, they'll have plenty of help," Fox grumbled.

"But they don't really care who is nailed."

Russlynn watched a slug of ash grow behind the ember devouring the cigar. Fox pulled the clipped end over his moist lips and tried to wave away his troubles with a dismissive hand. Russlynn drummed up just enough indignation to catch Fox's attention. "The people have a right to ask who is responsible for this debacle." The ash tumbled from the cigar and shattered exhausted cinders on Fox's lapel.

"We do not air our dirty laundry in public," Fox pronounced.

"We don't. That is the function of journalists."

"The Department cannot authorize such a publication."

"Of course it can't, but it can't stop an enterprising reporter from finding out."

Fox looked at the two neat piles, "The story is too big for any newspaper to get right. Stimers' assessment of the damage to the ironclads is over one hundred pages."

Russlynn raised his head from the desk to Fox's almost pleading eyes and told him. "A newspaper would be encumbered with all these pages."

Fox wafted his cigar over his desk, and Russlynn lowered his eyelids to one title, "Engineering and Repair, South Atlantic Fleet." He sighed his regrets at the catalogue of wounds the boats had suffered. "Quite useless to a busy editor, such as Mr. Greeley."

"Greeley would eat this up. He hates Lincoln."

"If I may judge from the editorials in the *Tribune*," Russlynn added, "It is a sentiment which Mr. Greeley extends to Du Pont."

"Who else?"

"Mr. Fulton."

He let the name sink into Fox's confusion, until the possibilities sounded like a fog horn warning of treacherous rocks. "There is no better authority than your accredited observer of the battle."

"Fulton was scathing of Du Pont."

"The truth will set your free."

"Fulton has only produced half as much verbiage as Stimers."

"Still too much."

"What would these editors require?"

Russlynn pressed his fingertips together to form a thoughtful steeple, leveled his concerned glare directly at Fox, and told him, "A simple summary of one page for each report."

Fox stared into the distance, grasping for any reason to follow Russlynn's lead. When word got out, there would be such shuffling that the cabinet office would sound like a gambler's table. Congress would howl for resignations, and accusations of "treasonable incompetence" would flood the Committee. Du Pont's defeat at Charleston was now Welles' catastrophe in Washington. Fox was determined not to sink with the Secretary. He stood to his full length, scraping the chair legs behind him, and fisted the cigar between whitened fingers. He glanced at the reports on his desk and looked directly into Russlynn's eyes. "I leave the matter in your capable hands." Fox took a relieved puff at his cigar and walked out of his office.

Whenever his business took him to the War Department, the constant clickety-clackety of the Telegraph Room captured Russlynn's attention. At first, the metallic chatter had been an annoyance, and the infernal racket reminded him of looms spinning in a cotton factory. But he had bumped into the devices everywhere on his travels, in dispatch offices, private businesses, government agencies, train depots, and even some of the better department stores. They had given him an idea, but he needed someone who knew about the machines. A confidante whose trust he could control would be ideal - someone intelligent enough to supply his needs, but certainly not a personage important enough to appropriate his idea.

The War Department jousted with the Navy Department for public attention and government funds. When the armies stalled on yet another fruitless campaign, "On to Richmond," the Navy picked up the battle-cry, "On to Charleston." Russlynn delivered Fox's messages to the Telegraph Office and had noticed one diminutive telegrapher with a dour face. He had made a point of offering a cheery "Good morning" to the man, for he might someday be put to good use. Russlynn passed by the man standing in the corridor outside the Telegraph Room, stopped, and asked, "Andy, isn't it?"

"That's what they call me," Andy replied, and Russlynn ignored his surliness.

"May I have a moment of your time?"

"If it is just a moment."

"I would like to learn something about telegraphy."

"I can recommend a professor who teaches Morse Code."

"I am more interested in the whole system."

Andy looked up to catch the friendly gleam cascading over him, but did not move his eyes from Russlynn's face. Hustlers had frequently approached him with lucrative offers for information, but they all wanted something specific they could convert to cash. One of the telegraphers had sold the details of a new sharpshooter's telescope to the rival of the inventor. The fist-fight at the Patent Office was amusing, but the telegrapher had a year in prison to think about the one hundred dollars he had accepted.

"Not interested," Andy said.

"I can assure you that my request is entirely serious."

"All of them are."

"And legal. I don't want to know the content of a message."

Andy stood defiant as a tide-smoothed rock. His taciturn stance forced an introduction. "I am Allen Russlynn, and I work for Secretary Welles."

"I know who you are."

"We haven't met, have we?" Russlynn quizzed.

"I see your signature on requisitions."

"Then you will know that my interest is in the service of the government."

"So, why the War Department? I thought you Jack Tar Johnnies didn't like the land service."

"Ah. Such rivalries are for children. I want to know something about the system."

"What do you want to know?"

"Is it possible to send one message to many people at the same time?"

"You mean simultaneous telegraphy?"

"Yes, the very thing." Russlynn enthused.

"Of course it is."

Andy had learned to keep his mouth shut and his ears open. He considered this a blessing for he knew he was not the most talkative of men. Questions about the technical aspects of the telegraph were most unusual. He stood behind his silence as a shield and gleaned impressions. Fox's office boy was not trawling for useful information or angling for commercial advantage. It was only common sense that this mannequin already had what he wanted to know.

Russlynn was not used to subordinates dismissing his requests, but he swallowed his exasperation with a question, "How exactly does it work?"

"Different wires and instructions."

"So you have to install more wires for more messages?"

"No."

Russlynn was seething at the little nobody's monosyllabic defiance. He asked in his most personal tone, "What brought you to Washington?"

"Train," Andy grunted, and Russlynn wanted to punch the man's insolent face. "I meant, how did you get work in the telegraph office?"

"Transferred," Andy coughed.

When Andy saw the rage surging above Russlynn's starched collar, be dangled a few more words, "You can send hundreds of messages down the same wire. It is the destination which is important, not the number of messages."

"How is that done?" Russlynn encouraged.

"Just like railroad tracks. You only need one track between two places. If you have a good watch, you can send many trains down the track."

"That's what happens with the messages I send?"

"Approximately."

"How so?"

Andy sensed his questioner's attention and played out some more words. "Look at two train depots, say, one in Washington and the other in Baltimore. Put down five or ten or a hundred tracks and the business soon fills up the track. The telegraph lines between two cities follow the tracks, and they now have hundreds of wires wrapped around a core in a cable. Half the wires can be used to send messages, and the other half to receive. That way nothing crashes into each other."

"Unlike the trains."

"Soon trains of cars will have double sets of tracks, but the telegraph cables are growing by the thousands."

"But what if I want to send the same message to two different cities?"

"Then you merely send instructions with the message to forward it to the next address."

"It is as simple as that?"

"For your purposes, whatever they may be, it is that simple. It is a more complicated matter for the telegrapher."

"But it is possible."

"Happens every day," Andy assured him, but added, "on government business."

"What about private business?"

"That is not my business."

Andy gazed into the distance as if he were looking straight through Russlynn. He savored the awkwardness of the silence and waited for Russlynn to bite with the next question. "I could send the same message to Baltimore, New York, and Chicago and they would all receive the same message at the same time?"

"The same message, but at slightly different times."

"You mean hours or days?"

"Minutes or seconds."

"So fast?"

"At the speed of electricity."

Andy had walked into the hall to escape the endless tapes of death notices. Two or three dots and a dash or two could change a life. He looked away from Russlynn and stifled his desire to laugh behind his scowl. Since he already had the information, his problem was getting his message delivered, Andy reasoned. The timing of this message was important to this trumped-up lackey.

Russlynn was damned if he was going to waste any more time. Andy smiled at the edge in the voice demanding, "Look here. Who can send my messages?"

"I could, but I won't"

"Whom could you recommend?"

"Homer Bates."

"Who is this Mr. Bates?"

"He's the Chief Telegrapher of the Baltimore and Ohio Railroad."

"Would he be willing to do this?"

"I suppose so. His business is business. I work for the government. Homer will take care of your business."

"How quickly can he do this?"

"As long as the words take."

"One thousand words?" Russlynn suggested.

"Ten minutes. Homer has a good hand. Fast, steady, and accurate."

"Could he send the messages tonight?"

"Tell him I sent you."

"I am afraid I only know your first name, Andy."

"My name is Andrew."

"Certainly ... Andrew?"

"Carnegie."

Russlynn delivered a curt "Thank you for all your help," and turned to saunter down the corridor to the exit.

Andy calmly stepped back into the Telegraph Office and sat at his desk. He raised his finger over to the key, and in his fast, steady, and accurate hand, tapped out a message to Homer: "A fish is coming down stream."

Chapter 21

"Wigs on the Lawn"

Sophie was in a rare bad mood. She felt ashamed for the shortness of her temper. She had chided Philibert for not bringing her the mail before he could explain there was none to bring.

She protected her solitude, but her joy was the regular appearance of a smartly dressed young sailor delivering Du Pont's letter journal. But now she received only a stack of envelopes shuffled through Philibert's arthritic and nosy hands. The last ten days offered an annoying dearth of paper. Uncertainty always inflamed her ailments, and worries would crawl down her spine and scrape at her bones. One of her more sympathetic friends appeared with a pulp book listing every condition from Arthritis to Zimmerman's Disease and offering every remedy from Ambrosia to Zinc. Sophie had accepted the volume graciously, and she wondered what her friend would talk about without her list of complaints. She thumbed the pages to "W" and penciled in the margin, "Writer's Cramp." Beside the disease, she added the cure in bold strokes, "Shore Leave."

She had learned patience when he was in Italy or China, or worse, California. But blockade duty generated a letter almost daily, and she had grown accustomed to the regularity of the mails. This stoppage was worse than dyspepsia, and the little book prescribed no treatment for nervous bad temper. Her doctors had offered a bottle of promises containing the new miracle cure from Europe. She glanced at the bottle's ornate label and declared, "I am certainly not going to entrust my health to someone who can't even spell 'heroine.'"

Ten days of silence tormented her.

She caught a momentary delight of flowers swaying before the French windows and chuckled, "Once the Du Ponts all lived in chateaus."

Their grandmother had designed the house on a roll of wallpaper and had drawn the rooms around her family's crowded lives. If they were going to make gun powder in the valley below, she would build the house on a high hill. Ever practical, she had simply stated, "If the whole place blows to Kingdom Come, at least we'll be at the top of the pile." Grand Mamma had known what she wanted, but didn't really know anything about architecture. She did not think of a house as merely a building, still less as an investment, and certainly not as a "collective noun for a lot of dreary and hopefully deceased relatives." No. *Louviers* would be a refuge from the world of business affairs, high politics, and low intrigues. The Du Pont men were notorious for their ethics in business and in love. Contracts and wives were to be honored, for honor was the only protection against the sordid little assignations of swindlers and courtesans. Thomas Jefferson had understood this when Grand Mamma Irene had sent her drawings to him with a note, "As you have been so successful with Monticello, I wonder if you could aid my daubery?" Jefferson was charmed by the sender and challenged by the request, so he suggested "windows facing the valley, tall and rounded in the French manner to remind you of home." It was the least he could do for a family who had negotiated the purchase of Louisiana from Napoleon. He had been right. The Du Ponts were French to the core of their American lives, so they christened their home *Louviers* to remind them of their origins.

Sophie appreciated that a house must hold memories longer than the lives of the people who dwelt in it. When Du Pont came home from the Far East, they were taking tea on the lawn, and he explained to her, "The Chinese all have little lips on the eaves of their roofs." "How so?" she had asked, intrigued. "The roofs lift up at the corner to remind the people they were all living in tents when they were nomads."

Sophie hobbled around her sitting-room ignoring the insistent aches from her joints, collecting her journals and little books. She thumbed her copy of *The Daily Food* and mumbled a silent prayer of thanksgiving that she had received a telegram with the simple, "Bonjour, Mon Amour" and not the dreaded Bible verse of the next day. The relief had dragged a week of health through her bones until she felt quite sprightly. Then the ague had crept in like a drunken guest waking the house with his staggering and stumbling.

The footsteps creeping down the hall were not some long dead rake, but Philibert gliding towards her room. He walked through Sophie's sitting-room to the French windows and threw them open. "The day is lovely, Ma'am." Sophie knew resistance was futile, so she took his arm and stood to be led through her morning constitutional in the garden.

She pointed to a pile of newspapers soiling her table. "It better be." She forced her legs to follow her butler's lead and smiled to think she was Philibert's retainer, for there was little she could do without his strong arms. "And what is your opinion of this trash?" she demanded.

Philibert had read all of the reports of Du Pont's failure. He cast a contemptuous sneer and grumbled, "There'll be wigs on the lawn in the morning."

"What are you talking about?"

"Wigs on the lawn."

"You will have to pardon my ignorance and enlighten me."

Philibert's face flowed into a smile of long-suffering tolerance. Sophie knew to wait through the knowing twinkle in his eye for another of his bizarre tales.

"In Ireland," he introduced, "when men have one of their little altercations, they settle the matter like gentlemen."

"With fists?"

"Sometimes. They meet on the lawn outside the house, throw down their wigs, and start blasting away at one another."

"Ah. A duel?"

"Yes. A duel."

"With pistols?"

"Usually."

"Swords?"

"Rarely, but sometimes with rifles."

He waited for the image of enraged marksmen to ferment in Sophie's attention. "None of that back to back, ten paces, turn and fire nonsense. We get right to the point, throw down the wigs and have at it."

Sophie would not give him the satisfaction of her jaw dropping in amazement, so she suggested with reasonable skepticism, "You have witnessed this?"

"With my father's own two eyes."

"But not your own."

"Father was the most truthful liar I have ever met."

Sophie smirked at the pleasant absurdity, "So, they met on the lawn sans wigs and killed each other?"

"Well, not actually killing. It wasn't much of what you would call a knock down affair."

"So they purposely missed each other."

"Oh, no. They were quite serious about the business."

"Tell me what happened."

"They banged away fifteen times. That made thirty shots."

"And still they didn't hit each other?"

"They would both be dead, if they were sober."

The whole sorry thing brought peals of laughter. There were no rapier thrusts or slashing cutlasses. Just two drunks swaying over their guns and scaring the birds. Sophie never knew if his tales were a true record or the products of his kindly imagination, but they always made her feel better. If only there were such a simple solution to their present difficulties. How does one duel with newspapers?

Philibert conducted her through the garden and sensed she needed more than amusement. "It's a strange thing about those newspapers."

"Pack of lies."

"True, but they're all the same lies."

"You only need one," Sophie observed.

"That's what I mean. They all say the same thing about the ships being good enough to do the job and blame the Admiral for not getting the job done."

"That's the whole point of the dreadful process."

"Well, you'd think they could come up with something better," he almost shouted, "but they just repeat the same nonsense in different words, and some of those words aren't all that different."

Sophie agreed that the newspapers shared a striking similarity. She noticed Philibert stroking his whiskers, always a sign of reticence and an invitation. "What else have you gleaned from those rags?"

"Just the names," Philibert offered.

"You mean the names of the officers concerned?"

"Oh no. I know all those people from the guest lists. No. The titles of the newspapers."

"Titles?" Sophie questioned.

"They're a bit like boats."

"Now you are being purposely obtuse."

"Well, look at the front pages and just take off the name of the place. You have the *American, Times, Reporter, Herald, Constitution*. They all sound like the names of navy ships."

"And?"

"Well, the Admiral is used to fighting on the ocean. Now he has to fight these things on the land," Philibert said.

"So you see this as another battle?"

"Doesn't he see it that way?"

"That's what I fear," Sophie whispered.

"You, afeared of a fight?"

"No. I just think that the strategy involved does not translate."

"You mean it's different guns?"

"I mean it's a different sort of war," Sophie said defiantly.

She guided Philibert back to her sitting-room, for she could no longer evade the jumble of her desk. He took his leave, but his father's tale lingered.

The implied knotting of truth and falsehood in Philibert's little parable of dueling rifles was clear in the stack of newspapers before her. The skill of their insinuations was matched only by the vicious selection of second-hand facts. She sat before her desk and sighed to pull order from the clutter before her. She stacked the newspapers in the middle, where their headlines could leer at her, and searched for answers in the sheaf of letters.

For the fifth time she searched the letter from Lincoln to Du Pont. Frank had sent her the "presidential missive," but she could find nothing in it to cause his outrage. The president had been most courteous, and it was evident to her that he had chosen his words carefully. Clearly Lincoln wished to give no offense, but Frank had taken umbrage. She tried to see what her husband read into the letter, but the causes of his complaint were just not there.

She read Lincoln's words aloud, searching for any hidden jibe. "This is intended to clear up an apparent inconsistency between the recent order to continue operations before Charleston and the former one to move to another point in a certain contingency." Then she realized the answer was around the paper, not in it. This is a letter. There was always a telegram with orders, but this was personal. She looked at the date, 14 April, and realized there was a break in the time. Now she was worried. Who knew what mischief could be accomplished in ten days of silence?

She opened Frank's last entry in their letter journal and could feel the bitterness in his complaints. There was such hurt at the affront to his dignity. Lincoln was being Presidential in his order, and Frank would never question such an order, even if he thought it the worst damned silliness. He would obey just as he had at Charleston, even though he knew it was doomed to fail. But Frank's rage had blinded him to the kindness being offered with the order.

Her head swiveled between the letter journal and Lincoln's letter, and gradually she perceived that the danger to her husband

277

was coming from her husband. Lincoln had directly said, "No censure upon you is intended." Either Frank had ignored this or he hadn't seen it in the first place. The President was trying to smooth things over by getting down to the essential point. Frank was missing it because he saw only a slight upon his character and an insult to his reputation. That was firing him on, and the more he fumed, the worse he made the situation.

The President's order was wrapped in concern for the Admiral, but it was firm in its command, "Do not leave until further orders from here." The "here" meant Lincoln himself. Lincoln was clearly in command, but he left Frank in charge. It was a subtle but important distinction, so typical of the President. She gazed into the garden and said, "Fox and Welles were in charge and out of control." This had all the makings of a disaster.

She sensed Philibert's stealthy approach along the hall. "I do apologize for the intrusion and the delay, Ma'am." He stood in the doorway clasping an envelope in his gnarled hand. His care for the wooden floors explained his sudden and sometimes unwanted appearances.

When she was a young bride, she was shocked to see Philibert skating along the central hall. He had pulled woolen socks over his shoes and explained that he had invented a new way of waxing the "magnificent parquetry of the floors." He even organized the servants to spread the wax and then polish it with the same bizarre stockings over their shoes. Even though it resembled a skating rink, *Louvier*'s floors always gleamed like the pendants in the chandeliers above them.

She took the envelope but did not recognize the handwriting. Philibert saw her confusion and explained, "It was sent to 'Madame the Admiral Du Pont in the care of the Mills, Wilmington in the State of Delaware."

Sophie deciphered the ornate swirls and acknowledged, "Yes. That is the address. How extraordinary." She thanked him, but his legs had already shuffled him out of the range of his deaf ear, and he glided down the hall.

278

She slit open the envelope with her paper knife, and a whiff of cologne assaulted her nostrils. Her eyes ran over "My Dear, Sweet, Mrs. Admiral," and Sophie sighed, "Oh, that dreadful Simmons woman." She grumbled that "her salutations are as sweet as the sog-balls she called milfies." Not satisfied with assaulting Sophie's stomach, the woman now had to bend her ear and strain her eyesight. There was also something about socks and her charitable work for the Sanitary Commission. "We are selling thousands of pairs of socks and collecting a mountain of money but it isn't enough." Ah. Another letter begging for a handout.

What was this about feet? "I have noticed that our brave men of the water have problems with their feet." What was she doing with the swabbies' feet? "I have asked many questions, but nobody seems to know why they suffer so from itching." Now she was down to something about powders. "I had the good fortune to meet a man who knows all about toe fungus." Was there no limit to her disgusting interests? "I have also been told that this is not due to the sailors' slovenliness but has something to do with the coal dust on their boats." Simmons was starting to make some sense. "I have resolved to do all in my power to help these poor dears." But what did Simmons want?

Sophie sighed and read aloud, "I know what I do not know, which is absolutely nothing about toe fungus. I suppose a lady should not acquaint herself with such things, but these are very trying times, and we all must do what we can."

She rested the pages in her lap and gazed out the window. Simmons may be talking about something revolting, but to give her her due, nobody else would discuss such matters. Sophie was relieved that Simmons was finally getting to the point. "I think if I could find a smart man who knows something about chemistry and funguses, we could devise some way of helping the sailors."

Well, this was practical, and ignored. At least Mrs. Simmons' heart was in the right place, even if her head was a refutation of the thesis that nature abhors a vacuum. "I would be most willing to pay such a person for their expertise and to offer the necessary monies to find an answer to this most vexing problem."

Simmons was willing to pay for this out of her own pocket. "Do you know any such person?" A chemist. That's what she wants. Sophie knew she was just a stone's roll down the hill to the mill and could find "such a person" with one ring of her bell. Mrs. Simmons must be seen in a better light, if she is willing to do this and pay for it. "Perhaps I was wrong about her," Sophie said to herself.

Sophie sat reflecting on how, sometimes, she could be wrong about people. Paying calls was a chore, but it was a duty of her social station, as necessary as the knitwork in her reticule. In her mind, she saw the names of Secretary Welles, Assistant Secretary Fox, Mr. Stimers, Senator Davis, and Dr. Fulton on the place cards at a dozen Washington tables or on a score of *cartes de visite* casually entrusted to doormen. Social calls were the rewards of Mrs. Simmons' generosity. She was tolerated by the ladies who showered Mrs. Simmons with invitations to tea, balls, theaters, and charity suppers in exchange for her money. But this was different. Simmons herself was trying to do some good where those same ladies would turn up their noses. That may be the appropriate response for anyone who has ever smelled a messdeck, but Simmons was either too stupid or too good to care. Simmons would get nothing for herself from this project, except the sniggers of her hostesses. No. There was something quite genuine about this letter. Simmons had simply seen or, in this case, sniffed a problem, and decided to find an answer. Well, then. Sophie would help her, and she felt a little ashamed for ridiculing the woman. She stretched forth her hand and rang the little ceramic bell, and Philibert appeared like a shadow.

"Yes, Ma'am?"

"I need a chemist."

"Very good, Madame," and he was gone.

Sophie opened the lid of her escritoire and extracted her tablet of blank paper. She took her time to clean her pen and think about

280

her more immediate problem. Simmons was admirably concerned with feet, and Frank was about to lose his head. It was time for her to speak from the heart. She dipped her pen into the inkwell and let the nib drink its full. She would collect her waring thoughts, write her notes and, when the journal finally arrived, warn Frank about the dangers he was ignoring in his rage. She wrote out the heading, "Bonjour, Mon Amour."

There was more than enough blame burning the newsprint on her desk, so she had to assure Frank, "The Department did not intend to quarrel with you about the Charleston affair." The recriminations were being fired with ferocity and accuracy, so he had to put a stop to the escalation. Now, the fabricated scandal had become a vortex, devouring the damned and the saved alike. Senator Davis had involved himself in the controversy, "But the visit of Mr. Davis to the President, placing Fox in a vexatious position, roused his anger and hostility." Davis was a friend, but "his intervention has been an unfortunate one."

There had been a hint that Frank should take the blame for the Department because it could not bear the responsibility of failure. She knew it was this double-dealing that so revolted him. Frank's mistake was to think that Lincoln was the cause of the problem, when Lincoln was actually desperate to be part of the solution. This had become clear to Sophie, but Frank was still blind to the obvious. Sophie perceived the real danger. In his hurt, Frank would do something rash, and by rash she meant attack, when he should be falling back to get a better shot.

He was writing to those infernal newspapers like he was a young man on a boarding party. This only made him look foolish in the eyes of the fools who believed the stories. Sophie had learned never to underestimate the stupidity of people who were so willing to believe low cunning. There was little or nothing one could do with them, so it was best to give them a wide berth. They soon tired of being ignored and wandered off to pester other people. At least that's how she had learned to keep them at a distance.

Peace was what was needed in this fight. Frank should stop fighting, for the more he struggled, the tighter he pulled their nets around him. She read again Frank's complaint against the reporters. He hated each article with its "terms injurious to myself, unjust to the officers whom I have the honor to lead, derogatory to the reputation of the naval service, and utterly false in its most important particulars." She could feel his hurt.

She put down the letter and thumbed through the report Frank had sent her. The Navy had given Fulton permission to observe the battle, and he had written his observations for Fox. She compared the words in the report with the pronouncements in the newspapers. Philibert had been right; they all said the same thing. But now she knew that Fulton's missive was the source of the information. Fulton may have written the article, but Fox would have censored it. Sophie's eyes narrowed in hatred of the man her husband had mentored, then trusted.

She read again Frank's letter, railing about "refutation of his calumnies," and how he had "sent newspaper clipping to Welles," so he could defend the "honor and high standing of the naval service." She grunted the accusations aloud in her fury. "Welles? Honor?"

"As ever," she thought, "Frank is taking responsibility for his decision not to renew the attack." He was trying to reason with unreasonable people, and that was always a mistake. He was forgetting that people often don't act from reason, especially when they are looking for an excuse. She was proud that he had refused to renew the attack, for that would turn a defeat into a disaster. This was prudence, but they were calling it cowardice. She also knew that Fox and Welles were desperate for a victory. She scribbled down the dates of the letters and the articles, and regretted there was just enough time to make a thorough mess.

She pulled her writing tablet towards her. "My Beloved Husband," and paused, uncertain if she should be so blunt. She had to tell him. "I apprehend greatly you having taken a step you will regret." She continued softly, "I wish when you are angry

282

and worried, you would write to me more, and less to others, because it is safer, and after writing the first emotions to me, you are more likely to write calmly and collectedly to others."

Now was the time to take a deep breath, smile, and wait. Frank must step back, extract himself from the net, and then throw it back at them. That was what they had always done, and she wondered why Frank hadn't remembered this. That was the French way. That was their way. "Standing Back" is not "Standing Down."

Sophie heard the approaching swish of Philibert's shoes, and she breathed deep relief at the echoing accompaniment of thumping boots. She welcomed Philibert's irony, "Dispatches for MiLady," as he ushered the sailor into the room. The young man glowed with health and the hint of a blush to be in a lady's private room.

She immediately reassured him, "Don't worry, young man. Philibert will chaperone you." He stood before her with a flustered air, as she eyed him from top to toe. "How are your feet?" she asked.

"My feet, Ma'am?"

"Yes. I have been told that the men's feet suffer in the service."

"I don't know what to say, Ma'am."

"Tell me about any ailments to your feet."

"It's hard to say."

"Just describe to me what happens when your feet start to get itchy."

The sailor wanted to scratch both his head and his feet at the odd question. He stood clutching many envelopes and Frank's letter journal. Sophie felt his unease as he tried to find the words to describe Salt Water Swamp Foot to a lady.

The sun had slipped behind the house, and its last rays slid down the roof to flood a rhododendron bush. Sophie waited with a kindly grin for the sailor to master his awkwardness and, as he prepared his words, she admired the pink brocades bursting to scarlet, drinking their fill for the long night's wait for morning's bloom.

Chapter 22

Anaconda

Alfred's laughter echoed from the parlor walls, and Hannah's shrieks bounced off the ceiling. "That's about the stupidest thing..." she blurted through her gasps.

Alfred squatted on the bare floor. "And you've heard plenty of stupid." Alfred was wiping the moist merriment from his eyes. "Who dreamed up this nonsense?"

Robert pronounced the name through his mirth, "It's Mr. Sedgwick."

Hannah snorted, "My, oh, my, are we not the fancy pants? They're going to make you Governor of South Carolina."

"And is his other name Tom, as in Tom Foolery Sedgwick?" Alfred queried.

"No. It's Charles, and he's a Congressman from New York."

Alfred wondered why Robert knew so much about this stranger.

They settled just long enough to savor the absurdity of the suggestion presented in the House of Representatives, "To wit, that Robert Smalls be appointed the Military Governor of South Carolina, after the reconquest of that rebellious state."

Alfred begged Robert, "Plaze, Massa, you dun gwang to mak me a Aaaaadm'ral?"

Their laughter flared again, and Hannah rested her palms upon her knees. "Those people can't be serious."

Alfred pulled his face into a mocking grimace and chastised her. "Please have some respect, Mrs. Smalls. The United States Congress is not some back-alley jook house full of high-rolling sharks and skuzzy stinkies." That set them all screaming again.

Robert surfaced the question they were all evading. "Why would anybody suggest such a thing?"

"Out of their great respect for your many achievements," Alfred explained.

"And admiration of your fine character," Hannah assured him.

Alfred needed more, and he flashed his smile of ironic sweetness. "How come you know this man?"

"I don't," Robert admitted. "He's one of the Admiral's friends."

"And now he is one of our friends," Hannah added.

"Why is he so friendly, he wants to make you the Governor?" Alfred probed.

"We sent him a present," Robert reminded him.

"What present?"

"The shotgun from the boat."

"Digby's shotgun?"

"The very same," Robert laughed back at Alfred. "It wasn't loaded."

Their banter probed the mystery. Robert knew laughter unlocked understanding; he was willing to play the fool to find the truth. In the time it took to laugh, understanding crept in beside the joke. Hannah believed ridicule was the beginning of wisdom. All agreed you could only understand something when you could laugh at it. Robert remembered a drunken planter staggering along the quayside and boasting to his friends, "I laugh in the face of death," just before he toppled into the water. The incident was as stupid as the braggart, but there was also the hint that laughter could charm a catastrophe, sometimes.

Slaves had long discovered how the worst disasters bred the best jokes. Robert had once been fed a plate of pulled pork and gravy at a funeral. He had sat through the viewing with half a bread loaf piled high with pig, as the widow tearfully told the guests, "It was his favorite food. Not any more, but it was his favorite." Even when paying their masters' allowances, badge slaves added kindly wishes, "And I hopes you get to heaven on a string." Such quaint felicitations pleased the masters, who never understood it meant, "I hope you get hanged."

Lydia had tutored Hannah in the soothsaying of jokes. "You can tell a person's character by the way they laugh." Hannah's skepticism evaporated when Lydia pointed out the difference between a snort and a smirk. Lydia had also said, "Some say you can tell the future with laughter, just like tea-leaves and coffee grounds." That was an old wives' tale, but Lydia was seldom wrong about people. This was not so astounding. Some women would ask the wind in a tree if they were carrying a boy or a girl child.

Hannah and Lydia had watched a man look for the face of a would-be wife in the skin of a sweet-potato. With every disappointment his faith would mount up on desperate wings. The more they believed, the less the magic spoke. Silence was the only gift of their mute oracles. But still they believed, "except for that man and his Bible." Lydia explained to Hannah how one master would close his eyes, open his Bible, and "The Lord spoke to him in the line below his finger."

"You're joking," Hannah had protested.

"Nope," Lydia assured her. "But he gave up smearing his thumb through the Scriptures when he hit upon the verse, 'and there are those which have made themselves eunuchs for the kingdom of heaven's sake.'"

"So he stopped that foolishness!"

"Gospel truth!"

The greater the cackling and the more exaggerated the mirth, the closer they came to comprehending the things they most feared. Without the humor, the dangers would have made cowards of them all.

Hannah let them wipe their faces before she raised the truth beneath the laughter, "Looks like some people think a black man in the Governor's Mansion would be better than a white rebel." Alfred added, "Governor Robert would be a joke worth seeing."

Robert reminded him, "They don't share our humor."

If they were calling for Robert to be the supreme autocrat of South Carolina as a prank, there wasn't much funny in it. They

287

all caught the scent of vengeance in Sedgwick's offer, and they shook their heads in disbelief.

Alfred quieted and caught Hannah's eyes. "A year ago, you were a waitress at the Excelsior Hotel. Now you will be the First Lady of the State." Robert nodded. "When she was waiting tables, we were wharf rats and skiff shovers at fifty cents the day."

"And now we are a power in the land," Alfred snorted.

"Just because some white man says so," Hannah said.

They watched her look around the room as if she were seeing through the walls. Robert and Alfred followed her head as she took in all the world they had together. Alfred knew this house was their haven, but he was always apprehensive that someone would take it away. Robert was ready to hear Hannah pronounce, "This 'Bottom Rail on Top' nonsense has to stop."

When the bottom rail of a split-rail fence moved to the top, everything was turned upside-down. The phrase had bubbled up like swamp gas from the freedmen's colonies, then the newspapers had grabbed it. Some gloried in vengeance; others exalted in joyful retribution. Few could see the consequences.

Robert and Hannah were wise to the temptations of revenge, for they would not hurt anyone who had not harmed them. Hannah's confidence blossomed from her experience, and when she married it to Robert's young belief, they survived. Alone, they wandered through uncertain fogs. Together, they could plot a more noble course.

Alfred accepted their code because he'd seen there was a limit to what any man could steal. He had refused to loot and told Robert, "I won't take anything I can't build, but woe the man who would take it from me." He despised the "Bottom Rail on Top" idea because such a fragile fence was a dangerous ladder.

But principle wasn't enough to live by in this new world. When they were slaves, they only had to listen to commands. Freedom needed the knowledge of people's ways. Alfred grumbled, "You never know what they're going to do."

"But they still do it," Robert said.

"One day they're drooling over you and killing the fatted calf."

"And the week after they wouldn't throw a cracker to a starving man."

"It just don't make no sense, no sense at all."

Understanding the people's motives for bringing Robert's name into their schemes would be the family's life preserver, but the answers were shrouded in unblinking silence. They needed to know why people did what they did, but those who knew the secrets of generosity or contempt were stingy with their knowledge.

"I just can't figure them out," Alfred complained.

"You got company there," Robert said.

"Look at this house."

"What about it?" Robert asked.

"Du Pont gave you the money to buy it, didn't he?"

Hannah rested her chin in her palms, and Alfred felt the withering of her nodding head. "I think I should bring you to accounts, young man," she commanded.

"I'm sorry, Hannah."

"No, I mean you have to know the accounts, the money."

"Half the house money," Robert explained, "was what we saved up to buy Hannah."

"The seller skedaddled and left us holding the bag," Hannah said.

"Du Pont got those Washington people to pay up the money for the boat."

"You got your share and we got ours," Hannah assured Alfred.

"So the house price is Hannah's bride price and our boat prize money," Robert added.

The arithmetic calmed Alfred's worries, but Robert knew he was right. Some things didn't add up. Robert sighed, and Alfred caught the sympathetic wheezing. Robert remembered an old

289

Bible saying from Lydia, "The wind bloweth where it listeth, and thou hearest the sound thereof, but canst not tell when it cometh, and whither it goeth." At least he could still trust that the wind knew what it was doing.

Finding the reasons for Congressman Sedgwick's hare-brained idea was more testing than predicting the weather and the waves. The wind, the water, and the land obeyed laws greater than themselves. You could get an answer, keep it for a rainy day, and know why it was raining. These white people made it all up as they went along. They made the laws, and the laws made them important. Robert and Hannah suspected that was the only reason for making the laws in the first place. Whoever made the law got what they wanted, and those laws made everybody feel like good, law-abiding citizens.

But they had something the law could neither demand nor comprehend. The laws and their makers could rearrange a fence, but they could not make a new person. Robert, Hannah, and Alfred cast aside the "Bottom Rail on Top" because they hated slavery enough to refuse to be the new masters. Theirs was a different revolution, a change of mind and heart which could never be legislated. The passing of the whip from one hand to the other was simply not good enough for them.

"Well, I don't want to be a stick to beat a white man's back," Alfred confessed.

"They could just as easily find another stick for our backs," Robert agreed.

They would not become the lords of fallen masters. If they were free, then all must be free, and that included their former owners. They had often wondered what had happened to Mr. and Mrs. McKee and hoped that they were not suffering too much. If Master Henry knocked at the door of his old house, Robert would have opened his arms as wide as his heart.

"That's so," Hannah said, "and that's why we should forget about this fool's notion. If they remember what they want when they've finished killing each other, we got better things to do."

"That's it," Robert agreed. "We'll just forget the whole thing. If they remember, we'll play too dumb to be trusted with the job."

"I can do that," Alfred bragged.

"You're the smartest dumb ass I know," Robert admitted.

"And that's why I'm still here, Governor."

Their thoughts continued to wander as they pondered. Their new lives demanded that they trust to others, even when they could not understand those people. Robert and Hannah had followed the Reverend French to New York, and he had not disappointed them. But such was not always possible. Robert and Hannah were left to leap into a terrifying uncertainty. They had leapt with Du Pont, and he had returned their faithfulness. They could not do this with everyone. If they did, they would have fallen long ago. Du Pont had been right about the sailors. All of them had kept their word, because they thought before they spoke. But not all white people wore blue, and few black people were asking the same questions. They had to be very careful with people's praise, for it was more dangerous than their condemnation. The faces on today's newspaper would be found in tomorrow's outhouse.

* * * * *

Rhind stomped over the gangplank and ordered Abe, "Cast Off!" Abe hurried to run the plank to the deck and heard Rhind hauling himself up the pilothouse ladder blowing curses like a rusty boiler. Robert was shocked to hear Rhind's demanding tone. "Get Going!"

Robert cast a soothing, "Aye, Aye, Sir."

Rhind had a newspaper tucked under his arm, and he paced behind Robert. Robert nodded assent when Rhind ordered, "Keep to mid-channel." Something had gotten Rhind's dander up, but this was not the time to ask for details. Keeping to mid-channel was as ridiculous a command as "Get the boat in the water," but

Robert let it pass, hoping Rhind's temper would ooze in the deeper water.

The usual morning run from Beaufort to Port Royal was generally a sleepy trip, but Rhind's foul mood seeped through *Planter*'s nooks and crannies. When it became evident that *Keokuk* could not be salvaged, Rhind had been ordered back to *Planter* until his wound healed. Rhind wasn't the jolliest man at the best of times, but he had always been considerate. Robert had noticed a gruff cloud around Rhind. The politeness had worn thin, and now there was little to hold back the aggression that made the man such a successful fighter. Robert had joked that his bad moods were his souvenirs of his trip to Washington, but Rhind's silent stare boded a troubled mind more than a wounded body.

Rhind watched every ship they passed, as Robert kept *Planter* on a straight and even course down the Beaufort River. He was glad to see there was not as much bandage peeping from under Rhind's hat and guessed the wound was healing nicely. There was no pink seeping into the white linen band.

Rhind shook his fist at the window. "God damn them to Hell!" Robert smiled over to him, "What's that, Sir?" Rhind drew the rolled-up newspaper from under his arm and wielded it before Robert's face like a policeman's truncheon. "This!" Rhind's furious fists balled up the newspaper. "This God Damned, no good pack of bullshit wrapped up in a whore's breech-clout." He threw the paper ball to the deck and kicked it at the far wall. "Gimme that wheel," he growled, and Robert stepped back to let Rhind take control of the ship.

Rhind's frustration slithered through the wheel's spokes, and *Planter* pitched to his impatience. Robert waited for the man's temper to cool to a dull rage. He walked over to Rhind's tormentor, picked up the jagged sphere, and unpeeled the pages to see Du Pont's wrinkled face scowling at him. Rhind's eyes turned to the offensive thing Robert held, but his anger softened under Robert's questioning brows. Rhind mouthed the words with studied disgust: "Rear Admiral Du Pont is to be relieved of command of the South Atlantic Blockading Squadron." Robert held his shock behind a silent mask, but Rhind spewed contempt through the words, "Admiral Dahlgren is hereby appointed to command."

Robert had to ask, "What the hell does that mean?" Rhind stretched his back and clutched the wheel handles to restrain his anger.

"It means that Dahlgren has friends in high places and the Admiral has enemies in even higher places."

Robert folded the pages to bring home to Hannah and waited for Rhind to set *Planter* on a more even keel. When the bow wash split evenly along *Planter*'s sides, he asked, "You mean they're going to get rid of the Admiral?"

"That's a nice way to say betrayal."

"But doesn't he go on to another command?"

"There is no other command when you're an Admiral."

"So where will he go?"

"Only place left for him is home."

"I hear that's not so bad."

"It's the way he's being sent home," Rhind explained. "This is the worst disgrace they can do to him."

Rhind swiveled his neck to soothe the tightness in his chest. He clung to the wheel and breathed deeply, but each breath was harder to hold than the last gulp of air. Robert looked at the heaving shoulders and wondered if a man could drown in the open air. If he could get the man to talk, he might find some relief.

"Why would they? And who is they?"

"The Navy," Rhind blurted, "That's who's 'they,' and we are right sick of 'they."

Robert's calm matched Rhind's fury, and he waited patiently for the fit to play itself out. Rhind twisted the wheel, and Robert heard the ropes coil tightly around the drum. Rhind jerked the wheel to the left, and the tension in the tiller ropes swung *Planter* towards a ship moored along the river bank. Rhind heaved his shoulder to the right, and the wheel drum screeched in the grip of the taut cables. *Planter*'s bow rose as she lurched away from the ship. Rhind gasped in shame that he had almost wrecked the boat.

Robert relaxed when his legs felt the rhythmic sway that told him the boat was steady in the water. He saw Rhind's fingers a tanned brown upon the wheel handles, and it was a better sight than the white knuckles at his first grasp. Rhind's shoulders slumped into the helmsman's easy slouch, but his voice blew frustration. "This tub is too slow."

"I know how to cut two hours off the trip."

"Really?"

"Sure."

Rhind chuckled ruefully at their old joke and told Robert, "Well, if you're that 'sure,' you take the wheel." He stepped to the side but was careful to change positions with Robert one hand at a time, to make a smooth transfer. Rhind leaned his forehead upon the wheelhouse window, grateful for the respite. Robert's hands lay light upon the wheel's rim and its spokes. He shrugged at Rhind, and *Planter* swayed in the stream like a carriage horse going home. Rhind queried in mock aggravation, "And just how are you going to save us two hours?"

"Just ahead," Robert said. "There's a creek. I think it belonged to somebody called Archer."

"I don't care if it is the property of Neptune's ass, s'long as we get to the Royal sooner."

"Why the hurry?"

"The captains need a pow-wow. We must work fast." He pointed a disdaining finger at the newspaper. "We have to tell the truth faster than these dogs can spread their lies."

They passed the last moored ships, and Robert commanded into the tube, "Ahead Four." Rhind felt *Planter* slow with the current. *Planter*'s stern swung with the flow, and her bow pointed to a wide gap in the bank. Robert whispered, "Ahead Two," and *Planter* gently pushed aside the rushes drooping into a broad creek. Rhind had always admired Robert's ability to weave through the inland shallows, but this short-cut was special. *Planter* had a foot of freeboard on each side, and Rhind chuckled, "Anybody looking at us from the marshes would think we were walking over the land." His eyes swept the wet ravine to watch the little veins seep swamp water into the creek. "How'd you know about this?"

"Common sense," Robert shrugged.

"It isn't on the charts."

"That's 'cause they don't need charts here. 'Sides, if you have two big rivers, they'll make a creek between 'em."

Rhind's nerves merged with "Ahead Two," and he calmed to the swaying of the swamp grass nodding in their wake. The shortened journey focused his attention. Robert felt the spreading calm and asked, "So what happens when we get to Port Royal?"

"I'll have to track down each of the ironclad captains."

"Wouldn't they be with their ships?"

"That's the problem. Three ships have been ordered to Florida. Two more have been packed off to New Orleans. One ship even got orders for both places at the same time. Nobody knows where anybody is."

"So everybody's scattered?"

"Maybe not yet. We got another order from the President himself, telling everybody to stay put."

"Sounds like a real mess."

"Tell me about it," Rhind grumbled. "This mess is good for some and bad for all."

"So what are you going to do?"

"We must write to the Navy Department, but we must all do it together."

"I guess that's reason enough to hurry."

Robert watched Rhind's chest dance in time with *Planter*'s paddlewheels. Now the man was talking sense, and Robert imagined *Planter* leaving a trail of hurts behind her stern wake, like throwing useless cargo overboard. He was as attentive to

Rhind's complaints as he was careful to avoid scraping the creek banks. Rhind told Robert, "I have to find them before they set out on dispersal orders. Some of them might already be gone, and it will take time to recall them all with the President's order. At least nobody can make a pig's mess out of that."

"When Hannah has this sort of problem, she always makes a list."

"This is not a shopping trip," Rhind joked.

"No, but you could get mighty confused tearing around from boat to shore to boat to ocean."

The plan was seeping through Rhind's mind. Chaos had ridden into his life on his rage, but now he saw the danger in his fury. This battle of words would be no different from a skirmish at sea. They would have to identify the target, maneuver into position, and fire their broadsides together. Hannah's strategy was right, so Rhind would start this fight with a shopping list. "You got some paper?"

"On the chart table," Robert said with a smile.

Rhind looked at *Planter*'s ornate log book. It looked like it should be on a lady's dressing table. He thumbed the first pages and saw the name "Relyea" next to "CSS *Planter*." Now she was the USS *Planter*, and Rhind marveled how much Robert and Hannah and the rest of them had risked to change the "C" to a "U." What courage, and fear, and terrified hope lurked in the exchange of two simple letters of the alphabet. It felt bad to tear a page from the book and ruin the chronicle of their triumph. He found an old bill from some hotel in Charleston and decided to compose his list on its blank back. There was no use ruining the log book just because it was convenient.

He made a column of the ships' titles and scrawled the names of their captains beside each. He started at the bottom with *Keokuk* and his own name because he was the last ship in the line of attack at Charleston. Robert had been steady all the time they were in the harbor. When they broke off the attack, his skill had grounded them where they could be rescued and far enough from shore to evade capture. And so from last to first, from *Keokuk* to *Weehawken,* he dredged from his memory of that terrible day the nine doomed ships and their maligned captains.

They had all known that taking Charleston was impossible, but they all went willingly, knowing they would probably not return. He read down the list and scratched his bandaged head with the pencil stub.

All their lives had hung on Du Pont's pen. On that awful night, he had called all the captains to his flagship and asked for their opinions. Other officers would have ordered, but Du Pont had asked. In the graciousness of his request, they all knew why they we willing to fight again. He had been as willing to listen to them as they were willing to risk their lives. The next morning, he signed orders canceling the attack. Du Pont had the courage to say, "No more!" but his reward was to be branded a coward. Blaming him for failure was as senseless as the plan which could never have succeeded. If for no other reason, they must protest the disgrace of a man so considerate of their lives. Rhind looked again at his list and realized he had reconstructed Du Pont's order of battle. It was somehow fitting.

"Smoke." Robert jolted him from his thoughts. Rhind looked up to see a black cloud to their extreme left. It could be something burning in the marsh, for the trees obscured whatever was burning. Robert watched the smoke form itself into a dark cloud and said, "Ship." If a house were on fire, the smoke would rise in a straight funnel, but a circle of dark cinders could only come from a steam ship. Rhind saw another puff belch over the treetops. The vapor-ball was closer to their center-line, so it had to come from a moving vessel. But which one? Robert assured him, "Smoke that black means an ironclad." Rhind knew he was right. Green wood or the cheapest coal fueled paddle steamers. They spewed plumes of acrid ochre marbled with gray ash. The indigo blotches of coal dust upon the sky could only come from an ironclad. The next cloud was closer still to *Planter*'s bows, so whatever ship it was, it was headed upriver to Port Royal.

Robert spoke "All Stop" into the tube, and *Planter* slid to quiet repose. Rhind and Robert focused ahead to where the creek opened onto the Broad River. More clouds puffed darkly beyond the treeline and soon they saw the ironclad pass in front of them.

"It's *Weehawken*," Rhind sighed.

"She's headed back to Port Royal," Robert assured him. Robert knew the ship had been sent to New Orleans but asked, "Why is she going home?"

Rhind confessed with a happy grin, "Because Rogers is disobeying orders."

"I didn't think that was possible," Robert joked.

"It's impossible for us, but not for you."

"What do you mean?"

"We're Navy. You're contract labor. You can quit any time you want. We can't."

Robert was so glad he had remembered the short-cut through Archer's Creek to the Broad River and Port Royal, for it would also speed his way home to Beaufort, and he was itching to talk to Hannah.

Robert had heard some white people say they "had the wolf by the ears" but hadn't known what they were talking about. Whatever was the wolf, they could not let go of it. If they released their grip, the wolf would turn and eat them. Rhind and the captains were about to take the Navy by the ears. Robert hoped they would not be devoured. He had never seen a wolf, but he knew it was fearsome. Maybe Rhind came from snowy places where they were used to handling such creatures. When he thought of his family's own problems, he could only imagine they were riding the back of a water snake. Like those men with the wolf shaking its fanged snout, Robert, Hannah, Alfred, and all the rest couldn't let go and could not jump off. Wolf or snake, such beasts would turn on you and either tear you to pieces or drown you in their coils. You had to keep going and keep holding on.

Rhind had cleared a way for Robert's understanding. The man's rage fed Robert's determination just as Alfred's jokes charmed his fear. He could be angry without being stupid, and he could laugh and still be smart. Rhind's sharing of his own hates and hurts soothed Robert's own fears. Rhind's confessions had revealed something hidden beneath the curses. He had given Robert the most obvious secret, the clearest truth: a sailor was the Navy's slave. Hannah would surely appreciate such a wide-souled man.

Chapter 23

Door

Davey limped along Bay Street. The rest of the shore squad shunned their Silent Jonah, for he would not join in their pleasures. They were content to lounge against the row of brick walls and let him wander away.

When *Keokuk* finally sank, the healthy were sent to salvage her guns, and the wounded were shipped to the Sanitary Commission. When the sea refused to give up the treasure, the Navy scattered the crew among the surviving ironclads. The nurses did what little they could for the maimed in mind and body flooding the hospital sheds. A surgeon had dressed Davey's leg, perplexed by the strange holes. He visited his gruff patient because the lines of regular punctures had captured his curiosity. When the sailor refused to enlighten him, he shrugged off the oddity with a contemptuous, "just another malingerer." Infection set in, and Davey raved for a week. He was ordered to "lie in your hammock until the scabs fall off." The powders lulled him into a swaying torpor. Two weeks of horizontal rocking cured Davey of the fevers, and for two months he feigned just enough health to be assigned "light duties."

Guarding supply wagons plodding through their rounds of the warehouses, wharves, and depots of Beaufort was not demanding. He was supposed to protect the cargo from pilfering stevedores and the other guards, but his duties gave him much needed knowledge of streets and alleys. It was accepted that a few pounds of coffee would be liberated in transit, but the line was drawn at victuals and anything that would explode.

The anonymity of the town was no comfort. Onboard ship everybody knew him; ashore he knew nobody. He slowed his feet, trying to remember which house was the Smalls' refuge, but the hustling mobs of black and blue spilling in and out of the buildings and flowing along Bay Street confused him. He saw the door and raised himself to peer over the window. The hall was full of sailors on shore leave. There must have been two hundred men fisting expensive tots in tin can tumblers and waiting their turn for twenty women. The Smalls would never be in such a place.

Davey wove his way through the throng of the drunk and the desperate, pushing away the offered cups and enticing arms. The crowds frightened him, so he hid from their reckless joy in a doorway and turned his back upon the fumes of counterfeit revelry. He stood waiting for the squad to leave with their loads and longed for strong coffee, black and sweet, but he dare not show his face until the evening. When the wagon creaked away on swaying wheels, Davey walked into the street and away from his former haven.

He merged with a band of straggling sailors returning to the docks. He followed them along the quay until he saw the smokestack against the sunset and veered to the bollard by the dockside. He rested his foot on the stern rope, and it felt too taut for the tide. A tight rope on an ebbing tide would leave *Planter* hanging askew on her moorings. His foot twanged the rope. A scowling face popped up over the woodpile, but soon the lips spread into a welcoming smile. "You best give her some slack," Davey jibed, and Abe laughed back, "My, Oh My. Look what the water coughed up. Jump over."

Davey threw his best foot forward to the deck edge, thrust his arm to the rail, and dragged himself on board. Abe pumped his arm and made a show of examining Davey from head to foot. "We went looking for you, but you were nowhere to be found."

"They had me on the quarantine ship."

"They wouldn't tell us where they hid you."

"Glad to know you tried."

"It was a real Hide'n Seek. Bamboozled even Captain Rhind."

Davey was eager for news and Abe's chatter calmed his nerves.

"I heard he got it in the head," Davey said.

"Along the side," and Abe drew his thumb along the hairline over his ear. "But he's OK now," and added, "as well as he ever was."

Abe saw Davey scanning the deck and looking up to the wheelhouse. "Where's Robert?" Davey asked.

"Oh, he's ashore."

"You guys all by your lonesome?"

"I mess down with William on the saloon deck. We get extra for night guard duty."

"That's a good berth. Plenty of pay for nothing to do."

Abe rejoiced that Davey could come 'visitin, but the visit befuddled him. Davey was a "good'un," but right now he looked the proverbial fish out of water, so Abe had to ask, "So how come you here?"

"Shore leave."

"Oh," was all Abe could say, but he kept the lid on his suspicion. "You are such a joker."

"How so?"

"You coming back to a boat when you just left one." Abe heard the anxiety rustling under Davey's talk about Hannah and Robert.

"I been all over the place and couldn't find them."

"They got their own house now," Abe said.

"Where might that be?"

"I'll take you there."

Abe jumped to the dock and wondered why Davey was holding back. When he saw how carefully Davey followed, he noticed the limping. "You gettin better, but not yet best."

"Yeah."

Davey did not go into detail, for Abe would not have believed him. He could hardly believe it himself. The rows of slowly vanishing scabs were the only proof, but soon even those would heal, leaving no testimony to the fishy miracle. There would be just two rows of depressions in his flesh, but the memory was enough for him.

Davey strained to keep up, but when the pain winced up to his face, Abe slowed the pace. The throbbing spiraled up his thigh, and he had to rest by a white fence. Abe assured him, "Take your time. They won't be out."

"Who's they?"

"The whole tribe."

When Davey's breath returned, he looked around at reminders of his shopping trip with Hannah. The houses became familiar when he saw leaves fluttering through a hole in a roof over a porch. The last time he saw this, he jested that he would need only twenty nails. Now he would need a hundred. Such neglect would creep into even the best wood and rot it.

"We're here," Abe announced and halted them before a two-story house set back from the street. He remembered the gap in the hedge, but then he had kept to the back yard. Approaching from the street made the house unfamiliar. The front gate was missing, and the steps up to the porch were crumbling brick, but the place was solid, if a bit beat up.

Abe pushed open the door with his shoulder, and Davey winced at the shrieking semicircle it gouged into the floor. The house was dark, but he could just make out a staircase leading to an upper floor. He squinted at a candle flame walking down the hall to him and smiled to hear the throaty voice complaining, "How many times do I have to tell you to pick up that door when you open it? You want to dig a hole right through to the cellar? What you got?"

"Is that you, Miss Lydia?" Davey asked.

"Who else would it be," and she raised the candle close to Davey's face. "My, my. Look what the fair wind blew in."

"All the fairer for seeing you."

"You look hungry," and she turned to lead him to the back of the house.

He remembered the back porch and yard, but the summer house was now working, and Lydia bustled him into a makeshift galley. She blew the embers over a fire and threw a skillet onto the pyre. She glanced at the hunger in Davey's eyes, hinting at something her handful of eggs could not satisfy. "Fatback eggs fill that hole?" she proclaimed, and his eyes moistened at the kindness.

She set a bowl before him and poured sizzling fat and fried eggs over clumps of soda bread. He pulled a spoon out of his jumper, and it really was a very pretty dish to set before a starving sailor. She watched him eat and sensed there was something wrong. She couldn't help him because she didn't know his troubles, but they could wait. Trouble was always better on a full belly.

"You here for long?"

"I'm on shore leave."

"Hannah will be home soon, and Robert's doing some sort of merry-go-round with the big sailor men."

Lydia brought him a blanket and wiggled off his shoes. Davey wrapped his head in his arms and sank to rest. She looked down at the boy and felt his exhaustion seep into the floor.

She heard the door screech and ran on quiet bare feet to shush Hannah. Hannah saw the bundle on the summerhouse floor and shook her head to hear Lydia say, "Looks like we got ourselves a runaway."

The morning brought the waking bustle of chiding children and Lydia ordering the men to "get good and gone." Davey opened his eyes to see Robert smiling down at him, "Up and at'em, Sleepy Head." Davey burst from his wooly cocoon and grasped Robert's hand, almost spilling the coffee Robert was offering with the other hand.

Lydia shooed them out of her way, so Robert took Davey aside to gently pry from him what was going on. Davey gave his excuse of shore leave and not really knowing what to do with himself because he knew nobody in Beaufort and didn't want to waste himself on the drink and the stinkies, so he just thought he'd look up old friends and see what they were up to, and didn't Miss Lydia make a fine breakfast and all. Robert would not interrupt this string of waffling hogwash because he knew Davey was "not very good in the lying way." Robert searched for an excuse to keep the boy in the house. "That front door could use some attention," Robert said as he led Davey down the corridor.

Davey swung the door open. "The hinges are good." He knocked his knuckles along the door from top to bottom and side-to-side. "Wood's sound too, for now."

"What does that mean?" Robert queried.

"It has to come off to be scraped to bare. It should hang straight, so it won't ruin the floor every time it's opened."

"Can you do that?"

"Sure. Better than new. But I don't have tools."

"I guess you left them on the ship," Robert shot from under a cocked brow.

The worry creeping out from beneath Davey's eyelids told the whole story. The details could wait. "I think I saw a screwdriver and a hammer out back," Robert said.

Davey followed him out the door to the side porch and down the steps across the yard to an old shed on brick blocks divided into two rooms. The shed was piled with bits of broken furniture, old ropes, a child's sleigh, and odds'n ends Davey couldn't recognize. Why anybody would have a sleigh in Beaufort was a mystery for they had snow twice in a lifetime. Then again, the Smalls' whole set-up was a mystery, so Davey decided to glide along with whatever was going to happen. He didn't have much say in it anyway. They agreed that the house now had a carpenter. Robert thought, "That makes a start."

Later in the morning, Lydia walked up the path with her maybe to a hole in the front of the house where the door should be. "Guess it went for a ramble," she mused, and heard a distant drum-roll tapping in the yard. She leaned over the porch railing, and Davey looked up from his labors with his hammer poised over a hinge. The door was in pieces, and L'il Robert was playing "Peek-a-Boo" behind long planks leaning against the walls.

"You got to work early," Lydia complimented.

"You make a breakfast fit to send a man to work."

He looked happy as a boy at the beach, and Lydia remembered him fussing over them at Bay Street. He had exchanged his pistol for a hammer, and he was no less welcome for the trade. She could smell his pleasure in the wood shavings crunching under her feet and in the sawdust wafting in the air between them. Lydia heard L'il Robert's squeals escape from his lean-to and called him over. "Come here, child. Help our Big Boy work." L'il Robert defiantly squatted in the dirt to search for nails, but Lydia knew Davey would let no harm come to his little assistant.

"What's this?" L'il Robert demanded.

"That's a muntin."

"Muttin what?"

Davey picked up a thin, six-foot long stretch of grooved wood. "It's the middle of the door." He grabbed up a shorter plank and held it across the muntin, "This is the rail, and when you put it all together, they make a door."

"What bad?" the boy demanded.

"It got wet and all bent out of shape."'

Lydia thought it strange that Davey was talking about pieces of wood as if they made up a spoilt child, but the man certainly looked like he knew what he was doing. L'il Robert lost interest and wandered back inside for a feeding. She stepped closer and ran her fingers along the wood Davey held. "So this thing is really the door." She looked at the pieces against the wall, and Davey explained, "First you put it between the top and bottom rails, and then you put in the side rails." Lydia watched the boy's pride blossom with his lecture. "So, you gotta build a door from the inside out." Davey beamed pride, "Start with the muntin and finish with the lock."

306

She knew Davey was hiding something, but she was patient to winkle out what he was really up to. She picked up his knife and turned its edge to the sun to let it gleam. The edge was silvered sharper than a scalpel, and Davey could slice through heart pine with a gentle nudge of his thumb.

"How did you get this so sharp?"

"Spit and stone."

She stayed to watch Davey work, so she could study his face. When he inspected the different pieces, his artistry emerged. The glass had long given place to crudely nailed boards, but the outline of their recesses intrigued him. The door panels were evenly spaced to hold two columns of six small windows.

He had seen such doors before. The windows were placed to form a glowing cross when the lights shone in the house. "A cross-window door," he told her, "is for churches or pastor's houses and such-like religious people." For a moment he thought the door might have been from a poor house or an orphanage, so he ran his thumb along the central shaft of the door frame. The carpenter had purposely composed this door with three deliberate rows of two squares of glass. He tried to figure out what it meant and imagined the door with light glowing through frosted glass. This was not a cross. Then he saw that the lateral joists were exceptionally thin. He tapped them with a curious knuckle and leaned an ear to catch the echo. The wood was solid and hard, so this was integral to the door and not something added later. He stepped back, and his imagination saw three open books one above the other in the design of the doorway. In the door he saw that he could not stay here forever. The books were open, so he had to open himself to something new. It was just like Johnny reading from the story-books; he always stopped just when you wanted more.

"This is a very fine house. Solid," he said, hoping for more.

Lydia saw he was about to bust a gut with curiosity, so she told him, "Robert is the master of this house."

"I don't mean you're just staying for a while."

"Neither do I," she said. "He owns the house."

"How is that even possible?"

"Money."

"Just money?"

"And a whole lot'a luck."

"How can a slave own a house?" Davey asked, as embarrassed by his question as he was anxious for her answer.

"We ain't slave no more, so we can own whatever we can buy."

"But how could you buy this place?"

She smiled long and slow to make Davey even more attentive. "Seems the previous owner didn't pay his taxes."

"So."

"He went off in the great skedaddle and abandoned his property, the house and me."

"You and the house?"

"Yup. And the summer house and the trees. Hannah even showed me listed in the deed to the property."

"But how did it happen?"

"Well, seems if you abandon your property to fight against the government, you still have to pay taxes. The old master didn't pay the taxes, so the government sold off his house."

"And Robert had the money to pay the taxes?"

"That's it. He cleared the account with the money he'd saved to buy Hannah. Since he stole Hannah along with himself, he had the cash left over, so he got his house, his wife, and his mother."

"His mother?"

"That's right. Robert is my son."

The next morning, Robert returned from a night trip to see Davey stoking his mouth with oatmeal for the day's work. "Boy's a mite hungry," Lydia explained, and Robert smiled at their new house guest. Davey nodded and tried to get Robert's name over the oat lumps blocking his mouth. They giggled, and Robert waited calmly to find out more. He could ask Lydia, but her ostentatious preoccupation with her housework told him, "You find out for yourself."

Robert sauntered up to Davey and said, "Boy, you sure are hungry."

"Nothing Miss Lydia can't take care of."

"She sure knows how to fill a man."

"Nice place you got here."

Robert turned to Davey, "You sure know what you're doing with the timber."

"I supposed it's a gift. My daddy was a carpenter, and he made me work the wood before I could walk."

"Guess you don't have to do much walking in this trade?"

"Nor in the sailor's line."

"So how come you walked over here?" Robert edged to the point.

"I couldn't figure anywhere else to go," Davey confessed.

Robert wanted to cuddle the boy, for the man was struggling with his own soul. He knew there were times when you should leave well enough alone, but this was not one of them.

"I thought you were on the sanitary boat, getting better."

"I am, but it's too close to be better."

"Then what?"

"They're sending us all back to the tincans."

"All?"

"The blind can go home. Some think they're the lucky ones."

The edge to Davey's tongue told Robert that Davey envied the dead. They all knew what ironclad work was and how little chance they had of survival. He would stand beside Davey as much as he could, but he would not stand behind him pushing the man to a place he did not wish to go.

Davey was wrestling with his own limits. Robert waited for the man to make up his mind.

"I just can't take it any more," Davey admitted.

Robert thrust a firm hand on Davey's shoulder to calm his shivering fears. "That's good enough for me." Davey stood rooted to Robert's eyes. But this wasn't enough for the man, so Robert forced himself to say what neither dared to speak. "Everybody has his limit. This is your edge, but I will not condemn you for it, and neither should you."

As the sun slumped behind the trees, Davey reassembled the door and laid it over two boxes. He had found a piece of cut glass and used the straight edge to remove decades of paint. Robert left the expert to his labors so he could talk over the problem with Hannah and Lydia.

Hannah was confused about why he had come to them and a little irked that he had brought his problems to their home. "We don't want them nosing around here."

Lydia laughed, "As if we have anything to hide. Why, the place is picked clean as a Gospel Bird." Their talk danced the "maybes" and the "what ifs" and the "I don't knows" around Davey, but they could not tease a solution out of the tangle. Clearly, "the boy should not be here." It was equally obvious that, "we've got to get him back before they know he's gone."

Robert saw that the problem was bigger than their knowledge, "We have to find someone who knows about these things."

"If you don't soon find the right someone, that boy will pay for our ignorance," Hannah pronounced. She was right. Davey's presence was a problem they could not solve because they had never known of a sailor hiding out in a Navy town. They were ignorant of the regulations which would decide Davey's fate and knew not what to expect from the service. Hannah came up with the string of an answer. "What about Johnny?"

"What about him?"

"He can help us," Hannah said.

"Why Johnny?"

"He's our only other sailor friend," Hannah said. "He will know what to do. This can't be the first time a sailor went on the loose. It's just our first time keeping one."

Hannah, Lydia, and Robert stood pondering with their hands upon the hips and a thoughtful rubbing of chins. Hannah said, "A thread can pull a ribbon." Lydia teased their thoughts through the maze of their problem, "And a ribbon can pull a string." Robert chimed in, "A string can pull a rope," and Lydia finished their poem. "And a rope can pull a wagon." Robert capped the sequence: "Or a boat."

Hannah and Lydia looked to Robert, and he had to tell them clearly, "I'll find Johnny."

Today was all they could offer Davey. Tomorrow was another day and they would think about Davey's problem and figure some way out of it. After all, people said they were heroes because they had figured a way out when nobody else could think of a way in.

Chapter 24

"Hic Sunt Dracones"

Nichols knew what he had to do. The duty did not involve molly-coddling Johnny Webb. The boy's face was like grimy stone that perfectly matched Nichols' scowl. They stood on the mail boat deck, and Johnny wondered if he had made the right decision. Trusting Nichols might end with Davey's neck stretched from a yardarm.

It took Robert almost a week to find Johnny and ten minutes to tell him Davey's troubles. Johnny explained the "grace week," but Robert was in the dark. "If you jump ship for less than a week, you're Absent Without Leave and you get punishment on the boat. But if you're away for more than a week, you're a Deserter, and they hang you." If they could smuggle Davey back aboard quietly, there was a slim chance he would get three months' hard duty. They had to find an officer who would "make it all good," but time was running out. "What about Rhind?" Robert suggested.

"Could work," Johnny mused with much scratching of his hair beneath his hatband.

Robert recalled the attack on Sumter. "He wouldn't have a head to wear that bandage, if you hadn't tackled us." They agreed that Rhind could be trusted, but when they went looking for him, Rhind was nowhere to be found. The Navy had swallowed him into reassignment. They could not go to Du Pont, for he had enough troubles of his own.

They had to find an officer who shared Rhind's hard head and soft heart, so they set out to pump sailors about their commanders. Robert so wanted to help Johnny find someone who could help Davey, but he knew that asking questions would give away the game. Hannah and Robert had learned early that white people were very poor judges of their masters. Robert reasoned aloud, "Let the sailors complain." Johnny dismissed the suggestion. "We'll just get messdeck grumbling." Robert assured him, "But we'll also find out about their captains."

Johnny grinned at the ploy and set a course for all the sutlers' dives of Beaufort to collect as much scuttlebutt as he could muster. He quickly learned that finding an officer he could trust was like searching a whole ocean for a single ship. Nobody had anything good to say about their captains. The sailors' opinions taught him to curse in three languages, but he had not figured out where to go with Davey's tale. One pair of captains gave him some hope, but they were just sentimental, and he told himself, "That type would weep at your funeral."

Then he remembered how Nichols had made the replacements hold on to that steaming gun barrel. When Postlethwaite had slipped off the ratline, Nichols stayed with the boy while the surgeon took off the foot. Officers had better things to do than hold a sailor's hand. Nichols had then transferred Postlethwaite to a hospital. Johnny figured that Nichols was the best hope they could find.

Onward had been ordered to Port Royal for the change of command, so Johnny wormed his way on board and asked for a "private word with the Captain." Nichols had nodded and listened.

Nichols called Murphy to the quarterdeck and commanded, "Half crew on shore liberty." Johnny heard the surprise in Murphy's voice with the perfunctory "Aye Aye, Sir," and Nichols walked to his cabin. He left Johnny waiting at the gangplank, stranded by his own words. He had just told a superior officer of a desertion and asked that officer to help the deserter. He must be crazy. It could go either way. Determined boots thumped along the deck, and Johnny looked up to see Nichols striding towards him and folding a fistful of papers into his jacket pocket. "Where is he?" Nichols growled, and Johnny was struck dumb. "Are you deaf or just wasting my time?"

Johnny launched his trust with the single word, "Beaufort."

Nichols nodded to the gangplank and commanded, "Lead the way."

Johnny followed him along the line of tethered ships until they found the *Cicero* ready for the afternoon run to Beaufort. The Midshipman in charge was chuffed to hear a captain politely ask, "May we come aboard, Sir?" That "Sir" bought more goodwill than a peremptory order, so *Cicero*'s only officer was "happy to oblige, Sir." Nichols and Johnny hopped from the dock to the deck, and the little boat tugged at her moorings like a donkey jerked from a pleasant slumber. The bows forward of the wheel left just enough room to lean against the rails. Johnny judged *Cicero* a steam-powered skiff. Nichols looked over this water taxi, and it reminded him of "a cracker box with a tin-whistle and an egg-beater hanging out of its ass." The Midshipman offered coffee to the only two passengers who had ever asked for passage and advised, "Gets a mite chilly when we round the peninsula." The single sailor who comprised *Cicero*'s crew fired the boiler, yanked the mooring line like a cowboy untying a steer, and shoved the boat into the stream with one push of his foot.

Johnny stuck close, eager for any hint revealing what Nichols would do when they arrived in Beaufort. The only ray of hope was when Johnny had asked if he should draw a sidearm from the Master-at-Arms, and Nichols grunted, "Not necessary." Nichols quizzed Johnny about the rescue of *Keokuk*. Johnny saw he was more interested in the crew than the floundering ship, so it was a relief to give a candid answer.

"I couldn't see anything from the gun post, but when we got on deck, we had to crawl to the side on all fours."

Nichols nodded, "I suppose nobody could stand at Abandon Ship stations."

"I got forward to fire the flares."

"We saw those and launched the boats."

"And none too soon," Johnny said with a sigh.

314

Nichols caught Johnny's relief and shared, "We picked up thirty-six from the water." The rest had straggled up the ladders to collapse on *Onward*'s deck, looking like bloated cod sliding over a fishmonger's tray. "You took to the oars as soon as they plucked you," Nichols recalled. "I didn't see Collins in the water."

"He was on a sandbar. We took him up last 'cause we didn't see him behind the wreck."

"I heard he had an adventure between the stern and the sandbar."

Johnny was surprised Nichols knew so much and said, "Yeah. I couldn't believe it when he told me."

"What convinced you he wasn't lying?"

"The holes in his leg. They were tooth bites."

"Some would call that providential," Nichols suggested, but he assured Johnny, "I'd call it luck."

Port Royal to Beaufort was a mere eight-mile trip as the crow flies, but the men joked, "any crow flying over the islands would have to carry his lunch in his beak." When Du Pont captured the sound, he had given the Union its first victory at sea and its only deep-water port. Nichols understood the strategic reasons for its capture, but he could not comprehend why the rebels would "risk life, fortune, and sacred honor" for such a string of stagnant swamps. Port Royal had grown into a repair depot and coaling station simply because the river could float the largest ships. A fifteen-mile jaunt down the Broad River, around Parris Island, and up the Beaufort River was shorter and safer than slogging through the snake-infested marshes. The sailors had christened Beaufort "the Shit-Hole Capital of the Glorious South."

Cicero approached a wide stream on the left, and Nichols inclined his head to Johnny. The boy's face flushed with some unspoken pleasure. He had read enough of Webb's letters home to his mother to judge the man's character, so Nichols ruled out reveries of grog-shop brawls over howling stinkies. Nichols said, "You seem to be enjoying the trip."

"Yeah. I like to look at the colors."

"Colors?"

"Yeah. The water changes colors."

Nichols looked over the side to see the turquoise fluid wrapping itself around *Cicero*. Nichols savored the water's magic. He was glad to see that, even though Webb was so young, the boy was already acquiring the mariner's delight in the element they both served and feared. "What do you like about it?" Nichols prodded.

Johnny hesitated just long enough to cast aside his fear of looking stupid. "There are so many different colors."

"You mean like over there?" and Nichols finger shot to the shore line.

"Yeah. The water is coming out of that stream sort of pinky-beige."

"That's low tide run-off. When the tide goes out, it sucks the loose earth out of that runny. In a few years, there will be a wide channel between the two islands."

"So that's why the colors," Johnny said.

"The tides sluice out the sand, and it combines with the red oxide. Like brick dust and old mortar on land. The water takes on the colors of the earth."

"It's still pretty."

Nichols smiled to hear his science wrapped up in simple pleasure and decided to drift with Webb's curiosity. "I saw an old map of this area," he shared. Nichols remained silent, and Johnny waited through the pause. "Somebody wrote 'Uncertain Ground' on the old chart," Nichols said, "in the shallows around Hilton Head and St. Helena Island."

Johnny caught the hint below the statement. "I've been told old map makers just put in something about sea monsters, when they didn't have a clue what was really there." Nichols grinned and added, "That's right. They used to fill the empty spaces with guesses and the warning, "Hic Sunt Dracones." Johnny's

316

eyebrows rose to wonder if Nichols' had the hiccups, until Nichols explained, "Here lie dragons."

Even though it was twenty years ago, Nichols could still feel the sharp rap over his knuckles for translating the Latin as "Here lie dragons," and his nose recalled the man's breath reeking of spirits no less ardent than his rage and railing, "Monsters, you fool, not dragons." The shame had stung deeper than Master Grubbins' cane, and his revenge had ended his days at school.

* * * * *

Young Nichols had rummaged in the few shelves the school called the Library and found a book with illustrations of monsters. He opened Sir John Mandeville's *Travels* to strange lands with stranger people. Nichols eyes lingered over their bizarre and outlandish bodies. He took the book to the schoolroom and knew what it would cost, but he was willing to pay the price. Grubbins was making the students translate, which meant they would pretend to read, while he snoozed at his desk.

Nichols had said in a loud whisper, "It's not a monster."

Grubbins spluttered himself awake to demand, "What's that?"

Nichols held the book open, displaying the page of pictures to the class. "It's a skiapod. A man with one leg and one foot." The boys' giggles rippled through their recognition of their teacher's gimpy leg. Grubbins' raised arm silenced their derisive howls, and Nichols pointed to another picture, "And here's a cyclops. It has one eye in the center of his forehead." Grubbins raised himself from the chair, the legs squeaking behind his shivering frame. "But the best of the lot is the blemmyes," Nichols continued, "And it's a woman." The picture fanned Grubbins's ire, and his arm lunged for the cane, but the threat only goaded Nichols to more defiance. "See. She has no thing."

Grubbins shuffled towards Nichols, waving the cane over his head. Nichols stood his ground, pointed to the open page, and yelled, "She's got her mouth at her stomach!" Grubbins' purple nose wheezed fury, but Nichols proclaimed, "Her nose is in the middle of her chest." The boys whooped, and Nichols stepped back two paces. He arched back, and Grubbins' cane whistled past Nichols' face. "Her eyes are up at her shoulders," Nichols yelled, and laughter exploded through the school room.

Grubbins lurched into his attack. Nichols jumped up on a desk and launched himself past the infuriated master. "It's surely a woman." Grubbins stomped back down the aisle between the desks, slashing from side to side, but Nichols dodged every swipe with a deft leap to the next desk. Nichols' defiance fired his voice as he yelled to his howling classmates, "She's got no tally-wacker." Grubbins's fury rose with his arm. "She's got huge tits dangling on each side of her nose." Grubbins kept hobbling after him, but Nichols kept jumping and screaming "Tit Face!" Nichols' foot slipped and he sprawled under Grubbins's blows, but he could not stop laughing. The phlegm spluttered from Gibbons's nose and mouth. Nichols wondered if he took just a few more strokes, Grubbins would fall dead. But he didn't.

Grubbins punched with his left hand, and Nichols parried the cane thrusts with the book. Grubbins' blood was up, and the class taunted his prey. Grubbins' arm sliced to Nichols' head, but Nichols closed the book over the quivering cane and would not let go. Master and boy played tug-o-war until Nichols pulled the stick from Grubbins' grasp.

Grubbins doubled over, his nose bleeding onto the chair he clutched. Nichols raised his leg and thrust his most vicious kick into Grubbins' thigh. The man spun on one shaking leg and collapsed to the floor, his head recoiling off the side of a desk. Nichols stood looking down at the pool of blood spreading from behind Grubbins' head, and silence roared through the room.

Other boys ministered to their fallen tyrant and cast accusing scowls at Nichols, but he hoped Grubbins would die. He turned and walked out of the classroom. When his parents came to collect him, they spoke not a word. His father honored an exorbitant bill and simply said, to his son, "Cheap at twice the cost." A month later, Nichols boarded the strange world of USS *Constitution*, offering a letter from his Congressman recommending that the captain accept "the bearer as Midshipman, Unpassed."

*　*　*　*　*

Nichols threw back his head and shouted "Ha!" into the Atlantic dusk. The laughter quivered from his head to his hand grasping *Cicero*'s bowrail. Johnny cringed at his Commander's unnerving hilarity. Nichols waggled his jaw and chortled to remember the boy laughing at the picture of a woman with no head, happily walking long-forgotten woods. But now the man was caught between the women at *Onward*'s bow and stern, and her figurehead was no less buxom than the headless woman quietly smiling out of her stomach.

Cicero churned down the Broad River, and the deeper water raised Nichols' spirits. His mind glared at the problem before him. They would have taken the short-cut through Archer's Creek and steamed straight across the peninsula, but this boy was not so experienced. Rounding the point would add two more hours to the trip and give Nichols time to grapple with what he had to do.

Johnny looked over the side at the brown wash leaving them. After serving on *Onward*, *Keokuk*, and *Planter*, this boat was like being caged in a baby's carriage. "Feels kinda funny," he grumbled, and Nichols responded, "What does?"

"This fifty-foot tub," Johnny said. "It's a mite tight." Nichols smiled to think of a ship like new shoes pinching your toes.

"As long as it gets us there, it may as well be a Class I frigate."

Johnny knew Nichols was a strange man, but his gruffness couldn't quite hide his kindness. *Onward* had taught Johnny and Davey never to get on his bad side. He would have his reasons for discipline, but you would only discover them after serving your punishment. He didn't need a whipping boy.

Cicero pushed herself into the open ocean at the tip of Parris Island and turned into the evening gloom flooding the Beaufort River. The tide pushed them forward over the sandbars, but Nichols and Johnny felt the keel juddering beneath their feet, like sliding over a washboard. He noticed Johnny grimace and said, "A few groundings and that boy will learn to ride the tides." Johnny nodded agreement and keenly felt the acceptance of Nichols sharing the obvious with an Able Seaman.

More ships crowded the river bank, so they knew Beaufort was not far ahead. *Cicero* wended her way down the tunnel of masts, and Johnny remembered a summer walk down an avenue of trees with their branches meeting over his head. Fires flared from the forges of repair shops carved into old hulks, and Nichols' eyes followed the red threads shooting over the water. They passed the *Powhatan* and watched mechanics noisily winch a boiler through her forward hatch. "That's the picture they should put in the papers," Nichols scoffed. "Have you read the newspapers?" he asked casually but was curious for Johnny's opinions of the "Scandal of the Seas."

"Yes. It's all bullshit."

"That's what sells newspapers," Nichols said. "Are the men in agreement with you?"

"Nothing worse than squabbling over prize money," Johnny exclaimed, with an angry edge that caught Nichols' attention.

The Baltimore Sun tempted its readers with the promise of an "astounding exposé" and then published the amounts of "public money paid for capture of the prizes." The figures paid to Du Pont and the other senior officers were almost accurate, but their investigation into the "blockade business" was a web of malicious messdeck gossip proven by the "opinions of experts." The only facts were a list of captured ships, but the reporters claimed the Navy was letting ships through the blockade so they could be captured with more profitable cargoes running out of Charleston. The accusation could not be disproved because the Navy would not release the accounts of the prize courts.

Common sense said it didn't matter if the cotton caught going out could not be used to pay for the weapons running in. Every ship captured drained the enemy of the ability to kill the readers' husbands, sons, and fathers. But nobody was listening. The public was outraged that "Du Pont and his like are risking the lives of our loyal loved ones to make money for themselves, when they should be making war on the rebellion." The dollar signs shouted louder than the casualty lists, and the other papers joined the "crusade against corruption on the high seas."

"Do you think he's been cooking the books?" Johnny asked.

"Du Pont? Never."

Nichols explained that the reporters "praised the sailors' danger and the toil, but there wasn't a lick of justice in the whole mess." Nichols had read with glowing indignation how Du Pont was portrayed as both vicious and barbarous, a pirate hiding beneath the Constitution. The reports gutted his reputation of any element of virtue, claiming he fought for selfish ends instead of for the common good. They were revolting to all Nichols' finer feelings, but he was powerless to right this wrong. He knew justice could never bloom in such a garden of lies.

"What do you think, Sir?"

"I think we would not be here today, if Du Pont had ordered us back into Charleston."

"That's what we all think."

None could deny they all owed their lives to Du Pont's decision not to renew the attack. The politicians and the papers screamed "treason," but every man in the ironclad squadron knew what the decision had given them and what it had cost Du Pont. Nichols gazed straight into the sunset and said, "When I was a kid we had to learn something by heart. 'Courage is the virtue which champions the cause of right.' We can't fight for Du Pont, when everybody thinks he is in the wrong. That's the real poison in the broth."

"What's going to happen to him?" Johnny asked.

"Tomorrow he's finished," Nichols sighed.

"Can't Washington help him?"

Nichols laughed out loud, "No use complaining to a hen-house full of foxes that you have no chicken."

"It just isn't right," Johnny complained.

"How can it be right when we have more laws than justice, mainly because we have more lawyers and crooks than honest men?"

Johnny's head swiveled from bank to bank, his eyes jumping from ship to ship. They were sailing down a corridor of the most advanced fighting ships the world had ever seen. "You'd think we could do better now that we have such machines," Johnny complained.

Nichols assured him, "Arms are of little value without wise counsel at home."

The Midshipman tooted *Cicero*'s little whistle and bumped the hull to the dockside at Beaufort. Nichols jumped over the gunnel and onto the dock, and he hoped the pain shooting through his knee was the discomfort of the journey and not old age. Johnny seemed to know where he was going, so Nichols followed him through the maze of discarded bricks and blowing sand that was the town. The crowds thinned when they strolled down an alley separating white frame houses. Johnny slowed before a house on a slight rise and said, "Here it is."

Nichols took the lead down the path and up the stairs to a newly repaired door with frosted glass windows. He knocked, and soon the swelling glow of a candle filled one of the glass panes. The door opened. Nichols looked into Robert's eyes and asked, "May we come in, Robert?" Robert stood aside, and Hannah faced Nichols and Johnny as she had more than a year ago on *Planter*'s deck.

"Well, Sir, not so much water between us this time," she said. Nichols's eyes blinked slow recognition, but little friendliness. They brought him into the front parlor and offered him the only seat in the room. Nichols cast his glance over a church pew rubbed smooth by generations of congregants, and he shook his head to decline their invitation to sit. "I hear you are harboring a deserter," he said, and then commanded, "Bring him here."

Robert's footsteps shuffled out of the parlor and down a corridor. Hannah was left to the terror of waiting. Nichols watched her nostrils flare and moist beads collect on the sides of her nose. He could not relieve her, so he tried small talk, "That's a fine door you have."

"Davey fixed it," she whispered through pursed lips.

Nichols assured her, "He was always an excellent craftsman."

She cringed to think this man held Davey's life by a thread and he was talking about some stupid door. The fury rose in her throat and strangled her outrage. Nichols caught the hurt in her eyes, and they suffered silently through the eternal minutes until they heard two pairs of feet in the hall. Johnny sidled over to the door and nodded to Davey as Robert led him into the room. They stood frozen.

"Carpenter's Mate Collins," Nichols intoned.

Davey held his jaw rigid, "Yes, Sir." Nichols' hand rummaged in his coat pocket, and he pulled out a folded sheet of paper.

"I have a duty for you, sailor."

Their eyes were glued to the copperplate handwriting signaling Davey's doom.

"This is your Order of Transfer to New York."

"Transfer?"

"Despite you self-assigned shore duties, you are still on *Onward*'s crew list."

"I don't understand."

"It is simple." Nichols explained. "This order authorizes your transfer to the Navy Yard. You will go to New York."

"Is this real?"

"Look at the signature."

Hannah thrust her face at the paper, quick to stall Davey's illiterate shame. "Du Pont," she said.

"Tomorrow, you will join the crew of *Penguin*. She leaves for repair and refit."

"But she's in Port Royal," Robert added.

"I presume that *Planter* will be partaking in the ceremonies tomorrow."

"Yes, Sir," Robert said.

"There shouldn't be any problem for *Planter* to hail *Penguin*."

Nichols pulled a wallet from his pants pocket. Johnny thought he was looking for money, but Nichols extracted a *carte de visite* from a little slot and framed it between thumb and forefinger before Davey's eyes. "When you get to New York, you will go to this address," and added, "Number 16, Gramercy Park." Nichols caught the confusion rippling over Davey's face and made him repeat the address until it was etched in Davey's memory. His hand swiveled on his wrist, and the card revealed the photograph of a middle-aged man sitting in his finery for a portrait. "You will ask for this man. His name is Mr. J.J. Zuille. Repeat all that."

They stood listening to Davey recite as if he were a rather slow schoolboy, "Number 16, Gramercy Park. Mr. J.J. Zuille."

"They will ask who sent you. You will say, 'Transferred from the Red Ribbon.'" Nichols drilled the name of USS Red Ribbon and then warned Davey, "That is all you say."

"Then what happens?"

"How should I know, Sailor?"

"Who is he?"

"Looks like some rich fellow to me."

"But how do I get to him?"

"I'm not going to wipe your ass. You get there the best way you can. It's not my problem."

Nichols recoiled from his show of temper, and they all sighed relief. He wanted to find some way back to the boy, but all he could say was, "That was quite a time you had on *Keokuk*. I was surprised to know you had survived."

Robert and Hannah stood as shocked as Johnny and Davey. The world was upside-down, and all their worst fears had floated away on this man's dangerous kindness. He knew what he was doing, and he also had help from a man who was rich enough to ignore another's need, but who chose not to. Robert thought of Mr. McKee and all his kindnesses, and Hannah recalled the night they stepped over the broom. Nichols had something of those times in him and was willing to share it with Davey.

Nichols' face mirrored the astonishment in Hannah's moist eyes. She wanted to wrap her arms around this man, but Nichols' stiff stance repelled such intimacy. If he could not return her joy, he could at least quell some of her confusion. He took Hannah's hand as though to shake it, but he turned up her palm to show the red ribbon wrapped around her wrist. "Don't be so surprised when a white man also touches this." With that he raised his hat to all and turned on his heel. Johnny followed him through the door and into a cloud of questions, knowing they would never be answered.

They marched back to the dock, where *Cicero* waited for them. The Midshipman looked like he was about to fall asleep, so Nichols asked, "Are we keeping you up?"

The boy yawned back, "All in a night's work."

Johnny was still reeling from their night's work. He had confided in Nichols, hoping to smuggle Davey back on board ship. He had never heard of an officer helping a sailor to desert. Nichols was chuckling at something, but Johnny saw nothing funny in their situation. If word got out, they could all hang. He was seriously considering whether Nichols was crazy.

The Midshipman waited for his single crewman to boil steam. Nichols and Johnny grabbed the rails as the little boat lurched into the stream. They chugged past the wooden walls of the fleet moored on either side of them, and Nichols could name every commander and give the sea record of each ship. The thousands of men they passed had given their all to the service, but Davey Collins had gone beyond all limits. Collins had been honest enough. What good would it be to stretch the boy beyond what he can do? If Nichols had done his duty as the Navy demanded, Davey would get a fair trial, then get hanged. A wounded mind was more dangerous to the ship than a missing limb. "It's not like we are going to win or lose the war on one man," he mumbled aloud.

Nichols tried to remember the days when he was as young as Webb and Collins. From the moment Nichols set foot on deck, treachery had been the greatest evil. He had seen cowards at sea feted as heroes ashore; they had the cunning to convince the gullible, eager to believe in sham courage. Reputations, built on lies, had created fortunes, and fame had filled many a purse. Du Pont was different. With him, there were no tales of derring-do, no swashbuckling with a cutlass clenched in gleaming teeth swinging from a rope onto the deck of a Tripoli corsair. There had just been the quiet and unsung heroics of doing right. But now the foul accusations and whispered calumny made the crews mute. No voice could be raised in protest, when all demands for the truth were damned as disloyalty. Nichols and all the captains had been warned of the "consequences of interference with the Protocols of the Department." He knew from bitter times upon red seas that when one is commanded to listen, one is forbidden to speak. There could be no justice in such disgusting silence.

Nichols saw the heaviness in the Midshipman's face, so he took the wheel and commanded, "Watch where we go." The Midshipman watched Nichols order Johnny, "Webb. Keep your eyes peeled for Archer's Creek." He saw Johnny stand at the apex of the bows, holding onto the rail with one hand and guiding them with the other. The hand waved them to the right, and the Midshipman gazed along a silver ribbon, shimmering under a full moon. Nichols swung the wheel with expert panache, and they entered the creek. "This will take two hours off each journey between Port Royal and Beaufort." The Midshipman quickly calculated that his work day was cut in half, and he wondered why he'd never noticed this short-cut.

Nichols was eager to get home, but his mind would not stop steaming ahead. He had been trained that the honor of the service was the supreme good. But honor had been perverted, twisted and

326

deformed into anything of advantage to those who could demand their service. He looked over Johnny and thought of *Onward's* crew. So many of them with only one leg or a solitary eye. The headless were finished. The longer the war continued, the more the crew would become monstrous, until drunken skiapods danced along the decks. She would become a floating bestiary, with dead eyes forever seeking an ever receding shore.

Nichols' mind railed at those who measured life by their own pleasures. Morals helped us connect with others, but the selfish were a whirlpool over quicksand, drowning anything they could not smother. No. Even it if meant disobedience, Nichols would be ruled by his better nature. They could hang him for what he had done, but if he shirked this duty to a broken mind, he could value neither friendship, nor justice, nor generosity. No. He would not acknowledge pain to be the supreme evil, nor saving his own skin the supreme good.

They were to keep their mouths shut. Well, tomorrow they would have to listen to the voices of *Onward's* guns. Dishonor was the supreme evil.

Johnny heard Nichols chuckling behind his ears. He heard bits of words as Nichols mumbled, "virtue," "no good," and "bastards" wiggled through the laughter. Nichols was talking to somebody who wasn't there, and Johnny was getting a bit worried.

When the Navy had cut the men's rum ration, *Onward's* crew had written a formal protest to the Admiral. Johnny had been their scribe because he had the neatest handwriting. Nichols had sanctioned their appeal. Du Pont sent a polite but firm note to Nichols, chastising him for not following the chain of command. A week later, a ships' chandler bumped his rowboat alongside *Onward* to deliver four barrels of Jamaica spirit. When Nichols asked for the order to sign, he was told, "nothing to sign. This is on the Admiral's own account."

Nichols laughed, and Johnny shrugged his shoulders at the jollity. Nichols approved of Du Pont's devious ways of doing good, and he admired how the man worked quietly, without expecting praise. Nichols had kept Du Pont's note, and the autograph was very much like the signature on the Order of Transfer for Carpenter's Mate David Collins.

Johnny looked back over his shoulder when he heard Nichols again shout "Ha!" into the night. They would soon get back to the ship, Johnny hoped, before Nichols started howling at the moon.

Nichols' laughter rippled through the night, and he savored the sly mischief. Even Du Pont would never know that his last written order as Commander of the South Atlantic Squadron was a complete forgery.

Chapter 25

Maybes

Hannah closed the door and leaned her exhausted back against it. She tried to sigh away the evening's surprises, but they nested in her mind to breed exhaustion. She grumbled to herself, "Just when I thought things were going to settle down," but stood straight and walked into the front room to confront whatever they had to do. One look at Davey told her, and she practically screeched, "You can't go to New York looking like a lost sewer rat. Gimme them clothes."

Davey's face appealed to Robert but found no relief when he said, "When a lady tells you to take off your clothes, you best do as she says." She stood before him and glowered over folded arms, as he gingerly peeled off his jumper and shirt. She stretched forth one arm to receive his castaways and commanded Robert, "Get him cleaned up out back." She sailed down the hall to the summer kitchen calling "Lydia," and demanded, "boil up a pot big enough for a man and his skivvies."

Robert smiled over Davey's naked embarrassment and held the remainder of the clothing bundled in his arms. "I'll meet you in the yard." Robert left for the kitchen. Davey did not wish to pass the ladies, so he went out the front door and pussyfooted along the porch cupping his wedding tackle in his hands.

Robert soon appeared with buckets of hot and cold water. "Scrub down and we'll soon get you decent. Hannah doesn't think you're dirty. She just wants you spruced up for the trip." Davey picked a bar of lye soap wrapped in an old cloth out of the warm bucket and set to swabbing his flesh in the moonlight. Robert took the soap rag to Davey's back but let the boy clean his face, chest and legs. He could see the worry in Davey's face and offered a set of his own underdrawers. "Put these on when you're finished and get a warm-over in the kitchen." Davey was relieved that Hannah would not see him naked.

Lydia laid out Davey's trousers and jumper on the floor and sat crosslegged, pulling thread through her teeth. Hannah appeared with three pairs of Robert's socks and a very large fannuh. She tossed the woven circle on the floor and threw the socks into its center. "Not much to show for the road." Lydia suggested, "Two of Robert's old shirts and this one he's been wearing." Hannah hummed and complained, "He's too big for Robert's britches," and Lydia opined, "Just have to see what that New York fellow has in his closet."

Lydia cut blue squares from a Navy blanket and folded them to fit the worn patches in Davey's pants. Hannah was always amazed by Lydia's eye, and she looked down to see the patches fit perfectly over the threadbare seams. Lydia's fingers softly pierced neat rows of stitching along the trouser seat and down the legs to the knees. It did not take her long to have the pants ready for Davey's legs. She was glad that he had both legs, and the thought inspired her to pull the stitches flush with the material.

Hannah attacked the jumper with a brush and whale oil and scrubbed salt out of the underarms. She curried the sleeves until the oil seeped into the wool, and she wiped away the raised dirt with a damp rag. Each time she brushed out the soiled blotches, she rinsed the rag in the hot water bucket. With an hour's care, the water turned black, and the jumper gleamed a fresh sheen. She handed the jumper to Davey. "Now you won't look so tattered walking down that street. What's its name?"

Davey knew she was testing his memory and proudly stated "Gramercy Park. Number 16."

Lydia smiled up at him. "Now you're fit to go a calling."

Robert's eyes told Hannah that it was close to "sailing time." Hannah bustled around Davey, and he took her commands as kisses, but she kept busy enough to hold back the tears. Lydia dumped a pan of cornbread and bacon onto a sheet of newspaper and folded the mess into a steaming circle. She waited for Hannah to finish sorting Davey's "traveling suit." When the bread package had cooled, she rested it on top of his shirts. Lydia pulled the four semi-circles of the fannuh together and secured it with an old boot lace. Hannah told Davey, "Keep that close and don't lose it." Davey lifted the squared circle with his hand and whispered to Hannah, "Now I have my own maybe."

Robert grabbed Davey's hand and piled it with twenty golden dollars. Davey saw it was a small enough amount not to attract too much attention, though it added up to more than a month's pay. "Just in case," Robert assured him with a gleaming smile. They had known the kindness of strangers and the cruelty of friends, but they also knew, when you couldn't tell one from the other, it was best to have something shiny in your pocket.

They walked him to the door, but he could not thank them for the words choked in his throat. Hannah hugged him, and Lydia whispered, "You remember how to get back here from wherever you go." They stood for a moment, breathing strength from each other, until Robert touched Davey's sleeve and they stepped over the threshold. Hannah watched after them and felt flushes of hope for the boy carrying all he had in his maybe.

*   *   *   *   *

Du Pont sat in his wardroom, savoring the comfort of Rogers' company. The desk was cleared and its drawers were empty, so they rested their glasses on Du Pont's packed sea-chest. Rogers looked through the wardrobe's open door to see the Admiral's dress uniform hanging from a hook. The heavy epaulettes made the coat's shoulders slouch into a tired droop.

The fleet had been ordered to stand-to the next day. There was to be no Transfer of Flag ceremony because this was merely a change of command. Rogers and Du Pont had joked that it was a strange transfer when he had not been offered a command. Rogers had ceremoniously hauled down the Admiral's Flag from the masthead at evening service and had carefully folded it. When he presented the neat square of golden stars on their deep blue bedding, he had quipped, "This patch will cover many a wound."

331

Du Pont would take his flag with him when he started the journey home in the morning.

They had lounged and chatted as only old friends can, but when Du Pont opened the cigar box, a sheaf of folded paper jumped up at him. "My, my, Rogers. You've given me a Jack-in-the Box."

Roger sucked his cigar and told him, "My sister sent it, expressly for you."

"You have heard from her in England?"

"She sends you this instead of a long letter."

Du Pont unfolded the paper to reveal an inscription in an ornate hand. "This is the Byng Memorial," he said, amazed.

"None other."

Every officer knew of the sad end of Admiral Byng, a British hero hailed the protector of Britannia's shores. He had been given ten ships to defend the island of Minorca from a French invasion fleet. He knew the task was impossible, yet he sailed into certain defeat, flags flying and guns blasting. The Parliament started a whispering campaign calling for Byng's court martial. Then they executed him.

"Your sister has a fine hand," Du Pont said.

"She went to his tomb and copied down the words." Rogers hesitated but knew he had to obey his sister. "She instructed me to inform you that she now understands everything."

Du Pont read the date of "March 14, 1757," and sighed, "It was over a hundred years ago. They shot him on the quarter-deck of his own flag-ship."

"To the perpetual Disgrace of Public Justice," Rogers recited.

"Martyr to POLITICAL PERSECUTION," Du Pont continued.

"It is the last line which sticks in my throat," Rogers whispered, and he declaimed with suppressed anger, "BRAVERY and LOYALTY were Insufficient Securities for the Life and Honour of a Naval Officer."

They sat staring at one another through the smoke and whiskey fumes, their silence as eloquent as the inscription. Du Pont felt the kindness of Rogers' sister rise from the paper she had sent across the ocean. She was such a lady that she did not have to waste words of embarrassed commiseration. She knew all and understood perfectly. That she could remember Byng and make the pilgrimage to catch these words inspired Du Pont's admiration and his resolve. There had been acidic jokes about living in a civilized country without unusual punishments, while this punishment was cruel enough. He had been tempted to envy Byng's end. Still, it was a kindness he would ever remember, when there was so much he would rather forget.

"She actually went to his grave." Du Pont remarked.

"Yes. It's a family vault in an English village. Very quaint, she says." Rogers waited a moment for he wanted Du Pont to know that Byng was still remembered in his home. "She also tells me that every year at noon on March 14, they ring the church bell, 52 times. Once for each year of his life."

Du Pont savored the gesture and hoped the people of the Brandywine would remember him in generations to come. Rogers leaned out of his chair towards Du Pont, a bit unsteady on his haunches. "Trust not to class."

"That's an odd thing for you to say," Du Pont answered. "Since you were the head of your class at the Academy."

"Hm," Rogers snorted. "And how many of my classmates are we now fighting?"

"It was a sad day."

"They betrayed us," Rogers almost shouted. "Their damned patriotism for their states."

"Now their states have betrayed their loyalty."

"I was thinking more of Byng," Rogers explained over a slurring tongue. "He trusted to his friends and to his king. They shot him."

Rogers was getting to that point in the bottle where men confess their true feelings, knowing that the morning will blow away some of the hangover and most of the confidences. "I wish I could remember where I read it, something about 'one musht distinguish between a man's school, his college, and his character.'"

"I have heard that as well," Du Pont returned, and searched his memory for those words. "In France. It was some saint, about six hundred years ago. Bonaventure, I think."

"If we remember the words and forget the man," Rogers mused, "then he was probably right all long."

"Strange," Du Pont thought aloud, "how we forget the most important things."

*   *   *   *   *

Murphy knew something was very odd as soon as Nichols jumped onto *Onward*'s deck. He had returned with Webb, but Webb was no longer mustered with *Onward*'s crew. It was past midnight, and the two young officers left in charge were smart enough not to question Nichols' command to "Raise Sail!" The second night watch was roused, and soon the crew were crawling up the ratlines to get *Onward* under sail to wherever Nichols decreed. As softly as a nursemaid, the anchor was hauled and the top-gallants spread with just enough billow to move *Onward* into the channel.

Nichols called the officers and the Chief together and told them, "We will take station at the Port Royal bar. Make sure we are to seaward of the bar." This was so unusual that they sent questioning faces through the circle, but Nichols explained, "We will wait for the Admiral's launch. He will come out on the morning tide, so we will need seaboard to maneuver."

Nichols turned to Murphy. "Have all gun crews man their stations at first light. Double powder bags will be brought up from the magazine." Murphy had to ask, "Doubles, Sir?" Nichols looked at him as if he were deaf, laughed ruefully, and repeated,

334

"Doubles." Now there was apprehension at Nichols' precise orders, but the hint of madness in his insistent manner worried them. They would obey, but at least he had given them clear instructions, which they would remember when he was hauled before a Court Martial.

Chapter 26

Crossing the Bar

Du Pont stood before his wardroom door. He adjusted his collar and hooked his sword onto his belt. He was a little groggy from the previous night, but it was so like Rogers to show up unannounced bearing malt whisky and good cigars.

The evening had demanded such fellowship. He paused, for this would be the last time he would step through that door; an Admiral can be relieved of his command only once. He would keep his flag, but it would never fly from any ship's mast. His replacement would bring his own most coveted emblem of advancement. Rogers opened the door, nodded once, and escorted him to the ship's rail. Du Pont stood by the gangplank with his sword in one hand and his flag in the other.

Rogers called the crew to attention, the bosuns flared their shrill pipes, and the men forced the customary, "Three Cheers for the Admiral" through gravelly throats. Du Pont thanked Rogers for his smart salute and assured him, "Sophie hopes to see you very soon at *Louviers*, as do I." Rogers watched Du Pont walk down the plank to the launch and saw he was very unsteady on his legs. The Admiral stopped, and the wood creaked under his weight. He forced one swollen foot past the other until a very polite Petty Officer helped him into the launch. The bosun cast off, and the little boat chugged away from the flagship,

This was not the time for blame or self-pity. He had so often repeated the phrase, "Woe unto you, scribes and Pharisees, hypocrites all!" But now the words simply bored him, for it was cowardly to continue such bleatings. He recalled the other part of the verse, "You have omitted the weightier matters of the law, justice, mercy, and faith." It was now time to attend to the weightier matters, and not leave them undone. He thought, "But it does feel bad to be so hard done by after all these years. Maybe

I should have stayed at home and worked in the business? Was it worth a life?"

*   *   *   *   *

Robert called down to William, "Steam up." A quiet whistle in response told him the boilers were full and impatient to go. They had positioned *Planter* downriver and found a berth between the two largest warships in the fleet. Even from the pilot house, Robert had to look up to see the decks of *Planter*'s companions.

He opened the window so he could better hear any engine thrumming down the river. He could barely make out a small boat in the distance, plying its slow way down the tunnel of masts lining the banks. Davey was on deck, his sharper ear tuned to the river traffic. Hannah had been impressed with the boy's ability to hear a conversation across a busy street, so they had placed Davey at *Planter*'s stern, where he could pick up any stray sound of an approaching boat. Robert looked back and thought how strange it was that Davey should be standing today in the very spot where he had thrown that flaming powder keg into the water. There was no doubt about his strength, but even a strong arm can wither when the mind is hurt.

*   *   *   *   *

Nichols stood behind the Number One Gun, his eyes bouncing from man to man, standing to rigid attention around the gun. He looked up to see the top-sails blow big in the offshore wind. The stern anchor was holding firm. *Onward* was ready to lunge forward when he commanded the anchor weighed. Johnny was grabbing the flagstaff and leaning over the taff-rail so he could see whatever was headed towards them. Nichols smelled

337

distant smoke, then Johnny raised his arm and bellowed, "Vessel dead astern. Two miles." Nichols drew his sword.

*　　*　　*　　*　　*

Du Pont admired the workmanship of the launch. The planking was not the usual parallel of rough-cut planks. Each timber was carved and shaped to follow the graceful curves of her sides. The decking converged to meet at the bow point, as lovely as the pointed arch in a cathedral's window. Her bow rose gently to meet the waves, and it struck him as odd that such care should be taken with a harbor launch. It was a fine example of the shipwright's art. There was a strange yet familiar smell about her that tickled his memory. It was like seeing a face in a crowd and being too shy to ask, "Where have we met?" She was a beautiful screw cutter, but her stern was not the usual cheap square cut. Her beam rails were not quickly and sloppily varnished; someone had made the effort to polish her timbers. This boat was not the child of a miser's purse. The stern bulged to wallow over the swells. Clearly this ship was meant for open waters. But there was also the scent of wax surfacing through the coal-smoke.

He turned to the young Captain and said, "This vessel seems very familiar."

The Captain maintained his rigid stance and sullen gaze. "She was converted to steam last year, Sir. Before that, she was the *Porpoise*."

Du Pont's youth surged up before him. When he was posted to his first command, *Porpoise* was their sister-ship. He had spent a year sailing the California coast during the war with Mexico, and *Porpoise* was their constant companion. She was small for a fighting ship, but she ignored her stature and fought alongside the three-decker giants. Now, those same giants and their spawn silently lined the river banks. The launch pushed down the river between the forest of masts, and Du Pont was unceremoniously left to his thoughts.

338

*   *   *   *   *

Davey closed his eyes the better to hear the steady hum through the racket of machinery clattering from the neighboring ships. His ear caught hold of the rhythmic pulses. They were growing louder, so he called back to Robert, "Here she comes."

Robert calmly spoke "Ahead, Two," into the tube, and *Planter* poked her nose into the current. He waited for the launch to pass them. The side paddles slowly revolved to let *Planter* glide into the mainstream. Robert's legs lurched to the side as the outgoing tide pulled her bow into the flow. He raised his hand above his head to grasp the whistle cord.

*   *   *   *   *

Du Pont looked ahead to see the line of white ripples spiraling over the sandbar at the mouth of the river. Beyond the bar, the sea gently billowed in green swells laced with taffeta foam. It was so calm, he could imagine walking upon those wet little hills all the way home. Once over that ridge of little waves, there would be no turning back. He would board the *Vermont* and, three days later, she would set him ashore in Delaware. There are many worse places to be stranded.

He heard a ship's whistle blowing behind him and turned to see what dared to intrude upon his meditations. He heard three short blasts, and as his eyes sighted the little boat, a fourth long moan escaped from *Planter*. Familiar faces lined the boat's rails, and they were all waving at him. He could make out that little man Abe and the taller William, who had guided him to a most revealing dinner with the Reverend French and Miss Laura. At the stern, a smartly dressed sailor waved his hat in most unsailorly fashion, carrying a vague memory of a pistol on the beach and a pipe flaring at night.

The whistle blew its boisterous chortle a second time, and he saw Robert tugging on the cord in the pilot house. *Planter* was keeping an even keel with them, and Du Pont thrilled to have this escort. When the fourth blast spread over the water, he remembered, "It was a damned fine joke." Robert had used the codes of his captors to escape their ignorant bondage, and Du Pont heard in the steamy laughter the echoes of his own future. He would follow Robert's example and turn the weapons of his enemies against themselves.

Du Pont peered over the bar to a ship riding at anchor under steadying sails. He wondered what it was doing in deep water, when it should have been docked with the rest of the fleet.

*   *   *   *   *

Nichols clenched his sword and stood to attention behind the Number One Gun. The crew were rigid at their places, and double powder bags stood within easy reach. Johnny shouted from the stern pole, "She's at the bar." Nichols raised the sword once to his face, and when he dropped it to the deck, the gun fired.

He paced the eight steps to the Number Two Gun. His sword tip almost touched the wood beneath his feet, and the gun roared. The gun crews worked in time with his march, each gun firing, recoiling, and reloading as if the whole ship were a Swiss clock.

*   *   *   *   *

Du Pont saw the cannon flash before he heard the explosion. The semi-circle of the concussion expanded upon the water, and he knew the strange ship had fired directly at *Porpoise*. The ripples ran over the sea, scattering diamond points in its wake upon the swells, growing ever louder as they rushed toward him. Only a double charge used in battle could stir such a heaving on a

340

calm sea. Du Pont braced himself for the iron ball that would follow.

The spray rushed over the bows. *Porpoise* lurched away from the shock, but no metal wrenched her asunder. He heard the booming pass over him like a departing train, and then the ship fired again. He looked to the right and saw *Planter* keeping pace with them. The ship to his left fired again, and he saw the flag unfurled from her stern mast. It was silk and flowed freely with the following wind. He had seen this supple ensign only once before, and knew the ship was *Onward*.

*　*　*　*　*

Robert blasted the whistle twice and sent the signal back to Nichols that all was well. They had arranged this farewell in ways that would not call them to account. It was a fitting thing to do for the man who had done so much for them. Robert's heart lingered in the memory of all their meetings, knowing he would probably never see the Admiral again. But who knows? Just over a year ago, he would have laughed at any soothsayers who might have cast such an improbable future for him.

Hannah had been right to judge the man by what he did and not by what he said. He had used his own money, when the government was tardy in supplying wood. Without Du Pont's dollars, they would have starved under the trees. Hilton Head was not the only freedman's colony to thrive on Du Pont's wise generosity. He had forced the government to honor its contract with Robert and all the crew and he had ensured that they had received their due for commandeering *Planter*.

But it was more than money that made this man. He had seen the pitfalls before Robert fell into them, and had warned him about the enthusiasm of people who only wanted to use him. That was his most impressive quality. Hannah said he could see through to the person, and she had been right. Robert had learned how to navigate the shallows and the depths of their new lives, but it was Du Pont who had told them to "keep sailing, no matter what." It was a good joke. He told them, "If you want to avoid the rocks, you have to know where they are." It was as simple as that. Just keep sailing and stay away from anything that would sink you.

*   *   *   *   *

Du Pont counted the rests between the shots. They were regularly spaced, so the captain was pacing the gundeck. That was the only explanation of such amazing drill. *Onward* was firing the full eighteen shots of an Admiral's salute. This was no random act of disobedience. He chuckled to himself, "The Navy may have stopped their rum ration, but they have kept their spirits." They were telling him they were not to be crushed, and neither was he.

Welles and Fox had concealed the knife behind their poisoned smiles. "But who were they anyway?" They would be gone in two years and soon forgotten, but the actions of these men and these ships will last forever. The heroism of Robert and Rogers and the cheek of Nichols and Rhind are worth more than the schemes of politicians. "If only they would spend half the intelligence and energy fighting the enemy as they did each other, the rebellion would have been crushed long ago." He finally admitted to himself, "I am past caring about a puffed-up toadfish such as Fox. Sophie was right: our friends are for a season, and the season ends with their pleasure." The same lips which whisper such venom would cheer the firing squad. Du Pont vowed to himself, "If they tie me to a rock, I will slash the waves until they drown me. Byng was not a Du Pont."

He looked from port to starboard, from sail to steam, and knew he was on the cusp of a new age. How different this was from the first time he had stepped on deck. Then, determination and loyalty were all that was needed. You could trust the captain's judgement, for his years of learned service were freely given. Now, firmness of purpose was insufficient for the fight. The enemies were those who would pervert the ideals he had fought so hard to preserve. These men on either side of him were the new heroes, men who would weigh their chances and who had the courage of defiance.

Robert's signal reminded him of the best characters the war had produced. Robert had launched himself to freedom, but he was not alone. A lesser man would have abandoned his family. Robert rose with his. Three little toots and a drawn out wheeze were his nose-thumbing overture to the life the law refused him. Nichols knew the emptiness of such laws that unjustly bind because he so loved the freedoms of justice. Such people could be trusted to keep their promises because they had vowed to keep their faith. They were the best of sailors, and their honor was all the tribute Du Pont needed, or wanted.

Porpoise chugged alongside *Onward*, and he peered over the gulf to see Nichols pacing slowly as the guns followed his step. Du Pont grasped his sword in its scabbard and thrust his fist high above his head. Nichols would know the meaning, a sailor must keep his sword sheathed, until it is needed. The cannon flash caught the silver motto in the sword's handle and proclaimed in light, "Rectitude."

Onward and *Planter* escorted *Porpoise* to the *Vermont* two miles from shore. The trip was shorter than the time it took for the echoes to fade, but this was all they needed. Du Pont turned to *Planter* steaming steadily beside him and waved his flag at Robert. Du Pont's chest swelled with pride and hope as he gazed into the eyes of the man who stole himself.

343

Acknowledgments

So many people contributed to the writing of *The Man Who Stole Himself* that it is impossible to thank them all.

My first awareness of Robert Smalls was when a teacher told us the story of a real hero when I was eleven years old. Fifty years later it is time to thank Fr. Seamus Murphy, SJ, for sharing his understanding and compassion with the ignorant fools he had to teach and making us less ignorant and, I hope, more compassionate.

Adam Kissel, of Virginia, is responsible for the developmental editing. Adam's amazing eye for detail and his magnificent sense of aesthetic proportion kept the Man from sinking.

Lucas Clawson, archivist of the Hagley Museum, and Jeanne Solensky of the Winterthur Archive and Museum, were vital in supplying information about Admiral Du Pont.

Bede Mitchell, Dean of the Henderson Library at Georgia Southern University procured the books which were beyond my grasp and made the writing possible. Vanessa St. Oegger, Reference Assistant at the Special Collections Research Center at Syracuse University Libraries, supplied me with a letter of Charles Sedgwick, which clarified an intriguing aspect of the friendship between Robert Smalls and Admiral Du Pont.

Barbara Moore and the staff of the Franklin Memorial Library, Swainsboro, Virginia Bolton, Ann Buxton, Gladys Collins, Karen Hidlebaugh, Windy Ward, and Willene Williams deserve special mention for their invaluable help in acquiring books through the Georgia Pines Interlibrary Loan System.

No book can be birthed without the keen insights of Beta Readers. Very special mention must be made of the excellent Beta Readers: Amy Blumenthal, Arlys Ferrel, Shelly Good, Elizabeth Goode, Barbara Holliman, Jennifer Baker-Matty, Kim McFarland, Stephen Preston, Gina Renee, Karen Sollars, and Eldred Spell. Their perceptive minds and applied imaginations are to be celebrated and valued.

Anna Thibeault is the source of all inspiration and perspiration in writing *The Man Who Stole Himself*. Without her love and belief, this would have been impossible.

Thomas Thibeault

Born in Canada, raised in Ireland, lives in the United States, Thomas has retired from a thirty year teaching career which has taken him to Russia, the Middle East, and the Far East.

Half a century of wide reading, wider traveling, and concentrated thinking have provoked Thomas into writing.

Those travels involved working as a deck hand, soldier, truck driver in Africa, art model in Ireland, train brakeman in Canada, and a tour guide at the pyramids.

Thomas brings a wealth of experience to writing which expresses our primal experiences.

He lives in Georgia with his wife, Anna, and their fourteen cats.